MY BROTHER MICHAEL

Also by Janis Owens
  Myra Sims
  The Schooling of Claybird Catts

Y BROTHER
MICHAEL

Janis Owens

PINEAPPLE PRESS, INC.
Sarasota, Florida

Inquiries should be addressed to:

Pineapple Press, Inc.
P.O. Box 3889
Sarasota, Florida 34230

www.pineapplepress.com

Library of Congress Cataloging-in-
Publication Data

Owens, Janis, 1960-
  My brother Michael / by Janis Owens.-- 1st
Pineapple Press pbk. ed.
      p. cm.
  ISBN-13: 978-1-56164-343-1 (pbk. : alk.
paper)
  ISBN-10: 1-56164-343-2 (pbk. : alk. paper)
  1. Brothers--Fiction. 2. West Florida--
Fiction. I. Title.
  PS3565.W5665M9 2005
  813'.54--dc22
                                    2005016658

10 9 8 7 6 5 4 3 2 1

Design by Carol Tornatore
Printed in the United States of America

for WRO: Thank you for
letting me be myself

A historian is a prophet in reverse.

Friedrich von Schlegel

Chapter

1

O n the day my brother Michael died,
I was standing at a lectern surrounded
by fifty-seven bored freshmen scribbling notes to my concise dissection
of FDR and New Deal politics. With no knock, no warning at all, our
department secretary, Mrs. Weeks, walked in with a small yellow telephone message that said simply: *Call home.*

Before I could react, before I could even ask why she had taken it
upon herself to interrupt my honors-level American history class with a
routine phone message, she said, very gently, "Dr. Catts, your brother
has died." She paused to let the news sink in, then: "I'm so sorry. I know
you were close."

Seeing my stunned face, my tears, my total lack of control, she
dismissed the class and, with remarkable Yankee efficiency, had me on
a plane to Tallahassee within hours. She even packed me a suitcase,
though to this day I don't know how she found my apartment (I'd just
moved) much less the socks, the underwear, and the dark funeral suit,
still clean and crisp in a dry cleaner's bag.

But whatever her method, she had me in Florida late in the afternoon of his death, renting a car in Tallahassee and driving west to the town of my birth, arriving with two days to spare, but checking into an interstate motel room quite anonymously, refusing to let the family know I'd arrived. For they have long memories, my people do, and are not the kind to forget old indiscretions, no matter how far removed. And with Michael dead, dead at forty-three of pancreatic cancer that was only diagnosed during routine gallbladder surgery in October, I could not imagine them in a very forgiving mood and was too broken myself to withstand them.

So I stayed holed up in that seedy motel room for the better part of two days, drinking whiskey for courage, sometimes dialing Michael's home phone, but hanging up when unfamiliar voices answered, for despite Mrs. Weeks' kind words, my brother and I had not spoken in eight years. We had not communicated at all beyond a quick visit by his daughter Melissa when she flew out of LaGaurdia on a student trip to Europe a year and a half earlier and the standard Christmas cards, quite impersonal, his name printed in calligraphy, as befitting a small town aristocrat, an impatient signature scribbled below. But not another word until shortly after Thanksgiving when he called from his hospital bed to remind me of a promise I'd made him the last time I ever saw him alive.

A promise that was causing me actual physical pain as I dressed for his funeral, for I am a Tagamet addict and, what with the whiskey, had gone through a week's supply in three days. By the time I'd knotted my tie and started for the church, I was actually spitting blood and hoping to God I wouldn't do something humiliating at the service, like pass out. It would really be too much for these God-fearing folk to bear—the prodigal son stealing the limelight at the funeral of the older son—so I forewent the family section to take a seat among strangers in the back row, slumping passively and quietly bleeding into my handkerchief like the gentleman my mother raised me to be. I could see Mama, in fact,

seated twenty or so pews ahead of me in the front and corner of the
mob that packed the small sanctuary. Despite her diminutive size, she
had a distinct set to her shoulders and a headful of white hair that made
her easy to pick out of the line of bowed heads on the family row.

My brother's widow was not so easily discerned, for her brown
hair that showed red only in the sun was covered with a fine netting, her
body was clothed like half the other women, in solemn, pagan black. But
I tried. I have to say I tried. Even at his funeral, God help me, and if her
brother Ira had seen me, I believe he would have killed me for it.

But providentially, no one noticed me there in the back, with the
place packed to perhaps twice that of normal capacity, folding chairs
blocking the aisle, even the choir loft filled with sobbing mourners, all
in evidence of the fact my brother was a mover and a shaker, a man of
ideas. The owner of the town's most prosperous factory, president of any
civic organization he ever cared to join, the largest contributor to any and
every charity in town—and those are just the laurels the first speaker, Dr.
Winston (once GP to every snotnose and dogbite in the county, more
recently, mayor) could get out before he was overcome by emotion and
gave the pulpit back to the preacher. I was surprised to see this was still
Brother Sloan, the same pastor who'd weaned us on salvation and damnation as children, who, with his fifty-odd years in the ministry, might
have been expected to have something fortifying to say, but didn't, only
standing there an uncertain moment, then blowing his nose and asking
Brother Cain, the AME pastor, to please come to the front.

It was the first time I'd ever seen a black man without a tool belt
step foot in Welcome Baptist, and I listened with a little more interest
as he managed to sputter a few things about Michael, how he had hired
the first black manager in the county, how that small act of tolerance had
unlocked doors they never thought would open. He was trying to make
some statement, some plea this practice not be abandoned when he,
too, was overcome, not really crying, but shaking his head and returning

to the deacon's bench that was packed with ministers of every description, all mourning in various degrees of sincerity. Fresh from the land of rationalism, I couldn't help but wonder if they weren't weeping more at the death of those computer-generated checks than at Michael's actual passing, but this small cynicism did not distract me as our old childhood friend from Magnolia Hill, Benny McQuaig, took the pulpit and managed between snorts and shuttering breaths to spin a pretty accurate eulogy.

Foregoing the titles and civic niceties, Benny painted a truer picture of Michael, a portrait of a man who was a natural optimist, a pragmatist who was born poor but worked his way out of it one grinding, clocked-in hour at a time. Randomly jumping here and there, he recalled the summer Michael tried out for the majors in Sarasota, his lifelong love of the Braves, the tough years in the seventies when the plant had almost rolled over—years I was away, years I came back, years I wasn't so fond of remembering.

Benny's flat country sincerity, along with his red face and many pauses to cry unabashedly, was whipping the audience into an even greater frenzy of remorse, but I was suddenly diverted by a flash of red hair in the front pew and for a moment was too mesmerized to bother anymore with grief.

But it wasn't her; I could see that fairly quickly. The red was bright carrot orange, not deep auburn, edging close to brown. It was—yes, surely—it was Melissa, my niece, the one who had dropped by between flights last year. On the pew next to her was a tall young man—that would be Simon, the oldest son, named for our father, and next to him Clayton, the baby, his hair fair and light. And next to him was an averted head, bowed in prayer or prostrated by grief, I could not tell, as my heart began its old relentless gallop.

From the moment I spotted her till the last amen, the service slipped by with unexpected ease. There were the usual hymns and a fast, predictable sermon by a young minister I'd never seen before. Then suddenly, we were all standing, singing "Amazing Grace" a cappella and then filing up the aisle for the last viewing. In this, my careful retreat to the back betrayed me, for the ushers brought us out first, herding us up like so many sheep, trying to move things along so the family would be spared a prolonged wait. But I would not be hurried. I was too stunned for that and walked on heavy, leaden feet past pews and pews of people I'd left once, twenty years ago, then again, nine years ago, and never with many regrets, for we were not so compatible, my hometown and I.

But I paid them no mind that day, my eyes on the long oaken casket that was so amassed in flowers that the air was almost stifled with the particular waxy smell of the florist shop. Roses, carnations, arrangements and sprays, all pressed in such profusion that it bewildered the eye, and I had paused to see, in wonder, how they covered the very walls, when someone hit me from behind in a powerful, hysterical embrace.

For one incredible moment I thought it was Myra and was filled with a fast scramble of emotions: shock, shame, and yes—I won't lie— pure joy. Then I heard my mother's voice, rough, country, telling the world, "Gabe, Gabe, I knew you'd come. I knew you'd come—my son, my son—"

And while she punctuated her every word with a solid knock of her hard little West Florida head, I turned and found myself facing my brother's family: Melissa, with a red, shattered face, who stepped forward to hug me over Mama's head; Simon, dark and controlled, offering his hand like a grown man, though he was hardly more than a child, just outside sixteen, a vague breath of a memory of Michael, only taller and broader through the shoulders, a legacy of his mother's blood, of the hardy frame of the North Alabama Celt.

But that was all, no one else stirred, for the younger son, Clayton, was a stranger to me, watching me with level, neutral eyes that were mad and sullen, young enough to be petulant with something as relentless as death as he stood at his mother's side, supporting her in her grief. And though she was very close, barely an arm's length away, there was no recognition at all in her face as she looked at me, only a blank silence, and something in her very immobility reminded me desperately of the day her bastard of a father broke my wrist for showing her how to make a hopscotch board in the dirt of her backyard.

She had backed away slowly that day, one baby step at a time, till she was flush against the fence that marked the iron-clad border of her hellish little world and stood there passively, with no word of protest spoken, none allowed. And just as before, when I had been too afraid of that monster of a father to do anything but stare, I abandoned her, giving in to my mother's embrace and turning and looking on the corpse of my brother Michael.

And instead of the true confession I was afraid I might blurt out, or the useless words of regret, I only blinked at him, then murmured aloud in a very plain, controlled voice, "God, he looks like Daddy."

Now Daddy was a yard man.
And a mechanic. And a painter
and a cook. Daddy was, in fact, a job-hopper and a dreamer, and my
mother has excused my behavior many times by pointing to my pro-
genitor. But I never complain, not me, for he was also a man of great
sensitivity and fine intelligence who had the great financial misfortune of
being born in Coffee County, Alabama, during the Depression. Not the
Great Depression, as I was once fond of telling my students up north,
but the *Great Depression*: the one that arrived with the first pioneer in
South Alabama and was still not over, last time I looked. Not that anyone
ever laughed as loudly as I at my little joke, for no one in the Ivy League
gives a damn about the South, except, of course, for Faulkner, who in
my humble opinion they quote more than is necessary to impress—but,
here, I'm digressing. I was speaking of my father.

Simon William Catts. No relation to Sydney, though Mama would
have loved to have claimed him. No relation to anyone in West Florida
for that matter, but merely one of a thousand rural immigrants driven

from the land by the boll weevil and lured south by the commercial appeal, namely a job in a Washington County turpentine camp that he managed to hold onto until perhaps 1937, when he moved into town and began his great round of semi-permanent employment, trying his hand at whatever struck his fancy: machine work, farm labor, street sweeping. It was only when he met a defrocked Baptist preacher's daughter, a tiny blonde girl of fifteen, who was warned not to marry him, that he settled down to a regular job and a mill house on the northwest end of town, the house where my sister and brother and I were born, the house my mother lives in to this day.

But back then, in '42, it may have been seen as a purely temporary situation; temporary, that is, till the babies came, the first daughter in ten months, the second, a boy, arriving the month my father was called up to active duty. Michael Simon, he named him, in what he thought might be his last act of fatherhood. The next week he left for the Islands, where he spent two bloody, vicious years as a private in the infantry, doing the dirty work at MacArthur's back.

But he survived—for we are nothing if not a family of survivors— and returned home to bestow on my mother one final child, another son, who she named Gabrielle by mistake, intending Gabriel, though she was too stubborn to admit it, and when anyone would subsequently point out her error, she would cock her head to the side and ignore the spelling of the matter to say defiantly, "These boys looked like angels when they'se borned and I named them for angels." Never explaining why she'd named me in the feminine form, never bothering to write and have it changed once she'd discovered the mistake, and such was the rock solid power of my mother's convictions that people would never argue, but merely smile and nod and say things like "How nice."

So that's how I came to be born to a mill worker and his wife in a five-room Cracker house on an orange dirt turnaround called Lafayette Street in a section of town literally across the tracks known locally as

Magnolia Hill. Now God alone knows who first applied this ridiculous antebellum tag to the area, which was not exactly a slum but not quite middle class either, the small houses haphazardly built of wood or block or sometimes tarpaper, the yards hardly ever grass, but the overall effect softened by monstrous trees, live oak and camphor and pecan, that grew in abundance, for we lived on the tip of the Florida aquifer, and there was never a tree that died from lack of water, not on Lafayette Street. Nor was any child lonely, unless it was by choice, for if there were one thing these people were adept at, it was producing children. At one point in my life I remember having nine best friends, all of whom lived within a two-block radius of my house, all of whom attended Welcome Baptist at the corner, where Mama taught Sunday School and Daddy took us out back if we misbehaved. Which we seldom did, for Mama was a consummate storyteller, and the Old Testament stories of Samuel and Saul, David and Bathsheba, Balaam and Samson were the height and depth, the circle and moral circumference of our pale little world.

Blighted is the sociologist's term. Magnolia Hill was blighted, but the adults were children of poverty themselves and never seemed conscious of the bare, tree-shaded squalor, as they went about the business of desperately holding onto jobs and raising thin, crew-cut children, with no talk of regret, no brooding over might-have-been. Perhaps they were too busy with the routine landscape of their lives, the doctor bills and rent and putting food on the table, but I suspect they were also tired. Bone tired, for there is nothing more exhausting than poverty, and my earliest memories of my father are of him sitting at the dining room table every night after supper and patiently cutting new soles for his shoes out of cardboard box. Every night, without exception, then, with his feet properly outfitted for another day, he'd go out and sit on the porch till bedtime, for there was nothing else to do when it was too hot to sit inside, too hot to do anything but rock and pull up chairs for neighbors and listen to the strings of gossip that stayed fairly innocent until the children were sent to bed, then delved into the realm of head-shaking shock.

I had an appetite for innuendo, even then, and late at night, long after the other children had been exiled to bed, I'd wait till my brother Michael was snoring, then creep into the front bedroom and press my ear to the window fan and listen to news of the underbelly of Lafayette Street. And it was there, sometime in the summer of—oh, it must have been '60, when I was twelve or so—that Mama and the other women first began discussing the Sims. Endlessly, endlessly, and I could not understand why it fascinated them so.

"Said she fell down," Mama would intone dryly. "Third time this month. I tell you what, the Law's gone step in, it happens again."

There would be a chatter of light agreement, then someone else would offer a further tidbit of damnation: "Children skinny as rails. State ought to take them is what I say, and I don't care who hears me either, their Mama too sorry to light the fire—"

And I'd wrinkle my forehead against the cold screen, perplexed, beginning to see there was something wrong on Magnolia Hill, something I had no name for yet. All I recognized was the name Sims, which belonged to our neighbors to the left, newcomers to Lafayette and virtual strangers to me, for Mama didn't like the looks of Old Man Sims the moment she laid eyes on him and wouldn't let me play in their yard. But I only had Mama's bad impression to go by, for despite the rumor of unease in the porch talk, to my eyes there was nothing so wrong with their narrow, two-bedroom house, nothing to set it apart from any other house on Magnolia Hill, except that it still had an outhouse for a toilet. But that was all.

In fact, my friend Ira lived there. Younger than me by a year, he was three years behind me in school owing to the fact he only made it maybe three out of every five days. But despite his educational deficits, there was something very likable about his carrot-red hair, his thin country voice, his very bouyancy of spirit. In the brief time they'd lived on Lafayette, he'd firmly established himself as the neighborhood clown, the lovable idiot who'd eat insects and be dared into anything—peeing off the porch in broad daylight, smoking grapevine under the porch at night, stealing penny candy from the corner store. These attributes alone would have been sufficient to win our approval, but coupled with his grinning fearlessness, he spoke a peculiar East Louisianan dialect that the rest of us hicks found old-fashioned and charming. He called a furnace a *stove*, used words like *et* for ate and *kindly* for kind of, and most of his sentences began with either *it were* or *it weren't*.

Harmless and country, we thought him, but it was a compilation of these very attributes that led to the first domino fall that would eventually change all our lives on Magnolia Hill, though it really wasn't Ira's fault at all; it was my cousin Randell's.

Now Randell was fifteen, and every July when my sister Candace (I see the Faulknerian irony here, but what can I say? It's her name, or actually the shortened version of her name, which is—no joke— Canadasier) went to youth camp, he would come down by Greyhound bus and spend two weeks with us. A year younger than Michael, he was a long, tall boy with a big mouth and an eye for the girls, and at some point in the summer—maybe it was the Fourth of July—he had the great fortune of taking Lynnie Hall out in a boat during a Sunday School picnic and, in order to escape a sudden thunderstorm, of spending two hours, unchaperoned and well-excused, in an abandoned boathouse across the lake.

Now before I proceed any further, maybe I need to clarify our sexual development on Lafayette Street. A lot of literature has been written that seems to point up the Southern working class as a culture with an easy access to early sex, but whether this image is incorrect or whether we were an enclave of repression there on Magnolia Hill, I don't know. All I know is that my nine best friends and I were as ignorant of sex as the potted plants on my mother's back porch. We knew it had something to do with us *down there* and girls *down there*, and we liked to look at women's breasts (*titties*, we called them), and maybe a few of us had figured out the ways and means of masturbation, but that was about it. By some genetic fluke, breeding on Lafayette had produced families with a high ratio of younger sons, so there were no girls our age to experiment on or with, no interaction to spin us on to higher revelations. And as far as open, frank discussions where sex was concerned, I can only say that asking my God-fearing mother to explain the strange urges and curious surges I was experiencing hourly was about as easy as asking her to do a dance on the dining room table. I never did, and I know damn well Michael never did, and neither had anyone else by the looks of blank interest on their faces when Randell, fresh from Phenix City, Alabama (where, he said, and I quote, the girls were *easy*), rowed back into the swimming area, and while he assiduously helped a wet and shaking Lynnie Hall into the arms of her worried mother, turned and gave us this *wink*.

Well, we didn't know what to make of it, and Randell's subsequent winks and hints only perplexed us more, though we were too proud to admit it and only grinned back like the fools we were. All of us, that is, except Ira. He was too young, too stupid, to be ashamed; his only problem was that he was too ignorant to frame the question.

We played together all morning the day after the picnic, setting shingles on the amazing Swiss Family Robinson mansion we were constructing in the low-hanging limbs of one of the live oaks in our backyard, and I could see something was on Ira's mind. Something very pressing that had his face flushed and absorbed, and I was hoping he'd break down and admit his ignorance so the rest of us could be enlightened over what exactly might have happened between a boy and a girl in an abandoned boathouse that would subsequently give the boy cause to wink, but he didn't say a word till Mama called us in to dinner.

She always invited Ira in to meals, for she was convinced his mother didn't feed him, not one crumb, and, indeed, you could see the bones of his ribcage under his T-shirt and the very clear outline of his kneecap in the middle of his toothpick legs. So he was a fixture at our summertime table, and I must say I begrudged it, for we ate out of two pots, one fresh vegetable, one starch, and Ira could by God put a dent in both. I have never seen the likes of it in all my life: from the time his tail hit the chair till the food was gone, he'd be whipping that fork back and forth, back and forth, talking the whole time, unless Daddy happened to be home for dinner. He'd listen awhile, then murmur in a light, heatless voice, "For God's sake, son, hush a minute. I cain't hear myself think."

Ira would only grin wider, not breaking his pace, but keeping his eyes on the food, being very polite about seconds (and thirds and fourths), always saying "pleasema'm" and "thankyousir."

But on the day after the picnic, with Randell still there, still winking and saying things like "Boy that was the bes ride I ever took in my life, I tell you what," Ira was quiet and preoccupied, even when Mama brought in the food and prayed and told us to begin.

That's when Randell, the big shot, was sly enough to slip one by, right under Mama's nose: "Thet picnic, now, I tell you what, I have never enjoyed mysef more."

He said it with a wink to Michael, and Mama was making some reply, saying something about how glad she was he had enjoyed himself, when out of the blue, little Ira, his neck pencil-thin, his face an agony of inexpression, asked in a high, country twang: "Ran-dell? Didju *ponk* her?"

Well, he'd finally found a word, *ponk*, and where the hell he'd come up with such a euphemism I'll never know, but in the context of the sentence, we could all pretty well figure its rough translation, even Mama. For perhaps ten seconds she looked at us, one at a time, then carefully laid her napkin on the table and requested Randell's presence in the living room, please.

They left in perfect silence, Randell casting a murderous glance at Ira, who had begun eating again, attacking the squash with his usual frenzy, only turning once, to Michael, and asking again in that flat, astounded voice, "Did he *ponk* her?"

Michael was as paralyzed as I and could only stare, but Mama heard him through the wall and came out and told Ira he'd have to leave.

"But I ain't et yet—" he began, so she put his plate in his hands and pushed him out the back door, then sent us to our room.

We laid crossways on the old double bed in perfect silence, haplessly listening while in the next room, Mama was taking Randell apart, piecemeal.

"—a good, fine girl, her Daddy was to hear you'd talked about her that way, he'd *have your ears*—"

I guess she considered him too old to whip and was getting her pound of flesh by stark terror, but I was shaking in my shoes, for I knew intimately that I was by no means too old to whip and could feel one coming on.

Michael was lying beside me with his face to the ceiling, rubbing his eyes, crying, I thought, until I felt the bed vibrate. Nothing more than a tiny, tiny shake in the springs, and when he felt my eyes on him, he turned and looked at me a moment, then cocked his head, and in brilliant imitation of Ira's wiregrass twang, whispered, "Didju *ponk* her?"

Well it was the difference between night and day, I can tell you that; suddenly, Randell's fate at Mama's hands was funny, funny; it was the most hiliarious thing I'd ever heard in my life. I laughed so hard Michael had to gag me with a pillow, while in the living room, Randell was groveling like a dog, begging Mama not to call his mother.

"—we didn't *do* nothin Aint Cissie, I swear to God. You can call her and ast—"

Mama answered levelly, "Well I just might do that. Ask her what *she* knows about this—*ponking*—bidness—"

It was too much, even for Michael. We lay there and laughed like wild men, beating the mattress with our fists and holding our sides, even when Mama came in with the belt and tried to get us back on the straight and narrow by lashing at us and telling us we were a disgrace before God, and so on. But it made no difference. She could have come at us with a blowtorch, and we would have still hollered like idiots. Maybe it was nervous tension or hysteria, but we simply laughed all afternoon, calming to bare reasonableness at times, till Michael would wrinkle his nose and cock his head and we'd be gone, Mama yelling that she was calling Daddy, calling Daddy at work, we didn't hush *this minute*.

The next morning poor Randell was shuttled back to Phenix City in disgrace, and Daddy did indeed whip us, not over the *ponk* business, but for what he considered back-talk to Mama. However, rumor of the incident spread to the neighborhood, and all the frustrated virgins on Magnolia Hill finally had a word for *it*. The word was *ponk*, and we used it incessantly thereafter, for it opened up a whole new world of conversation, enabling us to connect the bits and pieces of evidence into an achievable act, the act of *ponking*.

In fact, I think it might have remained our word of choice for copulation, and I might have spent the remainder of my life calling slow drivers *motherponkers*, and asking colleagues with beautiful but incompetent assistants, what was the matter, were they *ponking* her? if not for Myra, dear Myra, my love, and because of her, the very word became a curse, and what had been a child's naive grasp of an adult mystery became a catchword for evil, a keyhole into an abyss.

Chapter

3

yra was Ira's sister.

His baby sister, and for the
first few years they lived on Magnolia Hill, we never saw much of her.
For one thing, she was shy; for another, she was not allowed off the front
porch or outside the backyard, and thanks to Mama's edict, we were
separated by a four-foot-high, pig iron fence.

So the environs to the rear of the Sims' house were her private
domain, and there she seemed content to remain, a quiet, colorless
child, somewhat more healthy-looking than Ira, with dark hair carefully
braided down her back, and eye color that was undetermined, as her
face was perpetually downtilted to her feet. The closest we ever came
to actual social contact was when she'd sometimes fall into step behind
us boys on the way home from school, not close, if we could help it,
for we were all a bit more worldly by then, still virgins, every one, but
beginning to see a light at the end of the tunnel in the form of a new
girl at church named Cassie Lea Scales, who in her first month in town
had French-kissed everyone but me. So we were careful that Myra not

overhear our blatant ponk-talk lest she run her mouth to Brother Sloan, but when we'd shoo her away, she never fought back, only stopping perfectly still till we were a block away, then walking again, quietly, her face still averted, her feet taking her straight up the front steps into her narrow, sagging, old house, where the door would close behind her till morning.

Now I was a fairly sensitive child, given to tears and pouts rather than cruelty, but snubbing Myra Louise Sims never gave me a twinge of ill-conscience, for everyone on Lafayette knew she was the Sims' undisputed *babygirl*, which in West Florida dialect meant *princess*. Most of the families had one, either as mother or youngest daughter, prototypes of feminine sweetness to be fought over and cherished, catered to and spoiled, with no apologies to anyone. Already, Myra showed signs of the beginnings of a long and pampered life. As I've said, she was healthier-looking than Ira and stayed home for meals and lived, so we all could assume *she* ate there, and furthermore, she was her father's pet— blatantly, unashamedly so. I had sat there more than once and watched the Old Man (a traditional title, incidently, for he was not old—perhaps as young as thirty) come home from work, calling he had a present and when Ira and Myra came to the porch, smile and hand Myra a small treat, usually ice cream of some sort, then go inside, leaving Ira bare-handed and green, not saying a word, only watching in a pale, breathless silence as Myra sat on the steps and ate it slowly, losing most of it to the heat, his mouth moving like he could taste it.

Mama happened to be planting roses at the fence one evening when this little scenario played itself out in all its miserable inequality, and I thought we in the Catts household would never hear the end of it. For days, at supper, at dinner, on the porch before and after curfew, her voice would rise and fall, for, as she put it, *it just beat all she ever seen*.

From that moment on, she drew Ira even closer under her warm maternal wing, making him desserts and giving him hand-me-downs, and when the Fourth of July picnic rolled around again, she somehow finagled Mrs. Sims into letting him tag along. It was one in a string of calm, hot summer days, the sky a light robin's egg blue, the lake tepid as a drawn bath, all of us boys, now somewhere in the neighborhood of thirteen, shamelessly ponk-conscious, watching the girls in their bathing suits with many comments on who was flat and who was not, and when Cassie showed up in a two-piece, we were rendered totally speechless and had to back off to the trees and talk about this thing.

It was agreed she had cleavage. It was agreed her navel was show-ing, but those were the only conclusions that could be safely drawn before Brother Barns started blowing his whistle, announcing the relay race, and we had to line up under the trees and wait our turn to swim to the float. By luck, I was the last in line on the boy's team and Cassie was last on the girl's, and summoning my courage, I asked her if I could kiss her. After all, everyone else had, from Ira down to Benny (the first of us to start in on acne), and I was in no way prepared for her answer, which was an unequivocal *no*.

"Why not?" I asked, thinking she was shy and noting the trees afforded privacy, and it was not the first nor the last time in my life that I have ever regretted my inability to take no for an answer when she clarified the situation with a wrinkled nose and a simple explanation, "I don't like fat boys."

Then she crossed her arms and moved up next to Lynnie and giggled something in her ear, and I had a pretty good idea who the joke was on and wandered back to the parking lot and lay down in the back of Uncle Case's old Buick in a haze of humiliation.

Growing up in a family of wiry people had always been a source of worry to me, since I was—well, fat is not the word—chunky, I guess you'd say, and Cassie's words had confirmed my darkest fear. I'd rather read than play baseball; I was fat; I had curly hair; I was the only boy at church who'd never kissed a girl: I was, in short, homosexual; and in

1962, in rural West Florida, it was not what you'd call a divine revelation, and one particularly hard on me because, by God, I loved the girls, and the thing with being queer was you didn't get many girls. I mean, it was just a sad fact of life even a sheltered church-boy like me knew to be true, and I was lying in the breathless heat of the closed-up car sinking under the weight of the thing, when suddenly, Daddy jerked open the door and shoved the ice chest onto the floorboards, calling to Michael and Candace and Ira that it was time to go home.

Mama was with him, her face pale and stunned, and for one blank moment, I thought it was because of me, that Cassie had told the world, but Daddy, speaking aside in his low patient murmur, told me Mama was feeling poorly and needed to go home. Around our house, "feeling poorly" was synonymous with menstruation, a curious facet of femaleness we Catts men catered to nervously (and in Mama's case, anyway) about fifteen days out of the month, but I was grateful to be spared the horror of facing Cassie Lea over dinner and felt my despair lift a tiny bit as Ira ran his mouth all the way back to town, poking it full of fried chicken and deviled eggs, but not stopping for a breath, not once. When we got home, I took to my bed and sulked the day away, oblivious to everyone else, till Michael woke me up late in the night and told me what had really happened down at the lake: how that after the relay race, Mama decided they were getting too much sun and called them in from the water to to rub them down with hand lotion (nobody used anything else back then; I don't think sunscreen had been invented). First she did Candace, then Michael, then she told Ira to pull up his T-shirt and when he did, she gasped aloud.

For all across the front of Ira's bony little chest, from shoulder to shoulder, there were a dozen or so little round holes, some fresh, some healed over, all a little bigger than redbug bites, and when she asked him what in the world had he gotten into, Michael swore Ira just grinned that silly grin and fingered one on his shoulder. "Oh, thet's where my daddy, he put out his cigarette."

Mama just knelt there rubbing the excess lotion into her hands, looking at him, just a blank uncomprehending stare; then she turned him around and when she saw his back, she stood suddenly and called Daddy and Brother Sloan. Michael said they stood around him a long time, talking in low voices, shooing the other children away when they tried to sneak a peek, Daddy trying to pat Ira reassuringly on the back, but not quite able to find a place to lay his hand, finally settling on a tousle of the hair; that's when Brother Sloan took out his handkerchief and blew his nose and said maybe it'd be best if we went on home.

So back to town we came, Michael smelling like a girl from the lotion, me feeling like one after Cassie's two-second surgery, and Ira, undaunted by it all, chattering like a magpie.

To tell you the truth, it was so strange, cigarette burns and a strong reaction to an unseen back, that at the time, I didn't pay much attention to Michael's story. However, I was diverted enough from my own troubles to sneak to the window and press my ear to the fan and see what the larger community's verdict would be, but found only Mama and Daddy there on the porch.

She was crying, Mama was, low, bone-wracking sobs that Daddy was trying to comfort, but she had a stuffy shake to her voice like she'd been crying for hours and planned to cry hours more before all was said and done. "Why does God allow it?" she kept asking. But Daddy was only repetitive, saying gently, over and over, "Hush sugar, the State'll take care of it. You done what you could. Hush—"

But she would not be soothed and waited on the porch with a handkerchief balled in her fist till the gray car with the state tags pulled up around eleven the next morning, and then and only then, would she go inside.

I was in the backyard with Ira at the time, nailing shingles on the treehouse, somewhat recovered from the weekend tragedy (Cassie's words, not Ira's back, which only perplexed me), still sad and listless and damned, but trying to make a go of it, when Mrs. Sims interrupted our work, coming to the back door and calling Ira inside, then depositing Myra on the porch steps.

From my perch in the tree I could see that even that late in the morning, she was still in her gown, a pale blue one, polished batiste, the kind old grannies wore, except she didn't look very grannie-like in it, she looked—I couldn't have told you how she looked. All I could have said was that it was just her, Myra Sims, my good friend Ira's spoiled little sister, sitting there on the back porch steps with her knees to her chest, not looking like herself, but not looking grannie-like either, despite the gown. Then finally I realized the difference: it was her hair. It was unbraided for once, unraveling in tiny krimps below her elbows, and for the first time, I saw it in the direct sun and noted that it wasn't brown at all, it was red. Deep auburn, the color of something—I couldn't have told you that, either, as I set my hammer down and dropped to the ground, inching to the fence, afraid I'd scare her, for she had not seen me, not yet.

"Hey," I finally called when I was within speaking distance. She was startled at first, but quickly calm when she saw it was only me, not at all embarrassed at being seen outside in her gown, only smiling a very kind, very sweet smile, saying, "Hey Gabrielle."

I don't know why she called me that, no one ever called me anything but Gabe, and she stretched it out to three syllables, so it sounded like Gay-bree-elle.

Well, what can I say? I was charmed and crept closer, leaning on the fence with studied nonchalance, casting about for an opener and coming up with something tried and true, asking her what was up at school.

But she didn't have a chance to answer, her mother was suddenly at the door, calling her inside in a harsh, frightened voice, and to my great teeth-gnashing despair, it was the last time I saw her for many weeks. Apparently, Mama's call to the public health nurse had embroiled the Sims in a child abuse investigation, and though we could see no actual results in terms of a healthier-looking Ira, Mr. Sims now hated our guts and refused to let either of his children leave the house. It was a cruel, calculated move, one the public health authorities did not challenge, though on the rare occasions we saw Ira, he was horribly emaciated, his eyes sunk deep in his head, but his smile still jaunty, as if spending twenty-four hours a day under the same eight-hundred-square-foot roof was all a matter of routine course.

As for Myra, I could only catch infrequent, unanswered glimpses of her till August finally crept by and September was upon us, when we could walk to school together while the Old Man was out of sight— nursing a hangover or at work unloading luggage at the bus station. I found if I timed it just right, I could usually manage to walk more or less at her side, careful to maintain a casual discretion, for until now, the other boys had been as foolish as I in overlooking her charm, and I wasn't too eager for the competition since they were growing more experienced by the week at the hands of Cassie Lea while I remained as untouched as a nun.

Not that we talked as we strolled along. That had been strictly forbidden by the Old Man, and Myra and Ira were nothing if not obedient, but just being there at her side was enough. In fact, after Cassie's hard words, a passive, voiceless girl with red hair and a sweet curved face was my idea of The Perfect Woman, and by Halloween, I was almost sick with love. Drunk with it. Eaten alive. Every morning at five o'clock sharp, I'd wake suddenly in the silent chill of the old frame house and lie perfectly still, my eyes following every tick of the clock till it would finally ring at seven, when I'd jump up and dress and whip through breakfast so I could be on the porch by seven-thirty, casually falling into step with Ira and his sister, saying "hey" very pleasantly, politely ignoring their inability to reply. I'd accept Ira's skeletal grin and Myra's shy, downcast eyes without missing a step, knowing in my heart that if she'd been allowed to speak, she'd have lifted her sweet face and said: "Hey, Gay-bree-elle."

But she couldn't and wouldn't till sometime after Christmas, Christmas of '61 or 2, when my mother had finally had enough. For six months she'd waited on the State to do its duty, then, being the consummate guerrilla fighter she is, abruptly shifted tactics. And though she never changed her opinion of either of the adult Sims, referring to them privately as "that woman what lives next door" and "that thang she lets lay up over there," to the casual observer she became their very best friend in the world. "Bent over backwards" is one way of putting it. "Held her mouth right" is another.

It was the box that did it.

On Christmas Eve, she'd seen Old Man Sims come home with a box, a large, obviously present box, and throughout our Christmas Eve feast, Mama had repeatedly expressed a heartfelt desire that box enclose a gift for poor Ira.

Well, she should have known better, and sure enough, bright and early Christmas morning, Old Man Sims was out on Lafayette, pushing Myra around on a brand-new, fire-engine-red two-wheeler while Ira sat on the curb and stared. I joined him there, trying to be happy for her, though the idea of walking to school with a grinning, silent Ira while Myra flashed by on a red bike was a powerful burden to bear, and I abandoned my walkie-talkies and *Mad* magazines to take to my bed with a stomachache from sheer angst.

Mama took to her own bed later in the day after she went out to throw the torn wrapping paper and finished bows into the burn barrel and saw Ira across the fence in his backyard, playing with the big box Myra's bike had come in. She watched him in silence, shaking her head, probably again reflecting on the nature of God, but when he saw her watching him, Ira jumped up and broke his five-month forced silence to point proudly at the box. "Look a-here what I got me for Christmas, Sister Catts," he said without a shred of irony. "Got it *bran' new*. Come from Sears."

And poor Mama, it almost unhinged her mind. She was country Baptist, the kind that celebrated Christmas with a vengeance bordering on insanity, selling her soul on credit to the Dollar Store and Western Auto to make sure her children had a tree and a turkey and a few wrapped presents. And there Ira stood, so very proud of his *box*.

Well, Old Man Sims had his way that Christmas, but every dog has his day, they say, and after a few more tears on the porch over why God let things like this happen, Mama proved her skill as a minister's daughter who'd learned to live with more than one congregation of fickle Baptists.

The next morning she was out in the yard before breakfast, cutting back her roses, her hair tied up prettily in a bandana, and the moment Mr. Sims showed his face on the porch, she called over gaily, "Why, good morning, Mister Sims. Thet was a mighty pretty bicycle you got your girl Myra. Just where did you get it, I was wanting to know. My boy Michael's been a-wanting one."

The Old Man knew everyone on Magnolia Hill hated him for what he'd done to Ira and had paused a moment in stunned amazement, then ducked by, ignoring her in a flat snub that deterred Mama not in the least. She was a Baptist with a mission, and every morning or afternoon when she knew Mr. Sims would be coming or going would make it her business to be on the porch or in the yard, a smile fixed on her small, pretty face, her voice smooth as silk. Sometimes it was the routine ("Why it's coming up a cloud, I do believe—"), sometimes, blatant flattery ("Yessir, that baby a yours, thet Myra, she's just pretty as she can be—"), and by Easter, tensions had eased to the point that Ira was once again a fixture at our table, much as before, consuming rice and potatoes like a machine, and since he'd seen his back, Daddy never told him to hush anymore, no matter how much he talked.

And though Myra never again walked to school at my side, she was again allowed outdoors, and in the six-month exile, she seemed to have blossomed from a faint childhood prettiness to the very early signs of a serious, head-turning beauty. Suddenly, every boy on the block was Ira's best friend, and the Sims' front porch—where Myra would sometimes sit and watch the sunset—a popular hangout. And though Myra herself seldom spoke, we could have cared less; she was the queen and we were her slaves, and if she'd have told us to eat dirt, we'd have been knocking on Mama's kitchen door, asking to borrow spoons.

Among ourselves, we frequently discussed whom she favored, but it was Jack Krane, a skinny boy new to Magnolia Hill by way of Tuscaloosa who considered himself a fair hand with the ladies, who pressed the question. After a night of kissing Cassie during a missionary film, he was brazen enough to ask it right out loud, right in front of everyone. The rest of us froze, but Myra only continued to kick her heels on the edge of the porch, her eyes on the mauve sky, consciously or unconsciously ignoring this bit of confrontation.

But old Ira, he was there too and, not being anyone's fool, could see his newfound popularity had more than a little to do with his sister and, being the natural survivor he was, began playing it up, making the most of it. Drawing his dirty feet under him, he answered Jack in a playful, sing-song voice, his eyes cutting aside to Myra's downcast face.

"Naw, Jack," he said, "she doan love you."

Jack, of course, tried to argue, but Ira's voice was still light, making a game of it for the entertainment of all his dear new friends. "She doan love no *Alabama* boys."

Still, Myra's face was averted, and Ira began making his way across the porch on tiptoe, teasing her slyly. "Myra doan love no *brown*-haired boys. She doan love no *base*ball-playing boys."

Well, that cut just about everyone but me and Benny, a redhead, and Albert, a black-haired third cousin of mine, and I could feel my heart beating in my neck as Ira continued his little dance over to his sister.

"Naw, Myra likes her boys sweet. She like sissy-boys, dontchu, Myra?"

She still gave no indication she'd heard a word he'd said, but I was thanking God fast and furiously for my light hair, my reputation as an athletic non-starter, even my Truman Capote leanings, when Ira finally clinched it with a toe prod to Myra's leg and a wink.

"Myra doan like boys at all, she likes *angels*, dontchu, sweetpea? Writes their name all over the closet."

Well, it was me. Undoubtedly, unexpectedly me, beating out a dozen faster, taller boys: boys who'd kissed a girl who wore a two-piece, boys who'd done more than kiss her, if you believed their talk, and my face was suddenly as red as a beet. But Myra's was even redder, almost scarlet as she looked up and met my eye in one panicked flash, and there was no doubt at all Ira was telling the truth. Singing it, in fact, as he pranced around the porch: "Myra and Ga-habe, sittin' in a tree, K-I-S-S-I-N-G—"

The other boys joined in with relish, trying to vent the pain of rejection by dishing out a little humiliation, and though I made a face of great disgust and told them what idiots they were, it was the sweetest little tune I'd ever heard in my life. After a few swings at her brother, Myra retreated inside, and the other boys wandered off to join a late baseball game at the corner, but I had plans of my own right there on Lafayette and retired to the backyard with all the infinite patience of a hundred-and-thirty-pound spider.

I knew she'd be out, she had to be out (they had an outhouse, remember), and just before full dark descended, my perseverance paid off when the back door opened and she went down the path. I stationed myself at the fence so I could face her on her return trip and tell her not to worry, that I loved her too, but my eagerness seemed to scare her off, and she ignored me completely, hurrying up the steps without a word and closing the back door firmly behind her.

I was disappointed, of course, but not crushed, deciding Myra was not only beautiful, but a lady of rare refinement, and the next morning, a Saturday in late January, the air crisp and Florida-cold, I tried a gentler approach, reading with my back against the old sweetgum tree, creating what I hoped was an air of friendly indifference. The book in my hands was my all-time favorite, *Gone with the Wind*, and I hoped she noted the size, for I'd read it twice already and was to Reconstruction the third time around, an accomplishment that stunned and amazed my family to the degree that rumor of my superior intellect was circulating nightly through the porch grapevine.

But again, she passed by without a word, and I was afraid my strategy had erred on the side of subtlety, when she paused on the bottom step and, after a moment, turned, and in a thin, country voice, asked, "Gabrielle? Whatchu readin' there?"

With a yawn and a small stretch, I laid the book against my chest. "*Gone with the Wind*," I said, then, slyly, "It's to the good part now. Scarlett's back at Tara. In a minute she's gone shoot this Yankee in the face." I paused, then threw out the real kicker as if in afterthought, "I remember from the *last time*."

It took a moment for the implication of this enormous revelation to sink in. Then Myra's eyes widened. "You read it before? That big ole thang?"

"Oh sure," I said with modest deprecation; then after a moment, "Well, actually I read it *twict*."

I could tell by her look of blank amazement that the matter of my good sense would never be an issue between us; that I'd nailed that one down for good, and after a moment, she murmured, "What in the world's it about?"

27

"The Civil War," I replied with oily confidence, as this was another area of my expertise, but she only retained that blank stare and asked without shame, "What's thet?"

"The Civil War?" I asked incredulously, for around our house it was a subject only slightly less revered than the Resurrection, and when I determined her ignorance was genuine, I sought to rectify the matter with a two-hour sermon on the Gospel according to Margaret Mitchell.

"All this," I began, waving my arms to encompass the orange-sand yards, the thin rusted wire of the fence, "use to be plantations. White people lived here growing cotton and whatall, and the niggers were our slaves. They did the work while people like us had barbecues and daInces and things."

I daresay it was as pretty a little fiction as was ever conceived on the hard ridge of survival known as Magnolia Hill, but Myra was charmed by it all and never tired of hearing of life way down yonder in the land of cotton. All winter long and into another azure summer, the mimosa scenting the air sweetly, like light powder, we'd sit across the pig wire fence, sometimes eating cookies I sneaked from Mama's kitchen or reading aloud, but usually just talking. Me doing most of it, occasionally standing to emphasize a point or draw maps in the dirt, and when I'd exhausted the Cause, I expanded to tell her of the French Revolution and the Napoleonic Wars, finding her a good listener, her eyes quiet and distant, the color of dark, still water.

Now I was a born historian, but I think it was during these evening lectures in my backyard in the summer of '62 that the seeds were sown for my life's work as a revisionist, for I was still deathly in love and felt no compunction at all in reorganizing the facts a little when it suited me. Napoleon, I told her, was short, blonde and stocky, and while I left Scarlett pretty much intact, Rhett became the golden blonde and Ashley took on the black hair and the mustache. Myra never questioned me, never, for my hard-headed obsessions seemed to have overwhelmed her, and it was only when autumn had come around again, the warm smell of burning leaves softening the sharp evening chill, that I grew confident enough of my disciple to let her lead the play a little more.

Well, she was beautiful, she was priceless, she was the heart of my heart, but she was still just a girl, and I found her taste ran to the childishly mundane, mostly hopscotch and house. But I was man enough to go along with it, and late one afternoon, it must have still been autumn as the cold had not yet driven us indoors, I set about designing her a truly tremendous hopscotch board in the dirt under the old sweetgum by pointing over the fence with a stick. What had begun as a spur-of-the-moment idea had stretched into an afternoon project, since either my directions were faulty, or Myra's grasp of geometry inadequate, and no matter how carefully I told her to draw a circle, a cir-cle, Myra, a *circle*, she'd eagerly scratch out a rectangle or a square, then look at me expectantly. Tedious, it was, but I never lost my temper, for as I have said, I can be a regular fountainhead of patience when it suits me, and finally, the noon sun long gone, the cold shadows of early twilight upon us, she was finished, her knees red from the sand, her hair unraveling from its tight braid, but there at her feet, a truly remarkable eighteen-square hopscotch board.

"Now, go and getchure rock," I told her, my elbows on the fence, my pointer stick tapping the yard. "Make sure it's flat. A roundun'll roll."

Obedient to the core, she went kicking through the sand under the live oak, and I was yelling further instructions when suddenly, without warning, I was hanging in midair from my wrist, my toes a good inch off the ground.

"What'sat arm doing in my yard?" A soft voice whispered in my ear, and I could smell the whiskey before I could see him, my eyes still on Myra, who was kneeling in the dirt, shouting, "Here, Gabriel! A nice flat—" But she never got it out, for when she turned and saw her father standing there, her face blanked, suddenly, like a blown bulb, the nice flat rock still clutched in her hand.

There was a soft grating in my wrist that I could hear rather than actually feel, and I was feebly trying to shake myself loose when our back door opened with a pop, and my mother came down the back steps, her machete of a voice coming before her.

"Put my boy down, let him loose. I'll call the Law, you drunk sorry piece of trash," she said, emphasizing the words in a venomous sing-song that sounded like: putmyboyDOWN, lethimLOOSE, I'llcalltheLAW, youdrunksorryPIECEofTRASH, and such was her ferocity that even Mr. Sims wilted before her, letting me crumple to the dirt.

He tried to offer a sullen explanation: "—in my yard, not given permission to come in my yard—"

But Mama was mad, mad, mad; her baby Gabe had been touched, and if it cost poor Ira all the rice in China, she couldn't be stopped, poking her little face over the fence and letting six months of forced silence break like a dam: "SEE if I doan call the Law! SEE if I doan tell my husband, he'll kill you, he'll shoot you like the dog you are, putting your HAND on my CHILE—"

Then she picked me up, all one hundred thirty or so pounds of me, while she probably tipped the scales herself at ninety-eight, and carried me inside, her voice as loud and grieved as a prophet, telling the world, "Tired of putting up with trash, TIRED, won't stand for it no more."

She laid me on the couch while she called the doctor, and as the numbed nerves in my wrist came back to life with a sear that set my teeth on edge and sent involuntary tears streaming down my face, I could hear Mr. Sims outside, not yelling at Mama, but shouting in a shaking fury, "Git in this house this minute, young lady. I have to tell you agin—"

At the moment, I was too overcome by the shock of pain in my wrist to understand the significance of these words, but later, years later, the memory of them would sicken me when I realized that Myra had been disobeying her father on my behalf, indulging in a protest in a small helpless way that she'd live to pay for, pay dearly. By then, of course, everyone on Magnolia Hill had come to understand a bit more of the mystery of Ira and Myra's relentless passivity, of the idiotic grin in one and the glazed blindness in the other, and none of us could believe it, still can't, to this day.

For we were a poor but good-natured lot there with our hymns and our paper soles and our virginity, and none of us had ever looked into the face of evil before, so it's really no wonder we didn't recognize it, not at first. Not till it raised its head and laughed in our faces, and by then, I don't know, even now, sometimes survival doesn't seem like enough.

Chapter

4

*M*ama was not mouthing idle threats when she promised to call the law on Mr. Sims, for all the good it did. Later that evening a deputy came by and filed a complaint, and Mr. Sims was questioned, but the general consensus was that a man had a right to protect his property, and while breaking a thirteen-year-old's wrist was extreme, it was by far not the worse thing that had ever happened on Magnolia Hill and nothing to worry the legal system with. So he was let off with a warning to straighten up and lay off the liquor, and Mama's second threat, that Daddy would shoot him, was sidetracked by the combined efforts of Brother Sloan and Uncle Case and Mama herself. Once she'd gotten hold of her temper, she began to see that this small run-in had the capacity to explode into a serious, life-threatening confrontation, for shootings and knifings and near-fatal fistfights were not unheard of occurrences on the Hill. And though she still hated Mr. Sims and told everyone who came by just how sorry he truly was and always would be, she wasn't mad enough to risk her husband's life and had the far-sightedness to have the preacher and her brother there when she gave him the news about my wrist.

Some of what came before and much of what came later has faded to me, but that night stands out so clearly in my mind: the smell of the oil-burning furnace in the living room, the murmur of voices on the porch, the stark white cast on my hand and forearm which in my drugged semi-sleep I kept banging on the mattress and headboard. I remember how they stood around my bed in the chill half-light when Daddy finally came home from work that night, his shirt sprinkled with paint from the good job he'd recently landed with a contractor, and how he'd kept his voice very calm, waking me to ask one quiet question: "Son, didju sass him?"

I gave as truthful an account as I could remember, while Uncle Case rested his hands on Daddy's shoulders and Brother Sloan kept his eyes on Daddy's face—nervous, darting eyes that searched for any flicker of that fatal stab of anger, but it never came. His expression never changed at all; he only stood when I finished and kissed my forehead and told me to get some sleep, then allowed himself to be led into the living room, Uncle Case still resting his hand on his shoulder, Brother Sloan quoting Jesus, saying something about going the second mile.

What Daddy's reply was, I never knew. Dr. Winston's pills kept me in a narcotic haze that lasted the better part of a week, and when I was finally on my feet, everything was back to normal, except my forearm was still immobilized in the cast and Myra was out of my reach, seemingly forever.

She wasn't in the yard, she wasn't on the porch, I could never even catch her en route to the outhouse, but no one seemed overly concerned with her absence, for Ira had gone unaccountably unpunished this time and continued to visit our table as regularly as clockwork, his jaws working hell for leather, his chatter never stopping. At first, I asked after her constantly, but he was vague and happy, saying she was busy at home helping with the chores, then requesting another biscuit, pleasema'am, and I was too profoundly terrified of the Old Man to press the issue. Late at night, while the rest of the neighborhood slept easy on the crest of a mild, frostless autumn, I tossed and turned in restless dread, afraid to cross the border to sleep, when I'd again feel the sour, nasty breath on my neck and the merciless voice in my ear, not speaking in threat, but in friendly confidence, whispering hideous secrets I could never face in the clear, red-leaved light of day.

So in a way, you could say I abandoned her; we all did since Ira's face was filling out nicely, and I still had Scarlett and Rhett to amuse me, and at church, my cast had somehow given me the romantic air of the wounded soldier, changing Cassie's mind about liking fat boys. Early in November she began making sly advances toward me, pressing against me in the hall, grinning at me in choir, and when the youth group took an overnight trip to Mobile, she smiled coquettishly, and in the full hearing of seven of my nine best friends, said, "I'm riding with Ga-habe."

I guess she thought I'd weep at the chance, for there was a regular folk-history brewing over the joys of sitting in a dark car with Cassie Lea Scales, but my heart belonged to poor absent Myra, and I only shook my head. "I'm riding with Brother Sloan."

This was the only car Cassie knew better than to practice her craft in and, all in all, a shocking pronouncement to say the least. My seven best friends, who knew intimately how sweet the rewards of Cassie's favor could be, were stunned speechless, and something in their wide, incredulous eyes must have signaled to Cassie that her control was slipping, for with all the boundless viciousness of an insecure thirteen year old, she hissed, "Well, that's just fine with me, Gabe Catts. I know all about boys like you. I know what y'all are called. My Daddy told me."

My seven good friends were looking at me with even more interest then, as if calculating how something like that might complicate how fast they got dressed around me in gym, but my love for Myra had given me the upper hand on old Cass, and with titanic control, I crossed my cast to my chest and lifted my face to the stars. "Yeah, well, that's OK with me, Cassie Lea Scales. That's just fine, 'cause my *mama* told me the name for girls like you."

Everyone, even Cassie, was looking at me now, and as I started for Brother Sloan's car, I went in for the kill. "And if you keep on doing it like you been doing it, you may get good enough to make some money with it when you git grown."

Well, poor Cassie. In that day and time I could have thrown gasoline on her and set a match to her hair and caused less damage, and on the way to Mobile that night, I remember being a little shocked at my cruelty, for I'd seen a glimpse of something like it next door, and though it frightened me, I still had no name for it. Only a feeling, a rumor of gigantic unease, that had no basis in reality at all, but could sometimes be seen in the abstract, as when I sat on the back porch the day after Thanksgiving and watched a violent winter rainstorm pulverize Myra's carefully numbered eighteen-square hopscotch board, leaving nothing but a dirty, reflectionless puddle that froze, then dried to blank, unmarked dirt.

But that's all, nothing material, nothing that could lure the sheriff back to Magnolia Hill, and it wasn't until Ira let the cat out of the bag quite accidentally that the law was finally forced to step in and do its duty.

It was January by then, the flat, snowless days of bitter Gulf-blown winds, the oaks shedding, the pecan trees long harvested of their crop, leaving Magnolia Hill in a state of rare ugliness, loose panes rattling in their windows, small victory gardens blank rectangles of faceless, fruitless dirt. Ira was eating supper with us that night, an event that was becoming somewhat less common since Christmas when he'd found a job stocking shelves at a corner grocery store and would take as many hours as they'd give him. But for all his labor, he never seemed one penny richer, still wearing not one stitch more than what came out of the bags of hand-me-downs Mama handed over the fence every few months, and I knew his continuing poverty had not escaped Mama's eagle eye, when, halfway through the meal, she asked him what he was doing with all the money he was making down at the store.

"Give it to my daddy, Sister Catts," he said solemnly. "Every penny I give to him."

Daddy looked a little sour at this, but I guess he could find nothing technically wrong with a son helping support his family, but it must have rankled him, for he asked in a very mild voice, "He ain't give you namore them whippings, has he?"

Now, as I have said, Ira was nobody's fool and must have remembered the last interest we had taken in his welfare had almost led to his virtual starvation, for he was pathetically eager to reassure us everything was fine, shaking his head emphatically, saying, "No sir, no, not atall—"

Daddy just watched him, and Ira, in a desperate attempt to be reconciliatory, added, "Never lays a hand on neither a us, Brother Catts, me nor Myra one. Not no more. Shurff won't let him."

The fact that the law was finally stepping in and doing its duty seemed to satisfy Daddy, for he turned his attention back to the food and Ira, pleased with his success, asked for seconds, pleasema'am, and expanded grandly as Mama filled his plate. "Course, he never did whip Myra. Nurse couldn't find a mark on her, not a mark. He never has touched ole Myra—" he paused as he took his plate, then, "'cept to *ponk* her."

He grinned at me when he said it, for this little contribution to our vocabulary had come to be known as his most famous creative achievement, and while the rest of us stared at him in stunned, blank silence, he rolled along without turning a hair. "Daddy gits mad, he locks her in the closet. But never a mark," he said sagely, "is laid on her back."

We were still in total shock, Daddy's fork stalled in actual midair, but Ira hadn't taken a breath as he inhaled the corn and tried to put an anecdotal twist on his story. "One time,"—he grinned—"one time, he clean forgot her. She stayed there a solid week." He laughed, for this was nothing to him. He was the human ashtray, remember, and molestation and closets and beatings with electrical cord were the furniture of his twelve-year-old world. "Mama let her out to pee, but right back in she went. Would a stayed till she died, I reckon, Daddy hadn't sobered up—"

That's when my father stood—all in one smooth, joined motion, his chair scraping the wood floor, his napkin falling to the floor untouched, ignoring Mama, who had stood too, and was saying, "Simon. Simon."

She gripped his arm as if to stop him, but he only looked at her, his paint-flecked face blank and set, and I knew that Mama could cry and we could cry and Brother Sloan could talk about the second mile till hell froze over, and it wouldn't stop Daddy from walking out that door.

Mama must have seen it too, for she spoke no further word of protest, only dropping her hand and not even watching as he left, keeping her eyes on the half-eaten food on the table while she waited for the slam of the screen door, closing her eyes a moment when it hit with a flimsy crack that bounced back once, then twice, then was finally still. Then, being the rock-solid, born-again pragmatist she is, Mama gave Ira his plate and sent him out the back door, then went to the phone and called, not the sheriff nor the preacher, but the ambulance.

By the time we made the porch, he already needed one, for Old Man Sims outweighed him by a good eighty pounds, and whatever Daddy had said in that thirty-second interval had so enraged him that he had not been content to merely knock him off the porch but had   followed him down to the yard, where he was kicking the life out of him, one tremendous blow at a time, laughing, I swear to God, *laughing* while he did it. Michael shook off Mama and took the fence in one bound, and Candace and I screamed like the terrified children we were as Mr. Sims turned and took him down with one blow, one vicious hammer of a backhand to the face. He may have started in on Michael then, kicking him, if Brother McQuaig (Benny's father) had not heard our screams and crossed Lafayette with a shotgun in his hands, describing in a calm, light voice just how much he'd love to blow Mr. Sims' head off if he made one more move, just one.

Then the ambulance was there and the sheriff, who tried to get a statement from Mama, but found her teeth-chattering hysterical as she tried to nurse Daddy back to consciousness, only able to point at Mr. Sims and scream, "Him! Him!"

So the sheriff couldn't arrest anyone till Daddy made a statement, and after the ambulance roared away, all was particularly quiet on Lafayette Street. Mama was in the bedroom, changing into her good dress to go to the hospital; Candace was on the front porch, holding ice on Michael's eye; and I was in the dining room, looking at the remains of supper, finally realizing the name of the evil that lived next door, but still not very sure what to do about it, when there was a soft knock on the back door.

I answered it, cautiously opening the door with my good hand and seeing it was Mrs. Sims, standing there with a pale, sagging Myra pressed to her side, half-buried in the skirt of her old housedress. To this day, I cannot properly remember Mrs. Sims as a young woman, what she looked like or how she spoke, for her husband's personality dominated the household so completely that she was rendered a mere afterthought. But that evening, I do remember two things about her very distinctly: a neat row of fresh red circles on her chin and neck, as if she'd been slammed against a wall with an open hand, and the way her hands shook with a small motion as she spoke in a low, hoarse whisper. "He's leaving. Leaving tonight, gone take my baby. Tell your Mama, ast her if she could—if she might—"

I understood in one horrified gasp and ran to the bedroom and pulled Mama, still in her slip, to the kitchen, where Mrs. Sims, her face expressionless, repeated her low, urgent request. "Leldon's going. Going to Texas. Says he's a-taking her. Please, ma'am, please—"

Without waiting for another word of explanation, Mama took Myra and pushed Mrs. Sims out the door, her voice a fierce whisper. "Go. Go. Not back there—the church—no, the tracks—no, I'll keep her, *go*—"

Mrs. Sims turned and started off the porch in the clumsy, mincing stride of a grown woman, while Mama shut the door with her knee and began going room to room, looking for a hiding place, her eyes white and frantic as a voice next door began yelling, "Myra? Myra Louise Sims! Eloise? Eloise!"

Then, in one of those grotesque ironics that seem to haunt our household, she chose the best hiding place she could manage in such a pinch: the rattling old chifforobe she and Daddy used for a closet. So poor Myra was out of the frying pan and into the fire, in a manner of speaking, but showed no sign of worry, only watching in a pale, wordless silence as Mama dug out the shoes and hats and Sunday suits and pushed her in—then, seeing me at the door, told me to get in and be quiet, or she'd kill me. Then she shut the door and locked the catch, and all was quiet.

I guess I was to be Myra's guard or company or prayer partner; there was no time to explain with Mr. Sims just beyond the flimsy wall, so close we could hear the shake of anger in his voice as he stood on the porch and yelled, "Myra! I'm gone beat you till blood runs down your laigs, you don't git to this house this MINUTE!"

I later learned that Mama, being the brilliant tactician she is, threw on a dress and sought to divert the attack by crossing Lafayette and standing on Sister McQuaig's porch, crying into her handkerchief, telling the handful of women who'd gathered there that she'd called her *daddy* and her *brother* and they were on their *way*, but I knew nothing of this at the time, for my eyes had adjusted to the darkness, and I was watching Myra.

Sitting in a closet must have indeed been routine to her, for she didn't look affected at all, only leaning a little bit forward, her shoulders slumped, her face blank and white. As her father's rampage gained momentum outside, she would occasionally close her eyes a moment, but was in no way the crying, peeing-in-the-pants baby I was, even having the ability to communicate, reaching out her hand to touch my cast, whispering, "Gabriel? Didju hurt yourself?"

My tears subsided a moment, for she'd been standing right there when her father had done the job on my wrist, but before I could answer, someone was on the porch yelling. Then what sounded like a mob was there. I could hear potted plants crashing and furniture flying. Then there was the squall of another siren, then silence. Long, unbroken silence, like the eye of a hurricane, that Myra finally broke with her small, kind voice: "Gabriel? Didju fall?"

When she asked it this time, there was a hiss outside the door and Mama's voice, low and harsh, telling us to hush. So we were perfectly quiet for another good hour, and at some point I reached out and held Myra's soft little hand, for her comfort or mine I don't know, and just before Mama opened the door, I told her that I loved her, too. Then I bent my mouth to her ear and whispered that if she wanted to, we could wait till we were married to kiss, but if she wanted to, we could do it now. She didn't answer by any word or gesture, but only leaned over and pressed her lips to mine for a bare two seconds. The impact of that dry little kiss sent a shock clear to my toes, rendering me speechless, and I still had not recovered when Mama opened the closet and pulled us out, ignoring me to press Myra to her chest, crying so hard the torrent of tears wet Myra's tightly braided hair and rolled down into her eyes.

I stumbled out behind her, blinking at the glare of the lightbulbs, seeing that night had fallen on Magnolia Hill, and Uncle Case was back, a shotgun cradled casually in his elbow, and Brother Sloan was there too, carrying no weapon other than his Bible, but looking like he'd enjoy beating someone to death with it.

"She's got a fever," Mama murmured to him over Myra's head. "Somebody get Dr. Winston. She's hot as a firecracker—"

Uncle Case left and Brother Sloan led me out to the porch, where Michael, with a grotesquely swollen eye, was sitting in a rocker discussing the Yankees' chances in the American League with Benny and Brother McQuaig. The endless pots of begonias and geraniums and ferns that usually balanced themselves along the porch rail were scattered and broken on the ground, and another shotgun was propped against the door with no explanation at all, but other than that, all was much as it should be, the night fine and warm for January, the men in their shirtsleeves. After I hugged Brother McQuaig and told him I loved him (which was the least I figured I owed the man who'd saved my father's life), I took a seat on the porch swing and found myself watching the Sims' house, which stood across the rough, sagging old fence in near darkness, the front door slightly ajar, the sidewalk strewn with pieces of boxes and bits of trash and a sock or two, all signs of a hasty exit. So it was gone, the evil in that house, and I could have wept from sheer relief, not realizing until then what an awful weight of dread had gathered over Magnolia Hill while that man lived there.

Then I closed my eyes and thought that soon we'd have to start getting dressed to go visit Daddy in the hospital; then Mrs. Sims would be back and arrangements for Ira and Myra would have to be plotted out, and Mama would have to call Daddy's boss and tell him Daddy wouldn't be in tomorrow, maybe try to talk him into holding his job for him.

Soon, the dry, boring details of life would be upon me, but for one sterling moment there, I was alive and well in the here and now. For the evil that had hidden next door had been put to battle and bested, and

Myra was safe in Mama's arms, and as I listened to the rise and fall of the calm, familiar voices on the clean, mild night, I had a sure, shining feeling in my chest that the bad was behind me now—that I had survived it unscathed, and it would never touch me, not ever again, as long as I lived.

I was thirteen years old.

Chapter

5

A s a child, *I was so often deceived* by hope that I grew into the cynic I am today, and that night on Lafayette, the sight of that still, empty house lulled me into a false calm. For within the month, Myra was nothing more than a shake of the head and a murmur of regret on Magnolia Hill, something for the adults to discuss with genuine horror on the porch at night after the children were safely tucked away in bed.

Now, had I been older, or heir to even one grain of my mother's hard-nosed practicality, I would have seen the inevitable coming, realizing that though Mr. Sims was out of the picture for the time being, Mrs. Sims couldn't afford to wait around for him to get drunk enough to come back and finish her off. But I wasn't, of course. I was too busy being relieved, spending my afternoons knocking on the Sims' front door and finally being allowed inside the scantily furnished, dimly lit living room, whiling away the cold twilight playing Old Maid over a battered old TV tray with a mysteriously ailing Myra, making jokes, reading books, trying desperately to recapture some of the happiness we'd conjured out by the fence on the warm summer nights before the fall.

A valiant effort that went mostly unrewarded, though Myra did grow a bit more animated when her fever broke, occasionally laughing or, once or twice, when her mother was next door making one of her endless phone calls, letting me kiss her again, full on the mouth. An exercise in heart-thumping, hand-sweating ectasy that almost paralyzed me, but left her pretty much untouched, only sitting there with the Old Maid in her hand, and the Barber and the Ballerina, reaching out to pick another card, calmly assenting when I asked her to marry me, equally assenting when I insisted she get rid of the red bike, so when she started back to school, she could do it the way the good Lord intended, walking by my side.

In a pattern that was to follow me the rest of my life I was making plans, big plans, over that rattling old tray, while behind my back, the larger world churned out plans of its own, plans I was blissfully unaware of till mid-February, Florida spring just beginning to make a sly inroad on the pale, leafless winter, when I came home from school one afternoon and found a truck blocking Lafayette.

It was a moving van, Candace told me, though I didn't connect the pieces, even when Ira came to the back door carrying some toy or book I'd left over there, his face scarlet with excitement.

"We're going now," he said. I still didn't get it, thinking Myra had a doctor's appointment, when he added mysteriously, "Myra says bye."

She'd spent two days in Jackson Memorial that month—I didn't know why, Mama wouldn't say—and still had to go back to the county health nurse every so often, for blood tests, she told me, holding up a bandaged finger as evidence. So I didn't think much of Ira's message, only reorganizing my afternoon, and when I finally emerged late in the evening, the naked tree line a delicate etching in black against the mauve of a winter sunset, I was not worried as much as I was perplexed when no one answered my knock.

The curtains were drawn, the house perfectly still, a trash heap of cans and torn newspaper and boxes piled in the corner of the yard, but nothing else amiss, and I waited and waited, wanting to ask someone what was keeping them—didn't the doctor's office close at five?—but there was no one to ask. Mama had taken the bus downtown to haggle with our policy man over Daddy's disability benefits, and I hesitated to leave the porch to ask one of the neighbors, afraid I'd miss something. So even after full dark had descended, neighborhood dining rooms filling with light, mothers coming to the porch to call their children, I waited, going to the door every so often and knocking again, then listening, listening with every nerve in my body, not allowing myself the luxury of anger, but caught in a pale, breathless patience that finally broke when I heard the brakes of the bus at the corner.

Late it was, past eight, Mama's cloth coat shapeless and gray against the houses as she made her way slowly down the dark street. When she heard me calling, she stopped a moment; then with no wasted words, only a great, a profound deliberation, she came around the fence through the Sims' front gate, and it was only when she was right at the foot of the steps that she answered my loud, querulous questions, standing there with one hand on the rail, looking up at me with a tired, drawn face. "They're gone, baby," she said quietly. "They're gone."

For a moment I only stood there blankly, trying to think of another question, one that would make it all right, one that would change Mama's answer and bring Myra back. But nothing came, and after a moment of desperate groping, I jumped flat-footed off that high, rattling old porch and ran away, refusing to come in to supper, refusing to listen to one more word because I really didn't need to: I knew already and had ever since I'd first knocked on that hollow, empty door three hours before. Knew that she was gone, that I'd let her go without even answering her good-bye.

And though I couldn't face it, refused to discuss it, even with Daddy, talk of their departure filled the length and breadth of Magnolia Hill, and for the first time in three years, the balmy, velvet nights were once again full of the name *Sims*.

"Moving to Birmingham," everyone said, to live with a cousin—or maybe it was an aunt. Anyway, it was kin, and there was a communal sigh of relief among the good folk on Lafayette, who had long grown accustomed to sins like fornication and adultery and theft, but were left nauseated and plagued with guilt over incest, berating themselves for not having seen the signs long ago: the favoritism, the obvious violence, the liquor. It wasn't the first time such a thing had happened, and the women especially, many of whom had been victims themselves of some form of molestation or another, beat their breasts and vented their rage by suggesting creative tortures for Mr. Sims, should he ever show his face on Magnolia Hill again.

But their fantasies of revenge remain unfulfilled to this day, for Mr. Sims never came back to Lafayette, and we eventually heard he died in Sliddell little more than half a dozen years later after a particularly nasty bout with diabetes. Literally rotted to death, one limb at a time, we heard, and my mother frequently voiced a sincere joy that his death was long and lingering, not just because his kicks had ruptured Daddy's spleen, sending him to the hospital for four weeks, thereby landing us more or less permanently in poverty, but also because she'd held Myra in her arms. At least, that's the way she'd explain it on the porch, staring across the fence at the house that never again saw a permanent tenant, but after a few straggling rentals, fell to disrepair. Her face was blank as she murmured reflectively, "If I'd a never touched her, it just wouldn't a seemed real to me. I never would a b'lieved such a thing could happen."

But she had touched Myra; she and I both had, and neither of us forgot her, not for a minute, though Daddy healed fairly quickly and found another job loading crates on the line at Sanger. By summer, life

had returned to normal: Daddy sweating, Mama talking, Candace beginning to date boys, Michael playing baseball.

Always playing baseball.

Now, I have not written my brother Michael into Myra's story
simply because he did not appear in it until the very end when the Old
Man flattened him out with that one lethal punch. While I walked her to
school every morning, while I recreated history and played house over
the fence, while my wrist was being pulverized by her father, Michael
was playing baseball. In fact, it would not be too much of an exaggeration to say that at any given hour between the years of 1952 and 1961,
whenever my brother was not occupied with the necessities of eating
and sleeping and going to school, he was playing baseball. Out on the
corner lot behind the church, sometimes on different organized teams,
sometimes with a ragtag group of men and boys, or if all else failed,
nailing pitches into an old hickory stump, perfecting it to one smooth,
no-nonsense, hundred-mile-an-hour streak. Always playing baseball.

A natural athlete with a small, tight frame and even, balanced
feet, he was probably naturally gifted in the game, but a combination of
things like obsessive drive and precise timing had enabled him to hone
his skills to the point that I have seldom seen any player, professional
or otherwise, with such talent. Pitching eventually became his forte, but
he could do it all, catch, throw, steal bases. By the time he was fourteen,
he was so good no one would play with him, for he could score a dozen
runs off an opponent, even if that opponent was a grown man.

But having or not having competition never seemed to bother
him. He was not in it for the ego gratification, but for the sheer love of
the game that he'd occasionally try to share with me, never with much
success, for the sun made me weak-kneed and the idea of standing out
in it hour after hour was about as inviting as a trip to the dentist. I said
as much to him on many occasions, especially after my hand came out
of the cast when he thought pitching would be the perfect therapy. But
he never nagged too much, for Michael was a very accepting person,

and we were not close enough in age to be locked into the tight claw of sibling rivalry. The actual numerical difference was six and half years, but it was compounded by the fact we were opposites from the moment we were born, or so Mama says. He was dark, I was fair; he, muscular and wiry, while I agonized over having to wear husky jeans. To my knowledge, Michael never opened the pages of anything more taxing than the sports section of the *Democrat*, while I eventually abandoned *Gone with the Wind* for C. Vann Woodward and the Fugitives (not the television show, but I don't have time to explain it here—).

It is very odd, really, the difference between my brother and me, truly not some sort of romantic exaggeration on my part, but scientific fact, almost as if Daddy had undergone a chemical alteration while he sweated malaria in the Islands at MacArthur's back, returning home to Magnolia Hill with a DNA reversal. Of course, sociological factors had a hand in it too, for I was the baby of the family and Michael the oldest son, considered a man at fifteen and taking a night job at Sanger, whereas Mama was still making excuses for me when I was twenty-three and yet to be gainfully employed. So maybe it all comes down to the difference between late-Depression childhood expectations and those of children born in the great twentieth-century phenomenon known as the Baby Boom. Or maybe it all comes down to nothing more than chance; don't ask me. All I know and all I'm saying is this: we were never very much alike, my brother and I, and whereas he died early, I live on and bear the burden of both our histories, and I can assure you, the telling doesn't come easy.

Oh, Michael, Michael, I've turned him over in my mind so much I've lost my perspective and can only remember him in the flat, lifeless accolades they listed at his funeral. I can only remember him as my older brother, the rich one, who bought out the factory he worked in and withstood the town and the Klan to hire a black man as his manager. Who turned down a contract with the Reds to stay home and care for his parents. Who told me the night I left for college to pay no attention to all the family who thought it a criminal waste of time, but to do what I wanted, that I was as smart as anybody and if I wanted to mess with books all my life, well, it was all of my business and none of theirs.

My brother Michael, the one who married Myra.

An event, I am convinced, that would never have come about in the natural order of things, if not for my mother and a growing obsession she began cultivating at forty that any woman who'd withstood two decades of her own children had a God-given right to grandchildren while she was still young enough to enjoy them. It was the kind of irrational certainty that occasionally worked its way into Mama's little head, and by the time Michael was nearing his mid-twenties, still unmarried and spending every waking minute at (as she put it) "that fool plant," she was nearly frantic. Candace had a baby (and it'd be her last; a postpartum hemorrhage had nearly cost her life), but she had left for Germany with her husband, an Air Force lieutenant who couldn't guarantee he'd be Stateside within the decade, and as for me, I was an eccentric nineteen year old scratching my way through FSU with no girlfriends to speak of. So when a young woman knocked on our front door late one October evening in '67 and asked for me, you might have expected Mama to hand over my phone number or at least provide my mailing address along with a short, flattering summary of my honor-student status and unusually bright future. But no, that was too logical, too straightforward for Mama. It did not further her goals in any small way, and looking at the woman's small white hands and shy, agreeable face, she immediately thought of Michael, her eldest and dearest, who still lived at home and brought in a paycheck, while Gabe had hair to his shoulders and talked so crazy she was ashamed to take him to church anymore.

So instead of bothering with anything as trivial as the truth, she patted her hair and murmured something about me being gone, then invited the stranger to supper on the spot. While they sat on the couch and waited for Daddy, Mama was quick to note her age (seventeen, considered by Mama to be a woman's prime breeding peak), her yesma'ams and noma'ams—a sure sign she was from good people—and last, but not least, the small gold cross around her neck that had her pegged as Baptist or at least well-intentioned in that direction. I do believe that by the time Daddy was stomping his boots at the back door, Mama was already tabulating a guest list, and when he came in, she leapt to her feet, anxious he make a good impression on this unsuspecting prospective daughter-in-law. I can only imagine her surprise when, instead of merely standing and smiling, the quiet young woman crossed the room and held out her hands, "Mister Catts? My mama says you saved my life once."

Mama had been too involved in her matchmaking to even catch the girl's name, but Daddy's face, gray with fatigue from his backbreaking work on the floor at Sanger (his last and hardest job before the bastards worked him to death), softened to a smile.

"Why, Myra Sims, Lord have mercy. Cissie, look at her now." He took her hands. "Why, you've made up into a fine girl, a pretty girl—"

Mama had been stunned enough to get out her reading glasses and give her (in her own estimation) one more good look and agreed it was indeed Myra Sims, except her name was no longer Sims; it was Odom, for her mother had remarried in Birmingham, and her stepfather had adopted both her and Ira, who was now a drill instructor at Parris Island.

All of this came out over supper, and Daddy, glad to see the tragedy on Lafayette had come to a good end at last, asked, "Well, Myra, sugar, has Ira *ever* quit talking?"

Myra said no, but that he was so big now no one ever told him to hush anymore, and they all laughed. I imagine by then Mama had heard news of Mr. Sims' timely end and was in a very jubilant mood, glad to find there was a God in heaven after all, who not only punished sinners but heard the prayer of the righteous, and had sent her this lovely, devout daughter-in-law the way He'd sent the ravens to Elijah. When she found out that Myra was only passing through, en route to visit an aunt in Milton, she simply insisted she stay the night.

"It's already dark, and no woman should be out on the road at night alone—"

"I took the bus—"

"Well, that's even worst, what with the trash that lays out in them bus stations. Listen, shug, you call your aint. I knooow she'll understand; you can sleep right here in Michael's room. We'll leave him a note. He won't be in till late. He works down to Sanger, works like a dog, makes *good* money, got a *good* job down there—"

So Myra was neatly tucked away in Michael's bed, and Mama says—swears—she left a note warning him of the presence of a woman in the house and instructing him to proceed with all due modesty and caution, but Michael, who never had reason to lie about it, said he stumbled home after a bonecrusher of a twelve-hour shift, and in the face of a cold October dawn, decided to wait till morning for his shower. Peeling off in the darkness, he crawled into bed and lay there a moment, then gingerly felt something in the bed beside him. He said he thought it was me, at first, home unexpectedly, except that it was somehow different. It made the bed sag lighter, and well, there was this smell that wasn't no Gabe smell, and after a few more curiosity feels, he came upon something he recognized all right, and leapt from the bed, hitting the lights and saying aloud to no one in particular, "There's a *woman* in my bed."

The lights wakened Myra, and she sat up, shielding her eyes from the glare, and while Michael frantically pulled on his pants, Mama came in, her hair in curlers, her voice (he said) as calm as if they were standing in the vestibule of Welcome Baptist.

"Well, I see you've met Myra. You remember Myra, don'tchu son? Lived next door—Ira's little sister? Well, she's down here a-visiting her people in Milton. Ain't she made up into a pretty girl?"

Well, I believe I've mentioned my mother's matchless skill in the fine art of manipulation and am positively convinced, her self-righteous denial to the contrary, that she purposefully set Michael up, knowing once he'd laid his tired Baptist body down in a bed with a woman the approximate shape of Myra, it was all over but the crying.

And she was right. Before I knew what was happening, Mama was calling me in Tallahassee with the news Michael was engaged, and she was hoping it'd be a short engagement because the girl was living with them till the wedding and she was concerned with how it *looked*—

I interrupted her dissection of the morals of the matter with my shock, asking, "Who? How long's he known her? I didn't know Michael was seeing anyone."

Mama said well, it was a whirlwind sort of thing, but she was a good girl, she was—

"What's her name, Mama?" I asked, simply amazed, knowing Michael was not the sort of person given to whirlwinds, and Mama paused a moment before she answered.

"Myra, honey. Myra Odom—"

"Myra *Odom*?" I said, and must admit the name rang no bell of recognition, only conjuring up the image of a knock-kneed country girl with a mother named Lueller who'd want to move in the week after the wedding, and I was far from enthusiastic. "Why won't he wait? I can't come now. I'm right in the middle of mid-terms. I'll be there Christmas—tell him to wait, Mama. This is a serious thing."

My doubt was genuine, for I was desperate to see Michael get out of Sanger Manufacturing. I'd seen it suck the life out of better men than he, and a wife and gaggle of children sounded like the nails in his coffin. But Mama would not listen, nor Michael, nor even Daddy, and when I came home Christmas Eve, the deed was already done.

Michael himself picked me up at the bus station that afternoon, still in his work clothes, his face bland and satisfied, and after one look at him I said, "So married life's treating you well?"

He only smiled, throwing my bags in the flatbed of his old truck, and on the way home, I asked him the question that had been on my mind since I'd first talked with Mama. "You didn't knock her up, didju?" This being the only reason I could figure a man would marry a woman he'd only known two months.

But Michael didn't seem to follow the logic of the question, turning and looking at me for perhaps ten seconds, then saying in a very light, dry voice, "Gabe, don't you *ever* talk about my wife like that again."

I rolled my eyes at what I considered his patented Baptist prudishness, and thought *well son, you've made your bed and you'll lie in it*, but said no more about it, only asking after Daddy's declining health and steering clear of the pristine virgin bride till we got home and I saw her. She was standing on the porch, surrounded by the neighbors and relations who at that juncture of my life still liked me enough to congregate at my homecomings, and I remember Aunt Mag, Mama's oldest sister, calling out playfully as I came up the walk, "Michael, you better watch out now, she come here a-asking for Gabe—" She said it in obvious jest, for my peculiarities had set me apart as a queer of no small proportion, but Michael didn't laugh as his wife stepped forward shyly, and I finally recognized her, letting my hand drop in shock, saying, "Myra? My-ra Sims? You came back?"—then after an incredulous pause, "You married *Michael*?"

That was all I could get out before Mama, a little nervous, perhaps feeling a small pinch of guilt, hustled me inside, saying, "Gabe, quit that shouting, honey; give Myra a hug; she's family now—" then pulled me through the house, still talking in my ear, "—might be pregnant already, come up sick as a dog this morning—"

And while I hugged Daddy and shook my uncles' hands, I was still looking over my shoulder, murmuring, "Myra? Myra *Sims*?"

Myra who listened to me? Who loved me more than any boy on Magnolia Hill? Whom I waited on that day for an hour, then two, then Mama standing at the foot of the steps, telling me to go on and cry, baby, that she was gone, gone for good and it was for the best? She was back, and she was *married to Michael*?

But there was no time to discuss it that night; it was Christmas Eve, the house full of relatives and laughter and talk of the marriage, and when bedtime finally rolled around, I found myself exiled to the living room couch since Michael and his bride were living with Mama and Daddy and had taken our old bedroom for their own. The lights from the Christmas tree, blinking green and red and blue, kept me awake, and I lay there with my hands under my head thinking that if I heard one sound from our old bedroom, even one creak from that rusty old mattress, I was by God walking out that door and never coming back, never again.

But Michael (or Myra—I never knew) was kind enough to spare me that, and the next day, throughout the turkey and Lane Cake and presents, I found myself watching my old love as she went about her day, helping Daddy wind string on a new reel, trying on the new dress Michael had given her (*twenty-one dollars*, Mama said with a significant lift of her face), standing in the kitchen with the other women and discussing pregnancy symptoms. I found her shy with me, speaking kindly, like the Myra of old, but never looking me in the eye, which nearly drove me crazy, and always standing close to Michael, her shoulder or hand making bare contact, as if physically drawing on his support.

All in all, it was enough to drive me to tears, for she was no longer the porcelain-faced child who'd once listened so passively through the spokes of the pig wire fence, but a tall, soft-faced woman with pale skin and coarse, red-brown hair that hung from a finely drawn widow's peak to just above the straight line of her shoulders. Her early promise of beauty had not been denied, but was not the head-turning, gut-wrenching sort I might have expected simply because it was ignored, or better, denied. I couldn't exactly put my finger on it at the time, but it was as if the Lord had called Myra forth and in return for her hellish childhood had offered her beauty, and Myra, looking at the world and reflecting on the nature of man, had said *thanks, but no thanks*. What was left was a clumsy, neglected loveliness: earthy, common, somehow sensually maternal in her heavy breasts and strong thin arms and wild, uneven hair.

Such was the holiday crush that we had no opportunity to speak privately, even if she would have allowed it, but I did manage to glean bits and pieces of her life from casual talk—how she had indeed moved to Birmingham after she left Magnolia Hill and lived there in peace after her mother remarried, an insurance agent named Carl Odom, who was probably the one man on earth responsible for the lightness in her face and her frequent laughter—he and Michael, who was quietly, unobtrusively stone in love, watching her as frankly as I did, even following her to the bathroom, where I figured he was up to more than just washing his hands, and proved it the day after Christmas when I walked in on them quite accidentally and found him kissing her with his old relentless concentration, pressing her to the mirror with his chest, not turning, even when I backed into the door in my embarrassment, but only when Myra saw me and pushed him away, murmuring, "Michael—"

Only then did he turn, his face blank, then showing a flicker of concern, as if he hadn't planned on something like that happening and regretted I'd seen it. Maybe he'd seen my eyes following her and pitied me, as Daddy had. He'd spoken no word of it Christmas, nor the day after, but the next evening on the porch, after we'd finished our usual homecoming talk—Welcome gossip and company politics at Sanger—he'd stood and said it was late, he'd better be turning in. Then, standing in the door that was framed by Mama's cheap dimestore lights, he'd looked at me out of his deep, kind eyes and said, "Son, thet's yo brother's wife you been watching all day."

I didn't bother to deny it but only looked out on the yard, and he let the night stillness gather awhile, his eyes still on my face, before he was satisfied his point had been taken and went to bed. But his gentle rebuke shamed me more than a thousand angry words, and I tried to keep my eyes to myself thereafter, though it wasn't easy, especially when Myra laughed, which was fairly often after about day four when she lost some of her shyness and apparently found my particular humor very funny, throwing back her head and arching her white neck till it curved sweetly to her chest in a long, tense bow.

I'm sure she was very innocent about it, but I was so intrigued that I found myself transformed into Lenny Bruce, on stage twenty-four-hours a day, and after a while, the excitement began to take on an edge of torment that frightened me. What had once been simple infatuation had taken on the characteristics of actual hunger, and after a week of hilarious days and tossing, sleepless nights, I decided to leave early, giving Mama some excuse or another, but seeing in Daddy's eyes I hadn't fooled him, not for a moment, and he was proud of me for backing off.

He was careful I not be offended, though, and took off work to drive me to the bus station, hugging me at the turnstile, saying, "We'll see you Easter, son, get us in some fishing—"

I said sure, that would be fine, and told him that I loved him, which turned out to be the last thing I ever said to my father. He died three months later, asleep in his bed, from a cerebral hemorrhage so massive Dr. Winston said it killed him instantly, without one twinge of pain.

"It was a good way to die," he told Mama. "I hope I die like that."

Mama, of course, was not comforted; none of us were; it was too sudden, leaving us with all the tormenting private regrets that come on the tail of an unexpected death. My own personal agony was not lessened the afternoon of the funeral, when a slightly pregnant Myra, anxious to comfort me, recounted Daddy's last night. She said he'd gone to bed early with what he thought was a touch of the flu, but had stopped in the kitchen to take some soda, and said that, well, Easter was almost here, Gabe would be home shortly, he reckoned he'd have to get out the poles, that fool boy was too lazy to row a boat—

Everyone laughed when she said it, laughed through their tears, for Daddy's lifelong amazement with my colossal laziness was a standing family joke. "Wouldn't strike a lick at a snake if it bit him" was the way he usually put it, and someone, Uncle Case, I think, quoted it to another round of laughter, but I stood up suddenly and had to get outside.

The April air was suffocating, already as hot as July, and I walked down to the church, and finding it locked went around back to the old baseball field. Not a breeze stirred the line of oaks that circled the rough, already yellowing grass, and for the first time I realized the field wasn't very big at all, not nearly the monstrous stadium I remembered as a child. I was standing there puzzling over how things seemed to shrink as you got older when Michael came up behind me, still in his funeral pants, his sleeves rolled above his elbows, his pockets and hands full of regulation baseballs, just like old times, a glove under his arm.

"Wanna throw a few?" he asked, as if things weren't bad enough already.

I just looked at him. "You can't be serious."

"Do your hand good," he said.

"So would amputation, but I'm not planning on that, either."

He didn't argue, only pulling on the glove and turning his attention to the old hickory stump that had once stood five feet high, but thanks to his line drives, was now down to about thirty battered inches, and after a moment's pause, he began drilling in fastballs.

"Myra didn't mean to hurt you," he said, winding up, then letting go with a straight blur that popped the stump with a *thwack*.

"It's all right," I murmured, diverted by the perfection of his form, the way the ball hit like an arrow.

"So why'd you run like that?"

"I didn't run."

He let it go without argument, his eyes still on the stump, his body winding around his hand like a slow spring, then *snap*.

"I just never should have left," I said, and he looked at me.

"Why not?"

"I shoulda stayed at home like you. Took care of Daddy. He wasn't fit to work after that asshole beat him."

He looked at me even longer this time, not accustomed to hearing me use casual profanity, then turned back to his opponent, the beaten-down old stump, "So what good would you a been around here?"

"I'd have worked. Took a job at Sanger. Done like you—"

He smiled at this, letting loose another flawless pitch, then paused to wipe his forehead, murmuring, "Son, you wouldn't a lasted till first break at any job in this county—"

"Yeah," I said, "that's right. That's exactly right. I wouldn't work, I wouldn't play baseball, I never done a thing in my life Daddy was proud of me for, nothing, Michael, nothing. He was ashamed of me, you know he was."

For a long moment, Michael didn't reply at all, only hammered in the last three balls and watched the dust settle. Then, after a moment, he spoke again in that low, quiet murmur. "I don't know why you want to do this to yourself. You're just like Myra, always wanting to grind yourself over *nothing*—"

"Well it's easy for you," I snapped. "He loved you; he was like you. You understood each other."

At this, Michael threw back his head and laughed. "He was like me? He understood me? Gabe—" he looked at me with exasperation, "my daddy and me were about as much alike as *nothing*. He wasn't no working man. He never spent a day on any job he didn't know for certain he couldn't drop like a light when it suited him."

He started toward the stump to collect the scattered balls, and I was intrigued enough to follow.

"Daddy was just like you," he said. "He just didn't know how to read, couldn't get his hands on things. Why, it hadn't a been for Mama and Candace and us, he'd a been a sailor or something. Something he could roam with. Daddy was just like you. Restless."

It was the first time in my life I'd ever thought of Daddy in such a way, and I didn't interrupt as Michael picked up the balls, turning them in his hands, looking for signs of damage.

"Always looking for something," he mused. "You know what he told me the first time I handed him my paycheck?"

I shook my head.

"He said, 'Son, this is real nice a you to hep your mother and me, but are you sure it's for the best?' And I said yeah, that I'd thought it over and figured Sanger was my ticket off Magnolia Hill, and he just scratched his head, said, 'Well son, it's yo life, you can do what you please, just make sure when yo feet hit the ground they keep on running till you're somewhere you're satisfied, 'cause life is too short to go around hungry.'"

It was the kind of peculiar country advice Daddy was noted for giving. In fact it was the same speech he'd given me the night I told him I was leaving Magnolia Hill for good and never coming back, or at least not poor, and Michael had not gotten the words out of his mouth before I remembered my young, arrogant words, spoken to a man who never had a chance to get out, whose feet had only taken half a dozen steps before he was halted, and I started to cry again, out on the old church grounds, not from grief, but humility. Because Daddy hadn't argued that night, he hadn't even taken the opportunity to give me a little fatherly advice on how wanting and getting are two different things; he'd only smiled and let me go, and I knew even then how unworthy I was of such love, how far it was above me.

Michael only watched me cry, just like Daddy used to, and even said the same thing when I was finished. "You cry more'n anybody I ever seen in my life."

I didn't bother to apologize, but only asked him if he was satisfied. He didn't answer for a moment, only retrieving the last of the balls, then smiling very slowly, and I thought sharply, quickly, that he was thinking of Myra.

"Yeah," he said. "I ain't hurting."

He offered no more, and I did not press, for Myra was still a sensitive subject, one that I would have gladly put behind me, except that an argument with a department head over the relative worth of LBJ had cost me a scholarship, and with all my money going to books and rent, I had little or nothing left for food and found myself like Ira Sims, drawn to Mama's table out of biological necessity.

So I was around fairly often those next two years, there to see Myra produce what would have been Daddy's first grandson, named Michael Simon, but always called the latter, for he was Daddy's spitting image from birth, with the same dark eyes, the close-fitting ears, the sweet, patient smile. It was as if God had sent down an instant replacement, and we loved him, fought over him, spoiled him shamelessly.

When I was home on weekends, I'd sit on the porch and sing:

> *Dance up a boy, dance up a little,*
> *If you don't dance up, you cain't play the fiddle.*

It was a silly little song with about a thousand verses that my grandfather used to get me to dance to when I was a baby, and Myra would come outside to watch us, laughing and clapping as Simon danced till he dropped, and once she smiled at me out of her deep, kind eyes. "Gabriel, you'll make a good daddy. You need to find you a wife."

Simon had fallen into my arms, and I was holding him upside down, tickling him till he screeched, when I caught her eye. "I have found me a wife," I answered over his head. "Found her when I was thirteen. Problem is, she married my brother."

For one blank moment, her eyes had connected with mine, then she'd sidestepped me deftly, taking Simon, saying he needed a bath, and when I caught her in the kitchen later and tried to apologize, she jerked away and backed to the stove, her eyes averted, murmuring, "No—no, listen, Gabriel, it's fine. Don't touch me again, it's fine—"

By the time Michael got home from work, she'd already gone to bed, with a headache, she said, and I was disgusted with myself as I watched my brother eat supper with his dirty, nicked hands and tired, red-rimmed eyes, the kind you get after putting in seventy hours Chinese overtime, so disgusted I left early and stayed in Tallahassee and starved awhile. Not because of Myra's rebuff, but because of the shaking in her voice that held a note of desperation, as if she were feeling it too, that subtle surge between us that had never quite died out. Desperation, because that kind of emotion might be inescapable, and she was in a vulnerable spot there, with Michael gone so much, and Mama at church, leaving just me and her and little Simon for company.

And you know, looking back, I think that both of us realized, even then, that sooner or later the jokes and the laughter and the dancing up would have to come to an end, and if it happened to dry up while we were alone, what would we have left but betrayal?

Chapter

6

So I left and stayed away, for Myra's sake and my brother's, still unable to reconcile myself to the fact he was satisfied spending ninety percent of his mortal life inside the pounding walls of a furniture factory. A mill. A plant. Whatever you wanted to call it, it meant hell to me.

How can I describe the life of a mill worker in the South? The most compelling image that comes to mind is one of Michael I remember from this period when I went down to the plant to take him his supper one night. They were working shifts then, the place lit up like Cinderella's castle, but when I went inside, there was no ball, no prince, only row on row of saws and molds and lathes, all chopping and ripping and making such a racket I couldn't hear myself think. After screaming in the foreman's ear a few minutes, he motioned me to a small glassed-in break room where a handful of men sat huddled around a table, drinking coffee in the ninety-eight-degree heat for the caffeine, their faces paste-white from the hours and the fatigue and the sheer monotony of the hot, wasted night. Michael was not among them. He was standing alone in the corner with his back to the wall, and though I hammered on the glass and held up his lunch, he remained there, motionless, his cap pulled low over his eyes, and after a moment, I realized he was sound asleep, there against the wall, his arms folded on his chest, his knees locked, his face slack with a curious peacefulness. I went inside the little room that was only slightly insulated from the roar of the floor, and when I touched his arm, he was immediately awake.

"How can you do that?" I screamed into his face.

"Do what?" he asked, feeling around in the bag Myra had fixed him and pulling out a sandwich,

"Sleep!" I screamed. "Standing up?"

"Oh." He casually devoured the sandwich—something cheap, like bologna—in two or three bites. "I'm tired. Fifth night. Tell Myra I'm signed up for tomorrow."

"You can't work tomorrow!" I screamed. "You worked all night, all week, the overtime's fixed! Damn, Michael, don't let them do you this way!"

He just shrugged, eating the pathetic supper in fast, hungry bites, and I was enraged at his passivity. I mean, here was a man who'd mastered baseball so well that the Reds' scout had begged him to come to Cinncinati and try out. Had called every night for a week, but Michael had turned him down because Daddy was about to lose the house, and while the scout was sure, was positive, he'd make it, at least to the minors, he couldn't give him a contract till the manager saw him, and by that time, it'd be too late. So, with this pointless, hillbilly need to martyr his life away, he'd gone on full-time in this rattling monster of a soul-sucking furniture factory, putting in his hours miles from the sun and mowed grass of a baseball diamond, while his wife sat home alone and his little boy sometimes called me Daddy by mistake.

"Are you gone stay here all your life?" I yelled into his face, and he only shrugged, throwing his bag away and sliding his safety glasses back on.

"Just till I die." He grinned, amused at my outrage, but I didn't think it funny at all and turned and left without a word, slamming the breakroom door in a particularly ineffective show of anger, the mighty bang consumed by the din and roar of the machines, costing the men around the table not so much as a blink.

But Michael followed me, calling my name, and caught me just outside the door, his face still smiling, though he was trying to be kind.

"Listen, Gabe, I'm fine. I'll catch some sleep on my breaks. It's nothing, it's work, I'm used to it."

But I wasn't satisfied. I was madder than hell. It was so pathetic, the endless line of saws, the workers with their pale, sunless faces and mortgages and cardboard-soled shoes, and I stood with my back to the cool dense night and lashed at him. "No, you're right. You'll work here till you die, work like a dog to put a few more dollars in Old Man Sanger's pocket while Myra and Simon raise each other alone."

His smile disappeared. "Myra's fine," he said, then, with an almost sullen intensity, "she'll be driving a Cadillac in ten years."

I only looked at him, shaking my head at this pathetic poor-boy brag, sickened he was already so dehumanized by the factory shuffle that he could not speak in first person, but had to say his *wife* would have the Cadillac.

"Yeah," I shouted over the roar, "and in ten years I'll be pitching for the Yankees."

It was a cheap shot, even for me, bringing up pitching in the middle of this exhausting, dreamless night, but he said nothing, only watching me a moment, then turning and walking away. Watching him dissolve into the dust and roar of the floor, I felt even worse and ran after him.

"Michael, I'm sorry!" I shouted, grabbing his shoulder and turning him to speak into his face, "I believe you. A Fleetwood. Pink, with white-walls. Be the wonder of Magnolia Hill."

He smiled then, easily, accepting my sarcasm for what it was meant to be, an apology, and when I was almost to the door, he shouted, raising his voice for the first time that night, "Kiss Sim for me!"

I turned and waved, and when I was in the car, I paused a moment to watch the cold white lights that filled the monotonous row of windows. They still glowed with that air of light-hearted, fairy-tale gaiety, and it was hard to believe there was a God in heaven when flesh and blood men sweated seventy-hour weeks for the privilege of living on Magnolia Hill. Then I started the engine and went home and told Simon his father loved him and packed up, lock, stock and barrel and left for good, not returning home the whole time they lived on Magnolia Hill, preferring genteel starvation to lying on the couch every night and letting my mind wander around the corner to the iron bed where Myra slept alone, thinking how easy it'd be to slip in there and press my mouth to her neck and see for myself if the increasing desperation in her voice was nothing more than my imagination.

To further remove myself from temptation, I transferred to Chapel Hill for my master's, and if times were hard in Tallahassee, winter in North Carolina took on the rigors of Valley Forge. My thin Florida blood would simply not adjust to the cold, and the night Mama called with the news Myra was expecting again, I lay in bed with chattering teeth and thought, well, that was wonderful; I'm up here dying of hypothermia while Michael and Myra are way down yonder in the land of mimosa, plotting Cadillacs and making babies.

It hardly seemed fair, and when they sent me a photograph of a tiny, red-haired girl, I sent a polite letter and pleaded poverty in lieu of a present, then moved even further north for my doctorate, all the way to Boston, where, to my mother's everlasting joy and eternal name-dropping satisfaction, I finished it off at *Harvard*.

To this day I cannot properly explain why I chose Harvard of all places to take a doctorate in history with a specialization in the Southern contribution to the Civil War, since despite various fellowships and grants, the tuition alone landed me in perpetual, unresolved debt for the better part of two decades. I can only attribute the move to low self-esteem and a need to hook into the aristocratic, Faulknerian air the name, coupled with a Southern accent, evoked, though by the time I'd etched out my degree, I had grown very tongue-in-cheek about it, telling people at parties that yes, I was a Southerner and in love with my sister Candace, but my family had sent me up here to Boston, and at first I was a little depressed, but lately I'd started taking walks on the wharf, and God, I hoped everything worked out.

Then I'd laugh till I cried; I thought I was so damn funny and would entertain them with all my little gothic anecdotes from home. Like most Southern emigrants, I had a whole cherished repertoire, small eccentricities, like how a cousin of mine had shot off his arm for the insurance money; the ins and outs of Baptist courtship (in which poor Cassie Lea Scales featured predominantly); how my brother Michael, the poor hick, had turned down a contract with the Reds because he wasn't sure there was any *money* in it.

So by means of my hiliarious, confessional laughter, I nearly managed to dehumanize and de-sting them all, breaking every icon in sight till someone, a fellow student or later, a student of my own, would join in the fun by asking with a grin if I knew the definition of a Mississippi virgin? Then he'd wink and say, "a twelve-year-old who could run faster than her father." Old joke. I used to hear it a lot, and sometimes I'd just look at him, or if it was a student, take out my vengeance later in the semester with the red pen. But I never laughed, never, not even politely, for Myra was still too alive to me, her memory too fresh. I could still remember her ocean-colored eyes over the fence at twilight, and how she and Mama had cried so much the day Simon was born that they'd gotten me started, and we'd passed Kleenex and sobbed like old women at a funeral all afternoon long while Michael only shook his head and smiled.

Sometimes I wondered whatever became of her hellish memories of Magnolia Hill, and how she'd ever brought herself to move back, one house, one pig iron fence, down from her own Auschwitz revisited. Once, when I was still at FSU, I remember coming home unexpectedly and seeing her outside, standing under the edge of the old sweetgum we used to play under as children, her face calm and blank as she looked across the fence at the rotting old house the absentee owner had let fall to disrepair, the yard a wasteland of waist-high brush, kudzu creeping down the wires to take hold of the sagging roof.

She was so still, so vacant, that I went down the steps and stood next to her, putting a foot up on the fence and saying lightly, "So, Myra, wanna draw a hopscotch board?"

But she paid me no mind, only stood there without the barest flicker of response until she turned and she saw me there at her side and was as pleasantly surprised as ever to see me, smiling, shaking her head at my hair, leading me inside to show me Simon's new tooth.

So I figured even the worst wounds healed with time, mine and hers both, and was a bit more accepting when Mama called with the news that Michael had been promoted to foreman, and they'd bought a house way out on Thomasville Road, ten miles or so out of town. An old house, she said, but they were fixing it up, and she thought it'd be right pretty when they finished, though Myra was having some female trouble; she'd been in the hospital, but was all right now.

By then, I'd finished my degree ("And about time," as Uncle Case was fond of saying. "Never a day he's worked, never a day in his life—") and accepted a nice entry-level position at Boston College that entailed reading so many freshman essays that I can say without fear of contradiction that I know more about the Continental Congress and Western Expansion than any man, woman, or dog in the state of Massachusetts.

It was a combination of the essays and the New England winter (I thought UNC was bad) that made me give it up after only a year, and I looked around awhile before settling at the Archives in Washington, doing research on a grant from the Smithsonian. It was a safe, boring job that hardly paid anything at all, but did allow me to dig through trivia in my spare time and begin the first draft of my great *American History of the War of Rebellion*, a book I had long since roughed out and occasionally toyed with, but had never gotten around to the actual meat and bones of writing. I was too busy, I told myself, but did manage to churn out a few articles for historial reviews that kept my fellow historians hopping, especially the Southern ones.

Somehow, for no very clear or understandable reason, I'd developed a lasting hatred for two of the great paragons of Southern mythology, Nathan Bedford Forrest and Jeb Stuart, and my obstinate opinion of their relative worth was tantamount to calling for desegregation in Biloxi in '62. A self-hating Southerner, they must have thought me, and I received actual hate mail for my assertion that the most creative act Robert E. Lee could have done in 1863 was to stick Jeb Stuart's jaunty feather up his nose and so asphyxiate him. As for Forrest, he was as cunning a soldier as he was slave-trader. My only problem was that I'd somehow identified his proud, high-cheeked face in the fading sepia daguerreotypes with none other than Old Man Sims, and once I'd made the connection, I could never again look on him as anything more than an antebellum Nazi.

Perhaps it was this connection between Old Man Sims and Nathan B. that first got me interested in nosing through the old slavery records that were salted away in the upper stories of the Archives, and from their black and white sureness, a shocking portrait began to emerge, one that would eventually pull the rug right out from under me, so I could never again refight the great battles at Manassas and Vicksburg and Chattanooga with such vigor.

It is my heartfelt conviction that the spark that drives any historian forward is a certain fascination with the solidity of the past and a tiny obsession with the wistful realm of might-have-been. This is surely the case with Southern historians, who have refought the same old battles a thousand times, writing reams of papers on the near misses, the coincidences, the whole ghostly domain of *almost*, as if such conjecture were capable of moving them closer to what they wished had happened, a Southern victory.

At least, that was the case with me, until I began innocently tracing the slavery records and saw such a ruthlessness emerge that I could never again get very excited over how very close a pacifist administration came to being voted in in '64. After all, it would have meant the continuation of the very real evil that was slavery, and though in debate my colleagues were quick to point out what a small percentage of CSA soldiers were actual slave owners, I was equally quick to bring up the Missouri Compromise that got the ball rolling in the first place. Then we'd go back and forth over states' rights and rural versus city and industry versus agrarian, and all the other dimensions, but I'd stand my ground till they shrugged and said, well, I could be like that if I wanted to, and I always had a feeling they privately added a small mental note along the lines of Cassie Lea Scales (*Well I know what boys like you are called, my Daddy told me*).

Philosophical musings aside, the long and the short of it was that after eight years of higher education and a truckload of money, I was still out there looking for my niche and beginning to get a little desperate. After all, I was twenty-five, and it occurred to me that at twenty-five, my father had not only fathered three children, but had seen Iwo Jima and lived to tell about it.

Not the man my father was. The old phrase sometimes echoed in my mind, and as another year passed in passive somnolence, the sound of my footsteps in the cold marbled halls of the Archives began to take on the hollow ring of an undertaker's in a mausoleum. By then I was officially within spitting distance of thirty, and increasingly tormented by a growing obsession that if I didn't make a move soon, I'd die among the microfilm and be quietly filed away for some other poor bloodless research assistant to stumble upon in the twenty-first century and report to the main library—"Yes, I've come upon a perfect specimen of, I think, a twentieth-century male. Looks to be a repressed Protestant from, say, the post-Vietnam era. I'll have to verify it in coding."

So I quit. Cold turkey. Memorial Day weekend, 1974, and went to my apartment and gathered all my notes and maps and files full of documentation, and with nowhere else to go and the registrar at Harvard still in possession of my social security number, headed home. Twenty-three hours on a Greyhound bus it was, and the first thing Mama said when she saw me at the door, was: "Lord, Gabe, you done quit yo job."

Not "hello" or "glad you're back" or "my son has returned," but: "You done quit yo job, son. What'll you do? Have you ever thought of going to work at the bank? They doan pay much, but the hours are good. You'd be off Christmas—"

I wasted no time in nipping this in the bud with the pronouncement that I was home to write a book. A concise, broad-based, well-documented dissection of the Civil War that would sidestep no issues and set things straight once and for all—but Mama wouldn't let me finish. "Well, sugar, that's fine, but you cain't stay here."

"Why not? I'll only be here awhile. I can't afford rent. I'm still paying the Yankees."

Mama conceded that might well be so, but she'd knocked down the walls of the little bedroom and converted it back to its original intent (the last ten feet of the back porch), and as for the other bedroom, my niece Lori was staying there until Candace and Ed came back from Germany in September.

"She'll be eleven in June, and that's too old for an uncle to be sleeping on the couch, walking around in his underwear."

"She was raised on an army base," I argued. "She's lived around men in their underwear all her life."

But Mama wouldn't be budged, and I was lying on the couch with a headache when she finally relented, saying, well, Michael was coming to dinner, maybe he had room. . . .

"How's Myra?" I asked, after she had finally bestowed on me a kiss of welcome and began cooking dinner, filling the house with the sharp smell of summer: white corn and butter beans.

"Spent a lot a time on thet house," she answered vaguely. "Refinished every floor herself. I told her she could a laid carpet for what she spent on varnish."

She was still harping on those wood floors, how hard they were to maintain, how cold they'd be in winter, when Michael came in for his lunch hour (apparently a Friday ritual), and he, at least, seemed genuinely glad to see me.

"Why didn't you call?" he asked, hugging me.

Mama called from the kitchen. "He done quit his job, needing a place to stay, wanted to stay here; I told him he couldn't; Lori's here, she's eleven—"

"I'm working on a book," I inserted as we sat down at the table, and his face in no way took on that here-we-go-again grimace.

"Well, listen, you're welcome to stay out at our place. We got plenty a room. It's a big old house, built in 1903, off Thomasville Road."

When I told him I didn't remember a house of any description on Thomasville Road, he said, "Neither did I till the realtor showed us. It's set off the highway a good quarter mile, Clarence Thurmon built it for a summer house."

The Thurmons were county aristocracy, blood kin to the actual *Sangers*, and I remember being a little surprised. "A Thurmon house? Really?"

"Yeah, it's a nice house." He paused for a fraction of a second. "Myra's done a fine job of restoring it."

"Working her fool self to death," Mama inserted as she set the food on the table; then, in a sly aside, "Of course, a little hard work never hurt nobody, thet's what yo Daddy useter say—"

"Are you sure I won't be any trouble?" I asked, ignoring her.

Michael began eating, "No. No trouble at all. Might be doing me a favor." He paused for another fraction of a second, then, "Myra'll be glad to see you."

For the rest of the meal, we caught up on the news: how Candace and Ed were moving back to town in August, how Sim and Missy were faring, and though Michael spoke no word on his own behalf, I could see he had prospered. His hair was cut close to his head in short, clean layers, not the old scalp job Myra used to do on him in the kitchen with Mama's sewing scissors; his hands neat and free of the tiny rips and scabs of the wood shop; his clothes so pressed and sharp he reminded me of the prep students in Cambridge, with their button-down shirts and pleasant, even faces. It was a startling transformation, in a way, and when I went outside, I stood by his car in shock.

"A BMW?" I asked. "This is yours?"

"Yeah, I got it second-hand at the auction. It was two years old, only had 12,000 miles—"

"How much they paying at Sanger these days?" I asked as I threw my bags in the trunk.

He was vague. "Just the usual. There's a big shake-up going on right now, a union trying to raise its head—" he slammed the trunk, "but I'm doing all right."

"He's the new manager!" Mama hollered from the porch.

I looked at him. "Are you serious? How long?"

"Oh, awhile," he said, and though he didn't seem interested in pursuing the matter, I was undeniably impressed. Management at Sanger wasn't small potatoes. It was the best job in town, maybe the best in the county, and I could hardly believe Michael had taken it at the tender age of thirty-one.

But my surprise at his new red car and his manicured hands was nothing in comparison to the true and actual shock of his new house. From Mama's hints I'd expected something interesting, a steep-roofed Cracker house or gabled Victorian, but as we rounded the final loop in the drive that wound like a snake between unchecked growth of twisted yellow pine and native willow, I began to catch glimpses of a house so well suited to the encroaching jungle that it was almost obscured by the rampant, unrelenting green.

Built along old-fashioned, turn-of-the-century lines, it was two-storied, but carefully so, the size not distracting from the graceful design that could perhaps be described as Spanish gothic, with touches of Queen Anne in the porch and ornate moldings, but Territorial Florida in the graceful arched windows and buff-colored stucco, long ago stained green by the dense overhang of a huge, spreading live oak. It was a style that was enjoying a modest renaissance in the tract-house subdivisions of South Florida, but as Michael helped me carry my bags onto the deep, shaded porch, I saw that this was no cheap reproduction, but the genuine article. Old Florida, as old as you could get, short of a chickee, and I followed him through the ten-foot door in honest wonder, finding the shotgun hallway cool and wide, with what looked like twenty-foot ceilings and shining white oak floors, the ones Mama wanted to cover with carpet.

"This is the most beautiful house I've ever seen in my life," I murmured as I followed him through the typical Georgian four-square layout, ending in a long sunroom that was bordered by three identical arched French doors that looked out on a small yellow pool. "How high are these ceilings?"

"Sixteen foot and a pain to heat," Michael answered, opening one of the French doors and going out on the deck. "I thought you could stay out over the garage. Used to be the servant's quarters; I thought about fixing it up for Mama, but she won't leave the Hill."

73

I nodded, still in a daze, wondering how anything as vulgar as Sanger Manufacturing could produce such a stunning house, and when I had taken a few steps across the deck, I came to a dead stop.

"This pool is marble."

Michael, half-way up the stairs, turned, "Yeah, that's all they built them with back then. It's nice. Easier to clean than concrete, somebody told me."

Easier to clean than concrete? I thought. A yellow marble pool and the best he can say for it is that it's easier to clean than concrete? But I said nothing, only followed him up the creaking wooden stairs to a small two-room apartment that had lower ceilings than the house, but the same shining floors and a claw-foot porcelain tub.

Aside from that, the furniture was spare, a table and chair and a narrow bed pushed next to the window, and Michael was apologetic. "It's all we've done so far, the house has taken so much—"

"No, no," I said, looking out on the pool. "This is great. A table, a chair, a bed, that's all I need." I turned and smiled. "Where's Myra?"

He checked his watch, "She's still upstairs with the children, taking a nap; she'll be down to swim soon. Listen, I gotta get back to work. I'll run up and tell her you're here."

When he was gone, I lay down on the bed, gingerly feeling the mattress, finding it packed cotton, the kind we slept on as children, lumpy and buttoned and smelling of endless hot, humid nights. But the sheets and the nubby cotton spread were fresh, and I looked around the room and thought if there was any place on earth I could do The Cause justice, it was in a house surrounded by live oaks, overlooking a marble pool.

But for some reason, my broad, easy optimism didn't pan out, and after a moment, I felt my smile fade. I couldn't put my finger on it, but somehow, something was wrong. Curiously wrong, in a subtle, elusive way that made me lie uneasily on the bed, frowning at the beadboard ceiling. Maybe it was the sheer perfection of the place, the symmetry of the arched windows, the cold shining floors; maybe I was thrown by it, or maybe—maybe nothing. Maybe I was just tired from the horrendous trip. I closed my eyes and thought of sleeping when I heard her below the window.

"Melissa Ann, not till I get out there. You know what Mama told you, not without the life jacket—"

I sat up and saw her through the wobbly, beveled glass, standing at one of the French doors, holding it open for a dark-haired little boy (Simon, surely, though he had grown tall and spindly), her face averted, looking down at a small red-headed child who was resolutely headed for the water, despite her mother's continued warning.

"You'll go inside and take a nap this minute. You take one more step, young lady—"

The toddler paid her no mind, stepping point blank into the shallow end, and though she bobbed up immediately in a tight, efficient little dog paddle, Myra went in after her, her voice never pausing, "Bad girl for jumping in like that, a *bad* girl—"

Sim brought out small, child-size life jackets, and the whole time Myra strapped them on, her voice continued. "Water'll get in your lungs and you won't be able to breathe. That's why I want my girl to mind me, you hear me? Do it again and I'll tell Daddy."

The little redhead looked pretty undaunted by it all, sliding back in slick as a seal the instant her mother let her go, and with a small look of exasperation, Myra pulled herself up on the poolside and watched them swim.

From my aerie above, I was able to watch her unnoticed, and on first impression, found her much like Michael, familiar, yet changed, her hair cut in an uneven shag that circled and spiked off her face like a gypsy's, her skin no longer ivory pale, but oddly stained a light pecan brown, a concession to modern fashion that I looked on with distaste, remembering the pale, fragile porcelain of her youth. However, these details were a matter of momentary annoyance, insignificant in comparison to the most shocking change, which was her size. Even as a child, Myra had been curved and round, and after bearing two children, I expected her to be even rounder, but sitting there on the edge of the pool, she looked like a different woman altogether, lean and snake-hipped, with long tapering legs and a small tight chest. It didn't suit her, I thought, and as I made my way downstairs, I wondered peevishly why women starved themselves to death for the privilege of looking like prepubescent boys.

The strangeness, however, was greatly dispelled when she saw me and stood, her face kind and slightly distanced, the Myra I remembered from Magnolia Hill.

"Gabriel," she said, standing and hugging me, "you cut your hair."

I held up her chin and looked at her. "You been on some fool diet, woman? You're skinny as a rail."

"No, no—" she said vaguely, dropping her face, murmuring, "I been busy. With the house—" she turned and called to the children, "Simon honey, d'you remember your Uncle Gabriel? And this—" she smiled at the little girl who was bobbing up to the steps, "this is my baby. Missy, say hey to your uncle. Missy?"

The carrot-red head turned up for a moment, and I had a two-second glimpse of a fat little Ira Sims face before she resumed her bobbing.

"She looks just like Ira," I said, and we sat together on the edge of the pool, our feet in the water, our backs to the sun, and with a good deal more ease than with Mama (or Michael, either, for that matter), I filled in the boring details of my life since I'd packed my bags and left Florida for good.

I told her of Chapel Hill, of Boston and the Archives, but found her quiet on her own behalf, speaking mostly of the house, and all the work she still had to do. I noticed that it was only when she spoke of her children that she was lit with any spark of the animation, the wonder, that used to light her face when I spun my stories over the fence on Magnolia Hill. Even when I asked what Michael had been up to, her face retained that blank, inflectionless honesty.

"Michael works," she said, very simply, with no qualifier, no other explanation at all, and suddenly, I knew what was wrong with this lovely house and its perfect children and shining oak floors, but spoke no word of it, only wondering why in God's name Michael hadn't listened to me. Why had he forfeited the love of this good woman to become a slave at a sweat house? It was such a damn waste. I mean, what was the use of having a marble pool when your only concern was how easy it was to maintain, what joy the breathing space of sixteen-foot ceilings when they were nothing more than inconvenient to heat?

My suspicions were confirmed later in the evening when Michael stood us up for dinner. Myra had begun cooking early, remembering my favorites, setting out the good dishes and getting the children to pick flowers for the centerpiece. When the phone rang at seven, she answered it, her face very calm, very resigned as she listened a few moments, then hung up.

"Michael will be late," she told us. "He said to eat without him."

The children didn't seem too bothered by it, as if this weren't such an uncommon occurrence, and later, while I helped with the dishes, I asked, "Myra? Does Michael do this often?"

She looked at me. "Do what?"

"Work this late?"

"Oh," she said, then repeated her vague words of the afternoon, "Michael works."

She lifted her face to the high ceiling, the shining appliances, and shrugged. "He gave me all this. He bought me a car last year. He has to work. It don't come free."

I could have pointed out that there was more to life than cars and houses and marble pools, but there was a tired finality in her voice that was too beaten to argue with, so I only smiled and said something about what a good job she'd done with the restoration, then kissed the children good night and went upstairs.

I was still awake on the hard narrow bed, the window open to catch any breath of a breeze, when Michael finally pulled into the garage well past midnight, and let himself in the French doors. I watched his progress through the dark house by the lights he turned on, noting that his bedroom light never came on at all. Just the kitchen, then the hall, then the bathroom, then nothing at all, and with the darkness like an insulating blanket between us, I spoke aloud the word forbidden in this Baptist stronghold that had been recurring in my mind all day, ever since I'd first seen Michael's neat, perfect face at Mama's door.

I whispered: *Damn*. Then I went to sleep.

Chapter

7

*P*erhaps it was, in those first hours
home, that the groundwork was laid
for the rest of my life, but at the time, I was only interested in churning
out my book. Either Mama's words of reproach had sunk into my brain,
or Michael's labors had shamed me, and I was suddenly overwhelmed
with a burning desire to get on with the business of writing till I had one
clean draft. However, once I had established myself and gotten down to
the real pen-to-paper work, I realized why Shelby Foote had drawn his
narrative out into volumes, for the war in my head was taking up dozens
and dozens of legal pads with nothing more than dry, well-documented
facts that challenged nothing, covered no new ground, sounded pointless and repetitive, even to my own captive ear.

In retrospect, I can see that the phantom I was grappling with was
the small confrontation between reality and fantasy that comes at the
start of any long-dreamed-of, but just-undertaken project, but at the
time, I was simply baffled, baffled and depressed, reduced to spending
great chunks of irretrievable time doing nothing more than tapping a

sharpened pencil on the table and staring at my impressive stockpile of books and maps and secondary sources, trying to ignore the tiny voice of panic in the back of my mind that wondered aloud at the wisdom of embarking on life at the mercy of an older brother and a shaky wallet full of the credit cards all the banks had sent me once my name got on the Harvard lists.

Not that either of my benefactors, Michael or MasterCharge, ever went out of their way to remind me of my responsibilities; the latter so sure of my eventual earning capabilities that the very thought of demanding more than the minimal balance never crossed their minds, the former simply because he was never home. If I had not taken up residence over the garage, I doubt our paths would have crossed at all, for the most I saw of him was when the slam of his car door sometimes wakened me late at night, and when I'd occasionally join him at breakfast, which Myra prepared with all the skill and finesse of any other woman raised by a woman who was raised on a farm: eggs and grits and fried meats and little buttermilk biscuits, every damn morning, alongside jams and conserves and whatever produce was in season, tomatoes, now that it was May, and later, cold watermelon, cut in thin, sweet wedges, lightly sprinkled with salt. All of it set out on the table at six o'clock sharp, the back of the house lit against the gray pearl of the morning sky, the windows thrown wide to entice a thin stir of breeze to the hot kitchen, and though I was painfully conscious of being on the dole and trying to make my presence as little a burden as possible, once the lights had wakened me, I could not resist the temptation to creep downstairs and open the French doors on the sometimes awesome, sometimes bizarre sight of my brother calmly enthroned at a formal dining table, surrounded by mountains of steaming food, all nestled in china and silver, his busy, flushed wife, coffee pot in hand, waiting on him hand and foot.

So perhaps she was right after all when she said these things didn't come free, but I had little room to complain, taking a seat and making an Ira-like dent in the incredible feast while Myra waited on me as assiduously as she did her husband, her eye on my coffee cup, her excuses vague in answer to my repeated invitations she join us. Invitations I noticed her husband never extended. In fact, he didn't speak to her at all beyond an occasional question or request, though he did seem pleased with my company, setting aside his inevitable sports page to tell me news of his world, which had indeed shrunk into the pounding walls of Sanger Manufacturing. Union talk, mostly, though it was union talk with a twist, since Lafayette Street had long been infested with a small pro-union taint, unheard of in the South, and apparently just as unwelcome at the table of my brother, who made no bones about the fact that his late nights and early mornings were partly due to an all-out effort to nip this union nonsense in the bud once and for all.

When I tried to enlighten him on the roots and history of American trade unionism in an attempt to win his interest, he only went back to his breakfast with a laugh and a shake of his head. Something in the sight of Michael consumed in his opulence and Myra engulfed in her thinness and me and the poor suckers at Sanger left hung out to dry with our credit lines got me back in the writing mode, and one night in a fit of blind inspiration, I put aside my notes and retitled my manuscript: *Peculiar Institutions and One Lost Cause*, then, below, in one of those catchy subheadings popular at the time, *Why the South Lost the War of Rebellion*.

I was absurdly pleased with my little angle, one that would not only allow me to dissect battles, which was my specialty, but also insert a little provocative social commentary. The results might not be exactly objective, but Harvard was to blame for that, and I made no apologies to anyone, scribbling out my little popular history from daybreak till noon, surrounded by legal pads full of notes and texts for reference, pinning battle sites along the walls when it got too confusing to follow by ear. Rappahannock and the Rapidan Basin stretched from the kitchenette to the bathroom, the Petersburg Area filled the wall just above my head, and when I ran out of space in the living room, I stacked them two and three high, even in the bathroom, where I could ponder Cold Harbor and smirk at Stuart while I bathed in the old clawfoot tub.

But this was only necessary for the actual battles; the social commentary, namely a scathing exposé of the practice of chattel slavery, I wrote freehand, with only a few notations from my old Archives notes. From the first word to the last, I wrote with a vengeance, pleased in some obscure way with spitting in bulldogs' faces, for slavery was usually set aside as a cause and then forgotten, while I was drawing it in as not only a forerunner, but also an actual participator in the South's defeat. Which took a little doing, I can grant you that, but I managed to pull it off, at least in rough draft, then moved on to the fighting, where I took great inexhaustive pleasure in nailing Forrest's tail to the wall, but for some reason, found myself going easy on Stuart, deciding he was too easy game. I mean, everyone knew he was a poor ass; anybody who'd wear plumes like that was too stupid to take seriously. But Nathan B., now, he was pure delight, and I wrote actual reams on the Fort Pillow Massacre, then without missing a beat, accused him of losing Chattanooga for Bragg.

I truly enjoyed doing this little number on that son of a bitch, but whether the writing was going well or crawling, I always knocked off after lunch and went downstairs to sit with Myra and sometimes be talked into the water by the children, who, after their initial shyness, seemed to find me the best toy since Play-doh.

Starved for attention, I thought them, and spent hours flipping Missy off my shoulders, time and again, her face squealing and excited, while Sim waited on the board, bouncing and impatient, begging me to teach him to swan dive.

Myra herself seldom touched the water, unless Missy made one of her suicidal leaps into the deep end, but she was our ever-present audience, clapping for Sim, fussing at Missy, rubbing coconut-smelling oil on my back with small, warm hands that made my skin crawl and a slow heat burn somewhere in the pit of my stomach.

Something was building here, I could see that fairly early on, something that might catch and set this house on fire, and for a few days I sought to avoid it by saving my writing for the afternoon, making varied excuses to a disappointed Sim.

"But I wanna dive," he'd whine, standing on the stairs in his towel.

"Baby, I'm busy. I need to work. I got bills to pay."

"Grannie says you lay up here and sleep."

"Your Grannie doesn't know her tail from third base, and you can tell her I said so."

Then, seeing his downcast face, I'd relent "Call me when you're on the board. I'll watch from the window."

And all afternoon long, while the bruised gray clouds slowly lined up for a late evening shower, I'd sit at the window and outline troop movements at Chickamauga, while Simon's voice piped through the gathering dust, "Uncle Gabe! Look! Look! I'm ready!"

And I'd look all right, not at his clumsy little outstretched arms, poised above the steel blue of the water, but at his mother, sitting with her feet on the steps, her shoulders bowed, her face tired and empty, much like it'd been when she'd had her short reign as queen of Magnolia Hill. It was an odd expression, really, the vacant expectancy of someone waiting on a phone call, and I could feel a response beginning to gather in my stomach, a tiny lick of fire that kept my eyes on her long, drooping neck.

She was hurting, that much was clear, and it occurred to me that she had left the close, privileged borders of her childhood horror only to land in another Babygirl Paradise, this one complete with white oak floors and a marble pool and two truly lovely children.

But she never let on that anything was amiss, never mentioned Michael to me at all, much less to complain, and I thought her loyal, for if any man had ever abandoned a family for a career, it was he. That's why I was such an oddity to the children, an actual flesh-and-blood man who spent more than ten minutes a week around the house, and the next time Simon knocked at my door and I gave my excuses, I stood firm. Myra had begun wearing a bikini lately, a simple black one with a loose halter, but I was too old to enjoy being tormented by an untouchable body and preferred tracing casualty rolls and weather conditions of a hundred-year-old war to sweating a nipple by a marble pool.

On the third afternoon, however, Simon proved himself a very fine budding tactician, truly a child after Mama's own heart, when he forewent his usual outright begging to press his face to the crack under the door and call, "Uncle Gabe? Uncle Gabe? We're swimming now. We're down ther by the pool. We got us some brownies down ther, by the pool." There was a sly pause. "Pecan brownies." Then a final, desperate tag, "Right down ther by thet pool."

Well, the brownies didn't do the trick, but his shifting, conniving little voice did, and I opened the door and shouted into his face, "Brownies? Pecan brownies? By thet pool down ther?" And said to hell with it, what good was that hot Florida sun without a little casual lust around to give it that tiny sting? Hell, I was a grown man, I'd been around the block, I could handle myself. Hey, maybe it was time we sat down and talked about this thing—

But she wasn't even in her bikini that day; she was wearing a one-piece Olympic-inspired racer suit that was fairly modest when dry but had all the nail-tearing cling of a dripping T-shirt when wet. By chance or fortune, it was a day Missy chose to make her dive-bombs into the deep end, and as Myra pulled her out time and again, wet and worried and promising to whip her, I treaded water under the diving board, telling Simon to keep his neck arched, making a few promises of my own.

But not a word was spoken, not a glance or half-touch, until the children were being dried off and readied for their naps. Then, with the blood pounding in my ears, I told her we needed to *talk*, and she only looked at me mildly, with no surprise at all, just a calm, slow nod that made my heart beat so loudly I could hardly hear her reply.

"I have to read Sim his story first," she said, and I told her sure, fine, to take her time, that I'd wait downstairs.

So I kissed them good night and waited in the sunroom, pacing the length of the couch, the pound of blood slowly gathering in my forehead as I listened for her footsteps on the stairs. Ten minutes passed, then twenty, and still she didn't come, and as the minutes stretched out, I began looking around the room, at the carefully restored floors, the flowers on the mantle, and suddenly, I knew I could not do this thing to my brother in his own house. It was simply beyond me, beyond the borders of my own morality, and I left quickly, without a word, taking the stairs to the apartment two at a time, and bursting in on the airless little room that looked particularly vacant in the motionless glare of the afternoon sun, closing the door behind me and lying on the soft, narrow bed. The blood was still pumping in my head, but it had dulled to a flat, sickening headache that I closed my eyes against, trying to will away, when I heard something outside, a click. Not the click of a car door, but the muffled click of a carefully closed French door, and I stopped rubbing my eyes, straining to hear as a silence gathered for a few seconds, then was broken by the soft pad of bare feet on the old stairs.

Up, up they came, and when she made the door, she didn't bother to knock, but walked right in, calling, "Gabrielle?"

She was still the only person on earth who called me that, and when she saw me there, not answering, but only watching her, she crossed the quiet, sullen heat and stood beside the bed.

"Did you need to talk to me?" she asked. Then, "Are you all right?"

I couldn't answer, but only look at her: the sweet, flat eyes; the odd, sun-stained skin; the relentless thinness about her neck and shoulders that gave her always-melancholy face a slide into hunger, into despair.

"I love you, Myra," I finally said, whispered, in honest confession. "I'm tired of pretending I don't."

For a moment, she only stood there, looking down with a face of perplexity, softened by the kindness, the slant of worry. Then she smiled, a small, wry smile, acknowledging what couldn't have been a surprise to her, and hesitantly reached out one small hand and laid it against my cheek, her voice quietly singsong. "He looked like an angel when he was born and she named him for an angel."

It was as if she were making a tired, sad commentary on all our wasted dreams, on all the obstacles that had seen fit to separate us, and something in her gentle, puzzled reply bridged the gap between the then and the now and somehow became the words I'd waited for all those cold nights on Magnolia Hill, the words that took me around the corner to the bedroom where she waited alone, betrayed and voiceless, for my brother Michael.

They were the incantation that broke the spell of my reticence, and with no more words, no clumsy explanation or strained excuse, I caught the front of her bathing suit and pulled her to me and kissed her, slow and long and deep, for I'd waited long enough, thirteen years, and as she gave in to me softly, her stomach and chest resting against me, it was suddenly too late. Too late for discussion, too late for regret, too late for anything but the hard points of her breasts, her damp, silky, woman-smelling hair, her hot skin that I freed from the wet, clinging bathing suit in one clean jerk, and when I finally had her on her back, between the bed and the wall and the window, it was sweet, it was almost too sweet, it was right on the border of something unbearable, like the pound of an abscessed tooth. I couldn't think, I was so consumed by it; I couldn't call her name or be a lover. All I could do was get it out, get it out, and when it had all burst, the room hot and still and, I don't know, different (even the light subtly changed, the maps standing dimmer on the walls, the pool smooth again and reflectionless beneath the window), I was left with a small shaking in my body, like I'd lost something, given it away.

Something deep-rooted and familiar, some awful pent-up burden that was a relief to lose, and at first I thought it was the pressure of the long years of denial, but later, when she'd left to check on her children and I was alone again, a small Baptist voice whispered that perhaps it was my soul. But I cared not, not at all, for when it burst upon me like that, so white and hot that I cried aloud, I was through with death and history and commandments carved on stone. I was born again, alive and well and living in the land of dreams. And I was in love.

Stone cold in love. Heart-pounding, manic love.

Instead of satisfying me, her touch was like gasoline on dying coals; it burned, it burned, it made me twist on the bed, seeking a cooler spot. When twilight fell, I tried to write, but my mind was too centered downstairs, watching for a glimpse of Myra's legs through the French doors as she took care of her evening routine, cooking supper, caring for her children. I toyed with the idea of going down very innocently to borrow sugar or play with Simon just to be near her, but there was a terrible demon of honesty about me, and I was afraid if Michael came home early and asked how my day had gone, I'd smile and say fine, that I'd finally crossed the line to adultery, but it was the best thing that ever happened to me, and if he didn't mind, I'd like to live upstairs in the servant's quarters forever.

So I stayed holed up in my room like an animal, scribbling a few insights on Bragg between watching the French doors, just biding my time till one o'clock came around, when I could emerge on the deck in perfect innocence and play in the water with the children. At first it seemed like an eternity away, and I could hardly sleep. Then morning dawned and Michael left for work and I felt a little better. Then as the sun began its full possession of the sky, Simon was knocking on my door, asking me to pleeese come down and swim, that his Mama had brought out some Coke and said I could have as much as I wanted.

The very wording of this little phrase pleased me very much, and as I changed into my bathing suit, I told myself yes, and I was going to drink it up, every drop. Which I did, as often as I could, once, sometimes twice an afternoon, and after a fortnight, was satiated enough to be generous, in love with the world. Everything Myra touched was suddenly dear to me, her house, her children, even her husband, and I faced him without fear that guilt would betray me, joining him at breakfast, and again talking of routine matters, how the union was faring, the possibility the Braves might change owners, how such a change might affect their performance. The rationale that made me as innnocent and pure as a newborn babe was the determination that Michael's marriage was nothing more than a small legal technicality, while my and Myra's love not only outdated it, but had also stood the test of time and separation. I knew instinctively that with his business mind and sharp creases, he might not appreciate this small revision, but I certainly did. I understood it intimately, and it comforted me so much that I had no worries for tomorrow, just a brilliant glory in the day. Love had won. Neither perverse fathers nor scheming mothers had separated us, and when Myra dressed in the afternoon to return to her children, I'd get as manic as a wild man, stomping my foot, shouting that I loved her, loved her, loved her.

She'd only smile, not even shaking her head, and when she was gone and the room was quiet again, quiet and dull and smelling of all the things I'd introduced to it that day, coffee and suntan oil and sex, I'd go back to my books with a shrug and a smile, telling myself that it was just fine, it was OK, it was just some hold-over loyalty to Michael that made her stop short of saying she loved me. Nothing to worry about, nothing to let grind me in the night when the lights from their bedroom dimmed and the dark house hung among the Spanish moss like an old, sullen dreamscape.

However, as the weeks went by, my opinion of my brother did continue its imperceptible shift, and by early summer, his even features had begun to take on the relentlessness, the same pitiless glare, of my old nemesis, Nathan Bedford Forrest, as he squashed the Union single-handedly. I did not bother to hide my disgust the morning he calmly announced the vote had been sixty-nine to thirteen, though he only smiled and folded his paper,

"Boy, you been up north too long," he said as Myra poured his coffee, not bothering to give her so much a glance, but speaking only to me. "I can't have those idiots telling me how to run my business. Anyway," he sipped his coffee, "I got plans of my own."

Myra was replugging the coffeepot, frowning at a spark from the outlet, and I looked away, afraid my eyes would betray me, thinking *don't we all, brother, don't we all.*

However, it wasn't until summer was fully upon us, hot, humid, West Florida summer, the air thick and pregnant all afternoon long, but never giving in to water, only hanging there above the trees in clouds as ripe and pendulous as the belly of a cow, that I finally saw a glimmer of escape, when Ira, now a civilian machinist working for the Navy in Jacksonville, called one morning during breakfast with the news his wife had borne their first child, a son, but was feeling poorly.

"Youngun cries all the damn time," he told Myra, who'd answered the phone and was sympathetic.

"Try sugar water."

"Done tried that, tried everything. May try putting a gun to my head, I don't get some rest around here soon."

Once this image settled in Myra's brain, she was quiet and preoccupied, not even cooking or pouring coffee, so that even the General noticed and asked her why didn't she go over there and help Dana out? That she was good with babies, it'd give them a break.

Myra looked a little stunned at the possiblitiy, but I was suddenly as sharp as a tack, keeping my eyes on the newspaper in my hands.

"The children—" she murmured.

Michael, standing and stretching his arms over his head, said, "Mama'll keepem. She's always fussing about how she never gets to see Missy."

Myra was still reluctant. "It's so far away, I never drove that far alone."

That was when, with a total lack of guile that would have made my mother proud, I looked up. "I need to go to Gainesville sometime here soon. Can go today, if you need a ride."

Myra only looked at me, but Michael dropped his arms. "What's in Gainesville?" he asked, and I folded the paper back, giving it my full attention.

"The library at UF. I need to do some research on the war," I paused, "in Florida."

Michael was looking at me levelly. "In Florida? I never heard of no war in Florida."

"Son," I said, standing and tapping him with the newspaper, "there were all kinds of wars in Florida. Don't you know anything about your history?"

He kept looking at me with his mild, level eyes. "Apparently not as much as I should." Then he turned to Myra, "Call up old Ira. Tellem Gabe'll run you over. Stay as long as he needs you."

Once he'd given her the word, she immediately went into action, for she was still nothing if not obedient, and within the hour, we were ready to leave, Simon and Missy squealing and excited at the prospect of spending a few spankless days at Grannie's, Myra quiet and efficient, carrying a handful of suitcases around to the garage, telling Simon not to let Grannie forget Missy's cough medicine. Simon was assuring her he would not when we turned the corner to the garage. When I saw Myra's car, I stopped dead still.

Now, I am sure that sometime at Gettysburg it occurred to Lee that he was outnumbered, hopelessly and desperately outnumbered, and even as he went through all the elaborations of feint and thrust, he caught a small, distant vision of Appomatox, and as I stood there and looked at the tail end of Myra's new car for the first time, a similiar hollow dread hit me in the pit of the stomach.

"This is a pink Cadillac," I murmured.

Michael was, as usual, very low-key about it, saying no, it wasn't pink, it was *champagne puce,* a nice wide car for running the children around in.

But I only stood there and blinked. "It's a pink Cadillac."

He laughed then and admitted that yes, he'd thought of me when he ordered it, but it didn't have white walls, he couldn't go that far, and all the way to Mama's, I thought dully, "His wife is driving a Cadillac. A *pink* Cadillac."

Well, it wasn't 1861, but it was, in spirit and in truth, a declaration of war, and when we finally made the open road, whipping past the alligator farms and tobacco barns on U.S. 90, I could not concentrate on driving, I was wanting Myra so bad, trying to kiss her neck, while she wiggled away, saying, "Gabriel, stay on the road, you'll kill us both— Gabr*iel*—"

I didn't care; I'd rather see both of us dead than leave her for that damn Nazi. Once her father had bought her off with a red bicycle, and now Michael was doing it all over again with a pink Cadillac and a marble pool.

"Those who do not learn from their history are doomed to repeat it," I told her, but she paid me no mind, moving to the far end of the seat and watching the roll of the Chattahoochee hills till we were outside Tallahassee when she asked me to stop and buy her a Coke.

"I need to take my pill," she said, "before dinner or it'll make me sick."

"What pill?" I asked. "Why do you need a pill?"

"I been sick."

I tried to coax her back across the seat. "Crawl back over here, and I'll make you feel better."

But she was like Mama, boy, dead serious when it came to matters of licensed medicine, so I pulled over at a greasy Fina station in Perry and bought her a Coke from a machine, then watched in horror as she retrieved a quart-size Ziploc bag full of medicine vials from her overnight bag.

"What the hell?" I murmured, as she unscrewed the top of a small, tinted bottle and put a pill on her tongue.

"My medicine," she shrugged. "Michael said I shouldn't forget."

Now, I'd long been familiar with the phenomenon of prescription drug dependency in women whose religion forbade the comfort of whiskey (Mama took a nerve pill every morning of her life), but never had I seen such a varied collection. I held the baggie to the light and read the strange, exotic names, Thorazine and Mellaril, noting the dosages, how they were all large, then looked at Mrya, who was calmly sipping her Coke.

"You take this shit?"

"Some of it," she said. "Some of it's old." She shook the little bottle in her hand. "This is new."

I held out my hand, and she handed it over. The brand name was misleading, but she supplied the translation: "lithium." The name was vaguely familiar, with a connotation of a giant and lasting sleep. I thought, no wonder she's so expressionless, so unanimated. No wonder she waits on Michael hand and foot with such languid passivity. The son of a bitch had her zonked on nerve pills.

"Myra, you shouldn't take this shit; it's addictive, it fries your brain."

She looked at me over the rim of her Coke with the beginnings of a frown between her eyes. "But I have to, Michael *says*."

And something in the way she spoke his name with such assured familiarity, such boundless confidence, was suddenly intolerable to me, infuriating, and with a lightning whip of anger, I kicked open the door and threw the only pitch of my career, a ninety-mile-an-hour line-drive that shattered the little glass vial against the blank concrete wall of the gas station.

"Gabriel!" she cried. "That's all I brought, Michael said—"

"*Fuck* Michael," I told her, flinging the whole Ziploc to the oily pavement, then slamming the door and taking her face in my hand. "Myra? Do you want to stay shut up in some asshole's backyard all your life? Walk around like a zombie, waiting on him hand and foot?"

She only looked at me, her eyes bothered, but too distant to comprehend, and I kissed her, long and slow, trying to rekindle the bowed-neck laughter of the years I'd known her when Simon was a baby, before Michael had done his number on her.

But there was still no response, and I whispered, fiercely, "Listen, Myra, you don't have to live like this. You don't need a baggie full of tranquilizers to get you through the day when you've got me. I love you, do you hear me? *Love you.* I've always loved you, don't you remember? The fence and Napoleon and *Gone with the Wind?*"

I was still holding her chin up, so she had to look me in the eye, and when she answered, her voice was low and tired and curiously ashamed. "No Gabriel. I can't. Not the fence or Napoleon or *Gone with the Wind*. I lost it."

Lost it, she said, and the pathos of the words cut like a knife, filling my chest with grief, knowing she was not lying, but confessing an awful truth; that she had lost something back there, both of us had, and I tried to bring some of it back, whispering into her face, assuring her. "Well, I did. I loved you, loved you so much and you loved me and it wasn't a game, a child's game. I never forgot it and you never forgot it and it was real."

Then I kissed her again, closing my eyes, feeling the rise of the old relentless drive, and it was awful really, not like lust at all, but more like torment, and a few miles down the road, when we came to a small town past the Suwannee, draped and ballooned for a watermelon festival, I pulled into a strip motel and turned off the car, looking at her in the hot, still silence.

"You been a slave too long," I said. "You need a rest. Let's stay here, let's live awhile. To hell with everybody; we're getting old waiting on everybody else."

Then I signed us in as Mr. and Mrs. Gabriel Catts, and God in heaven, I loved that seedy, sleazy old motel. I can remember it today, the cheap pressed paneling, the worn cotton spread, the ancient, sagging bed. At thirteen dollars a night, seven dollars a half-day, the whole place smelled of indiscretion, of time rented by the hour, but I was charmed by it all, for to my eyes it seemed that Myra and I were transforming the cheap and worthless into something precious by the alchemy of our love. And while Michael had to give her pills and marble pools and pink Cadillacs to keep her, I was satisfying her where it counted, taking her right out from under his nose. A wise fool, I thought him, and when night settled on the storefronts and the ferris wheel lit the salmon sky, we went out on the town in search of something, I don't know what. Freedom, maybe, or laughter, or maybe nothing more or less than the childhood that had once been taken from our hands.

Whatever the reason, I have vivid memories of that night, memories time has not touched: of the smell of carnival food on the hot, river-damp air, fried elephant ears and sausage and the sound of hawkers on the midway, teasing suckers into trying their luck at the games, their harsh voices cushioned and softened by the rolling crackle of the organ music of the rides.

And Myra, of course, I remember her, for she was very beautiful that night, dressed like the WASP princess Michael had trained her to be, in khaki shorts and a white cotton shirt, and a face that began to show signs of wakefulness as we hit the puke rides, the Tilt-a-whirl and the Scrambler, over and over again, laughing and kissing, me putting my hands under her shirt in plain sight of everyone, but never seeing any raised eyebrows. It was carnival time, after all, the celebration of the harvest, and the hot night had an exuberant, pagan quality, a taste of Fasching among these plain, country folk, making them look kindly upon us, as if they understood intimately that this was the way it was between a man and a woman, so what did it matter? The night had plenty of darkness to go around, and the red lights of the midway only made everyone's private obsession seem hotter and riper and more full of promise.

It was past midnight when we returned to our room, and after we'd finished our evening there behind the locked door and the check-out sign, I lay in bed with my hands under my head, fascinated by Myra's bedtime routine. It was hardly exceptional, just the hair brushing, the bath, the putting on of a simple batiste gown, but it lent a feel of domesticity to the seedy little room, and when she climbed into bed beside me, it was so sweet, so right, that I held her face in my hand, and whispered softly, fiercely, "I need you to marry me, Myra. I want you to sleep next to me the rest of your life. I can't stand leaving you anymore."

There was a blank pause as I watched her, waiting for her answer. Then her face took on that slightly quizzical expression, and she almost smiled. "Gabriel, I'm married already. You know that." Then another pause. "I'm married to Michael."

The impact of her words didn't connect for a small, prolonged moment, and when they hit, it was like the blow of a mule kick, so hard I couldn't speak, couldn't argue, couldn't even cry, but only watch as she calmly went to sleep curled against me in apparent contentment, sometimes rubbing her face to my chest like a baby nuzzling a mother's breast.

After an hour or so, I carefully shifted her and got out of bed, going to the window where the lights from the ferris wheel had finally been pulled, leaving the town quiet and tired and ready for another year's work. Stale and spent, it looked, and I pressed my forehead to the cold glass in despair, knowing there was nothing I could do but fight. I couldn't give her up; I couldn't take her by the hand and make her love me. All I could do was hope and wait and show her that I loved her, that she could leave her boundaries without fear.

That was all I did. I didn't cry, I didn't sweat; I only stood there with my forehead against the cold glass and confessed to the darkness that I couldn't let her go, and I got back in bed, slipping my arms around her waist and sleeping till morning. Then, before we ever got out of bed the next morning, I made love to her again, much like before, with all the same heat and chilling release, then dressed and left the tip for the maid and the untouched condoms on the bedside table beside the Gideon Bible with no explanation at all; none requested, none given.

Chapter

8

he rest of the trip was bittersweet, the
bitter being the four days Myra spent rocking
her nephew in Jacksonville while I made a pretense of doing research at
UF; the sweet, the ride home, a drive of about six hours that I managed
to stretch into a two-nighter, staying at strip motels along U.S 90 with
names like The Journey's End and The Sunny South.

When we pulled into Mama's late Friday afternoon, the front door
opened with a pop, and Simon and Missy mobbed us at the car, hugging
Myra, hugging me, recounting their week on Magnolia Hill in a hysterical, breathless rush. I returned their kisses and gave them the small
presents I'd bought them in Gainesville, but Myra got a little unglued by
it all, holding Missy to her chest and crying like we'd been gone a year
instead of a week.

I tried to calm her, but there was a panic in her tears, something far
more intense than mere joy at being home, and it was only when Mama
came out and filled the air with her nonstop rattle ("Lori painted Missy's
fingernails ever' night and Sim found a snake in the shed, nothing but a

little green snake but I toldem he couldn't keep it, that I never had and never would let no old snake in my house—") did she stop, and later that night, alone in my narrow bed, I was swept with another wave of nervousness.

I loved her, surely, no question about that, but in a more practical vein, she was a woman who'd grown used to big houses and big cars and buying her children anything they wanted. And while she might be content to abide by my lifestyle, she'd surely be hesitant to accept such a life for her children. Once I'd considered it from this angle, her tears in the car were explicable, even expected, and I began to see that the business of separating a home, no matter how hollow that home was, could be an enormous task—one I was sure I could overcome, for I had no intention of hurting Sim or Missy. I loved them, too. As I lay in bed that night, I came up with a firm stategy and woke up early the next morning and borrowed Myra's car to run into town and call a few colleagues up north, asking about openings and possibilities, getting a few favorable leads.

One in particular caught my eye, a teaching position at the University of Virginia. It was straight entry-level American History, but in Virginia that meant the Colonies and the Confederacy, and since I'd always written favorably of Lee and Jackson, I'd have the inside track. I figured Myra would enjoy living south of the Mason-Dixon, and the very name *Virginia* conjured up Walton-like images of farmhouses and mountains surrounded by loving children.

Once I'd gotten the ball rolling, calling the department head and feeling it out, I was nervous and happy and broke my self-imposed exile to go inside to tell Myra the good news. I found her standing at her bedroom closet and came up behind her quietly, wrapping my arms around her waist, asking her how she liked Virginia, but she was frowning at a line of identical blue oxford-cloth shirts, the button-down kind Michael wore to work.

"What's the matter?" I asked.

Her face was intense with concentration. "Can't remember which ones are dirty. I need to do Michael's work clothes today." She was unrolling a cuff as she spoke, pressing the sleeve to her face, then pulling it out, murmuring, "This one smells like Michael—" and I jerked it out of her hand and threw it behind us.

"Dammit, Myra, forget Michael—what are you, his houseboy? Come on, come here." I pulled her to the edge of the bed. "Listen, have you ever been to Virginia?"

She shook her head, picking the shirt off the floor and folding it on her lap till I took it away from her again and threw it behind us.

"Then listen. I'm flying up there to see about a job. I want you to come with me. We can tell Michael we're going back to Ira's and take the kids and look around." I was too nervous to sit still and began pacing. "It'll only be a few days, we'll stay somewhere nice, somewhere the children'll like—"

"I can't," she said calmly, and I stopped, but before I could argue, she said evenly, "Saturday's Fourth of July, the family reunion. Mama's coming. Ira's bringing the baby. Everybody'll be there."

I had tensed myself for a major moral battle and laughed aloud at this small distraction. "Then I'll change the appointment, no problem. The thing is, we need to move soon. You stay around here much longer, you'll be comatose."

So it was arranged: I was to interview for the job a week from Monday and made reservations at a bed-and-breakfast inn in Charlottesville, booking two adjoining rooms, one for us, one for the children. Once everything was in motion, the pressure lifted a little, and I began eating breakfast with Michael again and was astounded a few mornings later when he casually mentioned he'd bought Sanger.

"Are you serious?" I asked. "Where the hell did you get the money?"

"Well, we been buying up bits and pieces of it all along. They been pretty crippled since the wage-and-hour people hittem and scared spitless of the union. Knew it'd sendem down like a sunk brick."

"I thought you broke the union. I thought they voted it down."

He chewed his toast with no change of expression, nothing but that fierce, quiet determination that he'd once used drilling line-drive fastballs into that old stump. "They did. Two days later."

I just looked at him. "Are you serious? Why?"

"They made too many demands. They were," he paused, "unreasonable."

"Oh, I see," I said. "Started asking for health insurance, did they? And decent money and overtime?"

"I'll have to pay 'em overtime," he said mildly. "Or the wage-and-hour people'll sink *me*."

"Well, bless your heart," I drawled, leaning over and tapping him with the paper. "You know how greedy those workers get, start wanting all kinds of shit. You know, educations for their children, good houses, a few hours a week with their wives—hey, soon the bastards'll be wanting to move off Magnolia Hill."

He was not at all touched by my sarcasm, only taking a final bite of toast, murmuring, "You talk like a Yankee, Gabe. You don't know nothing about bidness."

Yeah, I thought acidly, *but I know plenty about slavery*. And with no apologies, no subterfuge, said, "I'm taking Myra to the family reunion tomorrow."

He looked up, "Why?"

"Ira'll be there," I said, meeting his eye. "I haven't seen him in a while—"

Before I could finish, Myra came between us to pour his coffee, and her face was closer than ever to the Myra of old, flushed and excited, the pink in her cheeks making her eyes very light, almost cornflower blue.

"He's bringing the baby." She smiled, and Michael must have noticed the sweet liveliness about her, for he made the first open move of affection toward her since I'd been back, reaching up and feeling her neck with his hand.

"And he'll let you hold it all day and it'll spit on you and pee on you and you'll cry when they make you give it back," he said with a touch of his old tenderness that reminded me sharply of Daddy. Then he stood. "You have fun, baby. Tellem I'm working. I'll be there Thanksgiving."

Then he kissed her very lightly on the mouth and left to do his dirty work on the poor suckers at Sanger, and I was mad and desperate again, resenting that two-second contact, suddenly wondering if she'd been sleeping with him at night after the lights went out and the house was surrounded by that blanket of silence. The more I thought about it, the more convinced I was that it must be so, I mean, what excuse could she give? She couldn't say she had a headache four weeks in a row.

And damn, it made me mad. So mad I was afflicted all afternoon with my two perennial torments, a nasty headache and a screaming stomach. After Exedrin and Tagamet finally got me back in decent shape, I worked off a little nervous energy retyping my resumé, putting a little Virginian spin on it (de-emphasizing everything but Lee) and made plans to be at my best, most prosperous behavior for the reunion. I think I might have even ironed my pants. I was certainly desperate enough. I could tell Myra's family still wielded a powerful influence and figured if I could win them over and land a decent job and find a place to raise her children, then it'd all be over but the paperwork, and Michael would never lay his greedy hands on her sweet neck again.

So I dressed carefully the next morning, in what I hoped was the personification of the prosperous, agreeable son-in-law, pressed khaki and a white Lacoste pullover, at the last minute strapping on a Rolex I'd bought for seventy-five dollars from a starving undergraduate at UNC. Yes, I was dressed for success, but when we joined up with the larger Sims/Odom clan, I began to wonder if I'd overdone it a bit.

The reunion was being held at a spring on the river, the kind surrounded by cypress and water oak and a dirt parking lot full of trucks with rebel license plates and NRA stickers, and the moment I stepped foot into the swimming area, I remembered something I once knew, but had apparently forgotten: things like Lacoste shirts and pressed pants and Rolex watches didn't pull any weight around here. Not much weight at all, and even as Myra introduced me, I could see the glint of resentment in the eyes of the men, semi-educated farmers and laborers, who looked on my smiling face with self-induced blindness, seeing nothing but *Harvard*. God knows Mama had spread the word among them; she considered it my one bragging point, and there was just nothing I could do or say to detach myself from the awful stench, just talk and smile and tell the women their children were pretty.

Myra's mother, a tall gray-haired woman, much older than I expected, was very kind, though, telling everyone how well she remembered me, and what a sweet little boy I'd been, always telling stories and building things in the backyard. She went on to relate a few miscellaneous childhood anecdotes, with no mention of the wrist or the *ponking*, and to hear her talk, you'd have thought we were happy-go-lucky, close-knit neighbors there on Lafayette. In the interest of letting sleeping dogs lie, I went along with her, adding a few footnotes of my own, and by lunch, my determination to hold my mouth right was paying off, the men venturing to ask what the Kennedys were up to, the women commenting on my bachelor status, putting in good words for unattached nieces and cousins. I listened to their hints with nods of polite interest, though I doubt I'd have pursued them, even if I didn't have Myra, for all in all, the Sims clan was a big-boned, red-headed bunch, the women, with one or two exceptions, as big and wide as the men. And I'm not talking city-wide, either. I'm talking country-wide, size 24, 42DDD wide, with no apologies to anyone, wearing flowered bathing suits and keeping good-looking husbands in line with their loud wiregrass voices.

One of them was pressing food on Myra, telling her how *awful* she looked, how *skinny* she was, like she had cancer or *something*, when Ira and his wife arrived with a tiny infant in a blanket that Myra took without a word, jiggling and walking and anointing with lotions out of her enormous tote bag, with no attention left for anyone, including me.

Fortunately, Ira filled in the void, grinning his same old grin, slapping me on the back and introducing me to his very young wife as his good friend Gabe Catts, Michael's baby brother. I appreciated his open acceptance and talked of old times without pause, but it wasn't easy, for poor Ira had unexpectedly grown into the spitting image of his father, and for a while there, it really threw me. He had the same height, the same high, ruddy face, the same fox-colored eyes, and I didn't see how Myra or her mother could stand to look at him, much less hug him. But they seemed pretty oblivious to it all. I guess watching him change day by day had numbed them to this shocking transformation, and the image of the Old Man had been slowly replaced by that of harmless little Ira.

Late in the afternoon, when the crowd had thinned and the food was covered from the flies, he and I moved our lawn chairs down to a sandy loop in the river shallows that afforded a unobstructed view of the spring, where Myra stood knee-deep in the coral green water, watching her children swim, the baby still in her arms. She made an arresting picture there, the baby a tight bundle at her chest, Sim and Missy and the other children dancing through the shallows, throwing up arches of water that glittered like sapphires in the white slant of the late afternoon sun.

I was calmed and reassured by the sight, giving Ira only half an ear as he spoke of his years as a drill instructor at Parris Island, why he'd left to take a job with the Navy, and how married life was treating him, for he was a relative newlywed, only six months into it.

"Yeah, Junior there got me to the altar," he admitted with that same old shameless grin.

He must have noticed how my eyes were traced on his sister, for he finally turned and looked at her over his shoulder a moment, then sat back, unwrapping a fresh pack of Camels, his voice flat and friendly. "Yeah, old Myra. She loves them babies, now. When she come to see us, she didn't put him down a minute. *Slept* with him."

I smiled and again apologized for leaving before he'd come home, making some excuse or another that he accepted easily, poking the cigarette in his mouth and lighting a match with a small clean jerk of his hand. "That's all right. Dana understood. Hated to see Myra go, though. Nice having somebody to hang onto your baby for you." He paused to light the cigarette, then shook out the match. "Guess she has to, won't be hanging on to namore a her own."

This was news to me, and I drew my eyes back to Ira and met his levelly. "Why not?"

"Why not?" he laughed. "Well, I doubt Michael'll let her, after what she's put him through." He stretched his face into that skeletal grin. "I mean I might could handle a wife that laid the preacher, but listen, even I'd draw a line at the yard boy."

There was a blank moment there after the words hit when I could only watch him, not saying a word, just watch his auburn-colored eyes that lifted in surprise.

"You ain't heard?" he asked incredulously. "Michael didn't tell you?"

But still, I didn't answer. I couldn't, for without realizing it, his words had knocked the breath out of me, and I could only sit there and painfully inhale the sharp bitter smell of the river, while Ira, taking my silence for acquiescence, shook his head ruefully.

"I mean, old Myra, she's a good girl, but *damn* if she won't spread her legs for anybody that asks. I mean that yard boy, a goddamned kid, sixteen years old, doing it right in front of the children. Hell, it was Simon who told Michael—asked him one night at supper why Tommy'd lay on top of Mama every day while they swam."

I stood up then, suddenly, before I'd caught my breath, and turned my back on him, leaning my elbows over my head against the low-hanging limb of a water oak, trying to get one clean breath in my lungs, while his voice rang on, jovial and merciless.

"And listen, I'd a had his balls for it, but Michael, he said no, it wasn't Myra's fault. And he didn't even lay a hand on her. By God, I would have. I'd a ripped them fancy clothes off her back, beat her *raw*—"

I stood there pressing my forehead against the rough bark of the twisted old oak, wishing he'd stop, shut up, for God's sake, that he was killing me, but he didn't, his smoke drifting by in sweet wafting clouds.

"But that preacher, now, that was Michael's fault. Had her there for counseling, had her to this quack revival preacher, and everything was going fine and dandy till one morning he got a call from this screaming woman, saying she's gone kill his wife, the whore was sleeping with her husband—" He laughed aloud again. "And it was this preacher's wife. And that damn Michael, he had a man from the plant go and stay at the house when he went in to work at night 'cause that woman was dead on Myra's tail, wanting to kill her. And hell, if it was me, and Dana'd done that, shit, I'd a give that woman my address and set her out on the porch, lock the door behind her, tell 'em to *have at it*—"

"I think I'm gonna puke," I said lightly.

He answered just as lightly, "Go ahead. It's all private here. I seen men puke before, use to run 'em till they puked. Told 'em it was good for 'em."

For a moment I just stood there, unsure of what I was hearing. Then I turned and looked at him, and his red-tipped, fox-colored eyes were very bright, burning with a happy, carefree hatred as he blew a line of smoke into the air and tilted his head a little to the side.

"And then we come to the real icing on the cake. The *baby brother*."

I only looked at him, thinking with an odd detachment that wasn't it funny—there'd been another angel on Magnolia Hill after all, one Mama never named. And he had me right where he wanted me, regarding me with unabashed joy.

"Comes home to write a book, he says. Needing a place to stay. So poor Michael, that stupid sonofabitch, he says sure thing, move right upstairs, and bam, it ain't no time till he's not only in her pants, he's making plans. Big plans. Plans to meet the family, to steal away at twilight—"

At this, he threw his head back and laughed with such abandon that the women in the water looked up, Dana's face curious, Myra's calm and expressionless, dropping back to the baby, while Ira shook his head.

"You don't think," he said, "that for one minute we didn't know what you were up to ever since you drove up in that big old Cadillac with your gold watch and your *shit*-eating grin? 'Myra's got another stray on her tail,' I told Mama, and she's all worried, 'fraid this'll be the straw that breaks Michael's back and she don't have room for her no more. You got Mama all worried, Gabe."

I still didn't answer. It was just too unnatural, the children's happy squeals; Myra, knee-deep in the clear green water; and over all, Ira's silky, friendly venom.

"So listen here, Gabe, my *good friend Gabe*, who has helped maintain my sister's sterling reputation as a whore. You can sure have her, just feed her and pay her bills, but listen, *everyone else will* before it's over. It's just a matter of time. So enjoy it while you can. You sure stood in line long enough. God, you were hot for her when she didn't even have tits. Boy, you were ready for her then—"

"I love her," I finally said, whispered, trying to see if this honest truth would put some possibly sane spin on it all, but Ira only stood and pitched his cigarette in the river, lifting his arms over his head in a massive catlike stretch.

"Sure you do," he grinned. "We all do. Everbody loves little Myra, everbody always has. Shit, you think you're the only man she was driving crazy when she was ten?"

I hit him then, knocking him backwards into the shallows and diving in after him, rolling and sliding through the mud as I tried to get at his neck and not merely hurt him, but choke him, destroy him. To erase everything he'd said, to turn back the clock to four o'clock, when we were going to Virginia and seeing about a job and staying in an old bed and breakfast with a balcony that overlooked a salt marsh.

But Ira's time at Parris Island had been well spent, and it was only a matter of seconds before I was the one taking the beating. He fought like a machine, with no wasted energy, landing cruel dicing blows to the face and kidneys that had me lying face down in the mud after half a minute's uninterrupted pounding.

Then, showing very little sign of damage himself, just a rivet of blood from a gash on his forehead, he lifted my head by my hair and dispensed with the grin long enough to spit in my face. "You *love* her. You *love* her. *Shit.*"

He slammed my face back in the mud and started up the embankment, his voice lighter, reclaiming an edge of its vicious tease. "Boy, why don't you ask yer brother Michael about love? He's on to you and you know why?"

I was trying to sit up, coughing at the mud and filth in my chest, feeling the blood on my face with the back of my hand, and the laughter was back in his voice as he made the incline and turned and finished, "'Cause that stupid cunt *told* him. Think about that awhile, *shithead*. Think about what your Daddy would say if he knew."

Then he was gone, his footsteps playing across the fresh, sour smell of the river and the effortless squeals of the children, and I rolled slowly to my back and lay there in the black water, wishing he'd killed me. For I could take the electric sheer of the broken teeth, the agonizing grate of cracked ribs when I did puke, after all. What I couldn't stand was the news, the stunning bit of revision he'd given me with such massive enjoyment, for it was simply unthinkable, like taking a child in for a routine cold and being told it was leukemia. The same dull shock ("Was Simon what told him—"), then the calm of denial, then the sickening rebound ("—asked him why he'd lay on top of Mama while they swam—").

The nasty, awful kick of the words made me stand, suddenly, and dive into the river to wash off, then climb the steep bank, past the tables where the men watched me with flat, level eyes, but the women turned away, embarrassed at what a beating I'd taken. But I didn't care, I hated their stinking guts, every fat-assed, degenerate one of them, and when I called to Myra in the water, she turned, her face suddenly alight.

"Gabriel?" she called, handing the baby to Dana. "Are you all right? You're bleeding."

I turned and started for the car. "Can you get a ride back to town? I'm leaving."

She waded out of the water, running a little to catch up. "What in the world did you do to yousef?"

But I kept walking, quickly, past the tables where Ira stood with a drumstick in hand, grinning like the demon he was, and when I was close enough, I leaned over and spit blood at him, for I had nothing left to lose. I mean if he killed me, he'd be doing me a favor, but he didn't oblige, only jumping aside playfully, calling to Myra, "Come on, shug, leave the boy alone. You'll find you another one here soon. I got a friend at work been wanting to meet you. Got *sevral*—"

She stopped then and turned to her brother, asking him something, but I didn't stop to listen, going straight to the car and heading back toward town, taking the stairs two at a time to the vacant little room that was bright, too bright, in the flat yellow glare of the western sun, the maps full of red casualty pins and blue prisoner of war rolls.

Twilight fell slowly, painfully, as I lay there on the bed in my damp clothes and replayed every word, every glance that had led me to Myra's bed, and in retrospect, I had to admit that something was wrong. Bad wrong. Something past mere bad judgment and hitting into the realm of the unthinkable. Lying there in the fading evening hush, the smell of the river still on my hands, I began to feel the presence of something I had not felt in years, not years, and at first I couldn't place it, not until darkness had nearly fallen; then I remembered the hot, nasty breath on my neck, the soft, coy voice in my ear, *Whatsat arm doing in my yard?*

Once I'd pegged it, I was filled with a restless dread, standing and pacing, stopping to rub my eyes and try to put a name, an explanation, to Myra. What was she? A nymphomaniac? A drug addict? Some nameless, mysterious evil, her father's feminine counterpart?

Why had she told Michael?

I paced and spit blood and began to run a fever, chilled and stabbed and tormented by every demon in hell, actually jumping in fright when a car door slammed downstairs. I went to the window and watched Myra and a cousin unload ice chests and sleeping children, and when the cousin was gone, suddenly, I had to know, I had to be told, at whatever cost, and went down and knocked at the French door. She was still in her bikini when she answered it, her face creasing with concern as she opened the door. "Gabriel, what in the world didju do to your—"

"We need to talk," I snapped, my words muffled from the swollen jaw. "Where're the kids?"

"In bed," she said, closing the door behind me. "Fell asleep on the way home, had a big day, Mama said." She smiled when she said it, a smile that faded at the sight of my face in the light. She reached out a hesitant hand to touch my face. "What happened to your face?"

The ache in my side, the screaming questions in my mind were set aside for a moment by her touch, and I felt the old drawing, the pull toward her, and let her touch me, quietly, her eyes on my face, watching my reaction. Nervous, searching eyes that seemed to require my approval, and I had laid a quiet hand on her arm, when Ira's voice, full of that good-old-boy hilarity, came back to me: "*Simon's the one who told him, asked why Mama—*" and instead of a caress, I grabbed her high, near the shoulder, and shook her.

"Did you tell Michael?" I whispered. "Why did you tell Michael?"

She flinched at my grip, her eyes still on mine, her face very concentrated, as if she were trying to remember something, and after a moment, she said, very slowly, "Michael is my husband."

I shook her again. "Dammit, Myra, I know he's your husband," I snapped. "Is this some kind of game to you?"

"No," she said slowly, "it's not a game." Then, after another careful pause, "I love him."

That's when I did something that I have never been able to reconcile myself to. I mean, I am no saint. I have had my share of sins, both in the flesh and in the mind, but I'd never hit anyone without provocation, not even as a child, but I did then. Not a lethal blow of the Ira Sims caliber, but a whip of a vicious backhand that snapped her head back, splitting her lip with a shock of blood so sudden and red that I had not even swung through before I was apologizing, trying to take it back.

"No, baby, I'm sorry, damn, I'm sorry, Myra—"

But she wouldn't listen, pulling away frantically and backing to the couch, her face full of emotion for the first time since I'd been back in Florida. And that emotion was terror. I tried to catch her, to hold her and tell her I was sorry, but she escaped me till the couch stopped her and she fell back on it, still in movement, almost crawling over the back, till I caught and pinned her against the cushions.

"I love you," I said desperately to her face. "I'm sorry, Myra. I never hit anybody in my life. Are you all right?"

But her face never lost its terror till finally, she began to cry.

Noiselessly, the tears rolling down her face unchecked, and I hugged her in relief, for to me, tears were a sign of forgiveness, of surrender. On and on she cried, pulling her face to her chest, covering it with her fists, and after a while, I tried to calm her.

"Hush, baby," I whispered. "It's all right. We'll talk to Michael. Tell him we love him but we love each other, too. It'll be all right. These things happen, they work out, Myra, hush—"

But it was no use; she was engulfed in the crying in a way I'd never seen before. Noiseless, racking sobs that didn't seem to be dispersing anything, but only gaining momentum, and when words failed to calm her, I shook her, I shouted in her face, I finally even reached back and slapped her again, not in anger, but panic, for Simon had heard us and was standing at the top of the stairs, calling, "Mama? Mama?"

"Your mother's fine, Sim," I answered. "Go back to bed—"

"But we ain't had supper," he said.

I called desperately, "Well, go on to bed. I'll bring you something."

He padded back down the hall obediently, but still, Myra cried, rocking herself back and forth in a strange rhythmic tic that scared me so bad I tried to call Mama, but got no answer, and with nothing else to do, dialed Sanger. After about twelve rings, Michael himself answered, and I screamed into the receiver, "Myra's having some kind a *fit*. I don't know, Michael, she's crying, she won't stop, Simon's here—"

"Go upstairs," he said evenly, "and look in the top of our closet. There's a shoebox up there and a baggie full of medicine. Get out the Thorazine and give her one if you can get it down. Then stay with her. I'll call the ambulance. Just stay with her. For God's sake, don't leave her alone with the children. I'm calling Dr. Williams *now*—"

He hung up in mid-breath, and I ran up the stairs two at a time and told Simon his supper would be ready in a minute, I had to fix it, then went to their closet where I found the shoebox all right, but not the baggie full of medicine, and had a sudden memory of slamming it on the oily dirt of the Fina station while I told her she didn't need that shit, not as long as she had me.

I didn't even bother to curse, but went back to Myra, trying to lift her face so I could apologize again, but she was as rigid as glass in her strange, mad position. I was wrestling with her, trying to wipe the blood from her chin, when the knock sounded at the front door and I ran to answer it, flinging it wide for the ambulance attendants and their wide, high gurney.

"Here! Here!" I cried, leading them down the hall, almost as wired as Myra. They tried to strap her in on her back, but even their combined weights couldn't unbend her, and they were struggling on both ends, telling her to settle down, when suddenly, there was another voice in the room, Michael's, and he was slapping them away.

"Let her alone, you idiots. She's catatonic, can't you see that? Lay her on her side—"

They obeyed him, strapping her in curled to her side, and he followed the gurney to the ambulance and climbed in without a glance in my direction. When they were gone, the siren fading into the hush of the still country night, I closed the front door and went back to the couch, sitting there in a strange, bloodless void till Simon called again, and I fixed him something eat—I can't remember what—and that's all I remember.

Sometime later, maybe hours, maybe minutes, I heard a car in the drive and fled without thought, out the French doors and up the steep stairs to my room, not bothering to turn on the light, but lying in the darkness with a certain foreboding that for all the violence of this day, the worst blow had not been struck, not yet. That it was still being drawn back and would come from the hand of my brother Michael.

So I waited, waited quietly in the belly of the pitch night, sweat rolling down my face, chilling me, and when he came, it was much like that first afternoon with Myra, when I'd waited in the darkness for the inevitable to overtake me. First, there was the pause, then the feet on the stairs, then the voice at the open door.

"Gabe?" he called, and when I didn't answer, he crossed the room just as she had, but instead of coming to the bed, he went to the lamp and turned it on.

When he saw me in the light, he blinked. "Ira?"

I didn't bother to nod, and he pressed. "You all right?"

"Fine," I breathed, and he accepted it with a lift of his face, looking around the room at my maps and battles, then going to the window where the marble pool glittered under the new stars, and after a moment, he said very quietly in a calm, matter-of-fact voice, "Myra's schizophrenic."

closed my eyes when he said it, feeling this final blow fall much as Ira's had, quick and cruel, but oddly nonviolent: the slash of a surgeon's knife on a thin blue vein. Michael didn't pause to let me react, though, but continued, his eyes on the pool, his voice level and controlled, the same voice he'd used to describe busting the union.

"D'you know, Gabe, I only flew one time in my life. Thirty-two years old and never on a plane, but I had to go to Dallas, so I flew. Had this layover in New Orleans, and on a whim, rented a car and drove the rest of the way." He turned. "You know why?"

I shook my head, for the day's impact had left me as voiceless as a slaughtered sheep, and Michael made his way across the room, hands in his pockets, making a story of it.

"'Cause there's this town, this little Louisiana town right outside Slidell, where Myra's from, where her father's people are all buried. Well, I went there and spent about an hour finding the cemetery, and another hour figuring out which Sims was Myra's daddy. Then I spent about twenty seconds pissing on his grave, and then I turned around and come home."

He had taken a seat at my little table, still cluttered with books and battles and legal pads, and sat there mildly, his legs crossed, his wrists folded on top of one another as if he was in church. "'Cause that bastard's hand is still on my house. Twenty years and still reaching out, and I hate it, Gabe. I hate it. *God knows* I hate it."

"How is she?" I finally managed, and his voice grew calm again.

"All right. Right as could be expected. Doctor got her down with one shot and that ain't nothing to complain about. Had her tied to the bed, restrained, when I left, but she was sleeping." He lifted his face in a wry smile. "Kind of hated to leave her, she looks so good when she's asleep, kinda favors my wife. Not that *skinny woman* who keeps my children, and cooks and cleans and lays still when I want her to, but never offers much more. Can't very well, not with the drugs she's on."

His smile faded to a brace of set, bitter lines around his mouth, but he lifted his hand to make a quiet, understated point. "But I never let it get to me, Gabe. I never do. I don't forget that somewhere beneath that idiot smile there's the woman I married. This woman who use to iron my shirts ever' night 'cause I made her—I didn't want to be no factory worker all my life; who use to make me take her to the river to make love to her 'cause she didn't like Daddy and Mama hearing the bed creak." He rubbed his eyes and smiled at this, and the sheer normalcy of the memory was such a contrast to the dull, relentless evil of the day that I was taken out of myself a bit and carried along with his gentle, rolling words.

"Use to talk to me in bed at night, Myra did, back when I was so tired, so damn tired, all I could do was lay there and listen. But she'd lay there beside me, or if something really got to her, she'd sit up against the footboard, and her eyes would be so alive, so full of what she was saying. Telling me about people on the Hill, or church gossip and her opinion of it, or about books she was reading."

His hand came up again, pointing at me, trying to impress on me that this was a serious thing. "'And I don't mean little books, either, Gabe. I mean big books. Books she got from the libary. She'd readem while I was working, and at night, she'd tell me about 'em."

His face began to lighten again as he remembered something, and he shared it with me. "One night, she was telling me this story about this woman who'd married this rich man who'd been married before. His first wife was dead, she'd drowned, and this second wife kept being reminded of her—"

"Rebecca?" I murmured and he smiled.

"You read it?"

When I shook my head, he laughed. "Well, Myra sure did. Read it about a hundred times. She loved that damn book. She told it to me, one page at a time, it took forever, and when she come to the place they find Rebecca's boat, this voice cut through the wall: 'Did he kill 'er?'"

Michael laughed aloud. "And it was *Daddy*. He'd started listening to her at night and couldn't hep himself. It was so funny. He was so embarrassed, he kept apologizing. But he couldn't read. He'd never heard a such a thing in his life. That's when she made me start taking her to the river, figured if the walls were that thin, her running her mouth wasn't the only thing they were hearing out of her at night." His smile gradually eased. "But I didn't care, hell, she was my wife, and it was so good. It was like she was keeping me alive at night, taking me somewhere outside Sanger, beyond Magnolia Hill—those were the sweetest days of my life, sweeter than kissing her, just laying there and listening to her talk."

He sat there a moment, his face distant, caught up in his own story, then stood abruptly and began pacing the room, examining the maps on the walls, restless, a little frustrated that he had not found more fitting words to describe the incredible relief that comes when a desperate heart hooks up with a dreamer. But it was just as well; I knew all about it, and could see her so clearly, just beyond the pig iron fence, her arms crossed close for warmth, her eyes distant, intense, devouring every word, that for a moment, I lost the thread of his story.

"—found this house," he was saying. "Old, nasty. I didn't want no part of it. Wanted something in town, but Myra loved it. Loved it the minute she laid eyes on it, and they weren't asking nothing for it. It'd stood empty twenty years, the windows broken, the floor painted, the pool—dang, I thought it was a septic tank—full of all kinds of stuff, snakes and mud and algae. It took four trucks to haul it off.

"So it was rough at first, me working all the time and Myra making this place livable, then I got foreman, and it was like we turned the corner. Had us a house and a little money, and Sim, then Missy came," he paused in front of Shiloh, his face tired and curiously hurt. "And when she was, oh, maybe six months old, I woke up one night, and where was Myra? The bed was empty, the house cold. I found her downstairs in her nightgown, stripping floors. Told her it was late, to come to bed, but she was so excited, showing me the wood underneath, telling me whatall she had to do, with the floors and the windows. She was so happy, I just left her to it, didn't think much of it. And for a while, everything was still all right. The children happy, the house looking good a lot faster than I thought it would. The only thing was Myra—she was skinny all of a sudden. Her clothes starting hanging off her, and I could feel the bones under her skin when I touched her. Even Mama noticed it, took me aside one Sunday, told me to put carpet down on these fool floors, that Myra was working herself to death over them."

He moved down the wall to Gettysburg, reaching up to straighten a pin, his voice even. "That's how it went, all summer, I guess, five or six months, till one day—or night, I guess. Yeah, it was night, it was at supper, Simon looked up and right out of the blue, asked me—"

I sat up. "No—no, listen, Michael, don't—Ira already told me. I can't stand—"

"Yes, Gabe." He turned. "Yes, *you can*. I mean, you stood her very well, didn't you, when she was laughing and laying still? And you can stand *this*."

He faced me off evenly, and I was in too much pain to withstand him, lying back and closing my eyes, and after a moment, his voice calmed, reclaiming its even tread.

"Simon, he asked me why Tommy—this boy I'd hired to get the yard back in shape—why he'd lay on top of Mama every day while they swam." His eyes were still on the wall, but his voice grew very quiet, trying to make me understand. "And you know, Gabe, when he said it, Myra was sitting right there across the table, feeding Missy, and she didn't say a thing. She just sat there, stirring the baby food, her eyes real distant, like she was trying to remember something. And the longer she sat there, the scareder they got. Then, suddenly, she looked up and met my eye, and I knew, I *knew* it wasn't a lie, that Simon wasn't making something up, but before I could say a word, she jumped up and tore off upstairs.

"It was so quiet, so quiet when she left, Sim started crying; he knew he'd started something. But I cleaned up Missy and set them down in front of the TV, and the whole time I knew; I knew Old Man Sims was reaching out, out of the grave, putting his hand on my house. I could smell it, I swear to God I could. When I got upstairs, Myra was laying all curled up in bed, staring at the wall. I sat down beside her, and as soon as I said her name, she just flew up at me and grabbed the front of my shirt, grabbed it so tight the buttons went everywhere, and she was crying—

'My mind is going, Michael, it's leaving me, I know it is, I cain't remember Mama's name. I tried all day. I cain't remember how old Simon is, Tommy asked me, he's my little boy, Michael, why cain't I remember?'

"That's the way it was. No guilt, no excuses, just this wild, crazy talk. I got her to a psychiatrist—well, he's really an M.D., but one of his degrees is psychiatry, and come to find out, she hadn't slept in six months. Not a wink. Been keeping the children all day, working on the house all night. He said it was postpartum depression at first, then changed it to schizophrenia, but I don't know if I can buy that 'cause he says it ain't related to her past at all. Says it's just something that happens to people, like cancer or diabetes, but I know, I *know* her life. I remember her face when she was little, when she used to play out back. I know it's part of that and if I can just break it, break its back, my wife'll come back to me one day.

"Do you think she will, Gabe?" he asked suddenly, turning and looking at me on the bed. "Do you think I'm doing right by her? I mean, I could put her away, hospitalize her. Insurance would pay for it, and it'd be safer for the children. But damn, I just can't stand the thought of them seeing her once a week, sitting on some bench with that stupid smile on her face while they try to remember who she is."

"I don't know, Michael. I don't know." I whispered, for it was simply overwhelming. I couldn't pretend to understand.

He looked a little hurt I could not reassure him in this thing, then turned back to the maps. "Well, anyway, Dr. Williams put her in a week to stabilize her, said she was about to—I cain't remember the word—blow apart is what he meant. So we took her there and signed her in and she kissed Sim and Missy goodbye and told me she loved me, that she wanted me to remember that, no matter what, and you know, Gabe, that's the last time I ever saw my wife, standing there at the counter at Jackson Memorial, checking herself in with her little suitcase in her hand, looking scared and skinny, like a cancer patient going in for cobalt. The last time I seen her, I swear to God—"

He began crying then, possibly the first time in my life I'd ever seen my brother cry, for he was the stoic, and I was the one who got hysterical and had to leave the theater when Bonnie Blue broke her neck.

But this time we were quite reversed: him crying, me lying there racked by chills as my fever rose higher, but numb, so numb I could only close my eyes, and like Mama all those years ago on the porch, wonder why God allowed such things to happen.

"Come home like she is now," he said, getting the better of his tears, and resuming his inspection of the maps. "Smiling. Calm. Lights are on, but nobody's home. We tried everything, Dr. Williams and I, all kinds of medicine, enough to fill a room, and counseling and therapy, but nothing worked, and after a while I started getting desperate, thinking the longer she went this way, the bigger chance it'd be she'd never return. So when I heard about this preacher—"

"No," I said, sitting up. "No, Michael, it's enough, by God, I don't—"

"*No!*" he whipped around furiously. "No, it's not! You listen to me. I need to tell you, tell someone who loves her, who won't ask me why I didn't kill her. Someone who'll know she wasn't some bored housewife playing the whore— Now listen." He paused, his face worried but determined, speaking quickly. "A *preacher*. Who specialized in demonic possession. Now I know it just sounds ignorant, Gabe, but you remember Old Man Sims. There was just something so evil about him—not crazy—*evil*, that I decided to give it a try. She was seeing him a few months, doing a little better, I thought, when," he finally took a breath, "one night his wife called, pitching a fit. Said she'd found some clothes, panties or something, in his office, and she was on the warpath. I was afraid she'd come out here and kill her, had to get Sam to stay here when I went to see her husband, went out to his church, caught him in his office after the evening service, and as soon as I laid eyes on him, I knew it was true, that his wife was right. And all I said was: 'Why have you done this thing to me?'

"And you know, Gabe, he just fell over, just like I'd shot him. It was the strangest thing. Said for me to kill him, that he deserved it, but I told him the only person I wanted to kill was already dead, and the only thing

I could do now was hope and pray and try to keep her home because there's just no way to protect her and there's that *thing* about her. Sam calls it the *shark* thing. He had a cousin like it. Some uncle messed with her when she was little, and he says it's like they're wounded fish, bleeding in the water the rest of their lives, and there's a certain type of man who's drawn to them. Who smells their blood like a shark, that'll circle them and circle them, and when they get the chance, they'll *hit*, they'll *hit*, till there's nothing left."

Every time he said *hit*, he slammed his fist against the window frame, rattling the glass, and when the vibration finally stilled, his voice was quiet. "That's why, that's why I never thought of you, Gabe, as a threat."

I'd taken so much that day without any possible defense that now I was angry. I was more than angry. I was furious, coming off the bed, shouting, "Why the hell didn't you say something, you fool? You left us here, knowing—"

"I lived with Daddy a year. I never had to tell him to keep off my wife—"

"Not the same! I love her. I always loved her. You knew it, you knew—" But when I tried to stand, the weight of my body on the cracked ribs came up from the floor like electricity on a white-hot wire, making me slump back on the bed with clenched teeth, too proud to cry aloud. For a moment, the hot room dissolved into a kinder darkness; then I heard Michael, across the room, his voice quiet.

"Sit back," he said, his voice coming to me low and distant, as if he were standing across a field. "Lay back down. I'm not gonna fight you, Gabe, whip your ass and say we're even. Don't even try. Anyway," he turned back to the window, "you're right. I knew."

I just looked at him, not understanding, his back to me as he spoke.

"See, she just started on this new medicine. Lithium. It's what they maintain manic-depressives on. Dr. Williams has been wanting to give it a try. But between the old stuff and the new, there had to be a few days when she couldn't take nothing at all, till her system cleared, a drug holiday, he calls it, and I been dreading it so bad. He told me straight it was risky, said she could go catatonic like she did tonight, or manic and fry her brain a little more, or something we'd never even heard of. Could take a razor to herself, or Sim, or Missy, or all three of us, wouldn't be unheard of.

"So I been putting him off since Christmas. Then you showed up at Mama's and I figured you'd be around to keep an eye on the children, so I called him up, said it was now or never, and it was so strange. I mean, instead of getting worse, she started getting better. Sleeping six, seven hours a night, and sometimes I thought I could see tiny bits of Myra. Like when she'd talk about Ira's baby, she'd get this excited look on her face, like something was finally connecting. It was so sweet. It was like a light at the end of a tunnel, like this lithium was going to do a miracle here.

"That's why I let her go to Jacksonville, even though I had begun to suspect, shit, I began to know, that you were—" he paused. "Then Ira called the day you left over there, and you know Ira, he set things pretty straight. Told me you were, how did he put it? *Ponking* her. Ast me what I was planning to do about it, and when I said nothing, old Ira, poor old crazy Ira, he shamed me, Gabe, he really did. Because he got so damn mad, he called me names and you names and said he'd kill us both and you know, Gabe, till I heard all that damn screaming mad, I just forgot to get mad myself. Till then, everything with you and your little games was fine 'cause it fit my plans, but after I talked to Ira, I knew it wasn't all right at all. That shit, this was *Myra* we were talking about, not some knothole on the assembly line, that who the hell did I think I was, treating her this way?"

He sat down again, back at the table with the books and the legal pads and the box of reference cards, his face in his hands, meditatively rubbing his eyes. "And that's when I messed up. When I didn't meet you at the door and send you on your way. But see, she'd just been on lithium two weeks, so I figured, what the hell, what's done was done. If I could buy a little more time, maybe I'd reclaim a little more of her, a few more good days. So I gave you another week. One week with my wife. Right in my own house. Knowing you were with her, knowing you were making plans, 'cause I started getting these phone calls from people up north, telling me you were getting married and looking for a job. Then Myra told me herself. Said you'd asked her to marry you and wasn't that funny, you knew she was married already."

Without warning, the long torrent of words came to an end, and after their relentless pound, the lamplit room seemed dim and vacant as he finished, his voice quiet, his face in his hands. "So I was the one who played the whore with her in the end. Knew it wasn't right, but thought I could get away with it, right up till about an hour ago, when I was sitting there on a couch in the waiting room in the ER, when Dr. Williams came in and about bit my head off. Asked why I'd went and got her pregnant, that she couldn't take lithium, pregnant—"

I closed my eyes again. This had blindsided me, but he didn't pause, his voice still quiet, a little wry, as he sat back in his chair and looked at me. "And I guess congratulations are in order here because we been real careful, what with the drugs and all. Only thing is, when you pitched all her other stuff, you also pitched the pills, but really it's not that bad. I mean, I ain't planning to kill you or nothing. I mean, if there's one thing we're fixed up to do here, it's raise children—"

"No, Michael."

"Yes, Gabe," he answered just as evenly, standing suddenly, but keeping his voice even. "Yes, yes, indeed— See, I have this plan, this good plan, that may be my last chance. See, I'm gone hire this woman, this aunt of Sam's. She's the mother of this cousin of his. She's seen this kind a thing before, and she'll be able to deal with Myra and keep an eye on the children while she's pregnant. Then, just before the baby's born, Dr. Williams'll put her in the hospital and take it cesarean because he don't know what labor'll do to her. Then he'll keep her twilight-zoned till the baby's a few weeks old. Then," he finally paused for a breath— "then we'll bring her back home, have her back on lithium, see if it works out. I hope so, God in heaven, I hope so, 'cause if I lose her this time, I don't think I'll ever get her back."

"No, *Michael*," I repeated, knowing what was coming next, and he turned, suddenly furious again, shouting.

"Yes, Gabriel! And you'll go back where you come from—"

"No, Michael!" I shouted back, ignoring the pain to stand and meet him, "It's my baby. You can't tell me to leave, to run away. I didn't do anything that wasn't in love—"

"Love?" he cried. "Was it love that made you pitch her medicine? Her lithium level was nothing, nothing. She could have done anything, gone into a convulsion, getting cut off like that. You ain't talking about love, you're talking about how much you want her, and wanting ain't love. Screwing ain't love; if you loved her you'd leave right now. I wouldn't have to ask you twict—"

"—don't know *nothing* about our love—" I was yelling in his face, but he was as relentless as Ira.

"—but all you want to do is hang around, crying and showing your ass, biding your time till she's well enough to hit again, and hit and hit till she's gone, packed off to Chattahoochee just as sure as if that bastard'd taken her that night on the Hill—" His face was so close I could see the blood beating in his temples. "And he's the one who'll win, Gabe, cain't you see that? Myra'd never let you touch her, not Myra—all those nights at Mama's—did you ever touch her then?"

Her face in the kitchen that night, desperate, struggling to pull away (*don't touch me, Gabriel, don't touch me*—) was very close, very clear, but he didn't give me a chance to answer, speaking quickly, in a light, persuasive voice. "And this plan, I got this feeling, this good feeling, this lithium'll make her right—"

"Right?" I whispered, shaking with fury, "Right for *what*? To wait on you, to tell you stories in bed at night 'cause you work too hard to have a life of your own?"

The words were not out of my mouth before his hands were on me, gripping my shirtfront in much the way he'd described Myra's frenzied grasp, his eyes a bare inch from my nose as he murmured in deadly earnest, "Don't you try that shit with me, Gabe. Don't you talk to me that way. I had to work. I never had nobody telling me I'se smart, telling me I could get out. I never had a chance, but I believed in you. I spent money on you, I explained it to Daddy, but you never believed in me." He brushed a tear with an impatient hand. "Never."

"I did," I offered quietly, but he only laughed, dropping my shirt and turning to the window.

"Oh hell, Gabe, cut the bull. You know you didn't. Said I'd rot at Sanger. Ast me why I married Myra, asked if she was pregnant. Couldn't believe I'd busted a stupid, peckerwood union—hell, you used to look at me like you could smell how ignorant I was, like you laughed behind my back—yo poor hick brother, what a hard life he had. He just didn't know no better."

For a moment, the party jibes, the hilarious anecdotes came back to me (—*and my brother, my brother Michael, he turned down a contract with the Reds because he was afraid there wasn't any money in it*—) and I was no longer angry, just ashamed.

"I'm sorry, Michael—" I began, but he would have none of it.

"Sorry don't feed the cat," he said, pacing around again, his voice brisk. "Now what you're gone do is pack your stuff and take Myra's car to the airport in Tallahassee and leave it there and go on to one of these schools that keeps calling, wanting you to teach this war." He paused to look at Gettysburg again, then turned. "And what I'm gone do is work at a factory and take care of my wife and children. It's what you decided a long time ago, first time you took that bus out of town, and it's too late to change now."

"How can you be so sure?" I whispered, and he wouldn't look at me when he finished.

"Well, Gabe, two things make me so sure: one is the shotgun under my bed that I'm going upstairs and loading and coming back to kill you with if you ain't gone in an hour and kill Mama with the same bullet, 'cause she'll lose us both, and leave Myra and the children to the Sims, I guess. And two is, that despite what Ira and everybody else who knows what's going on and'll pull me to the side next week and tell me ways to kill you and get away with it, says—I do truly and honestly believe you love Myra. I always have. That's why I married her before you came back." He finally looked at me. "And you'll do it for her. Not for me. You don't give a damn about me. For her."

He went to the door then, but stopped with the knob in his hand. "I never meant to hurt you, Gabriel. If I have to shoot you, I'll do it clean, one to the heart. I'll hold your head while you die. I'll die too, but see—" he wiped another tear—"I cain't let you do this thing. Ira was right: it's wrong, it's wrong."

Then he was gone, his feet popping the old wood stairs, leaving me alone with my sixty-minute ultimatum, and I never doubted, never for a second, that he wouldn't do it, one clean shot to the heart, for his face had been that of Daddy's when he stood at the supper table the night Mr. Sims beat him. It was the face of a man with a clear choice before him, and as the minutes passed, I wished to God things were as simple to me. But they weren't. They never had been. I was too interested in maybe and might-have-been. Also, my fever was higher, filling my head with a pounding pressure that made it hard to remember everything that had happened since morning, when I'd strapped on my Rolex and went to conquer the Sims.

I lay on the bed, I paced, I beat my fist on the table and screamed aloud, for it was so damn wrong, leaving Myra to the hands of lithium and housekeepers while she carried our baby, maybe a red-headed boy, or a little girl who would look like me. It was so unthinkable, so unbearable that I paced faster and faster, reaching out to rip maps from the wall, scattering pins and paper at my feet, sometimes stopping to jerk the windows up on their water-swollen joints and scream at Michael across the darkness. Hard, unremembered obscenities that invited his anger, begged him to come and relieve me of the horror of the choice he'd laid before me. But nothing stirred the tropic malaise: the moss dripped motionless from the trees, the pool lay flat and blank against the pitch of the night, and with perhaps four minutes to spare, I left. Down the dark stairwell and across the yard to the highway, where I disdained Michael's careful plans and hitchhiked to Atlanta with nothing but the shirt on my back, leaving the books on the table and the maps on the wall for him to dispose of in whatever manner he pleased, for he was the victor, and the spoils belonged to him.

Now, I did not leave out of fear. Indeed, the shotgun and the one clean shot to the heart sounded pretty peaceful at that point, and I didn't leave out of any great faith in Michael's master plan. I left, simply and succinctly, because I didn't want me dead and Michael imprisoned, leaving Myra and Simon and Missy in the hands of those red-headed pagan Sims. It would forfeit the stand Daddy made and let Old Man Sims laugh in his face again as he kicked the life out of him in front of us all.

And I did it for Myra. The very word, *schizophrenia*, had a nasty, inhuman feel, and I had no walls to protect her, nothing but my love, and with Sam's shark theory in mind, I was beginning to question even that. Who knew what drove a man beyond the borders of his own morality? Who could say if it was love or the smell of blood in the water?

I couldn't, I couldn't; I could never see things as clearly as Daddy and Michael. But I knew I couldn't hurt Simon or Missy or Myra, not even if it killed me, so I did the only thing that occurred to my pounding, grieving heart. I left, even as I had come. And I can assure you, it was in love.

Chapter

10

or many years there was a phenomenon in the recording of Southern history in general and the Civil War in particular that I call the Great Gaps, where the major actions—the floor fights in Congress, the battles and maneuvers and strategic retreats—were dissected with such meticulous precision that no stone was left unturned, no possibility not painstakingly thought out, usually with that particular Southern knack for creating myth. Then, with no explanation, the books and studies would zoom on to the next major confrontation, covering the intervening days and hours and weeks with nothing more than a summary sentence or token generalization to bridge the gap. Hence, the Great Gaps.

It's an easily explained phenomenon, for historians are like all performers; they play to their audience, and while the scream of the rebel yell, the clash of the sword was exciting, hair-raising, slow death by dysentery and the relentless surge of pellagra was boring and easily forgotten. There was simply no reader, no ground-swell of interest for statistics like post-war infant mortality rates, no redeeming grace in an illiterate father, no tantalizing near-victory in land so poor, the old folks say, you couldn't raise a *fuss* on it.

The Gaps misplaced the history of the South for decades and perpetrated a false sense of grievance that I'd like to avoid by relating with all honesty and precision the years between my departure from my brother's house on foot to (eventually, three days and an overdrawn MasterCharge later) Washington, D.C., and the day of his funeral, when I stood beside his coffin and cried like a woman, out of regret, grief, and a tormenting guilt that I had somehow brought it about by my very persistence.

Ten years, it was. Ten birthdays and anniversaries, one-hundred twenty months of going about the routine of life, making phone calls, grading papers, getting out of bed on Monday and facing another week with no, absolutely no, interest beyond getting by. Living off memories. Living from week to week for Thursday night phone calls from Mama, who was outside the Sanger gossip circle and still believed Michael and Myra to be the picture-perfect couple, bragging on them shamelessly in a fast, breathless rush, for it was long-distance, and she, still, the eternal pragmatist.

"—a maid, some kin of Sam's, name's Louisa. I been a-teasing Michael, telling him he's got to be rich folk, hiring a mammy, but I'm just kidding. Poor Myra's about worked her fool self to death on thet old house, having a little hep won't do her a bit a harm—"

"How is she?" I'd ask lightly, lying on the couch with the phone on my chest, my eyes closed because it was so necessary, so painful, but so necessary, a needle in a vein, and Mama would answer easily:

"Fine. Fine. Getting big. I told her it's a good thing it'll come in March, there ain't nothing so miserable as being pregnant in June. But she don't care. Thet Myra'd stay pregnant all the day long. I never met no woman what loves babies more. Candace's giving her a shower. They've got real close, you know. They never were when they'se little, too much age difference. But they spend a right smart a time together now, I think it's good for them. Oh, and Lori's got her a boyfriend, and I tell you, son, he looks like an ape, an ape. Ed cain't stand him—"

On and on she went, hitting all the bases without pausing for a breath, and when she hung up, I had a few more pieces of documentation to ponder. So Candace and Myra were friends now. Good friends. Probably ate out together, went shopping in Dothan. Candace smiling, Myra, what? Distant? Blank? Mama never gave a clue, and I'd have to wait till the next Thursday at eight o'clock sharp, right after *The Waltons*, which never failed to put Mama in a sentimental mood, when the phone in my apartment would begin to ring. Not wanting to sound too eager, I'd let it go once or twice, then say hello casually and lay on the couch for my weekly hit.

"—big as the house, bless her heart, you know how she blows up when she's pregnant, but seems to be doing fairly well, fairly well. Say they're gone take the baby cesarean and I ask her why, she had Sim and Missy just fine, but she said that's what the doctor said. I tell you, son, these doctors anymore'll cut on you for anythang; I told Michael to talk to that man, that having a baby wasn't having cancer—" She broke off abruptly. "Did I tell you Ira stopped by?"

"No."

"Wellsir, he did. Sweet as he could be, but I tell you what, he looks sa much like his daddy I don't see how Myra stands to have him around, but he's staying with them a few days, getting a divorce, he says. Not married a year and already divorced and I said, 'Ira, how come to wanna divorce Debbie—'"

"Dana—" I murmured, but she didn't miss a beat.

"*Dana*? 'She's the Mama of your chile.' But he just grinned. Said he was looking for a woman what cooked like me, don't seem too worried about it. I told Candace I bet he beat that girl, he sure looks the type, and he worries me, Ira does. I wonder sometimes if his mind's not right, but

Myra sticks by him, never a word she says against him, but she's shore broke up over him leaving that baby, trying to see if Debbie—"

"Dana—"

"—Dana'll let her keep him in the summer. I told her she'll have her hands full with them three of her own and don't have no bidness trying to raise her brother's, too. Prob'ly her Mama's the one put her up to it. Did I tell you what she told me last time she was here?"

"No."

"Come by with that new husband a hers—never a word he says—and when I said something about the new baby, she just kindly sniffed, said she just wished Myra wouldn't have it. 'Wouldn't have it?' I asked, and she said, well anymore two childrun were plenty for any woman, that she should a went to New Orleans and took care of it before she was so far along. *Took care of it*." Mama breathed. "*I tell you what*. Trash, trash, trash. I knowed it the minute and the hour I first laid eyes on her. Oh, and Ed's run off the ape, told him to get a haircut; Lori's all broke up—"

While she unraveled the extended family's comings and goings, I fitted these new pieces of puzzle into the overall picture: Ira's divorce, Mrs. Odom's desire to see Myra salvage her marriage with an abortion, Michael's conspicuous absence from it all. He must be putting in long hours at the plant or Mama would be giving me his version, for she considered him a fountainhead of good sense and slavishly repeated his every word.

But nothing was said of him at all, till the call I was waiting for, in late March, the cherry blossoms in the mall whitening, Mama's voice piping and excited, with no inkling of the savage impact of her first, breathless, words:

"—another little boy, sweet as he can be, named him Clayton. Clayton Michael and Lord, Gabe, he's the prettiest little thing; I told Michael, 'See? Now you know why I named yo brother Gabriel,' but he just cried. He never cried with the others, but this'll be their last. Myra's had some kind a female trouble, still in the hospital, Michael brought the baby here himself. Poor little thang, cried the whole time; I give him sugar water and rocked him on the porch, that blame formula don't agree with him. I told Michael thet doctor didn't have no bidness separating a mother and a two-day-old baby, I cain't think what in the world he thought he was doing—"

"Do they need anything?" I managed in a fairly normal voice, for a suitable present had been one of my minor obsessions lately, but Mama only laughed.

"Good Lord, no, they got sa much already, enough for three babies. Candace and Lori give her thet shower, and you know Myra's always been so good herself about showers, that she got—oh, car seats and port-a-cribs and enough clothes to fill a closet. You just save your money, shug, that baby won't be a-needing nothing, not while Michael Catts has anything to do with it."

On and on she went, innocently grinding me to powder, and when I hung up, the after-effect was so bitter that I made plans to be busy next Thursday night. Take in a movie, go out to eat, maybe have a few students over. I was teaching again, under a grant at Georgetown that had the possibility of working into a full-time position, and my reputation as a recluse wasn't scoring me any points with the department. So I threw a big barbeque, and when Mama called, I told her over the pound of the stereo and the snatches of laughter that I was busy, we'd talk later. She said surely, son, to have a good time, and when I hung up, I made some excuse to run to the store for ice and cried the whole way, because the formula didn't agree with my baby, making him cry a thousand miles away, while I entertained a roomful of strangers. And there was simply nothing I could do about it. Nothing that wouldn't compromise Myra and alienate her houseful of Baptist women friends, who were showering her with presents because they knew she was fighting a battle for her mind, and giving her car seats and port-a-cribs and enough clothes to fill a closet was their way of going out in the front yard and doing battle with Old Man Sims.

So I distanced myself, or tried to, by scheduling a Thursday evening workshop, though Mama would still occasionally catch me by calling at odd hours, and I followed Clayton's progress reluctantly, until all the tiny bits of trivia ("—fin'ly got him on soy milk and now he sleeps the night—" or "—sucking thet thumb, I told them it'd make him bucktooth—") became a torment to me, and every time the phone rang I felt a tight claw of nervousness in my chest, afraid it was Mama and her breathless run of news.

It was sometime around the holidays, November or December, when the break came in the form of one of those insignificant chance-conversations that snowball into a watershed, when I found myself sitting next to a staff psychiatrist from Johns Hopkins at a faculty party. The husband of one of my colleagues, he was as bored as I with all the obligatory holiday socializing, and with nothing better to do, we fell to discussing schizophrenia, its patterns and its cures, while we sipped bourbon at the hotel bar.

As the evening wore on, I became loose (drunk, you might say) enough to discuss Myra's condition, cloaked in a deceptive nonchalance, referring to her as my sister-in-law, and describing the promiscuity, her pharmacopoeia of medications, the strange, noiseless sobs Michael called catatonia.

He recognized them all, sympathized, offered a few stories of his own, then, just as his wife tapped his shoulder and told him they could leave, downed his last shot and mentioned in an off-handed way that Myra's condition didn't sound like schizophrenia at all.

"True schizophrenia is really very rare," he said, "often misdiagnosed." He recommended my brother get a second opinion before he committed to long-term therapy.

I told him I would, but thought no more about it until late

Christmas night after a truly heart-warming evening spent in an anonymous blur at a neighborhood bar, when Mama called to wish me merry Christmas and describe in exquisite detail her each and every present, especially the one from Michael,

"—brand new; I told him all I warch is *As the World Turns* and *The Waltons* and they're just as good in black and white, but you know Michael, once he gets his mind set on something, he cain't be reasoned with. Went and bought Sanger outright, cost him every penny to his name, has a big shake-up going on over there, I don't know what all, a bunch a men done left, and I been a little worried, but I reckon he'll make out all right; there's been nothing Michael Catts ever set his hand to that he ain't made out all right.

"Bought Myra a ring for Christmas, with a gret big diamond; Lori says it cost a *thousand* dollars, says she saw one just like it in Dothan, and I tell you, son, I just don't see the sense in it. I ast Myra, I said, 'Myra, honey, how come you to want a new ring when the one you got ain't but seven years old?' And she just kindly shrugged. Didn't seem too impressed, only got eyes for that new baby of hers, pretty as he can be and spoiled? Won't let her leave him a minute, cries, holds her leg, pitches the worse fit I ever seen in any chile but you, and wouldn't you know, old Miz Odom was here for Christmas and she's got to make something of it, said what that baby needed was a good switching. Well, I told her right fast-like no baby that age gets a switching in *my* house and come nigh as a pea to saying, yes, and they don't git no cigarettes put out on them neither—"

I made the correct replies, but had slowly sat up on the couch, my eyes opening as I connected Mama's new evidence with the psychiatrist's doubt, and when Mama paused for a breath, I asked, "Mama. Listen. Have you ever heard of a Dr. Williams around there? A psychiatrist?"

"Dr. Williams?" she repeated, for she kept an eye on the local medical establishment, worshipping them in her spare time. "Well, son, the only Dr. Williams I know of is the one down to Sanger; Michael goes to him; he's the one who sewed up his arm that time, but he's no kind of—what did you call it?"

"No, no, never mind," I said quickly. "I must have got it wrong—" Then, "Listen, Mama, how's Aunt Mag? Did they let her go home?"

I asked it as a sly diversion, for Aunt Mag was seriously ailing, and Mama seized on her with a vengeance. "No, son, she won't be home this Christmas; poor Maggie ain't got long for this old world—"

When Aunt Mag was finally exhausted, Mama wished me another merry Christmas and told me I needed to find me a wife for the New Year, that I was too old to be single, it wasn't natural. I told her I had my eye on it, then hung up, leaving the small, white-walled room hushed and breathless. I sat tapping my fingers on the phone awhile, then went to the window that looked out on a blistering Maryland evening, and after a moment, whispered aloud: "*Damn*."

Michael, now, he was slick. What could you say? *Slick*. His brother comes to town; he sees the enemy and acknowledges it, and while I'm screwing around with the books and sweating the morals of it all down by the pool, he's making plans. *Lithium*, he tells his good friend Dr. Williams, who happens to be on the payroll down at the plant, have we tried that yet? See, my brother Gabe's in town, Myra might get *nervous*. We don't want that, do we?

"*Damn*," I whispered again and was mad enough to rent a car and drive straight through to Florida and set things straight. Use that shotgun on Michael, use that switch on Mrs. Odom's sorry ass, and rescue Myra and Missy and Sim and the little spoiled baby, who even at the tender age of nine months knew better than to let his Mama out of his sight; knew more than his daddy, that much was sure. *Schizophrenia*, my ass. Bad nerves, certainly. With Satan as a father and that bitch for a mother, who wouldn't have a rough time of it? But not a diagnosed schizophrenic. Just a tired woman in a bad situation, and I could have kicked myself for not going along with my own instincts, but buying into Michael's intense sob story. Sure he was worried, sure he was desperate, that's why his lies rang true. If the situation were reversed, I'd have sounded pretty convincing myself, crying and spitting blood and selling my soul to be rid of him once and for all. Why, even the real bone-crushers, the preacher and his angry wife, the yard boy and what Simon saw, neither had been verified or even alluded to by Mama or anyone else. All I had was Michael and Ira's word—Michael, who had a babygirl to protect, and Ira, whom I hated, whose mouth I would not piss in if his guts were on fire.

"Damn," I whispered, tapping the cold glass. "*Damn.*"

How had I been so gullible? How could I make it right, win her back with no blood loss, no bottom-line tragedy where those nasty, scheming Sims had the last word?

My answer came within a matter of hours, really, when Mama called sometime after midnight, crying, with the news Aunt Mag had died, and I knew what her answer would be before the words were out of my mouth: "Mama? Do you need me to come?"

I knocked on her door the next afternoon after a checkerboard of a flight all over the Southeast that concluded in a three-hour bus ride from Mobile, and this time, her welcome was much more fitting, with no mention of my job at all, just a vice-grip of a hug and a lot of tears on Aunt Mag's behalf. But seeing me seemed to calm her, and she began cooking supper as usual, talking and wiping her nose the whole time, not looking one day older than the last time I saw her: the same white hair, the same small, fragile bones, the same sure, country voice that worried aloud over the turnout for Aunt Mag's funeral, to her country eyes, a major indicator of relative success in life.

"Candace and Lori'll be there; Ed's working; I didn't hardly think he could get off, Michael sure cain't. They're giving him a fit down at that plant, just a fit; Myra might try, but I doubt Clayton'll letter go without a fight. He likes Louisa just fine till Myra takes to leaving, then he screams like a Indian."

I let her ramble, walking around the kitchen that always looked the same, too, except for a microwave (some earlier gift from the elder son) and a new table, courtesy of Sears and Roebuck revolving charge. While she chopped and fried and moved pots around on the old stove, I went out on the back porch that shook just a little more than I remembered and looked at the old Sims house next door. Kudzu had taken the whole back end of it, adding its weight to the already sagging roof and sending down curling tendrils to finger the dirty, reflectionless windows that still held an air of insolvent evil, as if the Old Man still lurked there, somewhere within the thin pine walls, his eyes fox-colored and attentive, smiling at me through the late-afternoon haze.

With a chill and a shake of my head, I went back inside, where Mama was setting the food on the table.

"Why doesn't someone tear that old house down?" I asked her as we took our seats.

She answered vaguely, "Lord, son, I don't know. Buddy Fischer owns it; I s'pect he don't want to fool with it; cost more than it's worth to tear it down, but it'd sho be doing me a favor." She paused to say the blessing with her lightning speed that sounded like *Lord-givus-grateful-hearts-fer-theseanallour-blessings*, then resumed: "—not to me, but to Myra. She don't ever mention it, but one time, let's see, it was last year, they come over, Myra and the children, and Missy climbed the fence and was jumping off the porch over there. Well it's all rotted, that place is, and I happened to see her through the winder and said, 'Lord, Myra, look at Missy, she done climbed thet fence; them steps is all rotten; she'll fall through—' And before I could move a muscle, she'd tore out the door, screaming, 'Missy! Melissa Anne! There's a dog over there, a *bad* dog, it'll bite you!'

"Well you know Missy's scared a dogs; she come tearing back, and

Lord, Gabe, you should a seen Myra's face, white as a sheet, pregnant and scrabbling to pull that chile over the fence. I run out there and took her by the shoulders, said, 'Baby, he's gone, he's gone.' I just felt like telling her—it's the truth before God—thet one's in hell, in hell; and it's like I was telling Sister Lee, I never cared much for hell till I met that man, but now it suits me *fine*."

I was only thoughtful, not answering, and after a moment, she retook the reins of the conversation, adding with a snort, "Then along comes Miz Odom, come here Christmas Day, and had the sheer nerving gall to speak to Myra about her children. I told Michael, I said, 'Son, thet woman speaks one more ugly word to Myra in my house and I've got a thang or two to say to her.'"

"What did Michael say?" I ventured, for he was my prey, but Mama only sniffed.

"You know Michael. Told me to keep it to mysef, said it wouldn't be doing Myra no favor to take up a fight with her mama. She'll be coming by here after while, has some clothes for Lori, *keeps* that chile in clothes—"

"Will she have the baby?" I asked, my eyes on my plate, and Mama laughed.

"You can bet on thet. Cain't take a step away from him, not a step, but he's a sweet boy, pretty as he can be, not a mark on him, says dadada all the time, makes Myra sa mad, she tries to get him to say Mama, but—"

She went on to explain the Cecilia Catts theory on why he would not (odd and varied, I can assure you), but I was having an information overload, beginning to feel numb, the blood-pumping excitement of the trip beginning to flatten to a dull, head-pounding, stomach-burning exhaustion. Mama paused long enough to notice my lack of appetite (a fairly unusual phenomenon at her table) and deciding I was not only pale, but *hollow-eyed*, insisted I take a nap.

So I closed myself up in the front bedroom and tried to rest up for the main event, but pieces of Mama's words kept running through my head. —*been nothing Michael ever set his hand to he ain't made out all right with*— and —*there's a dog over there, a bad dog, it'll bite you*— kept running through my head, keeping me on edge, listening for the sound of a car door or a knock.

But I did finally drop off. I must have, for I was awakened by the loud crack of the screen door and a high young voice, calling through the house. "Grannie? Grannie? Did Myra come? Did she leave the stuff?"

Mama was making some reply from the back of the house when another voice joined them, a woman's, hardly country at all, with an inflection I could not easily place. "—have to wear that old gray linen suit. It'll have to do. I didn't have time to run to the store. Myra's bringing one she says'll fit, but it's just a six—"

Candace, I finally thought. My sister, whom I hadn't seen in—how long? Not since Ed re-enlisted in '69—could it be seven years? I sat up, rubbing my eyes, yawning, when one last pair of feet hit the porch, and a final voice sounded, low and country, just outside the front door.

"I'm running late, got caught by the stupid train. Here, take him, Candace. The car's full. Lori'll have to help—"

It was Myra, talking fast, her feet sounding lightly on the steps, and I went to the window and watched them from behind the fan in much the same manner I had when I was ten and first heard her name. She was in the drive behind the lifted trunk, Candace on the porch, a few feet to the right of the window, so I couldn't actually see her, though I could hear the tiny voice of the baby in her arms.

"Dadadada—" it ran, on and on, till it realized its mother was gone, and began to break into a shockingly loud cry that my sister shushed playfully.

"Hush, you old spoiled egg, she's right there—"

And she was, Lori behind her, their arms full of dresses on hangers, Myra's face a little ashamed as she navigated the porch steps and dumped them into one of Mama's rockers.

"And these are just the hanging clothes," she told Candace sheepishly, then went back to the car for more. And more and more, at least half a dozen trips, Mama joining them on the porch, more amazed with every load, Lori jumping up and down, holding up a jean skirt or pair of shorts to her waist, her voice full of laughter, "I just love this. I remember when you bought it. Oh, Myra, you are *so good*—"

Finally, they were done, Lori's excitement infecting them all, Mama saying, "Curtis'll like this—"

And Candace: "Mama, quit with this *Curtis* business. She's thirteen years old, for crying out loud."

"She'll be fourteen in a month, and I was fifteen when I married your daddy—"

"Yeah, and you were a hick. Don't go putting ideas in her head. Ed's fit to be tied already."

Cornered by the clutter, Candace had moved over a few feet till she stood directly in front of me, the little boy on her hip so close I could have touched his fat cheek, if not for the screen. Mama had mentioned his beauty, so I was prepared for that, but his hair was different than I'd expected, bald except for a tiny edging of pale curls along the nape of his neck. He had seen me there behind the screen and was giving me an intense look out of his ink-colored eyes, and after a moment, reached out a small wet hand that stopped at the screen, his face perplexed, his fingertips running up and down the mesh a few times, then returning safely to his mouth, his interest averted, his voice a tiny baby-rattle beneath the conversation of the women: *dadadadada*.

It was too much; no one could have stood it. I leaned against the curtains and rubbed my face, trying to sidetrack the grief. For he was perfect, absolutely perfect, with his little white shoes and his two little teeth, and I already knew he was out of my reach, seeing with my own eyes that his mother, who stood across the porch not six feet away, was not the thin, smiling Myra of The Sunny South, but the other one: the solid size twelve, who threw her head back when she laughed, who shared Kleenexes with me the afternoon of Simon's birth and told her husband stories in bed at night. Gone was the fragile WASP princess of a summer ago, miraculously replaced by this laughing country woman who had the voice of a Cracker, but the look of an Irish peasant in her wild hair and sweet face and pale, sun-starved skin.

She was burrowing through the boxes, searching for a dress for my sister, assuring her it would fit, letting out a yelp of triumph when she found it, holding it to her shoulders and squashing any hint of patronization with a well-told anecdote:

"There are three of these dresses here. Three. Same size, same color. I bought them at Gayford's at the same time. When I was going through this stuff last night, I told Michael that saleslady must have thought I was *crazy*, buying three identical dresses, and he just looked at me and said, 'Baby, you were crazy when you bought them dresses.'"

She reached her hip over and butted Candace when she said it, for these were daughters of the black-belt, who couldn't converse without touching, butting hips or leaning together in casual embrace, and I closed my eyes, knowing I'd been beaten before I'd ever fired my first round.

Michael had won. Mama was right: there was nothing he'd ever set his hand to that he hadn't made come out all right, and he'd set his hand to Myra, and there she was: the lights were on and everyone was home. And they were country fundamentalist lights that would never look me in the eye again. Even if she loved me more than life itself, she would never leave Michael, for it would mean worse things than child-custody hearings and lawyer fees: it would mean hell, where her father waited with his patient, fox-colored eyes. And meanwhile, my son still watched me through the screen, sucking his fist, his round eyes placid and sweet.

I couldn't cry; it was past the crying point and on to the razor-blade stage, as the women's voices rose and fell on the late afternoon chill,

Mama coming inside, Candace taking the dress, saying, "I better try it on, I haven't got into a six since Lori—"

"It's a big six, more like a eight. God knows I'll never get into it again," Myra answered, taking the baby. Then: "Listen, I gotta run, Simon's at the skating rink." Candace went inside and she stuck her head in the door and called after her, "Cissie? I have to pick up Sim. Tell Uncle Pete I'm sorry if I don't make it. We sent flowers, white roses—"

Mama's voice answered from the kitchen, "Thank you, sister, don't you worry about it." Then: "Come back when you get Sim. Gabe's here; come all the way from Washington, taking a nap; wants to see the baby—"

For a moment, Mama's words seemed to elude her, then, just as she was backing to the first step, they hit, making her all but stumble, her eyes cutting across to the window where the midday sun on the thick old glass must have reflected back nothing but her own image, for the look on her face was one of blank, unfocused horror, the likes of which I'd never seen in my life. Without a word, she clutched the baby to her chest and fled, taking the remaining steps in one clumsy leap, and running across the yard, not stopping, even when Candace came back out on the porch in the black dress, calling, "Myra? It's a little tight in the waist, but it fits."

But she made no reply, slamming into the car and tearing off with such violence that she hit the curb, throwing up a spray of dirt and gravel on Mama's boxwoods, leaving Candace standing there on the top step, hands on hips, in a position of perplexity.

After a moment, she came back inside, her voice filling the house. "Myra left—must be running late. But this six fits."

Suddenly, the door from the living room opened, and a small blonde woman who bore a striking resemblance to my childhood memories of Mama was standing there, her eyes stunned at first, then, seeing my expression, filling with tears.

"Well, Gabe?" she whispered, darting a glance at the window, and I thought dully, she knows, she knows. Myra must have told her. Being a child of Mama's womb, she was a hugger and a consoler, and with no introduction, no words of explanation at all, she came around the bed and embraced me, crying on my shoulder, and once she'd gotten started, there was no question I was going to be able to stand there and take it like a man. Mama must have heard us, for her voice was suddenly at the door.

"Why, Lord, I forgot to tell you. He come for the funeral. Well, bless your heart, sister," she murmured, then spoke to someone beyond the door. "Ain't seen each other in seven years, bless their hearts." Then: "Well I just wished Michael was here."

Then she joined in, and we cried like disappointed children, and it was fortunate the evening's activities were solemn, for Candace and I could not look at each other without beginning to blink. Before long, we even had Lori going strong, and our pew at the funeral was so noisy with sniffles and sobs that the preacher made many pointed comments in our direction about what a long life Aunt Mag had enjoyed and how she had most certainly made heaven.

But we refused to be comforted, Candace and I, and I thought about cornering her after the service and getting the details of the past year from her, for she had apparently been given a pretty sympathetic version of my side of the story, but by the time we'd made it back to town, a sullen winter twilight had descended, and I was too tired to ask. After all, what could she say? I'd seen the absolutes of the situation on the porch and knew it was a no-win deal. If she told me Myra loved me, loved me but would not leave Michael, it would kill me, and if she said she loved Michael and our summer had been nothing but a comedy of errors she bitterly regretted, it would kill me more.

So I was dead in the water any way you looked at it, and the other possibility, the one I'd seen reflected in Myra's blank, terrified eyes, I simply refused to consider, affecting a cold so I could wheedle Mama out of some of her medicinal bourbon, and staying holed up on Magnolia Hill for the better part of three days, never going farther than the front porch, while the broken windows of the Sims' house seemed to grin at my torment.

The nights in particular were torturously long, the old house full of winding, chilling drafts that flowed room to room unchecked, like souls of the unquiet dead, and my last night, as I lay there and prayed for sleep, I thought about the years Michael and I had shared this room, this very bed. Years I trusted him, years I thought I knew him so well, when we'd slept on these same old sun-smelling sheets, each careful to stay on his own side of the bed, for we'd drawn an invisible line down the middle, and the penalty for fudging was a rat bite to the arm.

The notch in the old headboard marking the dividing line was still there. I reached up and felt it, smiling when I remembered how a punch to the arm had once been the penalty for fudging before I'd smartened up and insisted on rat-bites, since I was a poor puncher but an expert pincher. So we'd have pinch months and punch months, and according to the calendar, one of us would suffer from multiple bruises of the upper arms, for we showed no mercy when it came to territorial rights and both were unashamed bed hogs.

Bed hogs as children, bed hogs as adults, I thought, and my smile faded when I remembered that this was Michael and Myra's bed too, the first they'd ever shared, the one Myra had sat on with wide, excited eyes and told him stories and gossip and news of Manderley. If I closed my eyes, I could picture her so clearly, her face flushed, her hair wild and uncombed above her simple batiste gown, building to the climax in her low country voice: "—and then she goes upstairs, and she finds this bedroom, it looks out on the sea—wake up, baby—and all the clothes are still in the closet, just like Rebecca was alive—Michael, honey, listen—"

Keeping him alive with her words. Taking him off Magnolia Hill.

Showing him there were other worlds, other possiblities beyond the tight inertia of generational poverty: living dreams on a bed built for sleep.

But *damn,* I thought, sitting up and rubbing my eyes, it wasn't fair. There were Magnolia Hills in my life, inertias of my own I needed rescuing from, and nothing, not books nor degrees nor anything else had ever satisfied me the way she could. Why had Michael won? Because he was smarter? Because he'd turned down the Reds and stayed home so Daddy wouldn't lose the house? Was Myra God's reward for a job well done?

And Myra, why had she run like that? Was she terrified of me? Were our afternoons together, our two short nights, a degradation to her? Another nauseating shame at the hands of a man? Were we lined up together, three blind mice: the yardboy, the preacher, the brother?

And suddenly, I had to know, at whatever cost; I had to make it right. To beg her, to somehow convince her that it was never my intention to hurt her. That everything I'd done, I'd done in love. I wasn't a rapist, for God's sake. I was her lover, she had to realize that. I had to make her realize that, and as I dressed in the darkness, I thought feverishly that I'd tell her if anything ever happened to the baby—if he ever needed blood or bone-marrow or a kidney, she must call me. Call me, for God's sake. I'd do whatever they wanted.

Then I remembered the shotgun, and for some reason, the thought was oddly comforting—hilarious, in fact. And as I buttoned my coat, I laughed aloud, thinking waspishly that maybe one clean shot to the heart was like the lithium: just what the doctor ordered.

Chapter

11

I fished Mama's keys from her purse, and with bewildering speed, was heading east on Thomasville Road, my breath clouding the windshield, my heart beating so loud in my chest that it seemed to vibrate through the empty car. I was so nervous I even went to the trouble of formulating a plan. First, I'd drive around back and knock on the French doors, and when Myra answered, I'd tell her quickly, quickly, not to be afraid. Then I'd see if Michael was there, and *damn*—it wasn't panning out. I wanted to see her alone. Just for a moment. Just to speak to her as we'd spoken that summer, easy, nondemanding. I didn't want to have to stand there in front of Michael and pretend not to care, or laugh or cry or beg it off as a mistake. Maybe he wouldn't be home, I thought as I turned in the drive. Maybe he was still putting in the long hours at the plant, what with the big shake-up Mama continually spoke of.

The front of the house was dark, and as I pulled into the back driveway, I could make out the faint blue light of a television screen glowing somewhere beyond the sunroom curtains. Closing the car door softly, I followed the light across the deck to the French doors and with a gut drop of disappointment, saw Michael through the glass, lying on the couch, still dressed in his buttoned-down work clothes, but shoeless, his bare feet crossed on top of each other while he watched television.

He had something in his hands, a thin book that after a little maneuvering I made out as a *Sunday School Quarterly*. Of course, it was Saturday night. I was forgetting the old routines: supper and early baths and reading the Sunday School lesson while Daddy made a peep-box for Mama's primary class—Noah's ark or David and Goliath or Naaman dipping in the Jordan seven times and coming out clean.

Every once in a while, he'd lift his face to the television and watch a moment with intense concentration, then drop back to the *Quarterly*, shaking his head or smiling or once, throwing it at the screen, snapping "*shit*," which I must admit I found just a tiny bit shocking. I mean, here was your typical Baptist communicant, I thought, studying his lesson and *cursing*, and though years later my sniveling superiority would strike me as ironic in the extreme, at the moment I saw nothing at all wrong with not only spying on Michael and plotting to sneak in and see his wife, but also getting just a little judgmental over a bit of profanity I hourly compounded with every word in the English language. It even gave me the small edge of raw courage it took to reach up and tap on the door. The instant my knuckles touched the glass, his face was up. Then he was off the couch in one fluid movement, snatching something from the mantle, facing me nose-to-nose across the glass, a compact, very nasty looking little sawed-off shotgun in his hands.

"Who's there?" he demanded in a low, un-Michael-sounding voice, and I could only stand there and blink, thinking, *well, I can't say he never warned me.*

"Me, Michael. It's me."

"*Me?*" he said, then stepped back, and when the light hit me, his face went slack. "Gabe?" he whispered, then used the Ugly Word again and held the shotgun aside to open the door. "You *idiot*. Don't ever do that again."

"Do what?" I managed, my chest still a little tight, even though his face was not stiff at all, but slack and relieved and possibly even glad to see me.

"Sneak up on me like that," he said, closing the door behind me. "I could a killed you."

There was a tiny question in my mind over why he wasn't killing me now, for I was blatantly asking for the one clean shot to the heart by showing my face in his living room. But if he was going to be civilized about it, I sure wasn't about to argue and tried to be as nonchalant as he, watching him slide the shotgun back on the mantle, asking, "You always keep that thing loaded?"

It seemed like a pretty lethal weapon to keep lying around in a houseful of children. He turned down the television (where a college bowl game was in progress, which probably explained his sinful expletive) before he answered.

"Just at night," he said, then lay back on the couch, his bare feet back on top of each other, his arms folded on his chest. He seemed to be waiting for me to make the first move, but I could only look around, absently strolling to the edge of the kitchen, finding everything oddly unchanged. I had thought of this place so much in the past eighteen months that now that I was here, everything from the pool to the shining floors to the very smell of the place (Pinesol over coffee) held a strange, surreal numbness, like that of a dream.

Michael only sat there and watched me, occasionally glancing back at a play on the television, and I was across the room, almost at the foot of the stairs, when I spoke.

"Myra tell you she saw me?" I asked casually, and his eyes were on the game when he answered.

"No. No, she didn't."

I accepted this with a lift of the face and made my way back to the French doors, looking out on the pool that was murky and black in the night. "Well, she didn't actually see me. I saw her, though. Saw her run like a rabbit." I paused. "Is she afraid of me, Michael?"

"Of course she is," he answered easily. "She's scared to death."

It was so bitter, so bitter I couldn't speak for a moment, but only watch the pool where we'd once sat in the sun and clapped for Simon, knowing why he didn't have to bother with shotguns anymore—that he'd won. He was Michael. There was nothing he'd ever set his hand to—

"She thinks you're after Clayton," he finished.

I turned. "What?"

"Clayton. The baby. She thinks you're seeking custody. Terrified you're seeking custody. Ira lost custody of his boy in August, and she thinks it'd be a cinch for you to go before a judge, present her mental instability, have Clay on the next flight out."

I only stared at him, for in all my wild imaginings, the possibility had simply never occurred to me. Myra and her children were a unit, dividing them, unthinkable.

"And you ain't up to something like that, are you? 'Cause Peter Goodin's my lawyer, and we won't—"

"No. No," I said, waving him aside. "Damn, Michael, I can't take that baby away from Myra. Are you crazy?"

He smiled then, for the first time that night, and shook his head. "Gabriel, Gabriel," he murmured. "He looked like an angel when he was born and she named him for an angel." Then, easier, unfolding his arms and sitting up straighter on the couch: "That's what I been telling her, but she's been nervous as a cat, jumping evertime the phone rings. Listen, I got a registered letter yesterday—some screw-up, it was supposed to go to the plant—and she just fell apart. So did Lou and Sim and Missy. They called me at work, and I come racing home, expecting to find a body in the pool, and there they were, sitting around the table sobbing, this sealed envelope there in the middle. Turned out to be an order for microwave stands."

"I need to talk to her," I said quickly, and he answered me just as quickly.

"No," he said. "No."

I looked at him. "You don't have any right to say that. What are you, her daddy?"

"I'm her husband," he said. "And she's asleep and you ain't waking her up."

I only watched him a moment, lounging there so mildly, his wrists folded quietly on his lap, and closed my eyes, trying for patience. "I need to talk to her, Michael, tell her I'm not after Clayton."

"No."

"*Yes!*" I shouted. "*Yes*, Michael, and you can't stop me!"

He came to his feet. "*No!* Hush, you'll wake the baby—"

"I need to tell her I'm not after anything—"

"No."

"—that I never meant to hurt her—"

"No, Gabriel. *Shut up*. The children are asleep—"

"That I *love her*, Michael. I only told her once. That's why she ran." I took a breath, and finished quietly. "She probably doesn't remember."

Which was, of course, a lie from the pit of hell, and in retrospect, I can hardly see how such an argument might have convinced Michael of my need to see his wife. But before he could answer, the phone in the kitchen began ringing quietly, so quietly I didn't hear it, but only followed Michael as he went to answer it. He picked up the receiver, then hung up without a word, returning to our conversation with a little strain beginning to show in the tense lines of his mouth,

"Gabriel. Listen to me. You cain't see her, it just isn't possible."

"Yes it is," I countered slowly, turning to leave. "Wat—"

Watch, I would have said, had he not hit before I could get the word out, snatching my shirtfront with that catlike quickness and slamming me against the refrigerator, speaking to my face with a quiet, deadly earnestness.

"Gabriel," he whispered, "how much more of this shit do you think I'll put up with? Ain't I held your hand through enough of it? I mean, what do you want me to do here? Tell you to move back in, me take her nights, you have her weekends?"

He let go of me and held his hands up, palms out. "I mean, it's enough. I got a wife that screams evertime the phone rings, a brother sitting over to my mother's, plotting to steal her. I got a plant working half-capacity, the Klan breathing down my neck, on my ass twenty-four hours *a day*—"

"The *who*?" I asked, and he was still tensed, still prepared to block my way.

"The Klan. The White Knights of the sonofabitch Klan."

Well, it was clear *shit* wasn't the only profanity he was defiling the Southern Baptist Convention with these days, but at the moment I only wondered why in the world the Klan was concerned Myra didn't know I loved her.

"What the hell does the Klan have to do with this?" I asked.

Michael looked at me with an edge of tormented exasperation. "Well, *shit*, Gabe, the Klan doesn't have nothing to with *this*, but believe it or not, there's a larger world out there, outside this little fantasy you've made yourself, and I've had it up to *here*," he jabbed his forehead, "with you and them both."

He lowered his voice. "You know what they did? Last Sunday, I went out to get the paper and there was Missy's dog, Candace gave him to her, a beagle, she named him Speckles, and he was stretched out on the front steps, a fishing knife in his belly, cut like a pig."

I was stunned to silence at this, but he didn't pause. "Like a damn fattening pig, blood all over the steps. I had to bury him in the bushes, quick, had to dig him up to show the sheriff. It hadn't a been Sunday, it'd a been Myra opening that door." He looked at me. "And you know what would a happened if she'd a found ole Speck laying there with a fillet knife poking out his side? She'd be tied to a bed in Chattahoochee, is what."

"Why?" I whispered.

His voice was level. Level and tired. "Sam."

"Sam?" I asked. "Sam McRae?" And at first it didn't click. I mean I didn't know Sam very well. I remembered he and Michael used to play ball together on the county bush leagues, and though he was much like us—he'd grown up locally, his grandfather was a preacher, his father a sawyer at the heading mill—there was one difference that had forever barred him from my tight circle of very close, very beloved nine best friends on Lafayette Street: Sam was black. That's why he didn't count. That's why I was so amazed he had the capacity to create such a stir; that's why Michael's voice was even drier when he repeated, for my benefit:

"Sam, Sam McRae. I made him general manager when I bought the plant last year. Hell, I had to, he helped me buy it. And first they tried the union. Then we had a walkout and was riding a little low in the water but getting by, getting by. Then this stupid peckerwood klavern—five or six strong—started messing with it, and they been giving us hell. Dogging Sam, dogging me, calling here at night, threatening to firebomb the house—"

If the dog had scared me, this really gave me a chill, and I said, quickly, "Then listen, Michael, change his title. That's all they care about. Call him the Chief Production Clerk or something, anything. I mean, he'll have the same job. Hell, give him a raise, but don't open yourself up to this. You're right, Myra's too fragile—"

"No!" he said, slapping the counter with the flat of his hand and turning on me. "No, I won't. It's wrong, it's wrong, it's wrong." Then, in savage mimic, "*Change his title. Call him Chief Production Clerk*—shit, Gabriel, I'm ashamed of you, ashamed for Daddy's sake. You sound like one of my pissant account—but *no*—" He beat the counter again. "Sam's been there longer than anybody. His daddy worked it. His granddaddy helped build it. Hell, he knows more about running it than anybody, including me. Old Man Sanger hired me over his head, made him show me the ropes and it's wrong. It's wrong. I won't do it. I'll roll it over first. I'll tear it apart, saw by saw—"

"But Myra, think about Myra—"

"Yeah, Myra," he said. "Let's talk about Myra. Myra and Sam, and how he was the only man I trusted when she was acting out, the only one I knew wouldn't touch her. I mean, it wasn't the easiest job in the world. I seem to remember you lasting about a week at it—but Sam, he never said a word against her. He understood. He's just like that. He's always been there for me, and he's the manager of Sanger till it closes. I don't care what any jackass in a robe says. I'll break their backs over it, Gabe, *break their backs*, you just watch me. I will—" He paused for a breath, and after a moment of facing me off, seemed embarrassed at his vehemence, turning aside, murmuring, "I know you don't believe me, but I will."

"I believe you, Michael," I said simply, for I did. "I mean, next time I call, they'll all be joining the ACLU. I don't doubt it for a minute."

But he was too harassed to smile, only standing there, his breath still a little hard, and when the phone on the wall began ringing again, just barely, as if the bell had been turned down, he picked up the receiver and handed it to me without a word, letting me hear a fragment of a low, steady stream of venom: "—of a bitch and thet whore wife a yours think you are, moving into thet fine house, thinking you live above us—"

It was so vicious it made the hair on my neck stand up, but

Michael's expression was only one of exasperation as he took back the receiver and hung up.

"See? Every night. *Whore wife, whore wife.* But you just wait. Production's up, and when production goes up, profits go up, and when profits go up, I'm bumping the pay to the roof. Show those bastards what kind a bed they've made for themselves. They can rot on Magnolia Hill for all I care. They'll never work for me again."

There was a quiet ruthlessness about him that made me hesitate to ask, but I knew time was running out and was too desperate to worry with anything as trivial as fear, cornering him at the counter, and speaking to his face:

"Listen, Michael, I won't say a word to her about love, I swear to God, I just want to tell her I'm not after Clayton." He tried to interrupt, but I pressed on. "You can tell her till she dies and she'll never believe you—"

The phone began it's faint trilling again, and he reached for it, that harassed look back in his eye. But I didn't care; I'd rather he kill me than leave the echo of that profane accusation (*whore wife, whore wife*) unanswered.

"Five minutes," I begged. "Five minutes, Michael. Can't you afford that? I won't say a word about love. If she's asleep, I won't wake her, I swear on Daddy's eyes."

A childish proclamation, that, swearing on dead men's eyes—something we'd once done as children, little boys playing in the back-yard, fighting over toy trucks—and whether Michael took it at face value or was touched by a tiny shimmer of the memory of sandy dirt and pine-smelling straw, I don't know, but he picked up the phone and stood there a moment with the receiver cradled against his chest.

"Five minutes," he said.

Well, I didn't waste any seconds on the stairs or hall, and when I made the upper story and saw that the bedroom door was open, and the light still on, a surge of hope rose that fell like mercury on ice when I made the corner and saw her, for she was, as Michael had warned, sound asleep. Not as if she'd turned in for the night, but as if sleep had caught her in the act of reading, a book fallen from her hands, her hair still wrapped in a towel from her bath.

The reason for the deep, unexpected sleep was sitting on the bookshelf above her head, a tiny bottle with a long name and a big dosage, dated December twenty-sixth, the day I came to town. She must have gone straight from Mama's to the pharmacy for the refill, standing in line with the baby in her arms, waiting for her prescription, looking over her shoulder to see if I'd followed.

I sat down on the edge of the bed, hoping I'd waken her, but she was stone-cold unconscious, barely breathing, her face calm and peaceful. After a moment, I sighed and looked around the room. Nothing was changed since the day I'd sat her down and told her about Virginia, but for the first time I noticed the books. Shelves and shelves of them, in the headboard, stacked beside the bed: *Tender Is the Night*, *Brideshead Revisited*, *The Sound and The Fury*. Big books, Michael called them, and I wondered if she still told him stories in bed at night, if she'd come across *The Souls of Black Folk*, and Sam's promotion and the ensuing flak could be traced back to her flushed, excited face: ("And listen, Michael, there's a whole chapter on the black belt, right up there by Albany, and it's so sad, listen, honey, them people up there, they never had no chance—")

I sighed again, and looked down at her peaceful face, her small white hands, then lay down beside her, my face near her hair, the smell bringing up so many memories that I blinked. I was careful to keep my hands to myself and not get Sims-like about it, then relaxed and thought how this would be the way we slept at night, she and I, were we married. And I'd take it for granted. It wouldn't move me at all. She'd just be my wife, the mother of my children, someone I'd argue with over money with and sit with at weddings and face over supper every night, never realizing till she died how much I needed her, how that what had started out as two had indeed become one.

The time passed, five, then ten, then fifteen minutes, but still, I didn't move, for it was so sweet, and I'd never see her again, after all, never touch her, never smell the apple scent of her hair, not me. I knew I had to leave, go back North or East or West, and stay put, so that after a year or two, she could relax and resume a normal, stingless life of skating rinks and smiling sister-in-laws, with death and insanity so far removed they were appeased with florist flowers and self-deprecating jokes on the porch.

A life much like the one I once enjoyed beneath the massive oak and camphor of Magnolia Hill, the one her father had denied her, and yes, it was bitter I had to reap the sacrifice for his sin, bitter as gall, as Mama would say. But once I'd made up my mind, I was quite peaceful about it, sitting up and kissing her forehead very lightly, then going back downstairs, thinking if Michael would prove his love by staying, then I could prove mine just as well by leaving; prove it more, for Clayton was up when I got back to the kitchen, taking a bottle from Michael, who began apologizing the moment he saw me.

"He always has one at eleven. He'd scream all night."

"S'all right," I murmured, watching him clutch the bottle in his fat little hands, and when he'd sucked it dry, I asked Michael if I could hold him. I didn't think he'd let me, at first. Then I thought he'd hit me for asking. Then he set the empty bottle on the counter and handed him over.

"Careful. He's a puker."

But I made no precautions, cradling him clumsily against my chest like an infant, feeling his weight in my hands.

"He's fat."

Michael answered in the voice of an experienced father. "He'll lose it when he starts walking." He laughed. "*If* he starts walking. He won't even sit alone yet."

At the sound of Michael's laughter, it seemed to dawn on Clayton that he was in the hands of a stranger, his round little Gerber face beginning to pucker up in what looked like the prelude to a mighty roar. I handed him back to Michael, who took him easily, and changed the frown to a chortle of laughter by lifting him over his head and speaking to his face in a light, baby nonsense. "He's just an old lazy boy, aren't you, sweetpea? Daddy's gone put him to work at Sanger, toughen that old baby up."

He wasn't calling himself Daddy to underline any victories here, but the effect on me was pretty devastating, and I blinked and looked around the room one more time, impressing to memory the shining floors, the long arched windows, the piney, Christmasy smell.

"Well," I said after a moment, "I guess I need to be going." But still, I didn't move, but only watched Michael hold my son, thinking how well he did it, in its own way as flawless as his pitches. Then I remembered the kidney and bone-marrow business.

Michael nodded. "Sure, Gabe."

"And listen, Michael, never let that bitch Mrs. Odom keep him, d'you hear me? She'll switch him."

Michael smiled. "You been listening to Mama. Miz Odom's all right."

"No," I said. "Promise."

He sighed. "All right."

I stood there a little longer, and when nothing else came to mind, I said I guess I'd better be going and went out the French doors into the cold night that smelled of ice and wet leaves, crossing the deck and getting in my car when something else occurred to me, and I went back and tapped on the French door. This time Michael opened it without the shotgun or the baby, stepping out into the cold in his bare feet.

"And listen," I told him, "when he's grown, him and Sim and Missy, too, you sendem up North to school. I'll see about them. Get to know them, maybe."

"Sure, Gabe," he said. "We'll talk about it."

He was coatless in the December chill but walked me to my car, listening impassively as I spoke. "And you don't have to tell him anything about me, why I'm not married—listen, you can tell him I'm gay or something."

He smiled. "You'll marry."

But I demurred, "No. No, I don't think so—"

"Come on, Gabe, how old are you? Twenty-seven? Don't let this thing eat you alive. Go make a life for yourself. Find you a wife of your own—"

"*No*," I said, annoyed at his insistence that I settle for something less than the ideal, when God knows, he never had. "Why would I want to crawl in bed every night with a woman I don't love? You don't."

He rolled his eyes at this, the Michael of old, who used to nag me to play baseball. "*Damn*, you are stubborn—" he murmured. "You have always been so damn stubborn. I know where Clayton gets it."

It was an admission I could not understand him making and looked at him curiously. "It doesn't bother you? That he's not yours?"

Michael was standing with his arms folded against the cold, his eyes on the stars, when he answered. "Well, I figure he's either my son or my nephew, so we're kin one way or another—" He paused and I waited for his confession of uncertainy, his pronouncement of regret, but he only shrugged. "Anyway, that sweet little baby in there and whose blood is running in his veins is the least of my worries."

We'd reached the car, and I was opening the door, but stopped long enough to say, very firmly, "Yeah, well, listen Michael, don't you worry about that damn *Klan*. Listen, next time they call, you tell those stupid racist pigs if they ever step foot on this place again, and your *brother* hears about it, well they'll be *plenty* sorry."

Even as I said it, a small smile began playing around Michael's mouth, but he held it straight till I caught a glimpse of my white, uncalloused hand on the car roof and felt a smile forming on my face. "God, I know they'll be, *terrified*," I said, and we began laughing, both of us.

I mean, it was just so absurd, the Big Man doing his Big Talk, and we laughed and laughed, till suddenly, Michael was crying, hugging me over the car door, not whispering, but saying aloud in my ear, "I love you, Gabe. It's killing me to see you go like this. Remember us, remember us—"

Now, I have mentioned my ability to cry louder and longer than any woman I've ever known, and I was really going strong there for a while, finally having to resort to humor to get things back in line, blowing my nose, trying to smile, saying, "Damn, I hate leaving you moren Myra. Hey, listen, Michael, why don't *you* run off with me?"

He just shook his head at me, wiping his face with his hands, and I kept it going: "Hey, I can support you, I got a job. We can move to Virginia, buy a farmhouse, raise a family. Kind of a perverse Waltons—"

So I was laughing as loudly as I had cried as I got in the car, rolling down the window to call, "The only problem'll be Mama. I mean, listen, Michael, it'd be fun, but *how would it look*?"

I started the car and was pulling out when Michael pounded on the hood, and I rolled down the window. "If they get me, Gabe, promise you'll come back. For Myra and the children. Promise."

"They won't—" I began.

But he was insistent. "If they do—"

I nodded, and as I backed out, my headlights followed him to the French doors, where he paused to watch me go, barefoot on the cold marble, his arms folded against the night air. I could see he was crying again and thought that, yes, they will have to deal with me if they touch him. Then I pulled around the drive, past the house that looked like an old Spanish mission in the moonlight, the moss lazy, gently whipping in the light breeze, the yard dotted with yellow pine that stood pencil-straight, like Grecian pillars beneath the hard, clean Florida sky.

The peace of the place followed me back to town, filling me with a rare certainty that I was doing the right thing at last: the hard road, the one Daddy took when he stood from the supper table that night and knew he was beaten, but went anyway. It was a curious sensation, one I could not place till later, in bed, I realized it was pride—that I was proud of myself. I was carrying on a family tradition, and the next morning when I kissed Mama and put my suitcase in the trunk, I went to the fence and spat at the jagged windows and broken back of the nasty old house next door.

It was a childish gesture, and Mama laughed at me, but I only smiled and waved and thought in triumph that I looked like an angel and she named me for an angel. And I never looked back.

Chapter

12

S o another Gap ensued. Not such
a bitter one, not say, 1865 to '72, but
much longer in duration, comparable to 1872 to 1942, so maybe one
thing offset the other. Now, I can't properly explain everything I did in
these years but will try to recall some of the highlights as they come to
me in memory, congealed and softened, selected and dissected by the
satin glove of passing time: teaching class after class of freshmen, so that
I mumbled significant dates in my sleep (1492, 1607, 1754, ad nauseum),
moving on to Virginia State when Georgetown didn't pan out, where I
taught slightly more interesting Southern history (different dates, same
repetition) until 1981, when I finally settled on a job I actually enjoyed,
not in the classroom, but as a fact-gatherer for a statewide oral history
project at Indiana University. There I spent a majority of my days sitting
in frame houses in factory towns, interviewing slow-talking refugees from
the mills of Arkansas and the coal mines of Kentucky, who'd crossed the
river for the cash and spoke of their homes with such a mosaic of love
and hate and relief and regret that I fell in love with them. When they

heard the not-so-distant strain of Appalachia in my voice, they'd always ask where I was from, and when I'd say Florida, they'd ask about the beaches and I'd tell them, no, I wasn't from beach-Florida, I was from hick-Florida, and they'd know exactly what I meant.

"When we tell people we're from Indiana, they think we're Yan-kees—" they'd say, and when I asked them if they considered themselves Yankees, they'd be insulted. "No, no, we just come for the jobs. We'll be going back. My aint still lives in Trumann—"

Their fierce hunger for identity was so touching that I worked with near missionary zeal to document their heritage, so if things didn't work out and they never went home, their children would remember who they were and why they'd come north in the first place.

Which is all to say that I had some satisfaction in those years. It was not the grind I sometimes imagine—nor was it actually living. Once, sitting in an airport in Indianapolis, I caught a glimpse of my reflection in a glass door, and there was something very close, very familiar in my slumped shoulders, my patient eyes. Then I remembered Myra as she sat on the steps of the pool that summer, her face blank with the expectancy of someone waiting on a phone call.

But it was not really that bad. I had a close friend who died of cirrhosis during these years, and his very real suffering kept my small undulations in perspective, and for a while, I still had Mama's Thursday night calls to enlighten and sustain me.

So I was there, albeit, long distance, when Clayton took his first step at sixteen months (lazy, Mama was already calling him), when Missy broke her arm on the slide at school, when Simon began pitching in little league. And in bits and shadowy pieces, I knew Myra: Myra who joined a fitness center, who went to Barbados on her tenth anniversary, who became Mama's assistant in the primaries and bucked the WMUs and the deacon board to give a baby shower for an unwed teenage mother; Myra who had survived. And her husband, who had succeeded where better men than he had failed by spitting in the face of small-town racism and not only surviving, but going on to buy out a failing plant in South Georgia, where Sam McRae was not only general manager, but part-owner.

Any day I expected to hear he'd bought the Braves and turned them around to win the pennant, till abruptly one afternoon, with no warning at all, my supply line was cut when I answered the phone during an early supper to a hysterical rush of venom, not inhumanly vicious like the call to Michael's had been, but close and personal and peppered with searing maternal regret, "—never raised you to do such a thing. I'm glad your daddy never lived to see it. You shamed him, you shamed us all—" The overall effect was something like innocently answering the phone and getting a spray of machine gun fire in your ear, but I didn't argue. I didn't reply at all, but only stood there and let Mama's righteous anger burn up the lines a little longer. "—treated her like trash. Her mind wadn't right and you knew it. *You knew it*. You ain't no son a mine. Michael should a killed you for it—"

When it'd get too bad, I'd quietly hang up and breathe for a moment, but the phone always rang again immediately, and I'd answer it with my eyes closed.

"And how will he explain it to Clayton, tell me thet? It ain't even bothered you to just up and leave your boy for your brother to raise. You never should a come back in the first place. You stay up there with your Yankee friends. You never been a friend to nobody down *here*—"

With that, she broke it off herself with a colossal slam of the phone and a dead white silence that lasted the better part of seven years.

Her tenacity was baffling to me at the time, and for the first few Christmases, I'd looked for a conciliatory letter or a tentative phone call, but they never came. Finally, I reconstructed an explanatory scenario and could imagine how something—porch talk on Magnolia Hill or gossip at Welcome—had made her suspicious, and knowing Mama, she'd taken Michael aside after Sunday dinner and asked him point-blank: "Michael Catts? Didjure brother and Myra have a love affair? Is Clayton yours?"

And Michael, with his seemingly boundless capacity for shock, probably just stood there and picked his teeth, saying yes, but not to let it worry her, it wasn't keeping him up nights.

In the face of such incomprehensible passivity, Mama must have been outraged, furious at both of us, for she could not turn on Myra, dear Myra, whom she loved like a daughter. Mama is a wee bit eccentric, kind of a nut in the Aunt Pitty-Pat tradition, but she understands women (she had five sisters), and Myra's fight for control was probably realer to her than it'd ever be to Michael or me either one. After all, she'd thrown herself against Old Man Sims and opened her arms to her when she was a wounded child, and it wouldn't have made any difference if she'd have found out Myra was involved with half the men at Sanger. It'd be those sorry, good-for-nothing men's fault. Not Myra, never Myra, who held her hand at Daddy's funeral and took her to the doctor twice a month and worried over Michael's blood pressure and kept Lori in clothes. Never Myra.

It was an odd sensation, really, knowing that a nonsibling had taken your place in your mother's affections, but I never called her back, never made any excuses on my own behalf. I had an inkling that Mama's hard-headed, loud-mouthed defense was one of the pillars that supported Myra's remarkable recovery, and if it were shaken, even Michael would be hard pressed to repair it.

So I maintained my silence and my distance and was cut off, stranded at last, in Year Three of the Great Gap, and it was about two years later, while I was still in Indiana, that another incident occurred that I remember very clearly. It was in the spring, just as the term was ending, when one of my students dropped by my office to say good-bye before she left for Purdue to begin work on her master's.

She was very young, twenty-one or -two, very bright and aggressive, with an Arkansas drawl and a flat, country honesty that reminded me of Mama, and after thanking me for all the help I'd given her with my letters of recommendation and phone calls, she looked me straight in the eye and told me I drank too much. "I mean, I know it's none of my business, Dr. Catts, but I could tell you drink in the morning before class and that's bad. My mother was an alcoholic, and you don't want that kind of life for yourself."

Then she smiled and promised to write and was gone, leaving me to scratch my head and wonder if I was to spend my entire life with these children who thought nothing at all of saying something like that to your face, then smiling and telling you to have a nice day. However, her words had more than a little truth to them, though I honestly   couldn't tell if my alcohol consumption was unreasonable or not. I mean, sure I drank early, but I never got drunk, and after a few weeks of bouncing it back and forth, I grew curious enough to call an AA hotline and describe my drinking habits to a counselor who informed me that I was indeed an alcoholic.

"How can you tell?"

"You're dependent. You drink every day, all day. It's your life. I know, I'm one too."

I was not inclined to agree, for I was a professional, a man of letters. I paid an incredible amount of money every month in rent. But he was not impressed and suggested I give sobriety a try, then took my home number and promised to check up on me in a few days and see how I was doing with it. I told him sure, no problem, and for two days was stone cold sober, then felt a touch of a cold coming on, and when he called back, was still nursing it with my God-fearing, teetotaling mother's patented remedy, honey and lemon and eighty-proof whiskey.

"You're only fooling yourself," he said. "You're an alcoholic. Come to a meeting. You can quit."

Again, I demurred, explaining my cold and how I was not yet acclimated to the Indiana winter, that I was no longer Baptist, but Episcopalian, and could drink till I dropped and never see hell for it. But he would not be budged and told me I was an alcoholic so many times in two minutes that I promised to leave it alone until he called back.

"Sure you will," he said, and his needling doubt was so insulting that I went on a temperance binge, pouring out wine and pitching bottles, then sitting back with a good book and a glass of iced tea.

"There, now," I thought, looking around my living room and finding it very dry and safe and Baptist. "That will show him."

But the damn phone wouldn't ring. Every night I waited, I sweated blood, but the son of a bitch lay there dead and still and since it was between semesters, there was nothing to do but read or watch television, and since I usually read with a glass in my hand, I opted for television and, for the first time in my life, bought a *TV Guide*.

When Thursday night rolled around, I found myself watching *The Waltons* for a quick hit of nostalgia and could picture Mama, a thousand miles away on Magnolia Hill, looking at John-boy and wondering where she went wrong with me, and it was not a pleasant thought. In fact, I was sitting there thinking what a mess I'd made of my life, what a boring, endless mess, and began to imagine ways I could kill myself and cover it up so the insurance company would not suspect. Run a car over an icy curb. Take up gun collecting and shoot myself. Slip in the tub. Something relatively victimless. I'd leave my money to Mama (not a big item), my stuff to Michael. Maybe I'd leave Clayton my watch. It wouldn't mean anything to him, though. He'd probably show it to people, tell them his uncle left it to him. His Uncle Gabe, the fag professor who died in the car wreck—

The phone rang suddenly, a few inches from my head, and I snatched if off the cradle, shouting, "Where the *hell* have you been? I been waiting all week!"

"You're an alcoholic," he said quietly, and I sat there very still, gently pressing my eyelids with my fingertips, thinking, well, it was just one more step in my relentless quest to become as sleazy as Old Man Sims. Two for two. Molester and drunk. Given the chance, I'd probably be breaking children's wrists, locking students in closets.

"We're having a meeting at the Catholic Student Center. Come now, right now, don't think about it. Just put on your coat and pretend you're going to a movie, but come here instead."

Something in the quiet urgency in his voice spurred me to action and for about ten months, my Thursday nights were spent in the basement of the Catholic Student Union, making Protestant-like stabs at the informal confessional, and I think that I can say with all honestly that leaving the liquor behind was the hardest thing I've ever done in my life. My loss of Myra was eclipsed by it, my separation from Clayton; even Michael and Mama paled in comparison.

Looking back, I can't say how I made it, for I was a cyclic drinker who could go for weeks without a drop, but once I took that drop, I was right back in the belly of the beast. When I was actually drinking, I'd be contrite and humble, but during the dry spells, I wasn't an alcoholic, no, not me, I was a bone-dry Baptist, never drank a drop till I was nineteen. So they could never get me to admit I was an alcoholic on anything approaching a consistent basis, but I was so charmingly ingenious in avoiding it that my lapses seemed forgivable. Only Bill, the counselor who first spoke with me on the phone (a Catholic priest, I later learned, suffering from advanced cirrhosis) refused to laugh and would occasionally remind me of my fallen state: "You're an alcoholic, Gabe. You can forget it, but it won't forget you."

I'd smile. "I think that's what my mother used to tell me about Jesus."

He'd only shake his head, and I'd reassure him. "Listen, Bill, I haven't touched a thing in two months, I'm dry, I'm good—"

"Yeah. And my skin's yellow because I'm an Irish priest of Chinese descent."

Back and forth we went, till he died a fairly hideous death of liver failure, sending the rest of us screaming for Antabuse, which always worked well for me, since I'd developed an ulcer and vomiting was like gargling with Drano. So in fits and starts, I learned the fine art of maintained reality, and like Myra, dear Myra, whose face I could sometimes not recall, I survived: survived Mama's excommunication and the Whiskey Rebellion, and even the end of the oral history project when the money ran out and I was forced back into the classroom in New York, teaching urbanites at NYU because it was the only university in America that had never heard of the Civil War, which suited me just fine, because lost causes didn't move me anymore. I'd survived on my own with the aid of Antabuse and Tagamet, and digging up all the old losses was so dull and flat that I could almost agree with a student of mine who'd gone to Fort Lauderdale for spring break, and asked me what was with all the rebel flags down there.

I explained there was a war down there once, a hundred and twenty years ago, and that they still hadn't quite gotten over it, but his ancestors were Polish farmers in 1865, and he only looked at me. "Well, who the hell cares anymore?" he asked.

I shrugged. "Don't look at me."

One last incident occurs to me as the final, most perfect illustration of my life at the end of the Great Gap. I went to a party, I can't remember where, somewhere in Brooklyn, and sat around all evening sipping seltzer (which I detest), socializing with a congenial mix of colleagues. It was spring again, the city finally warming up to temperatures conducive to human hope, everyone laughing and easy, talking of jobs and projects and weddings, and sometime in the course of the evening, we fell to discussing restaurants. Now I am a nonstarter when it comes to cooking anything but barbeque, so it was a subject near and dear to my heart, and I fairly took the floor, waxing long and lovingly on the Italian cafes where I'd eaten pasta, the bistros where I'd consumed croissants. Then I remember getting really excited over this Cuban place in Little Havana where I'd once eaten paella in an iron pot with a lobster on top.

"A whole lobster!" I exclaimed, with an echo of the passion that I'd once used to defame generals. "Right there on the rice. It was incredible."

Later that evening, as I undressed for bed, I thought about what a nice time I'd had, that maybe it was a sign of personal growth, my seeking out human companionship. But later, in bed, I tried to recall the highlights of the evening and could remember nothing but talking about that lobster. I mean, everyone else was talking about flying to Israel for Passover or their daughter's marriage in June or how well their son was doing at Cornell, and the only thing I could contribute was a fanatical review of a dead shellfish. I mean, I talked about that damn lobster like it was the wife of my youth. ("Right there in the rice it was, I ate it with rendered butter served in these little cups—").

I lay there thinking I was worse than a fag. Fags were human; I was a nonenity. An amoeba. I lived to eat and ate to live. A small voice in my head had begun its relentless circling, reasoning that who cared if amoebas had problems with substance abuse? Everyone had their little weaknesses. Thorns in the flesh, the Apostle called them. I was beginning to stir beneath the covers when the phone on my bedstand rang, and it was a light, young voice.

"You probably don't remember me," she said, and I thought it must be one of my students from Indiana, for the accent was definitely country.

"No, I really—"

"It's me, Melissa. I'm here in New York right by myself."

"Melissa?" I repeated, the voice and name suddenly familiar, though I still couldn't place it till she said:

"Missy. Missy Catts. Your brother Michael's girl—"

"*Missy?*" I said, sitting up. "What the hell are you doing up here alone? You can't be, it's not safe—"

"Well, I'm with a group, really. We're flying to London. And Paris, France. With Miss Pitts, d'you remember her? She's my homeroom teacher, says she taught you English. Anyway, the stupid plane's late, and she says I can go eat with you if you come get me. Daddy said to call you if anything went wrong, but if it's too late—"

"No, no," I said, getting out of bed. "I was up. Where are you?"

"Let me ast," she said, then came back to the phone. "LaGuardia Airport, gate eighteen. You'll know me, I got red hair."

She could have had purple hair and I would have known her, for she was Ira Sims' female double, skinny and grinning, with a mouthful of braces and a headful of wavy red hair. Seeing her standing there in blue jeans and a big T-shirt made me feel like a very old man, but she only waved and grabbed a bag and told Miss Pitts she was leaving, then hugged me with no reserve at all.

"You shore don't favor Daddy," she said with a birdlike excitement as we went in search of food. "I'm starving to death, I really am. We had this awful food on the plane, it's the first time I ever flew anywhere. I thought I'd be scared, but—"

"This all right?" I asked, stopping at a snack bar.

She grinned. "Sure. Long as they have French fries. That's all I want."

And that's what she got, four bags of French fries that she consumed with true Ira Sims finesse, not missing a beat as she answered my questions and asked a few of her own.

"How come you ain't married? You need to come home, Welcome's got more old maids than any church in town, *nice* women, got *good* jobs, drive *nice* cars."

She sounded so much like Mama that I laughed aloud, but she was not embarrassed at all, only giving a little sniff and saying into the air, "Well, seems like to me you'd wanna do moren read all the time. That's what Daddy says. He says you used to read all the time, said you'se real smart. Said if we do good in school we can come up here to college, but I don't know." She glanced around the snack area. "These people look a little weird to me, some bald-headed ones about run us over in Atlanta—"

She didn't seem to require much in the way of reply, so I only sat there and watched her, seeing Myra in her small hands and ocean blue eyes. But whereas Myra's eyes were murky, distant, her daughter's were alive, snapping with excitement as she spoke of her trip.

"—and Tuesday we're going to Napoleon's tomb, right there in Paris. I love Napoleon. Mama give me this book about him and this woman who was his fiancée and I love it. I read it twict. I'm gone get my picture taken by his tomb if they'll let me—"

Napoleon and Josephine, I thought, and wondered if Myra remembered the Napoleon of our youths. Short and chunky and blond, who loved women with red hair.

"—they're all in a frazzle over Lori's wedding; they're getting married out by the pool the day I come back. I'm a junior bridesmaid, but the dresses are pink and I look pretty ugly in pink. I tried to get Lori to let me wear aqua, but no, she had to have pink, so I really don't care if I get back in time or not." She gave me a very Mama-looking smirk. "Just between you and me, they cain't afford to wait, if you know what I mean."

I didn't, and she tapped a French fry on the table and took a breath. "Well. Last week's when it all come out. I was helping Clay clean the pool—he never does it right—and up come Lori, crying her eyes out. Mama took her upstairs a long time, then Curtis come up, looking like death, then Aint Candace and then Daddy come home and took us all over to Grannie's. Had to stay there all day, not knowing what in the world was going on, then about dark, they all come over and announced Lori and Curtis were getting married *next* week. I mean, they weren't supposed to get married till June, had the announcements printed and everything, and nobody had to tell *me*, boy. I knew what was up, but pretended like nothing was wrong."

A smile began playing around her mouth. "But that stupid Clay, he got mad. See, him and Daddy were supposed to go fishing at Lake Eufaula next week, and he just wouldn't shut up about it. Kept saying how Sim got to go see the Braves and I was going to *Paris, France* and he never got to go nowhere, kept asking why didn't they wait till June? Everybody got married in June—" She rolled her eyes. "I mean, Uncle Gabe, Clayton will just not shut up once he gets started on something.

"So Daddy finally took him in the bedroom and explained it to him, but he was still mad, pouting all night, while everyone else was talking about where they'd live and what they wanted for a present. Mama wanted us to all go together to give them the down payment on a trailer or something, but Lori said they'd just like everyone to go together and send them on a nice honeymoon. I mean, that's just Lori all over. She don't have no sense when it comes to money, and she just kept at it all night, talking about the Bahamas or New Orleans, how she wanted to go somewhere romantic, till finally Clay—he was sitting in the corner sulking—he said, right out loud, 'Well why don't y'all save your money and go down to the drive-in? Looks like y'all been having pretty good luck down there already.'"

I was laughing, and she leaned over the table, beating her hand on it, saying, "He did, he really did, right out loud. Poor Mama was *humiliated*. She took him to the porch and whipped him, but Grannie had to go to the bathroom and put her face in a towel, she was laughing so hard. She loves Clay, he's her favorite—"

"Do you have any pictures?" I asked and she looked at me blankly.

"Of who? Us?" She slapped the salt off her hands. "Oh, sure—"

She rummaged around in her bag awhile, depositing curling irons and eyeshadow and gum wrappers on the table before finding her wallet and handing them over, each with a short commentary.

"That's Simon in little league. He still pitches, but his shoulder's messed up. He's trying to change to first base. And that's me; I hate that picture—look at them teeth. And this is Kristin, my best friend, and Heather, my second-best friend, and Joanna, my best friend at church—" She paused over a small, wallet-sized photograph. "And this is Clayton. He don't look like that now. He's going through an ugly stage, Grannie calls it—"

I held the tiny picture of a little tow-headed boy, maybe six, who favored both Michael and me with his light, cowlicked hair, but thinner, more pointed face. "—and this is Abe," Missy was saying, still dropping pictures on the table, "my ex-boyfriend—here, I think I'll just throw him away right now—and this is us. Lord, look at Mama's hair, had that awful perm, looks like Bette Midler."

It was an Olan Mills studio portrait, Michael grayer and heavier, much like Daddy around the eyes and mouth, Myra's wild hair full and curly, but her face relaxed, as if her life suited her, a daughter before her, a son on each side—one taller and dark, one young and oddly somber, his hand on her shoulder.

"You can have it if you want it," Missy was saying. "We got a ton of them. Mama got some deal, buy one, get a thousand free, or something—"

I looked at it a long time, then carefully put it in my wallet and felt a surge of emotion building and wondered how I'd ever explain crying to this happy child, but my tears were sidetracked by a fascinating bit of news.

Ira was in prison.

"Over in Raiford," she said, loading her bag back up. "Mama goes over and sees him when they let her, says it gives her the creeps because you have to drive under this sign like you're going into a concentration camp or something—"

"What's he in for?" I asked and she gave me another one of those Cissie Catts knowing looks.

"*Well,*" she said, "I don't know for sure. It's something too bad, but Simon knows, and he says to spare myself the details. Me and Clay figure it's got to do with women 'cause he heard Aint Candace telling Grannie that she didn't care whose brother Uncle Ira was, he'd never step foot in her house again, not while *Lori* was there." She had started on her fourth bag of fries and pointed one at me. "So see? Whatever it is, his trial took *forever.* Mama had to go over there and testify, but it didn't work, and to tell you the truth, I'm kinda relieved. I mean, everybody says I look like him, but he gives me the creeps, the way he's always smiling. I mean when Grandma died, he just smiled through the whole funeral. It was so weird."

I had not heard that Mrs. Odom was dead, but was more concerned with Missy. "You stay away from him."

She grinned. "You sound just like Mama. She says he takes after their father."

My sentiment exactly, but I wondered how in the world Myra had brought herself to explain such a sordid evil to a child, and looked at her curiously. "How do you mean?"

"Oh—" She finished off the last of the French fries and began folding up the bags. "—Mean, I guess. That's what she had to go tell the jury at his trial—about their father, how he used to beatem and stuff, not when they were little, but later, after they come to Florida, he become an alcoholic."

Well, talk about sharper than a serpent's tooth. "Not all alcoholics abuse their children," I told her firmly, and she only lifted an eyebrow.

"Really? Oh. Well maybe he just liked to." I was about to allow as that was probably the case, but there was no time. Her flight was being called, and as we hurried back to the gate, she tried to talk me into coming home for Lori's wedding.

"It'll be so fun. We're all going out to eat afterwards at the beach, just the family. Promise you'll come—"

I made my excuses and hugged her at the gate while a frantic Miss Pitts waved for her to hurry, then gave her all the money in my wallet.

"Buy em a present from me," I told her, "in Paris."

"Boy," she laughed. "Sure. I'll say it's from both a us. Nobody'll believe it. Clay will die. He hates it when I know people he don't."

I almost told her to buy him something, too, but hesitated, then remembered Myra and tried to think of an acceptable message, but couldn't.

So I only stepped back and let her go, watching her run to the plane, her bag bouncing against her back, her hair getting caught in the breeze as she cleared the outbuildings and ran out under the open sky. I kept thinking she'd turn and wave again once she made the steps, but she didn't, her eyes already ahead, on Paris and Napoleon and supper at the beach. There was a delay, and I guess I stood there fifteen, twenty minutes before it closed up and taxied into the bright artificial lights of the runway. Even when it had gone and another plane had taken its place, I waited, feeling for my wallet and taking out the picture she'd given me, smiling at the light in Myra's eyes. Kind, she looked, kind and accepting, a faint memory of the child on the porch steps who smiled when she lifted her face and saw me watching her.

Hey, Gabrielle.

Twenty-four years, it'd been, and I could hear her so plainly, not two steps behind me, and with her image a few inches from my face, I whispered into the impersonal semi-darkness of the gate, "Hey, yourself, Myra Sims. I love your daughter. She reminds me of you."

There was no answer, of course. There couldn't be. A thousand miles and another life lay between us, so I kissed her lightly, then bent and laid her gently on the hard dirty pavement and walked away. I abandoned her not in cruelty, but in craft, a wily enough alcoholic by now to recognize white wine when I saw it. Clear, innocent Chablis. Low calories, light. Good source of iron, some people said. Barely alcoholic at all, eleven percent at the outside. Perfectly harmless to most people. But not to me. Not to me.

Chapter

I made the break cleanly and was so
pleased with my fortitude that I allowed
myself the luxury of female companionship in the form of a colleague of
mine named Adele. A native of suburban Chicago, Adele was a clinical
psychologist when she wasn't amusing a roomful of freshmen with *The
Interpretation of Dreams*, and we saw each other pretty regularly for
about a year until I realized that maybe sixty percent of our conversation
dealt with mental illness and, in a rare moment of objectivity, decided I
was conjuring Myra at her expense. I eventually broke it off after many
hours agonized worry over how she would take it, worry that proved
singularly groundless, for she was not angry at all, only nodding a lot,
then getting her revenge in a very Midwestern kind of way, going on
to marry another colleague of ours who was not only richer and bet-
ter-looking, but who asked me to be an usher at the wedding. I tell you
what, it made me long for the good old days on Magnolia Hill, where
love was ruled by the Bible and the shotgun, and I was humbled enough
to keep to myself till the bright September morning four months later,

when, again without warning, my family reentered my life.

The phone rang while I was standing at the counter in the kitchen brushing my teeth at the sink, watching the early edition of *The Today Show*, and it was such an odd hour for anyone to call that I had an immediate gut-drop premonition that it would be bad news.

And it was.

Michael had cancer of the pancreas, Candace told me in a clear hard voice that was so calm, so precise, that I knew she was not being cruel but was simply in shock.

They operated on him yesterday, she said, for gallstones, but the lab results had come in at seven, and the surgeon had called the family to the hospital so he could tell them at once.

"They give him," she paused a moment, "give him," then another pause, "five months."

For a moment, the words were unreal, hanging in the air like some half understood joke, and when they hit, it was as if I'd been shot in the back. I slumped against the counter and lost it with such abandon that my sister was finally able to react, shouting over my tears, "He can't! He can't! I told Brother Sloan, no! But they told Sim and Missy anyway, they toldem he's dying. But not Clayton, and they can't, I toldem not to. They shouldn't tell children things like that—it'll scare him, he's too little. He can't—"

But he did. Not in five months, but three-and-a-half, and when he called in early December and told me he wouldn't make Christmas, I was drunk enough to tell him it was just like him to overachieve, even in death.

He laughed, a strange, rasping laugh that didn't sound like Michael at all, then spoke slowly. "Cabe. I need you da comb down here for da children. Remember? You probussed."

His voice was so strange, like he had a bad head cold; I could hardly make him out. "What? Michael? Man, I can't understand you—"

"Da children. Melissa and Claydon. Dere too young. Myra is drong, but da children are too liddle—"

I had the receiver pressed to my ear, but it was like a nightmare where you need to call someone, but can't operate a phone. "Damn, Michael, I can't—is it Myra? Is she all right?"

"Myra's bine," he insisted. "She's drong—" He broke off a moment, and I could hear the phone falling, then being picked up again, and when he spoke this time, his voice was hoarse, but normal. "Stupid tubes," he said weakly. "I hate 'em. Got 'em everywhere." Then, "Myra's fine, Gabe. She's always with me. And Sim's all right, but Missy and Clay are hurting. They're too little, but what can I do? I can't raise 'em in six weeks."

It finally occurred to me that he was asking something of me, and I sat down.

"I'm flying down Friday," I said lightly, knowing I hadn't answered his question, but having a hard time sorting it all out, for I was no longer used to whiskey and even a few shots got me over the edge.

"No." he said. "Don't come till the funeral. I don't want you to see me like this. I got hepatitis, and ascites. I'm skinny and yellow and sicker than hell. Everybody that comes by starts crying. I hate it."

For a moment, I was too stunned to speak, for I'd bought my tickets and made my plans and here he was, telling me not to come.

"I won't cry," I said. "I swear."

But he only laughed, and I grew desperate. "I swear to God, Michael. I'll be drunk, but I won't cry."

"No," he said. "That's all behind us now, and I ain't spending my last month on earth listening to true confessions. What's done's done. There ain't no secrets between us, Gabe. I love you. And I'm counting on you to keep an eye on my children—"

"What d'you mean, Michael? I got a job. I live a thousand miles away—"

"Then move—"

"But Myra, what about Myra? Does she know? You can't just set this up—"

"I ain't talking about Myra," he said. "I'm talking about my children. Missy's been talking about you ever since she come back from France. You're the only kin she's got, except for Candace and Mama. And Clayton," he paused, "he'll love you too, when he gets to know you. And Myra," he paused again, "what you all do is your bidness, I don't care. She won't talk about it. Can't. But it don't mean nothing to me. I don't want her staying a widow forever. That ain't no kinda life. But if you love her, that's your bidness. Just," he paused a final time, then sighed, "be kind to her, Gabe. She's been good to me."

I couldn't speak for a moment, and he tried to lighten his words with a little humor. "Toldju you'd cry."

"I'm not crying," I said flatly. "I'm dying, because listen, Michael, I'd do anything for you, anything at all, but you can't count on me for this. I'm not the man you used to know. I've changed."

"Changed? What do you mean, changed?" Then, "Damn, Gabe, this ain't some small favor I thought up to kill time. I need you, man. Don't disappoint me in this thing—"

"I'm an alcoholic," I said, and he seemed perplexed, as if he'd never heard of the term.

"A *what*?"

"An alcoholic."

"Well, who the hell cares?" he finally breathed, exasperated. "I don't need you to save their souls, just be there for them. Quit drinking, throw it out—"

"It's not as easy as that—"

"Sure it is. Throw it out."

"Michael, listen. I've thrown it out before. And been hospitalized and counseled and everything else in the world and none of it worked.

I'm drinking now, right now. I was sober four years."

He was quiet a moment, then sighed hugely, and when he spoke again, his voice was quiet. "Gabe, listen to me. *Throw the liquor away.* Never touch it again, or I swear to God I'll leave Clayton to Miz Odom and Missy to Ira. Good-bye—"

I was shouting into the phone that he couldn't, that Mrs. Odom was dead and Ira was in prison, but he'd hung up, and I slammed the receiver down and paced the room, saying, "Damn damn damn *damn.*"

Damn Michael. What was he playing at? Trying to fix us up into some kind of Brady Bunch to ease his conscience on his death bed? Didn't he realize that years, years and years had passed, and while Myra was still an enigma to me, she was nothing as firm as flesh and blood. Just a childhood memory and a summer of what? Love? Or was it just blood in the water? I still didn't know. And hell, these children were strangers to me. He'd been the one who'd made sure of that. He was the one with the shotgun and the one clean shot. Who did he think he was, picking up the phone and calling me like a dog? Well, he could go to hell; it was easy for a Baptist teetotaler to say *throw it out*—

I got his number from information and dialed his home phone direct, tapping my fingers on the table as the line cleared Florida, then rang, one monotonous drill after another. I was about to hang up when a small, unfamiliar voice answered, "Hello?"

"Is Michael there?" I said in a rush. "This is his brother. I need to speak to him."

"He ain't here."

"Well, *shit.* Can I leave a message?"

"He's at the hospital," he offered. "I don't know when he'll be back. They won't," he paused, "they won't let me see him."

The sadness, the blank loss in the voice was so palpable that I forgot my anger for a moment, and said, "Well, he probably doesn't want you to see him like this. He's got ascites." A condition I was familiar with from Bill's illness.

The voice was sullen. "What's that?"

"Ah, fluid in the peritoneal cavity. It can be pretty nasty—"

"I ain't going up there to ask him to the prom," he whined. "I just wanna see him. Simon got to."

My heart began its slow pound when I realized to whom I was speaking with such nonchalance, and I paused a moment, then said lightly, "I'll mention it when I call the hospital."

His voice was suddenly excited, "Yeah, and tellem—tellem I'm fine, that I won't cry, I swear to God."

Then we said good-bye, and I sat with the phone on my lap a few minutes before I dialed information, then the hospital switchboard, who transferred my call directly to Michael's room.

Here, the phone only rang once before it was snatched up and answered sharply. "Yes?"

Well, I recognized her, at least. The deep country voice, all inflection submerged beneath the weight of Michael's illness, but *coping, drong,* as Michael had said.

"Myra?"

"Yes?" she repeated, and I felt the pound in my chest again, that old relentless gallop.

"This is Gabe."

She made no reply at all, and I pressed forward nervously. "Is Michael there? I need to speak to him."

"No, he's not," she said, and it was the first time she'd addressed me in a normal, direct voice, the first time in a long time. "He's in surgery."

"Surgery? But he just talked to me, not ten minutes ago."

"He must have called from pre-op," she said in a low, tired voice. "They're in there now, draining the abdominal fluid. The doctor says if it's clear, he's got till Christmas, but if it's cloudy," she paused, "it could be tomorrow. Or tonight." Her voice dropped even lower. "Or while he's on the table."

I rubbed my eyes and felt that raw, blank unbelief in my chest. How could this be happening?

"I'm sorry, Myra. I don't know what to say. Tell him I love him, that I said yes. He'll know what I mean."

She said she would, and another silence ensued till I remembered Clayton.

"And listen, tell Michael to let Clayton come up there and see him. I called your house and talked to him and he's hurting, Myra. Don't leave him out of this."

There was a blank silence for a moment. Then she asked slowly, "You did *what*?"

I began to innocently repeat myself, and she burst through the line, her voice shaking with anger. "And who the *hell* do you think you are, calling down here, talking to my son, trying to tell me what to do?"

Her first words stunned me, and I only stared at the receiver, but suddenly, with no warning, the feeling was back, and I was mad. I was worse than mad, I was outraged, standing with the telephone in hand, shouting, "Your son? *Your son?* My son, too, woman!"

"He's no son a yours! Don'tchu ever say that again. Don'tchu even *think* it—"

"Oh cut the shit, Myra. I can't believe you're still playing the injured virgin. Listen, you can pull that shit with Michael, but I know, I was *there*—"

"Well, I'm glad somebody was. I sure as hell wasn't—"

"Oh *bullshit*. Don't even try that with me. Listen, I know crazy when I see it and I know guilty as hell and you were the latter. You can save your lines for the WMUs—"

"It's not a line. You know it ain't. You used me. You never cared for nobody but yourself, not me nor Michael either one—"

"Used you? *Used* you? I am sick of this babygirl bullshit. Sick of it, d'you hear me? I haven't seen my brother in ten years because of you. It was the worst night's work in her life when Mama hid you in that closet and didn't let your daddy take you—"

"—got that right—" she was screaming, "—Locking me in a closet with a horny little *snot* like you—"

I guess we could have raged on all night, screaming our accusations that were really not pointed at each other at all, but at betrayals worse than adultery—inadvertant betrayals, like sickness and pain and the merciless winnowing of death, but the doctor must have come in the room, for Myra dropped the phone, and I could hear voices, then finally, Myra, crying as she came back on the line.

"What?" I was shouting. "For God's sake, Myra, was it—"

"Clear." She cried and I sat down suddenly, the phone still in my hand.

"Thank God," I whispered. Then after a few moments: "Tell him I love him, Myra."

"Yes, Gabriel," she said, her voice even and normal and again, only tired.

"He won't let me come. I wanted to see him—"

"No," she said, blowing her nose. "Not like this. He's right. Listen, I gotta go, I gotta call Cissie—"

"Oh, yeah. Well, call me. Promise you'll call if you need anything."

"Yes. Of course. I love you, Gabriel."

"I love you too."

Then she hung up, and I felt curiously spent, not remembering, much less regretting, our hard, vicious words, only relieved Michael would be with us Christmas. Probably in the hospital, probably in extremis, but still listening to my excuses with no trace of doubt, triumphing over death as he had racism and adultery and insanity. Standing above it, refusing to succumb.

Then Mrs. Weeks came to my podium with her little yellow phone message the week before Christmas, and it was so cruel, as if something had been robbed from us all, and I went straight to the airport in tears. But not before I'd bought a bottle.

Chapter

14

*S*o *I was drunk at his funeral,*
standing there at his casket, leaning
on Mama, trying not to show myself, but having a hard time of it, for in
death, Michael was waxy-looking, thin, awful. Why, he wasn't Michael at
all, and I felt like turning on the congregation and screaming at these
people, asking them where my brother was, that I needed to speak to
him *right now*, this instant. But a small measure of control was with me,
and I only watched his still, sallow face for a long, interminable moment,
then turned and escorted Mama out the side exit into the quiet chill of a
white winter sun, tucking her into the family limousine, and pretending
to line up with the processional to the graveyard, but turning east at the
highway, once again fleeing with nothing but the shirt on my back, for
it was too much. Michael was gone, gone forever; I'd never talk to him
again. Myra was blank, and Sim and Missy and Clayton were looking at
me, but I wasn't there for myself, how could I be there for them?

The flight to New York was suffocating, endless, with three

layovers and all the holiday crowds making me deplane at every gate with a mob of crying passengers, running into the arms of loved ones, and by the time I had made my apartment, I was nearly insane. But once I was able to sleep (pass out, you might say), I felt better, and returned to work on Monday with no comment to anyone other than a thank-you to Mrs. Weeks for her remarkable efficiency in the time of crisis.

The winter quarter began early that year, on January third or fourth, and I was easily consumed by my old schedule: alarm at seven, office hours Tuesday and Thursday afternoons, lectures at nine and twelve and two-fifteen. The routine. I even went to a few parties, probably even bragged on my lobster consumption, I don't remember, because I was drinking at first, then I was sweating it, then I was back on Antabuse, scared as hell I couldn't maintain and dreading the puking if I messed up.

But I didn't, not for a while. Three months, then six, then summer came, dry and light, and I knew I'd turned the corner; not left the building, but turned the corner, and when autumn crept by and the holidays rolled around with all their gaiety and assorted temptations, I hoped to God Bill was recommending me daily to every saint on the calendar, for if I could maintain Steps One through Four in New York, I'd promised myself I would return to Florida for Five and Six, lean and mean and clean.

He must have been praying for me—someone must have—on the last day of the quarter, when a well-meaning freshman with a working knowledge of *Gone with the Wind* brought in Southern Comfort and crushed mint for juleps, which I have never liked, but after nine months (and three of those in snow) could have handled. Indeed, I was to that point of exquisite pain where my aftershave was beginning to look pretty good, but something, Bill's prayers or Michael's faith, sustained me, and I held out firmly but politely, even refusing the ice.

But it wore me down, drained me dry, and as I fought the traffic home that afternoon, I knew in my heart that I was not only about to lose it, but that I was, in fact, a Loser, and was about to prove it, as soon as I could find a parking place.

That's when the miraculous intervention took place.

On the George Washington Bridge, of all places, jammed tight between a bus and a rail, while I chewed my nails and scanned the radio, I came quite accidentally upon Dylan's "Lay, Lady, Lay."

It was the song of the summer in '68 or 9, getting about eighty-nine percent airplay, but a source of torment to me at the time, making me want Myra too much, back when I was still fighting it, still trying to make Daddy proud.

But now, the low, static-jabbed words came to me sweetly:

His clothes are dirty but his hands are clean
And you're the best thing that he's ever seen.

The ice still pelted my windshield, the barge-studded river smoked below, but I was taken back to Magnolia Hill, coming home from Tallahassee late on a Friday afternoon, the smell of butter beans and damp pine filling the living room where Myra waited, her face light-eyed and excited, throwing open the door, calling, "Did you get it? Did you get it?"

I'd pull it out of my backpack and hold it over my head, teasing her like the younger brother I was supposed to be, *To Kill a Mockingbird* or *The Hobbit*, or some other easy-to-read novel, and she'd wrestle it away and kiss me in thanks, quickly, thoughtlessly, and later I'd think about telling her to go easy on the touching, that it was killing me, but I never did, of course. It was too sweet, not just the smell of her hair or her breath in my face, but the wave of love and expectation that would come before her as she recognized my step on the porch and flung wide the door, creating a memory so strong it brought tears to my eyes, and suddenly, I realized how free I was. No bonds, no betrayals, no long nights spent tossing and turning on the razor edge between heaven and hell.

It was as if Dylan were sending me a personal message:

Why wait any longer for the world to begin
You can have your cake and eat it too
Why wait any longer for the one you love
When he's standing in front of you.

And in one of those day and night reversals I am famous for, my focus was no longer on whiskey at all, but on Myra, dear Myra, who lived alone, who was growing old while I screwed around in this idiotic Yankee traffic. I began beeping my horn, pounding on the side of the bus, getting as crazy as everyone else, till I was finally able to break free, and with the twin prospects of downtown traffic and Myra before me, I said to hell with it and took the next exit to Jersey.

About ten hours into the trip, I began to have serious second thoughts, but on sudden inspiration, I pulled off the interstate in North Carolina and found a copy of *Dylan's Greatest Hits* in a used record store, and whenever my nerve began to fail, I'd pop in the tape and feel my resolve rise.

Stay with your man awhile.
Until the break of day, let me see you make him smile.

I made town sixteen hours later, just after sunrise on a clear, cold Saturday morning, too tired to remember my name, much less why I'd come. It was for Myra, of course, but I just didn't feel ready for anything, and the town seemed hollow, honestly empty without Michael there to hug me, to believe in me, to tell me I cried more than anybody he'd ever seen in his life. I drove around aimlessly, finding everything pretty much the same—a new Wal-Mart on the highway, the old bowling alley closed, but that was all, and as my gas gauge began to dip, I remembered I'd never seen his grave.

So I headed out to the river where Daddy was buried, knowing instinctively that's where he would have bought his plot, and sure enough, there he was, way up on top of the hill, surrounded by ancient, black-trunked cedars and a whole city of tombstones.

Simon Michael Catts, June 5, 1943 – December 19, 1987 his marker read, and below, almost obsured by the winter rye, someone—Myra, surely—had inscribed: *He Walks With God.*

It was so simple, so plain, with no other grand words of praise. No mention of Sanger, or the money or the house, just: *He Walks With God,* and there was no question I wouldn't cry, because it was true. He walked with God if anyone did, and I sat down on Daddy's marker and cried and cried in that cold, wet dawn, and it was such a relief to do it there in private, with no one to see, no one to comment on the hypocrisy of it all.

Just me and Michael (and Daddy, if you wanted to get technical), and when I finished with the tears, I began talking, telling him all the things I wanted to say when he wouldn't let me come: how if I'd never believed in him, it was all my shortcoming and none of his; that I was proud of his house, his cars, his money; I knew it wasn't a fluke, but hard work and determination and drive, things I didn't have so much of, that's why I hated them sometimes. Then I told him that Myra and I, we had nothing to do with him, that I'd never touched her in his own house, never, not a hand (well, maybe a hand), but nothing more. And how I wished to God I hadn't even done that, because if I'd only have waited, it'd all be perfect, but now, now I wasn't so sure.

I discussed it with him the better part of an hour, not bothered by his inability to reply, pretty much predicting his laconic reasonableness, though a small cynical voice occasionally reminded me how stupid I must look, how *gothic*, sitting there talking to a grave. Why, it was the sort of thing I might have included in my own college repertoire ("—this guy, he screwed his brother's wife, oh, years ago, then his brother died and he's got such a guilt trip he goes up to the cemetery and *talks to him*. Apologizes. No, I swear to God, he really does—")

But I was truly past all that and didn't care if they featured me in a Smithsonian study—Hick Grieving Patterns in the American South, or the like. It felt too good; it set things right. As a matter of fact, even when I'd finished with the grief and the guilt and my chances with Myra, I still talked, mulling over recruiting prospects for the Braves, and how Florida State was really eating them alive again, for it was the kind of thing we'd discussed at every other homecoming of my life, the kind of thing I thought he'd like to hear.

The sun was fully above the horizion when I finally ran out of conversation, and I had paused to appreciate the fine Florida day, the sky Caribbean blue, the grass green enough that somewhere below a groundskeeper was pulling the crank of a mower, when I saw a car turn in the front gate and begin circling the hill—a dark blue Mercedes sedan, the diamond flecks in its rich metallic paint shimmering in the morning sun. As soon as I saw it, I knew it was Myra, not instinctively, but rather from a knowledge of the nature of local economics that bestowed fifty-thousand dollar cars on but a chosen few. I was parked on the other side of the hill and was able to watch, quite anonymously, as she got out, dressed the way native Floridians do in forty-six-degree weather, in a coat and boots and scarf, so that her whole personality was submerged beneath the weight of her clothes.

Clayton got out of the passenger side, stretching, calling something to her over the hood, and suddenly unsure of my welcome, I stood and with a quick glance left and right, ducked under the trees, thinking I'd better go to Mama's and check out the lay of the land before I made any moves. I backtracked quietly through the shaded tombstones, taking and holding a long breath as they passed me on the path, Myra talking, saying something about Curtis being there at ten, then a young voice, the same one I'd spoken with on the phone, answered he'd only be a few minutes.

The sound of their footsteps passed, and I waited long enough to give them a good head start, then stepped back on the path and was sneaking down the twisting, cedar-lined hill in strategic retreat when I came upon her quite accidentally, sitting on a little marble bench, a Christmas wreath held to her chest, her eyes on the pointed toes of the cowboy boots she was absently tapping in the sand, her face blank, not in the old way, not dead, but merely tired, oddly disappointed, as if she knew what she was getting for Christmas and was not impressed.

I stopped as soon as I saw her and looked around for another side-track, but there was nowhere to go except back up to the graves where Clayton was, or forward, so I took a breath and said, "Myra?"

Her eyes were up in one stunned second, her face so white I thought she'd faint.

"Gabriel?" she whispered, and as soon as she said it, I remembered the one characteristic my brother and I were said to share: we had the same voice.

I said, quickly, "Damn, Myra, I'm sorry, I didn—"

She didn't let me finish, coming off that bench in one gathered spring and hitting me with an embrace of such force that if I hadn't been such an anchor, it would have sent both of us over backwards. I had already put in two hours worth of sincere crying that morning, so, for once, was able to keep a stiff upper lip, pressing my face to her hair, telling her it was all right.

"He's gone, he's gone—" she cried, with almost exhausting relief, as if she'd been patiently waiting all year long for someone who could properly commiserate with how much she'd lost when she lost her husband Michael.

"I know," I whispered back. "I know—" Over and over again. There was just nothing left to say. He was gone and we were left, and when her tears did not abate, I eased her back to the little bench and tried to calm her. "It's all right. Hush, Myra. It's all right," like quieting a frightened child.

She finally began to slacken off, drawing back and fishing a well-worn handkerchief from her pocket but continuing to clutch my hand, and I was the one who was relieved this time, at her forgiveness, and had a sudden need to apologize for that tornado of viciousness the last time we'd spoken.

"I was drunk," I explained, as she wiped her nose and looked at me out of those calm, deep eyes. "I'm an alcoholic."

It was a landmark confession, really, one of the first times I'd ever admitted to being an alcoholic when I was actually pursuing sobriety, but she couldn't have been expected to understand the significance of it, and only nodded slightly and even smiled a little when I added, "But I haven't had a drink in ten months. Well, nine really. Nine months and eighteen days."

"You're doing better than me," she murmured, dabbing the mascara under her eyes. "I'm back on meds. Will be till I die, Dr. Williams has anything to do with it."

I thought it kind she mention her own emotional shortcomings as I unveiled mine, and smiled as I said, "That's not the same, though."

She finished with her eyes and drew close to me again. "Mama thought so," she said pensively. "Thought I was a drug addict or something."

I had a flash of Cissie Catts outrage. "Damn, your mother was a *bitch*," I said, and she stirred uneasily at my side.

"Don't curse my mother, Gabriel. You always hated her, and you never even knew her."

I murmured an apology, not meaning a word of it, and we were quiet again, sitting close for the sheer animal warmth, the distant, hollow whirl of the mower somewhere below, charging the air with a faint, wafting scent of summer, and it was amazing really, how easily we stepped back in stride. For it'd been so long since I'd sat down and spoken with the real Myra Sims—not the skinny one—and here we were, in

immediate contact, me defending her, her telling me to hush, me taking
it back, but not meaning a word of it.

"Where've you been?" she asked, and I looked at her.

"New York. Didn't Michael tell you?"

"I mean, this year. What took so long? Your Mama's been worried
to death."

I was pleased my absence had been a cause for concern among the
ladies and lifted an eyebrow. "What about you? You been worried?"

She looked at me a moment, then a small smile began playing
around her mouth, "Oh, I knew you'd turn up. Michael said you would."
She plucked at her handkerchief. "I been pretty busy myself. Got
married last week."

The effect was so awful I felt it down to my toes, but she didn't
appear bothered at all, that mad, cruel smile still playing on her mouth.
"Married your cousin Randell. He come down for the funeral, and we hit
it off. He divorced Cynthia, took a job at Sanger—"

I was sitting there with ice water blood, thinking this woman was,
in spirit and in truth, schizophrenic. Worse than schizophrenic: a suc-
cubus from hell, the scourge of an otherwise pedestrian life   when she
pressed her face to my chest, and I realized she was laughing.

"I'm teasing, Gabriel. I'm teasing. You should see your face—
Gabriel?"

I tell you what, I didn't think it was too damn funny after all I'd
been through, and when Clayton came back, I was still a little wobbly,
not saying much, just standing and shaking his hand, telling him it was
nice to meet him.

When Myra left to put her wreath on the grave, I looked at him.
"Your cousin Randell been around here lately?"

"Who?" he asked, still sniffling.

"Randell Chaffee. Fat guy with black hair. Wife's named Cynthia."

He shook his head. "Not since the funeral. They were here for
that."

I nodded, still a little shaken, and when Myra returned, she shook her head at me. "Well, Gabriel? What's got into you? You used to tease me all the time."

"I must have lost my sense of humor," I murmured, but she just laughed, putting her arm through mine and walking me down the path, Clayton falling in step behind us, and when we got to her car at the bottom of the hill, I remembered I'd left mine on the other side.

"D'you want me to drive you around?" Myra asked. "I've got to take Clay home; him and Curtis are going fishing. You need to go see your Mama. She's got the Salvation Army out looking for you."

It seemed so strange that just as I was regaining them, we were having to part, and while I was still distant from Clayton, unsure of my footing and trying to seem like a regular uncle, I had an odd, bone-deep premonition that if I let Myra out of my sight, I'd never see her again and made some excuse or another to tag along with them.

"Do you need anything from your car?" she asked. "A suitcase?"

"No," I said, getting in the passenger seat. "All my stuff's in New York." We were pulling out of the gates when something else occurred to me. "Come to think of it, I might have left the cat in. Remind me to call my landlady when we get to the house."

"Gabriel—" Myra laughed, shaking her head.

Clayton finally spoke up from the back seat, "How long you staying?"

I couldn't tell by his tone if he had an opinion in the matter and looked at him in the rearview mirror. "I don't know. Depends, I guess."

He didn't ask what it depended on, but only nodded and kept his eyes on the town that was tinseled and lighted for Christmas, the stores open early, the parking lots already full of harassed mothers and trailing children.

I put my arm up on the back of Myra's seat so I could talk to him over my shoulder. "So where are you going fishing?" I asked.

His eyes were still on the town when he answered. "Dead Lakes," he said, then swung his face around in one smooth motion till he met my eyes. "Curtis has a boat."

That gesture, the pause before answering, then the full weight of his eyes, was so much like Michael that for a moment I could only blink, then say, quickly, "Oh, yeah, we used to go down there a lot. Daddy and Michael and I. Had to rent a boat."

The town was still twinkling and festive around us, but I felt a story begin to develop as I covered my unease. "One time, I guess I was eight or nine, Daddy took us down there a whole week." I smiled at the memory, suddenly comfortable, drawn into the past. "I mean, we never went anywhere, but Daddy got a week off, decided it was time we had a real *vacation*. Boy, we thought we were *special*."

I laughed aloud and saw that Clayton's face was very arrested, his eyes dark blue, the same color and texture his mother's had been over the pig wire fence on Magnolia Hill.

"Decided to go down to the Dead Lakes. Daddy rented a cabin, and hot? Was it hot? I bet it was a hundred and three in the shade, and the mosquitoes—there were scads of them. You could hold out your arm and count fifty, but there was nothing you could do. There weren't any air conditioners. Hell, I don't think the place had screens, just a dirt floor and a refrigerator and a sink, but we didn't care. Boy, we were living high, we were on *vacation*."

Clayton's face had lightened a little, and even Myra was smiling, for I was conjuring Michael for them, bringing him back from that cold grave.

"The first night we caught, I bet, forty pounds of fish. Something was running, I can't remember what. Maybe reds. Anyway, we filled up the freezer, then slept all day and went out the next night, and they were running again, but there was no place to put 'em. The freezer was full, there was nobody to give 'em to, so we had to throw 'em back, then go back to that hot cabin and try to sleep. Well, I was already foreseeing a week of horror, but Daddy knew I was a whiner and made me swear on the Bible I wouldn't say a word, not a word, so all I could do was scratch and pray for Friday, 'cause I knew we'd rented that cabin a whole damn week.

"Well it went on like that for two more days. I bet we were catching sixty pounds of fish a night, then taking them off the hook and pitching them back and trying to sleep in that hot cabin with the mosquitoes. I was about to lose my mind. So was Michael; he looked like he had the measles. But he was a fighter; he didn't say a word. Then about eleven o'clock one morning, it must have been Wednesday, Daddy sat up on the pallet all of a sudden and looked at his arm—" I stopped, laughing too hard to speak, for Daddy's bewildered face was so real to me as he sat there in his underwear and looked at the two dozen mosquitoes lighting on his arm. "And he said, 'Boys, if this is *vacation*, well they can shore *have it*. Pack up the truck, we're a-going home.'"

(Incidentally, this entailed a small revision on my part. What he really murmured was: "Shit on *this*"—one of the few times I ever remember my father using casual profanity; but anyway, the sentiment was the same.)

Both Myra and Clayton were laughing as we drove out Thomasville Road, Clayton's face suddenly young again, as if death had never touched him at all.

"And the heck of it was, we had to eat them stinking fish for a solid month. Mama was mad we come home early, said we'd lost money on the cabin, so we had to make it up in groceries."

I paused as we turned off the highway, looking for the house, beginning to see glimpses of it through the trees, still old and lazy and quietly symmetrical beneath the massive oaks, a truck towing a johnboat parked in the drive.

"Sorry we're late," Myra called, stopping to let Clayton out.

"Gabriel's here. Gabriel, do you know Curtis?"

She was making the introduction through the car window, but Curtis got out with good country manners to shake my hand, saying, "No, I don't b'lieve so."

He was young and thin, somehow very familiar, and I squinted at him. "Do I know your daddy?"

"Sure you do," Myra said. "Clyde Simmons. Curtis is his youngest." Then to Curtis, "Did Lori get that coat I left her at Cissie's?"

Curtis was making some reply when I realized Clayton was standing by the car window, looking at me. "You wanna go?" he asked. "There's plenty of room. Sim usually comes."

Myra halted her conversation with Curtis to answer for me. "No, baby, he's been driving all night. He needs to go to bed. You go on. He'll be here when you get back."

He left without argument, and I followed Myra through the front door and down the long, high hall with a feeling of imminent satisfaction. Clayton liked me, for one thing, and Myra had said something about the *bed* for another, and I looked around the sunroom that was narrower than I remembered, and infinitely more cluttered, the cold wood floor covered with bright rugs, the walls full of pictures and   paintings and dried flowers almost ceiling to floor.

"Where's Missy?" I asked, and Myra sat down on the couch, a portable phone in her hands.

"She went to Helen with the Chapins," she said. "And Simon's camping on St. Joseph's with some men from the church."

"What's this?" I asked, as she began punching in numbers. "Who're you calling?"

"Your mother," she said over the receiver. "I'm serious, Gabriel. She's been worried to death."

But she let me take the phone from her, and for a moment, that very real, very palpable relief seemed to wash over her as I pressed my mouth on hers, and it was so sweet for a moment that everything else faded, everything but the woman beneath me, until she pulled back.

"What are you doing?" she murmured, feeling the front of her blouse.

What I was doing was unbuttoning her shirt, a seemingly inevitable step in getting to the bed, but when she felt her bra, she shoved me away.

"I can't believe you, Gabriel!" she cried, standing and rebuttoning her shirt with angry little jerks of her hands. "D'you think you can just blow into town and hit the hay in half an hour?"

She seemed to be waiting for an answer, but it was hard to be articulate with the blood pounding in my head. "What about the bed? You told Clayton we were going to bed."

"I said *you* were going to bed. You look awful. I'm going to get your mother, who's been spending about half her social security check every month calling around Boston looking for you."

"I been in New York three years—"

"I don't care if you been in hell three years. I'm going over there to get her while you take a nap."

"A *nap?*" I cried, then I rubbed my face and tried to get a grip on myself. "Myra, Myra," I said, "settle down. Mama's fine. Here, sit."

She sat down, not on the couch, but across the rug on the edge of the coffee table, and I tried to be calm, rubbing my face, thinking it was time we got a few things straight.

"I love you, Myra," I said quietly. "I always loved you. I came back as soon as I could, to marry you. You know that, don't you?"

Her face softened a little at the sincerity in my voice, and she smiled. "I know that, Gabriel."

"Well, do you love me?" I was bold enough to ask, and she met my eyes levelly.

"You know I do."

I put my face in my hands a moment and tried to smile, but I couldn't help it, there was a scream in me and it had to come out. "Then why the *hell* aren't we in bed? I'm thirty-eight years old, too old to be putting up with any more of this *shit!*"

She was on her feet in an instant. "I don't care if you're a hundred and eight, you can act right or you can hit the door. Who d'you think you are, coming in here, acting this way?"

I told her I was *Gabriel William Catts* as I hit the door with a flourish, but when I got to the edge of the deck, I remembered I'd left my car at the cemetery, and it only made me madder, having to go back and beg a ride.

I hammered on the French door, yelling in her face when she answered it, "I left my sonofabitch car at the cemetery. Gimme a ride to town."

She had been crying, maybe—anyway, her eyes were red, but she wasn't giving an inch, snatching her purse off the couch and stomping out without a word.

The drive back to town was—how can I put it?—viciously silent, me muttering that *yes I knew why they lynched people around here, why all the men drank, it wasn't any mystery to me, boy*—till Myra told me to shut up.

But she was crying when she said it, feeling around in her purse for a Kleenex, and by the time we made the cemetery, I was the one who softened.

"Myra," I said, as she idled next to my car, waiting for me to get out. "Here. I'm sorry. I didn't mean to yell at you."

She wiped her face without a word, but when I took her hand, she didn't snatch it back, and I pressed forward gingerly. "It's just that, see, I love you so much and I've waited so long."

"I know," she said softly, and I smiled and kissed her little white hand.

"And listen, I'm an alcoholic. It's not easy for me to stay celibate and sober, too. I mean, I can handle one or the other, but the combination's killing me."

She only turned and looked at me on that, then took her hand back and wiped her nose and began feeling around in her purse. There was something very deliberate about the way she was going about it, as if she were searching for something to give me, say, a house key, or maybe a motel room key, but as I watched, she only retrieved a fancy leather wallet and fumbled with the change purse, taking out a handful of crumpled dollar bills.

Then, with a very narrow glint in her eye, she began flipping them into my lap, one at a time.

"Here's your liquor money," she said after the third dollar. "And here's your whore money," after the fifth. Then she snapped the wallet shut and gave me a brilliant smile. "Welcome home, *Gabriel William Catts*."

Then, before I could even scream, she kicked my door open and hissed, "Now you get the hell out of my car, you manipulating little piece of shit, before I throw you out."

And before I knew what happened, I was standing on the gravel drive watching the Mercedes' brakelights flash at the highway, right back where I'd started at six A.M.: alone, with no one to talk to, not even Michael, because after getting whipped like that, I was ashamed to face him.

Chapter

15

I stood there awhile on that field of bones, then got in the car, congratulating myself on keeping a good, tenure-track job and being lucky enough to get out of this thing before it was too late. All I needed to do now was go see Mama, maybe set her down with a map and explain the geography of the world above Atlanta, and leave a message for Michael's children, telling them I was there if they ever needed me. But that was all. No more contact with any of those Sims, not if I could help it, for I found I didn't possess the missionary patience my brother had in dealing with those red-headed pagans, not even the babygirl.

As I passed through town and began the slow incline to Magnolia Hill, I saw that nothing had very much changed on Lafayette, a few trees dead or fallen, a few houses boarded up, a few painted, and someone had pulled a doublewide onto a vacant lot at the corner, but that was all. Mama's house looked better than it had in years, with a shimmering new tin roof and spotless vinyl siding, Michael's contribution, no doubt, but the effect was still country, for the whole yard was draped fence to fence with her usual Christmas trimmings, chipped reindeer and a plastic manger, and when I knocked on the front door, I could see through the curtains the twinkle of a Christmas tree that had probably been up since Thanksgiving. It restored a feel of simple innocence to the cold, bright morning, the donkey and the manger and the babe in swaddling clothes, and I was suddenly glad I'd come and knocked again. But still, no one answered, and after the third try, I went around back to look for the spare key, and found Mama in her old rocker on the back porch, shelling pecans for Lane cakes, and for the first time in my life, I saw she was finally grown old. Her skin was no more wrinkled, her hair no whiter, but there was a feebleness about her as she picked at the hard shells, the barren look of a woman bereaved.

"Mama?" I called from the yard, and she looked up, startled.

Then after a moment, she said lightly, "Gabriel?"

I cried when I hugged her, for Myra's nastiness had primed my pump, but she was only happy, her hands tight on my shirt, trying to speak normally, as if there weren't, and never had been, any Gaps between us.

"Son, son, you look sa good. You're losing your hair, baby."

"Well, thanks a lot, Mama."

"No, no—it suits you, baby, it suits you."

She had to cook, couldn't be talked out of it, and after biscuits and tomato gravy and anything else she could pull from her cupboard was duly baked, fried, and consumed, the strain of the trip began to tell on me, and I took her advice to lie down.

"Right here, son. Here in your old bed. Simon says it sags in the middle, but I hate to get rid of it." She was blank a moment. "You boys was raised on it, hate to just throw it out, like it was trash or something."

So within an hour of my long-awaited second coming, I was tucked away in the bed of my youth, three decades and still sweating the same woman, and it was hard not to be bitter. I found myself rehashing the sad memory of my ill-received proposal (my *third*, in fact) and felt very sorry for myself, wondering what deep-seated neuroses had prompted Myra to throw whiskey money at an alcoholic. The whore part, now, that could be seen as possibly funny, but the liquor struck me as a very *Sims* kind of thing to do, and I again congratulated myself on being rid of her.

But I was too tired to dwell on it, and hadn't realized how exhausted I was until I woke to a cold winter morning, the smell of coffee in the air and the sound of a vaguely familiar voice in the living room that I finally made out as Jimmy Swaggart, railing on the television. For a moment the shock was too much; it was as if I'd descended in a time warp to the days when Sunday was the day of early rising and last-minute lesson studying and begging Mama to let me walk down early so I could sit on the steps with my friends.

"Aren't you going to church?" was the first thing she asked when I showed up at the breakfast table, wrapped in a quilt.

"I don't have any clothes."

"Well, wear them you had on yesterday. They'll be fine. Nobody dresses for church like they used to. Clay wears *tennis* shoes."

"No—" I backed out gently, not feeling up to facing a church full of Baptists. "I'm still tired, that drive—"

"Myra'll be there," she said slyly, her eyes on her coffee, but I was vague, standing and wrapping up tighter in the quilt, wondering why it got so cold in Florida, for the old frame house provided all the insulation of a wet sheet.

"That's all right."

There was a line between her eyes when she asked, "Well don'tchu wanna see her?"

I just shrugged. "Listen, Mama, I'm going back to bed. It's freezing. Can we turn up the heat?"

She said she would, but the line between her eyes never eased, and I knew I was in for an interrogation sometime in the foreseeable future, but retreated back to the bed, feeling warm and guilty at the crack of the screen on the back door when she left. When I was a child, the only divinely-ordained excuse for missing church was an actual fever, and whenever the thermometer cooperated, Mama would set me up with a TV tray filled with medicine and Coke, along with many instructions to lie still and rest. I'd manage a weak nod of assent and wait till they were safely down the road, then pull out a book and read, while all around me Magnolia Hill emptied out, leaving the homes beneath the old oaks calm and peaceful, gradually filling with the rich smell of roasts and hams, slowly baking for Sunday dinner.

After three years in the city, I could almost taste the calm, and I put aside my grievance with Myra to lay there and savor it and wonder if it was about time I was coming home. Mama wouldn't be around forever, and I could live here weekends and teach somewhere close by, maybe Troy or FSU or Auburn. Somewhere within commuting distance, I thought, and after a moment, I realized I was reconstructing my youth, and if I succeeded, I'd be restoring 1963, living on Magnolia Hill with Mama, spending my days in a classroom, agonizing over Myra in my spare time.

I laughed at the idea, not really very shocked at my digression, and when I heard the low hum of a diesel engine in the drive, I knew who it was before she hit the porch. The front door opened with a bang, and she came straight in the bedroom without a knock, all dressed up for church with her hair curled and sprayed in place, her very beautiful, artfully made-up face harassed as she stalked toward the bed.

I didn't know what was going on, but her expression was far from pleasant, and I pulled the quilt to my chin, "Myra? What the—"

"The peepbox," she snapped, dropping to her hands and knees and putting her head under the bed. "Cissie forgot it."

For a moment I just looked at her tail poked into the air about a foot from the bed. Then I started laughing.

She straightened up and looked at me very narrowly. "Don't you start that crap with me again—" she began, but I only shook my head.

"Myra, don't you see what's going on here? Mama—" I laughed harder, "—she's fixing us up here. She knows I'm still in bed, so she turns up the heat and sends you over here dressed for the kill. I tell you what, if that woman'd been in the Pentagon, Vietnam would be the fifty-first state."

She only looked at me a moment, then ducked back under the bed, and after a little rooting, began tossing brightly papered shoeboxes on the bed.

"What do you call these?" she asked, and my smile vanished, disappointed in Mama, thinking she had indeed grown old.

"'Look for *Creation*,' she told me. 'The primary class is waiting.'"

I sighed and held the eyeholes to the light, finding all the old standards that had been rattling around the house since Daddy made them in the early fifties: *David and Goliath, Zacchaeus, Daniel in the Lion's Den*, but no *Creation*, and they were beginning to pile up on me when I finally peeped in on Adam and Eve, standing there naked in the garden, modestly shielded by a lion and a palm frond.

"Here you go," I said, and while she stuffed the other boxes back under the bed, I leaned against the headboard, the peep-box still to my eye. "You ever notice how there's always a lion standing there in front of Adam? And that very convenient limb hanging there in front of Eve's—"

She jerked the box out of my hand. "You ever noticed you need therapy?" she snapped, but I only laughed at her.

"I don't know why. If they were buck naked it'd only be scriptural. Hey, it'd increase Sunday School attendance by a hundred percent. Maybe you should give it a try."

She didn't bother to reply, only coming to her feet and heading for the door, but after a cursory peep in the box, she came to a dead halt.

"This ain't *Creation*," she said in disgust. "This is *Adam and Eve*."

"That *is Creation*."

"It is *not*," she said and went back to the floor, snatching out boxes. "*Creation*'s the black one with the moon and star cut-outs."

She ignored me completely this time, holding each box to the light, and when they were scattered all around her, *Genesis* to *The Revelation of St. John the Divine*, she sat back on her heels and murmured a barely audible "shoot," then went to the living room. After a moment, I could hear her, speaking quickly into the phone. "Brother Dorsey? Listen, could you run down and ask Cissie where the *Creation* peep-box is? Tell her it ain't under the bed."

There was a pause of about a minute, and when I got to the living room door, still wrapped in my quilt, she was sitting there in Mama's old easy chair, one hand holding the phone, the other rubbing her eyes. "Really?" she said, "Oh. Well, tell her I said thanks. Thanks a lot."

She hung up, but kept rubbing her eyes.

"What?"

"It seems," she said, "that Sister Catts remembered that she'd lost the *Creation* peep-box the *minute* I left the parking lot." She dropped her hand and looked at me. "However, she sent word not to worry, that she had everything under control, and Brother Sloan wasn't preaching, some missonary was, so if I was detained, everyone would understand."

My faith in my mother was instantly restored, and I laughed aloud. "See, see? You were supposed to find me in bed and wake me up and we'll be dressed again by the time Mama gets back, wrestling with guilt, promising it'll never happen again."

"You're serious, aren't you?"

I almost shouted. "Of course I'm serious! It'll make up for the time she set you up with Michael. Oh come on, Myra, quit being so damn stubborn. We still got time, hours—"

But she only looked at me. "Has anyone ever told you your mind's not right?" she asked. I finally saw that she wasn't budging an inch and collapsed on the couch, feeling a headache coming on.

"My mind's fine," I told her. "It's my liver and my prostate that's got me worried."

"Oh," she said, and kicked off her shoes, these high-heeled snakeskin pumps that I would estimate cost a week's salary.

I opened an eye and looked at her. "That lithium hasn't made you frigid or anything, has it?"

She stood up and began walking around the room in her stocking feet, her arms folded against the cold. "No, why? Did the liquor make you impotent?"

I raised up on my elbows. "I tell you *what*, Myra. Alcoholism is nothing for you to be making these smart-assed jokes about."

She turned and looked at me. "And manic-depression is?"

I faced her off a moment, then lay back down and closed my eyes. "I thought you were schizophrenic."

"I've been upgraded," she said. "PTSD. With manic components."

"What the hell is that?" I murmured.

She answered wryly, "*Bad nerves.*"

Then she strolled into the bedroom, and I heard the blinds being pulled, then no other sound for a long time. I finally grew curious enough to investigate and found her standing at the side window, looking out at her childhood home that stood desolate in the cold December morning, almost consumed by the kudzu, the roof caved in, orange stickers from the health department plastered on the doors and windows, pronouncing the place condemned. Suddenly, I was ashamed of harassing her, remembering Michael's words the night I learned she was pregnant: "—and a certain kind a man, and they hit on her, they *hit*—"

"I'm sorry, Myra," I said, sitting on the foot of the bed.

She glanced at me curiously. "For this?" she asked, with a nod at the house.

I tapped my chest. "For this."

"Oh," she said, then, after a moment, she shrugged. "It's all right. I'm getting used to it. I tell you what, I've heard more lines this past year than I did when I was sixteen."

"From who?" I asked, suddenly outraged, and that small smile began playing around her mouth again.

"Oh, men I been seeing."

"You been seeing *men*?" I shouted.

She looked at me. "What do you think I been seeing? Dogs?"

"Well, that's just wonderful: Michael's lying dead in the grave, and I'm sweating it out in New York, puking Antabuse, while you're down here living it up with the rednecks!"

She didn't seem too moved by my outburst, only looking at me. "Well, what was I supposed to do? You left the funeral in a huff, so drunk you couldn't *walk*—"

"I was *not*," I snapped. "I drove all the way to the airport. I was perfectly fine." I jerked at the quilt. "Who've you been seeing, anyway? That idiot Randell?"

"Good Lord, Gabriel, forget poor Randell. He weighs about three hundred pounds, has a wife and two grandchildren—"

"Then who?" I insisted.

She was vague. "Oh, just men I know. Mostly the new associate pastor, Carlym Folger. He's a nice man, Gabriel. The children love him. But he's only thirty-one—"

"Thirty-one?" I cried, then something else occurred to me, and I really howled. "And he's been giving you a line? A preacher? *Damn*, I hate these hicks. They always got one hand on the Bible, the other on their fly—"

She only laughed. "Gabriel Catts, you are the most outrageous hypocrite I've ever met in my life—"

"Hey, I'm Espiscopalian. We can do these things, we're allowed."

"Yeah," she smirked, "I bet."

I lay back on the bed crossways, closing my eyes, feeling a definite headache coming on at the idea of this unforeseen competition, while Myra continued easily. "Yeah, ever since Michael's obit hit the papers, they been calling, all kinds of men, all kinds of lines. They love me, love my red hair, love my children, love my—how do they put it? My *strong convictions*." She lay crossways beside me on the bed. "Love my *Mercedes*."

I opened an eye and looked at her. "Hey, don't look at me. I drive a Volvo. Sixty thousand miles and new tires. I ain't hurting."

She threw back her head then in the high arch I remembered and laughed and laughed. "Oh, I do love you, Gabriel. I do, I do. Maybe Michael was right. He said to wait, to give it a chance."

"Did he really?" I asked, and she rolled on her side and pressed up against me just like she used to do in the good old days in the servant's quarter, except back then she was usually naked, and today she was still in her coat, talking with that friendly confidence, her fingertips absently rubbing my chest.

"Yes, he did. I don't think he liked the idea of some stranger stepping in—"

"Myra, honey," I said, interrupting her, "if you aren't planning on being naked here in the next few minutes," I pointed at her fingertips, "don't be doing this."

"Oh," she said, and rolled to her back, "sorry."

After a moment, she sat up and pulled her coat around her, and in a much smaller voice, "I'm really not just being a tease here, Gabriel. I mean, I am a Christian, and I do have some convictions that it's the right thing." She shrugged. "Anyway, Missy's almost fifteen. What am I supposed to tell her? That it's all right for me, but not her?"

"You're a grown woman. She's a child—" I began, but she waved me away.

"Michael waited. So can you."

It wasn't that I was so hot to hit on her anymore, but simply that her argument was flawed, and I raised up on my elbows. "You were a seventeen-year-old Baptist virgin with Michael—of course he waited. We're adults; this is different."

"You're forgetting your ancient history," she said, standing and going to the window. "I was seventeen-year-old damaged goods. I'd been treated for syphilis twice when Michael met me." She paused to let the horror of that remark sink in, then finished. "And he respected my wishes, and so can you." She turned and looked at me. "I think."

The rotting old house loomed behind her and I sighed. "Of course I can."

She smiled very brilliantly then and held out both hands. "Well, we don't have to wait long. What's to stop us? I'll just have to call the children, and you'll have to go see Peter, our lawyer. Michael left everything all tied up. You'll have to talk to him. He'll have to explain—"

So Mama came home at *two* with some line about having been detained by Brother Sloan, and, finding us making wedding plans over the kitchen table, had a very smug look on her face, like Sherman telegraphing Lincoln from Savannah. Myra, of course, was still smiling the smile of the unvanquished, and I was left to chew my nails and wonder if this might not be the shape of things to come, but I had a damn-the-torpedoes fatality about the whole thing, and insisted we get the details out of the way before I lost my nerve. By evening I'd made arrangements with my landlord over my stuff (including the cat), and been tentatively released from my contract at NYU by my very sympathetic dean, a Jewish mama's boy himself, who understood perfectly my need to relocate when I described the horrid conditions I'd found my mother living in ("—rats everywhere, no heat. Boy, when I see my sister—").

Myra easily got in touch with Missy in Georgia and found her blessedly enthusiastic, only wanting to be a bridesmaid and wear an aqua dress and nothing more. Clayton, who'd come home from church with Mama, was equally accepting, only looking at me levelly out of his Michael Catts eyes, but not in an unfriendly manner, not the way I'd feared a child who'd once screamed when his mother left the room might react.

"Mama's last name will still be Catts" was his only observation.

So Simon, who was being wooed by the thirty-one-year-old preacher, was the last hurdle, but when he came home three days before Christmas, covered with red bug bites and hoarse from camping in the cold, he took this incredible twist to his seventeen-year-old world with true Simon Catts calm, saying congratulations in a barely audible rasp and shaking my hand.

"I remember you," he managed to creak out. "You taught me how to swan dive."

I hoped to God it was the only thing he remembered from the summer of '74, but was too nervous to worry it, for in the meanwhile, I'd gone to see the lawyer and found out why Myra's red hair was no longer her primary asset.

"Two hundred and fifty thousand dollars?" I repeated. "Michael left me two hundred fifty thousand dollars?"

"Well, it's not free capital, is the point, Mr. Catts," he said, showing me where to sign.

But I kept repeating, "A quarter of a *million* dollars?"

He was very patient, explaining taxes and investment strategies and withdrawal penalties, but I was miles out of my depth, and when he pulled out a prenuptial agreement, full of fascinating legal terms like abandonment and forfeiture, I was hesitant.

"It's not like I'm a con artist or something," I said. Then after a few more paragraphs: "Alcoholism is a disease."

The lawyer was tactful. "Of course it is, Mr. Catts, but Michael—Michael," he sighed, "was a detail man."

So I signed and didn't ask any more questions, figuring if Michael could afford to leave me and Candace a quarter of a million apiece, I probably didn't want to know how much Myra was worth, lest it strike me impotent for life. But when I left the lawyer and drove over to her house to get her approval for the suit I'd bought for the wedding, I began to entertain real doubts about this thing. I mean, it was clear that no one around here lived on Magnolia Hill anymore, and Myra, who'd always been my superior in many abstract, spiritual kinds of ways, was now incredibly rich. For some reason, it just didn't sit well with me, and that prenuptial thing—it gave the whole marriage a nasty business taint, making me wonder if all this talk of love and commitment was merely a clever way to die without paying taxes.

I was still shaking my head about it when I knocked on the French doors with the suit in my hand, and as soon as I saw her, it was suddenly all right again. She was rich, she was beautiful, she might have even grown into a little Sims-like nastiness, but she was still just Myra, her hair unbrushed at ten in the morning, barefoot in December, and when she opened the door for me, I kissed her neck, murmuring, "Here's the suit. I might have to take it back. I just talked to Peter and now that I'm a partial millionaire, I'm thinking about finding me a nice *young* wife, one without all those stretch marks and things—"

She only pulled away and smiled at me, and I finished, "—one that'll be deathly faithful in marriage, but a little slack on this prenuptial stuff—"

As soon as I said it, I realized Clayton was standing just around the corner, drinking milk from the jug at the refrigerator, grinning as if he'd heard everything.

"Hey, you're about two years too late," he said, wiping his mouth. "Lori's done taken."

I thought it was the funniest thing I'd heard in a long time, but Myra was not amused and sent Clayton to his room and me back to Mama's with such awe-inspiring dominance that all my old fears resurfaced. I mean, this wasn't sweet little Myra Sims anymore. This was a rich, red-headed Baptist widow, and by evening, I was entertaining so many doubts that Mama began to smell defeat and sought to close ranks by describing in great detail the sleazy lingerie Lori and Candace were giving Myra as a joke.

"They say they're underwear," she said, "but they don't look like underwear to me."

So I was hooked, scared but hooked, having to eat Tagamet the morning of the wedding, wishing to God I hadn't gone bad on whiskey so I could enjoy the comfort of one quick shot. Then, to top it off, Brother Sloan came down with the flu, and Myra's old buddy Brother Folger—a six-foot-four Knute Rockne type, with a butch haircut and a tight, mean face—had to perform the ceremony.

It was fairly obvious he was madder than hell about it, but Myra gave too much money to the church for anyone to try to tell her what to do, and the most he could do was glare at me and bite off his words ("*Dearly* be*lo*ved, we are *ga*thered here to *jo*in th*is ma*n and *wo*man in *ho*ly *ma*trimony—") with a tight, angry smile that left me feeling pretty shriveled, hoping that with my new-found wealth I could somehow persuade the Southern Baptist Convention to transfer his call to the mission field in the not-too-distant future.

Aside from that, everything else went pretty well, and though Myra and I were perfectly content to go home afterwards, Candace and Lori insisted we go on some sort of honeymoon. So we farmed the children out and drove down to the Redneck Riveria on Panama City Beach and booked the honeymoon suite of an off-name motel which turned out to be a huge maroon room with no furniture at all other than a king-size bed with a heart-shaped headboard.

Myra, who had been predicting something of the sort when I told her the price (twenty-six dollars double occupancy), laughed when I opened the door, saying, "Now, this is what I call a *honeymoon suite*."

She went out on the small balcony, letting in a breath of clean December air, while I brought in the suitcases and surveyed the stark room with more than a little unease, for the thing which I feared most was rapidly coming upon me, and when Myra came back inside, I was lying on the bed, rubbing my eyes.

"Myra, honey, I hate to have to tell you this, but after a week of repression and an hour's worth of venomous stares from Knute Rockne, I'm not at all sure I'm gonna be able to do this magnificent bed justice."

She just smiled and lay down beside me, her hands on my face, and I was prepared for some hideous remark about how whiskey had done this to me, but she was kind.

"It'll pass," she said, as if she'd seen this kind of thing before.

I opened an eye. "Michael ever impotent?"

She looked at me with tolerant annoyance, "Michael? *Never*," and began laughing, but I rolled away.

"You git away from me—" I said, but she slapped me playfully on the tail.

"Here. I've come on this trip prepared. You haven't seen my sleazewear yet."

I ignored her, lying with my face on the pillow, wondering why these things always had to happen to me, while she rummaged around in her suitcase, laying out a handful of odd pieces of black spandex and ribbon and feathers.

"I can't figure these things out," she said. "Me and Missy tried all morning." She held one of them up. "Is this the top or the bottom?"

"That's a G-string, you hick."

She looked at me, "Well, what does that mean?"

"It means it's the bottom."

"Oh." She looked at it a moment. "Well, what are the feathers and the whistle for?"

"Don't ask me," I said, burrowing back into the pillow. "I'm just a poor, fat, over-educated latent homosexual who can't even get it up on his wedding night. Call Knute, he probably knows."

"Idiot," she said, but with affection, then went to the bathroom, and after a moment, her voice drifted out. "I tell you what, my butt isn't what it was ten years ago."

Then she started laughing, and I sat up. "Come on," I said. "Let's see."

"No. I look like an idiot. Who wears this kind of stuff?"

"Please?"

"I look like a circus horse."

"Oh, Myra, come on—"

"You'll laugh."

"I will *not*." Then in a smaller voice, "Please?"

And of course it did the trick. I guess I'd gotten into such a humiliation mode that I could only be aroused by groveling and begging, but who was I to argue? It worked. It more than worked. It was so sweet I didn't want to leave the room, even for meals, and by the next afternoon, Myra was whining.

"I didn't eat anything but breakfast yesterday. There's a restaurant in the lobby. We'll come right back—"

"No, listen, baby, I'll go get something from the machines, some Cheetos—"

"I don't want Cheetos," she said. "I want food. I'm starving to death."

But she finally agreed to order pizza, and I was able to keep her to myself two whole days, and when we left that ugly maroon carpet and that hideous bed, I felt like I was abandoning a beloved child. And in the meanwhile, a few misconceptions had been cleared up, and I had a better understanding of not only Myra, but of my brother Michael as well.

For one thing, I understood his phrasing when he remarked that Myra would *lie still* when he wanted her to. At the time, I thought it was factory slang for copulation, but after a few nights with a sane Myra, I knew why she'd made Michael take her out to the river when she decided the walls on Magnolia Hill were too thin because, let me tell you, she did about everything *but* lie still. I mean, till I got used to it, it just beat all I'd ever seen. It wasn't that she'd fight against me or dominate the act, but she sure enjoyed herself, and by God, laughed more in the act of sex than any woman I'd ever heard of. And while the blank, smiling Myra of 1974 who gave in with such easy passivity had never struck me as abnormal, it was a far cry from this woman who talked and laughed the whole time without missing a beat.

The more I considered it, the more I marveled that Myra could enjoy sex at all, much less with such abandon, for it was on our honeymoon that she commented on, for the first and last time, any aspect of her physical relationship with Michael. It came in the form of an offhand, late-night remark that this honeymoon was better than her first one, but it hadn't been Michael's fault.

"I was just scared to death. I don't mean shy, red-cheeked scared. I mean crying, puking, calling-for-my-Mama scared."

It was dark in the room when she said it, the sound of the waves hitting the beach barely audible through the open window, and her voice picked up an echo of their mournful sweep.

"I just didn't want him to touch me. I mean, I loved him, I wanted to marry him, I just couldn't stand him to touch me. I thought it'd ruin it, ruin everything. I cried the whole wedding, and everybody thought

I was so sweet, the nervous little bride, but listen, there wasn't nothing sweet about it. It was sheer disgust." She paused a moment, then sighed. "And poor Michael, we only had two days, then right back to Sanger he went."

I could feel something wet on my chest and knew she was crying, but that was all she offered, for she kept her relationship with Michael very private and never told me how long it took him, how many nights of patience, how many years of relentless faith, to get her to the place she was now, where sex was reclaimed from the voiceless abyss of incest and restored at last to a talking, kissing, laughing, natural act of love.

Chapter

16

So the deed was done, the prenuptials signed, the post-nuptials begun, and it would be convenient to Gap the rest of my life to my death and chronicle how heartbroken Myra was, how she wept, but I am a historian by trade and feel a certain obligation to fill you in on the small matter of a few years' worth of daily living in between.

I suppose if I had one ounce of decency, I'd give the do-gooders of the world a little satisfaction by admitting I wasn't as thrilled with my wife or my new life as I thought I'd be; that the rats of self-doubt, of boredom and ill-ease gnawed me in the heart of the night, and I secretly longed for freedom from the very thing I had so long pursued, for such is the nature of man. However, I believe I've not only mentioned, but by now have succinctly documented my profound lack of the most common shreds of human decency, and with all honesty and shamelessness must confess that—what can I say?—it was fun.

I loved my life, I loved my wife, and most conveniently, I loved her children: Sim, who reminded me not as much of Michael as Daddy,

struggling with a dominant idealism and a Cissie Catts recessive pragmatism; Missy, a sane Ira Sims, whose only concern in life was her orange
hair and freckles, both considered a curse by local standards of female
beauty and a considerable thorn in her fifteen-year-old flesh, until I had a
stroke of genius and gave her all the Anne of Green Gables books for her
birthday and turned it around a little, so she had some hopes of growing
to be a handsome auburn-haired woman.

And then there was Clayton, little Clayton, who had to be kin to me
in some form or fashion, for we were so very much alike. Except that he
was thinner, his hair darker and not so cowlicked, he could have been
my double at age twelve: lazy, easy-going, only contrary when annoyed,
then lapsing into such a biting sarcasm that I could not punish him,
but like Mama, only go to the bathroom and put my face in a towel and
laugh, which was just as well, for Myra would have let me take a straight
razor to her before she'd have let any stepfather, even a blood-related
one, lay a hand on her children. I'd seen the writing on the wall pretty
early on and knew that no man would ever be as dear to her as the children she'd taken such risk to bear. Not me, not Knute, not even Michael.
It was just not her nature, and I knew instinctively that if the grim reaper
ever showed his face at our door and demanded a soul, she'd send me
downstairs with a kiss and a prayer and that would be the end of that.

Our first colossal battles were in this department, one over Missy's
shoes for the Sweetheart Banquet at Welcome, one over what Myra considered my corruption of Clayton's morals. Both occurred within two
days of each other, and for a while there I was hanging on by the skin
of my teeth, certain that by Easter my marriage would be nothing more
than a cause for head-shaking among my fellow Baptists.

Come to think of it, that was the first skirmish after all. Not Missy
and her ninety-six-dollar magneta-blue pumps, or Clay and *Hearts
and Minds*, but my presence (or absence, as it were) at Welcome
Baptist Church. It happened on my first Sunday back, five days into the
marriage, when everything was still looking pretty sweet, and I was fore-

seeing a life of uninterrupted bliss in my dear brother Michael's house. I was even toying with the idea of finishing the book I'd left a dozen years before, that Michael had never thrown away, never even bothered to take off the walls of the servant's quarters, the maps still hanging there in diffident silence, mildewed and curled and mostly pinless, but still intact.

With the rest of the week given over to adjustments like learning the furniture business at the hands of Sam McRae (I found myself chairman of the board, a courtesy title, I am sure, but I wanted to do it justice if I could), I decided Sunday mornings would be the perfect time to set aside for the Cause and was upstairs early that morning, painstakingly rearranging pins in Sharpsburg when Myra came to the door, dressed except for her shoes, her hair in hot rollers.

"Gabriel?" she said. "It's nine-fifteen. You better get a move on. We don't live on Magnolia Hill anymore. We live ten miles out."

I looked at her. "You need me to drive you in?"

She returned my look. "No, I don't need you to drive me in. Come on, I've got your suit laid out. Where're your shoes?"

It finally dawned on me that she was planning to fit me back into the family pew at Welcome, and with a lifetime of Sundays at stake, I sat her down on the narrow bed (same one, incidentally; sheets may have been the same for all I know) and tried to be reasonable.

"Sunday mornings are the only time I have for my book, and there's a good market for it now, a lot of interest in reenactments. I need to strike while the iron is hot—"

"You can borrow Sim's if you can't find yours—"

"No, listen, honey," I said, still maintaining my patience, "I'm Espiscopalian. The pants to that suit are too big. Brother Folger hates me—"

"I took the pants up last night," she said, standing, and I pulled her back down.

"Myra, listen. I attended Welcome Baptist three times a week the first seventeen years of my life. I've been saved, I've been baptised, I've been rededicated every time they preached hell. I know every hymn by heart, I can quote more of the King James than Jerry Falwell, and I will gladly give whatever percentage is the going rate in tithes, up to and not exceeding ten percent. Okey-dokey?"

She went to the door. "I can't find your socks, either. They must be in the shoes."

When she was gone, I decided my best defense was no defense and went back to Sharpsburg a few more minutes, till Clayton came in all dressed up, his hair slicked back with water.

"Mama says to come on, We're all ready."

"I'm not going, son," I said. (This was, incidentally, another courtesy title. I was finally to the age where I could *son* any male under twenty, and *boy* any white man—or any black man if I didn't mind losing a few teeth.)

He looked at me out of his Michael Catts eyes. "Are you saved?"

I sighed and repeated my defense and when I was finished, he said, "Oh."

Then he went back downstairs, and I thought I'd have another round with Myra, but with great relief, heard them drive away, leaving me to recreate Sharpsburg with only a few adjustments, then wander back to the house around twelve to see what was on for dinner. What I found was a cold kitchen and an even colder oven, and I wondered what kind of Baptists these people were, going to church without a roast in the pot?

But there was nothing for it, the house was empty, the television full of rattling fundamentalists, so I occupied myself as best I could, returning to bed with the *Democrat*, my eyes going back to the clock every few minutes, and being relieved when twelve-thirty finally rolled around.

By two I was sweating, by three, calling the highway patrol, and

I was riffling through the desk, looking for the Mercedes registration number, when I heard the key in the back door. With lightning speed, I ran back upstairs and hit the bed, so when Myra came in, she found me yawning over Safire, lifting my face for her kiss, asking how the service went.

"Fine. Brother Sloan preached," she said, talking as she undressed. "He's getting old, lost his place a few times, bless his heart. Carlym really needs to go on full-time."

She was standing there in a black bra and matching panties when she said it, and I suddenly understood we were at war here and turned back to the paper, asking casually, "Where're the kids?"

"Sim's at Keith's, Missy went to Dothan with Joanna, Clay's with Cissie. He always goes home with her on Sundays. They watch wrestling together." She hung up her dress and crawled in her side of the bed. "I take a nap."

"So y'all ate at Mama's?" I asked, skimming Buckley.

She yawned. "No. Not there. Took her to the Steakhouse. Go there every week with a few of the old folks. They never get out, and Clayton loves to hear them talk. It's just something we do on Sundays."

"Just you and Clay and Mama?" I ventured.

She rolled over on her side, "Yeah. And a few others."

As soon as she said *others*, I got the picture right away: the happy family at the Steakhouse, Clayton and the old folks and the church's richest widow, there with the young preacher, him holding her chair, complimenting her son, pouring her seconds from the tea pitcher.

"What others?" I asked.

She murmured, "Brother and Sister Sloan. Candace and Ed, sometimes. Carlym. Just the usual."

That was all she said, curling up and sleeping the sleep of the just, while I lay beside her, stir-crazy from being inside all day, hungry from missing dinner, and furious Knute was turning my flank. I knew instinctively that if there was one phenomenon on earth that could send me back to New York with my tail between my legs in abject forfeiture, it was the slick-talking preacher with his Pauline interpretations and cunning little scriptural directives ("Be ye not unequally yoked with an unbeliever—").

With nothing better to do, I went downstairs and ate a bologna sandwich, feeling very sorry for myself, then rejoined my wife in bed, watching her sleep, thinking she was far from finished. Her skin was very white against the sheets, with tiny lines around the corner of her eyes, smile lines, I guess they were called, her hair still thick and coarse, coming out of its stiff spray to spiral down against her cheek, a faint breath of the shy young bride whose downcast eyes had once driven me insane. After a while, she rolled over to her back so that the top of her bra showed, perfectly invisible black mesh—not the kind they recommended at Bob Jones, I could grant you that—and I sighed, knowing I was beaten without a single word, not a single volley fired.

When she saw me getting dressed for the evening service, Myra asked, "Are you coming?"

"Yes," I said, knotting my tie.

She looked at me, "Why?"

"Because I'm whipped, that's why."

She was confident enough to be generous, "You don't have to. Nobody's putting a gun to your head."

I made no reply, thinking that anyone who owned a factory and a Mercedes and a dresser full of black bras and matching panties didn't have to bother with anything as messy as guns, but held my peace and suffered through a fairly sorry sermon by Knute that took the better part of an hour—an hour in which I counted three significantly lustful looks thrown in my wife's direction, and that night in bed, I recommended we all convert to Catholicism.

"To *what*?"

"Catholicism. It's the last bastion of true Christianity in Western civilization. I mean, Protestantism is weeny, it's watered down, it's been intermingled with lesser beliefs."

"What lesser beliefs?"

"The charismatics. Calvinism. Not to mention the sleazeball evangelical circuit. I mean, really, Myra, anything goes in the Baptist Church anymore. Look at Jimmy Swaggart."

"But he's not Baptist," she began. "He's—"

"Same difference," I said, "Protestantism. It creaks at the seams. In ten years they'll be bleeding chickens on the altar."

Myra was looking at me with the beginnings of concern on her face, and I went in for the kill. "I mean, if you want to raise Sim and Missy in that decay, well that's fine, but Clayton needs to be somewhere they really believe. You know, hold fast to the teachings of Christ. Not swayed by societal mores."

For a moment there I had her in the palm of my hand, but in the heat of victory, I overstepped my bounds. "I mean, look at Welcome. Unashamed racists, cheat on their taxes, run around, the divorce rate is the national average, if not higher—" I chanced a look to see if she was still with me.

She was smiling. "Gabriel, you idiot," she said and turned over. "You had me going there for a minute. *Catholicism*."

I tried to salvage it. "No, no, listen. They have a centralized government. They keep a balance between the spirit and the letter of the law. They let the alcoholics meet in their basement—"

"They don't allow divorce," she inserted with a laugh.

I rolled her to her back. "And what's wrong with that? Read Matthew. Read Mark."

"I'm not arguing," she said, but it wasn't good enough.

"No, you're not arguing, but you're running around with a preacher, taking him out to dinner while your husband starves—"

"While my husband *pouts*."

"I was not. I was reading the paper. But I tell you one thing, I don't think it's too damn funny the way you're doing it right in front of the children."

This was enough to get her to roll to her elbow and look at me levelly. "I've been going out to dinner with Cissie and Clay and the others for years, and your presence or your absence isn't going to stop me from having a perfectly innocent—"

"Innocent, my ass," I snapped, and overrode her by simple volume. "Does he or does he not pull out your chair, pour your tea, ingratiate himself to Clayton?"

She answered patiently. "The waitress pours my tea, Carlym and Clayton are friends, yes, and he does pull out my chair, as he does for your mother and all the other ladies—"

"But I bet he doesn't enjoy looking down Mama's dress half as much as he does yours," I inserted, and her patience finally began to show a little strain.

"Gabriel, honey," she said, "if I was you, I'd spare myself the agony of applying my own lack of sexual maturity to every other man I met."

She had no more than gotten the words *lack of sexual* out of her mouth before I was kicking the covers off the bed, taking my pillow with me, and as I went through the door, I fired my last volley, a real killer, but what can I say? I was getting my tail whipped. "Yeah, Myra, well if I was you, I'd remember a little more of my ancient history, and how the last time you indulged in a little casual adultery, you not only wound up pregnant, but *catatonic*."

There was a sound at my back as if she'd thrown something, a pillow (or maybe the clock), and I found myself at the top of the stairs, faced with the age-old dilemma of where to sleep. The living room couch was the logical, time-honored choice, but it was way downstairs, so I crept into Clayton's room and crawled into the lower bunk of his bed.

He must have felt the movement, for he hung his face over the edge of the top bunk, a few inches above me.

"Gabe?" he whispered.

I sighed. "Yes."

He was regarding me very solemnly. "You and Mama have a fight?"

I sighed even louder, but what could I say? "Yes. You heard?"

"No." His head disappeared, but his voice was still close. "Daddy used to sleep in here when they'd fight."

I suddenly found myself smiling in the darkness. "Did he really?"

"Yeah," he yawned. "But he never made it till morning. Bed'd be empty when I woke up."

Well, that was Michael all over, but this was Gabe, and I settled in for a long siege. When my eyes adjusted to the light, I saw that the walls were covered with posters of Sylvester Stallone, whom I remembered from a boxing movie I'd seen in Indiana.

"You like Rocky?" I asked.

"Who?"

"Rocky." I pointed to one of the posters.

His voice was a tiny bit incredulous. "You mean Rambo? Ain't you ever heard a Rambo?"

"Oh. Yeah. Rambo. Yeah, I heard of him." However, I didn't tell him what I'd heard and tried to be agreeable. "They made a lot of them, didn't they? Two or three?"

"Three," he said. "They're filming the fourth one right now. In Israel."

"Oh."

After a few moments, he offered, "I like Vietnam."

It was a strange way to put it, *I like Vietnam*. I mean, what was there to like? It was like saying: I like Charles Manson. I enjoy newsreels of Buchenwald. I have a collection of human skulls.

His face was suddenly upside down again, watching me. "Were you there? Uncle Ira was."

Well, it was just the kind of war you'd expect Ira Sims to be involved in, and I shook my head. "Educational deferment."

"Oh," he said and disappeared again.

I had the feeling I was losing points here, and to Ira Sims of all people, and was irked enough to flex my historical muscles a little, throwing out bits and pieces of detail I remembered, not from the history books, but from the headlines.

He took it up with passion, getting very excited, stopping to hang his face upside down to make a point, or get bodily out of bed to show me a map, and when he finally ran out of steam around two, I was left alone in the darkness, tired and disappointed, wondering why the youth of America were romanticizing a stupid little piece-of-shit war like Vietnam. Nobody won; nobody should have; we didn't have any business there in the first place.

I sighed hugely and tried to sleep, but in the end, sometime around five, crept back to our bedroom to find Myra scrunched into five down pillows, sleeping like a baby, and at that point, I wondered why I'd ever been born.

"Myra," I said, shaking her, and she sat up.

"Gabriel? What's wrong, are the child—"

"They're fine," I said, then sighed again. "Listen, I'm sorry I said that about adultery. It was a cheap shot."

She was blinking as if disoriented. "What time is it?"

"It's five-fifteen. Listen, you can go to church all you want, but those sleazy underwear have got to go. You hear?"

For a moment she only looked at me. "You woke me out of a sound sleep to lecture me about my underwear?" she asked.

I nodded. "Yes. That's exactly what I did. No woman wears underwear like that unless she's asking for it."

She pushed her hair out of her eyes and looked at me a little longer. "That all?"

"Yes."

She curled back into her pillows and I lay down beside her.

"Well, are you getting rid of them?" I asked hopefully.

Her voice was kind. "No, I'm not. They cost too much for me to just to throw out, and furthermore I've got some sets that don't even have underwear, they're just garters, and I'll wear them too when it suits me."

I closed my eyes on this, knowing how Red must have felt when Temple Drake asked him to dance, knowing the bullet was as well as in his head already, and said, "Myra, honey, why do you want to do me this way? I love you."

"I ain't doing you no way," she said. "Whether or not you trust me is your business; it's nothing to do with me one way or the other. You want an enabler, get yoursef a dog."

And that was the end of that. She was asleep in two minutes, and I never closed my eyes a wink. So maybe that was why Missy's new shoes for the Sweetheart Banquet set me off at breakfast.

They were blue, magneta blue, and she told me she'd had to go to four different malls to find them.

"Why?" I asked, as in why bother, but she went and got her dress and held them together.

"See? A perfect match. Isn't it incredible?"

"Very nice." I allowed and was sipping my coffee when I noticed the price on the box. I set my cup down. "You paid ninety-six dollars for one pair of shoes?"

She was eating a granola bar, stuffing her backpack with books, and shrugged. "Sure." When she saw my expression, she paused. "They're John Jerro."

"Oh. *John Jerro*," I said and shook my head, then looked at her. "Missy? Do you realize how long it takes some poor sucker at Sanger to clear enough profit to buy his children shoes? Dimestore shoes? Two-dollar-ninety-eight-cent shoes?"

She shook her head.

"Well, it takes them forever because they never can, sweating seventy-hour weeks, living off bologna and credit, and if I was you, I'd think twice about living like a princess off their misery."

She took one of the shoes out of the box and turned it over in her hands. "They're magenta blue. I looked all day. They match my dress."

I stood up to pour more coffee. "Well, honey, you can wear 'em if you want to. I mean, they're your feet, but as far as I'm concerned, ninety-six-dollar shoes are an abomination before God, and people who wear them will burn in hell."

Myra came in on the tail-end of this conversation, and with the capacity for long suffering she must have acquired from her years on Magnolia Hill, made no reference to the conversation other than a polite request of my presence in the bedroom, please.

Something in her voice told me another battle was at hand, and I pretended nonchalance.

"Let me finish my coffee," I said, and she made no reply, only the sound of her feet as she went up the stairs.

I gave her a few minutes to stew, then found her upstairs, stripping our bed.

"D'you need to talk to me?" I asked. "I'm supposed to be at Sanger at nine."

She didn't bother to turn, only yanking off the pillowcases, her voice a story-telling murmur. "Gabriel," she said, "I never had anything when I was growing up. Nothing that didn't come out of a bag of hand-me-downs, or off the sale rack at the Dollar Store, and that was once a year at Easter." She paused to gather me in. "So when I had my children, I promised myself that one day when I could, I'd provide for them better than was provided for me—"

"Ninety-six-dollar shoes?" I interrupted. "Come on, Myra, you're turning Missy into a Cracker American Princess here—"

"*And*," she continued, "if it takes ninety-six dollars to make Missy feel pretty enough to go to one of these stupid banquets, I will spend it. In fact, I will spend five-hundred-and-ninety-six dollars if that's what it takes. She's my child and it's Michael's money and it's nothing for you to worry with," she tossed the stripped pillows on the bed, "one way or the other."

On that, she gathered the sheets in her arms and left to sort the laundry, and as she passed, I made one small counter charge, rolling my eyes to heaven, murmuring, "Once a *babygirl*, always a *babygirl*."

She stopped and looked at me a full ten seconds, then turned, but her parting shot was lethal: "And once a Mama's boy," she drawled, "always a Mama's boy."

Well, I had a nasty history with that little phrase, dating back to my days on Magnolia Hill, and it cut like a knife, so deep that I really laid in for the siege this time, foregoing Sanger to retreat to my maps and molding books with no word of explanation at all. I stayed holed up there all day long with no interruption from Myra, no conciliatory advances at all, noting she left in the car at one-thirty, and for all I knew could have been meeting Knute at the Day's Inn.

But when she finally returned, it was with a carload of groceries, so I figured Mondays must be grocery-store day around here.

Around seven hunger finally drove me inside, and I was nosing around the refrigerator for some of those brand new groceries when Mama walked in the kitchen, all dressed up in her Sunday best, and I straightened up. "What're you doing here?"

"The shower, baby," she said. "Where were you yesterday morning?"

"Whose shower?"

"Cindi Frye's. Myra's got the house sa pretty. Where have you been, anyhow? She said she's been at it all day."

"Oh," I said, eating a handful of grapes. "I've been upstairs. Writing."

Her face assumed its here-we-go-again roll, and I was annoyed. "Why do you get that idiotic look on your face every time I mention my book?"

She collected an armful of crystal punch glasses off the counter. "Son, how many of them books you ever written?"

"Well, I haven't finished it—"

"How many you ever published?"

"I said I haven't fin—"

"How many you ever made one red cent on?"

I just looked at her, and I guess she thought her point taken, for she took the cups and left me there for my wife to finish off. But when she came in for the cake a few minutes later, she said nothing at all, just a cold, pointed silence, till Clayton happened by, and she turned on him.

"Clay? I toldju to stay upstairs. It's seven o'clock; the ladies'll be here anytime. Now get going."

He said something about being hungry, but she was shooing him away till I had a sudden brainstorm and stepped in.

"Run get your coat, son. I'll take you to a movie."

He looked interested, but said, "I done seen it. Me and Keith went Friday."

"This is different. It's about Vietnam. We'll have to hurry. It starts at eight."

At the mention of the word *Vietnam*, he hit the stairs in a dead run, and I smiled. The movie I was talking about wasn't in the local theater. It was *Hearts and Minds*, a documentary I remembered being impressed with a hundred years ago, that I'd seen advertised in the *Democrat*, playing at the University Box Office in Tallahassee.

My kindness to her son seemed to have softened Myra, and she asked in a small, contrite voice, "Are you hungry?"

"No," I said and she came over and slid her arms around my waist.

"I'm sorry I called you a Mama's boy," she murmured against my neck, but I just leaned against the counter and ate the grapes.

"Don't worry it. I been called worse."

"Not by me," she said, and I would have liked to have sustained my cool aloofness a little longer, but she was standing there rubbing against me, admitting defeat, so I gave in and kissed her and was pressing for more, but she pulled away, saying, "Gabriel, Gabriel, here. The ladies are in the living room. Your mama's here."

Which might have been my point exactly, and I didn't let up till Clayton came back in his jacket, his face alight with excitement, and suddenly the evening was full of promise.

"Be careful," she said, walking us to the car. "Drive slow."

Then she kissed me again, lightly on the mouth, and suddenly it was a wonderful world: Myra surrounded by puritanical ladies who didn't approve of sex in general, much less extramarital; me and Clayton out on the town, hitting eighty on the interstate.

"I never heard of it," he said when I told him the name of the film, and I assured him it was the best I'd ever seen on Vietnam.

"Real footage, not that Hollywood crap."

Luckily, the Box Office hadn't moved in fifteen years, and we got there in the nick of time, just as the opening credits were rolling past. Half-way through, I again congratulated myself on the perfect selection, for the film was masterfully debunking all the romantic garbage associated with Vietnam, and Clayton's face was a puzzle of perplexity as Vietnamese women and children screamed over graves and an old woman described how American troops had destroyed her village.

Yes, I was feeling pretty pleased with myself when suddenly, with no warning at all, the camera was inside a whorehouse, showing buck-naked American soldiers and Vietnamese whores *in the very act*, and if Clayton had been mesmerized before, now he was hypnotized, his eyes the size of quarters.

Well, I knew I had screwed up on a pretty momumental scale and was faced with the split-second option of faking a heart attack or getting up and walking out, but for whatever reason, historical realism or shame at leaving, I stayed put, though the sweat was really beginning to pour as the scene stretched on in all its perverse jocularity, the soldiers making jokes about the girls back home, the whores' pathetic smiles never wavering.

Clayton didn't say a word about it on the way home, and though I considered begging him not to tell his mother, again I remained silent. After all, it was the truth; honest, hard-core Vietnam in the flesh, and if I apologized, it might lessen the impact of the film's message. I reasoned that if he was old enough for *Rambo*, he was old enough for reality, but I will admit to a very nervous slide in my stomach the next morning at breakfast when Myra asked him how he liked the movie.

"It was," he paused, "interesting."

"What didju see?" Simon asked. "*Lethal Weapon?* Is it still showing?"

"We went to Tallahassee," I said quickly, and was mercifully spared further detail by Missy's cry of outrage.

"Tallahassee? Clayton got to go to the mall? *Mama—*"

"My sweet," I said, grateful for the diversion, "there is more to Tallahassee than the mall."

"But nobody even *asked* me—"

So we were sidetracked by a little sibling rivalry, and when they left for school, I edged a little closer to the truth as I dressed for Sanger. "I hope it wasn't too intense for Clay," I said as I knotted my tie. "I mean, it was real footage."

Myra was unusually understanding. "I doubt it. You ever seen *Platoon?*" She made a face, and I tried to cover my behind a little more.

"That was Hollywood; this was real. But anyway," I added philosophically as I kissed her good-bye, "it was the truth, and I guess a little truth never hurt anyone."

A smug little platitude I was made to regret four days later when the real lowdown on *Hearts and Minds* surfaced via Clayton to Simon; Simon to Keith; Keith to his brother Kemp; Kemp to his mother; his mother to every woman at Welcome, including (but not limited to) Myra, at which time more truthful observations were made on my character than I ever wanted to hear.

They were made immediately after church in a loud voice in an airtight Mercedes, surrounded by our fellow Baptists, who were still milling around the front steps shaking hands.

"—can't believe you'd take a twelve-year-old boy to a pornographic movie, your own son, your own son—"

"Myra, Myra, listen—" I said, but she wouldn't pause for a breath, and when the people around the steps began to pause and watch us with looks of light interest, I drove us to the parking lot of the Piggly Wiggly and tried to reason with her.

"It was—would you shut up for one damn minute? It wasn't pornogra—Myra, for God's sake, SHUT UP. It wasn't a pornographic movie. It was two minutes of bare-breasted women—"

"—why he's been so quiet. You messed him up, Gabriel. You messed him up—"

"You couldn't even see what they were doing—"

"What they were *doing*?" she cried. "He's twelve years old. He gets embarrassed at *tampon* commmericals—"

"—toldju it was too intense, but no, you don't care about death and destruction. Boy, just a little sex has you uptight, you hypocriti—"

"Oh, shut up—get out of my car. Don'tchu ever even *talk* to my children again, do you hear me?"

My reply was prematurely curtailed by the slam of the car door, and there I was, stranded in the parking lot of the Piggly Wiggly.

Fortunately, it was within walking distance of Magnolia Hill, so I retreated to Mama's house and ate her leftovers in morose silence while my wife and children were being comforted by Knute at the Steakhouse ("For what fellowship hath light with darkness?").

I was finishing up, wondering what my next move would be, when Mama came in with the boys, all of them a little white-eyed, as if they knew something heavy was coming down.

"Where's Myra?" Mama asked. For Sim and Clayton's sake, I lied, "Home. Where's Missy?"

"Joanna's," she said, then told the boys to go see if they could find any clothes in the spare bedroom. When they left, I was prepared for another tongue-lashing at Mama's hands, as she had obviously heard rumor of my debauchery, but she only leaned against the stove and crossed her arms and asked, very seriously, as if she expected a straight answer: "Gabe, son, do you have good sense?"

I told her it was certainly a matter open to speculation these days and went to the bedroom to talk to Clay and Sim and try to uncorrupt them as best I could, but found them embarrassed and apologetic.

"Clayton's seen naked women before," Simon said in disgust.

I was shocked. "Where?"

"Playboy, HBO," he said defiantly, ashamed Clayton was making them look like such weenies.

Clayton tried to defend himself, lying on the bed with this hands behind his head, his eyes on the old tongue-and-groove ceiling. "You didn't see them, Sim. They weren't just naked. They were just so pathetic. These men were being so nasty to them, pinching their titties and making fun of them and all they did was sit there and smile. It made me wanna puke."

I was surprised he was so removed from the sexuality of it all, that he'd seen past the tits, as it were—something that I couldn't have done at twelve (hell, I barely did it at thirty-eight)—and I took it as an opportunity to instruct.

"That's right, Clay," I told him. "That's exactly right. See, *Hearts and Minds* was virulently anti-interventionalist. It purposefully showed the pathos of the war, the orphaned children, the crying grandmothers, the women having to resort to prostitution to survive. That's the symbolism, see? Vietnamese women being screwed by American soldiers like America was screwing Vietnam—see?"

I'd gotten a little excited with my interpretation, standing and pacing, and they looked thoughtful for about ten seconds till Clay seemed to come to some conclusion and lay back on the bed. "It still makes me wanna puke."

"Well, good. Good for you," I said, and catching a glimpse of the old Sims house out of the tail of my eye, the broken back of the roof, the sagging porch, I thought: *Take that, you bastard*.

But I said nothing more, only promising to square things with their mother, then went back to the kitchen and asked Mama if I could borrow her car.

"Why?"

"To find Myra. She kicked me out at the Piggy Wiggly."

Simon and Clay had followed me to the kitchen, and as Mama handed over her keys, Simon gave me a bit of parting advice.

"Tell her she looks like she's losing weight," he said. "It couldn't hurt."

"And tell her I've seen lots of naked women before," Clayton added, and I knew Mama wouldn't let that one hit the ground untouched, but left him to handle it as best he could, driving around town, not finding the Mercedes anywhere it should be, not at Candace's or Lori's or the Steakhouse, and I was wondering where Knute lived, when I remembered the cemetery.

She was there, of course, probably outlining to Michael what a disappointment I'd been, but when I found her, she was pulling weeds from the graves, the hem of her dress dirty, her face sad, but no longer furious. I took a seat on Daddy's tombstone without a word and tried to think of an apology, but I'd told her I was sorry so much lately that the words seemed cheap, and I only rubbed my eyes.

"This isn't working out so well, is it?" I finally said, but she didn't answer, only tearing at the bahia grass, and I finally broke down.

"Listen, Myra, I'm sorry. *Hearts and Minds* was a stupid choice for a twelve year old. I'd forgotten it was so intense. It shook me up too, and the way he talks, he's seen more nudity at twelve than I have at thirty-eight."

Her eyes were up in a flash. "Where's he ever seen nudity?"

I shrugged. "Don't ask me. Ask Mama, she'll probably have the goods on him by the time we get home."

She straightened up, slapping the dirt off her hands, then sat beside me. "Well, I'm sorry I screamed. I tell you what, I'm thinking about asking Dr. Williams to put me back on lithium. I just get so crazy anymore——"

"It's because you're in love," I told her, kissing her little white hand, but she was not so sure.

"I been in love before, and it wasn't like this."

"Not with me, you haven't," I said, and we were happy again, touching in the sun, the air cold but pleasant, the cedar still green, giving the air a sharp scent of summer. With the Sunday morning rush, we hadn't had a chance to talk all day, and instead of thrashing out the matter at hand, fell to discussing the incidentals—how many children she had in primaries, if the new *Creation* peepbox I'd made her was up to Catts family standards.

"The moon's too low," she said. "The children thought it was a beach ball."

I promised to rectify the matter and asked if I could put together an *Evolution* peep-box in the interest of balanced teaching.

"If you can get it past your mother," she said as she stood.

I laughed. "Poor Clay. I guess we better go see about him. She made me write John three-sixteen twenty times for inspecting one of Candace's bras. I can't imagine what the punishment is for blatant, unashamed voyeurism. She might have stuck him in the microwave or something."

"She'll probably sic Carlym on him," Myra laughed. "He's the newest form of punishment at Welcome these days."

I was not so pleased by Knute's intrusion into our intimate little conversation, and when we were almost to the car, I asked her if she really thought I lacked sexual maturity.

"Gabriel—" she said, trying to sidestep me, but I stopped.

"No, really. I won't get mad."

For a moment she only stood there looking at me, her head tilted a little to the side, a mannerism she'd picked up from Mama, I think. Then she smiled. "To tell you the truth, honey, I think you lack maturity all the way around—no, don't get mad—I mean it as a compliment. I think it's why I love you, why I always loved you, even when we were children, why I came back to find you when I was grown."

I could feel her fingers on my arm, her face lifted to the brilliant Florida sun. "I mean, you were so innocent, so sheltered. Your mama and daddy had made you such a happy little world there, with your books and your friends and your church. It was like you were a prince in a castle, enchanted, like nothing could ever touch you." Her smile faltered a little. "I mean me and Ira, we were never that way. No protection, no enchantment—but you were, and I think just knowing you showed me there was a better life, a salvation out there, if I'd just hold on."

Her eyes had grown very distant, but they sharpened. "I had a psychiatrist tell me that once. She said the difference between me and Ira was that he'd accepted cruelty as the norm, but I never had. I'd disassociated before I'd accept it." She looked at me. "And it makes sense to me. I mean, insanity is curable, but inhumanity? I don't know."

We'd begun walking again, and I let her talk, knowing how seldom it was that she could dredge up any part of her childhood in a positive way.

"And I don't know what you've been up to all these years, but the minute I laid eyes on you, I knew you hadn't changed, you never will. That net Simon and Cissie wove around you is still there, and it kills me when you and Candace talk about war and hate and viciousness—you don't know what you're talking about. You're both just so protected; it's never touched you at all. I've tried to make such a world for my children. Every child that's born should have such a world. That's why that movie bothered me. I mean, sure it's true. Nobody has to convince me of the reality of evil, but why not let Clay find out on his own? Why rush it? He'll see the underbelly soon enough. Let him be a child a little longer. Let's all be children. It'll all be over soon enough, anyway."

We'd reached the car, but her eyes were back on the row of cedars that marked the family plot, her voice suddenly grieving. "I mean, look at my poor Michael. Forty-three years old. Worked every day of his life, worried and struggled, and why? So his widow could drive a fifty-thousand-dollar car, and his daughter could wear ninety-dollar shoes. While there he lies, dead and turned to clay."

The abruptness of her descent startled me, and I took her face in my hand and lifted her chin. "What? *Dead and turned to clay*? Woman, I'm gone have to make you a new *Resurrection* peep-box, you keep talking like that."

She smiled at me, her eyes, as always, down-tilted and patient and kind as the sun. "See? It hasn't touched you yet. It *never will*."

Chapter

17

*I*n two short weeks, the lines were drawn, and I understood and accepted that I could say or do almost anything, work or not work, spend what I wanted, in short, carry on in whatever manner I pleased, as long as I abided by the absolutes: leave the children to Myra and attend Welcome Baptist without undo sarcasm or complaint. They were not such rigorous guidelines when you consider that I had not only inherited a beautiful wife and three lovely children, but a checking account that could handle outlays for ninety-six-dollar shoes without showing any strain at all. And anyway, I pride myself on my ability to adjust and overcame my unease and utter boredom at Welcome by taking over the men's Sunday school class and whiling away the sermons playing war on the back of the bulletin with Simon or Clay. At first, I beat them roundly, but after a while, both of them, especially Sim, would occasionally blindside me, and we'd tape their victories to the refrigerator, a practice which annoyed my wife.

"What if Carlym drops by and sees them?"

"He can take a hint and go back to the NFL."

"Gabriel—"

"—or take off a few Sundays and watch Jimmy Swaggart. I swear to God he's the sorriest preacher I've ever heard in my life."

"You're just jealous."

"I *am not*. Besides, he doesn't like me. He won't come to my Sunday school class."

"Nobody with good sense would go to *your* Sunday school class."

Well, that was gratitude for you. I'd only taken the stupid class in a futile attempt to kiss up after the *Hearts and Minds* debacle, and my first official act as teacher was to pitch the *Quarterly* and rename the class Current Dilemmas Facing Modern Fundamentalism, which meant: Running Our Mouths for Thirty Minutes Every Sunday on Issues at Home and Abroad. One week it'd be national politics; another, FSU football; but mostly it was a mix, the discussion moving along according to whatever hit a nerve. I'd estimate that no one in the class was under seventy, for the younger men attended Brother Kinnard's married class with their wives, or were more successful than I in getting out of it altogether, leaving the men's class to the husbands of the old ladies out in the Sunday school wing who taught children alongside Mama and Myra. Poor, cantankerous, and hard of hearing to a man, they'd been shuttled off to a tiny room behind the baptistry to be babysat till they died, and I like to think I breathed life into them, giving them something to look forward to on Sunday between breakfast and Championship Wrestling from Florida.

And I must say, I grew to enjoy it, finding them a surprisingly diverse bunch, from Brother Yonke, Russian by birth (before Communism, as he liked to say) to Jack Kin, a tall, red-faced old man who was rumored to have organized the county's most notorious lynchings. I never found out if this was mere speculation or truth, but he was a prejudiced old son of a bitch, and whenever our arguments touched on race, I'd reduce him to rubble with a few well-aimed scriptures and simple volume.

We had so many screamers in there that Brother Sloan, who traditionally meditated in his office during Sunday School (read the paper, I suspected) grew curious enough to join in the fray. He was the best in the bunch when it came to logic and would usually lead the charge against me. In time, they too, might have blindsided me, if not for their congestive hearts that would give in to angina and palpitations if I cared to withstand them, leaving me to carry the day.

One Sunday after I'd really played the devil's advocate, proclaiming the disciples to be rank charismatics (ever read the second chapter of Acts?), Brother Sloan had actually edged on to a heart attack, having to stretch out on the floor with a nitroglycerin pill, but still not backing down, just lying there amidst the flurry of damp washcloths, whispering, "You're wrong, Gabe. You're wrong, you're wrong, you're wrong"—which I have come to understand is the final Baptist argument when they've been right and soundly beaten.

The pill straightened him out without medical intervention, but Myra scolded me between services when I carried her boxload of primary paraphernalia to the car.

"He's eighty-one years old, Gabe. Leave him alone. Welcome's split six times over the charismatics. Even Candace left. Don't torment him about it. He's too old."

"Not too old for the truth," I said with a smile, for there was something very satisfying about baiting these old boys, and Myra slammed the trunk.

"Must you always win?"

"Only when I'm right."

She rolled her eyes. "Well, you're gone apologize during dinner. Bless his heart, he was white as a sheet."

I told her I would, but felt not one twinge of guilt, for despite their age, I knew these old boys were a wily, tenacious lot who could damn well take care of themselves, and forty minutes later I was proven right when Brother Sloan took the pulpit for the morning sermon and announced his text with glittering eyes: Second Samuel, chapter eleven.

Now, for the uninitiated, this is the Biblical story of adultery extraordinaire, David and Bathsheba, and with great relish, he described David's lust, his relentless maneuvering to obtain Bathsheba, and how from all appearances, he'd obtained her when poor Uriah was tidily disposed of by the hand of the Philistines. He kept his eyes demurely downcast for the text and introduction, but when he made it to the last line in the chapter, verse twenty-seven, he raised his face for the first time and met mine squarely across the nine-pew gap, his eyes as bright as a hawk's as his trembly old voice rang out, "But the thang which David haad done displeeased the Lawd."

Clayton was beside me, busy scribbling out boundaries on the back of the bulletin, not paying the least bit of attention, but my heart was beating hard as an anvil, and I could feel my neck growing very hot. I couldn't believe he was using the pulpit as a weapon, but he was, going in for the kill, preaching the body of his sermon on the consequences of David's sin, Tamar and her rape by Almon, then the tragic story of David and his son Absalom.

"O my son Absalom, my son, my son," he cried. "Would God I had died for thee, O Absalom, my son, my son."

The words settled on me like a curse as I watched Clayton's small excited face, frowning with concentration as he made his first move, and I tell you what, I came close to spitting on the floor and walking out.

"I can't believe it," I told Myra that afternoon in the privacy of our bedroom. "He nailed me from the pulpit, the ruthless old son of a bit—"

"Don't you ever—"

"Oh, cut the shit, Myra. He cursed me was what he did. Didju hear his voice? 'The thaang thet Daavid haad done displeeased the Laawd.'"

Myra was inexplicably unconcerned. "Gabriel, honey, it's just your own guilt talking."

"Guilt, my ass. Everybody knew what he was talking about, and I'll tell you one thing, that'll be the last time I ever step foot in Welcome Baptist, me or my checkbook either one, I can grant you that."

"Suit yourself," she said, but as the weeks went by, she'd serenade me at breakfast about how much everyone missed me.

"Brother Kin always goes out of his way to ask about you."

"Brother Kin," I'd tell her, "is a Nazi."

She finally let up, and I got a lot of work done on those balmy Sunday mornings, my first spring back, though Sim and Clay whined church wasn't the same without me.

"Play against each other," I advised.

"Clay's not any good. I kill him in two moves."

"You do not. I beat you once—"

"You cheated—"

"Boys, boys," I said, "I'm sorry. I've backslid. Give Knute my regards over dinner." Brother Folger had ceased to worry me as competition for Myra's affection. He was just too big and dumb. I couldn't see Myra putting up with him more than two hours at a time.

However, as the month passed, my departure from Welcome did present me with a small, unforseen problem, one that I'd seldom been challenged with before: boredom. I thought the book would keep me busy for at least a year, but once I got started, I found I couldn't sustain enough drive to keep me at it more than a couple of hours at a time, and after a few weeks of moody speculation, I came to the surprising conclusion that what was lacking was the classroom—the give and take, the questions, the whole noisy propellant of inquiry—and the next morning at breakfast, I announced I was looking for a job.

"Why?" was the general reaction, even from Myra, and I was a little hurt.

"Why? Because I'm the Big Man, the Breadwinner, the Daddy; I work. Bring home the bacon."

The boys accepted this explanation easily enough, though it prompted one solitary question from Missy, not addressed to me, but to her mother: "We don't have to actually live off it, do we?" she asked, no sarcasm intended, and after advising her to quit spending so much of her discretionary time in the company of her grandmother, I put on my wedding suit and my Rolex and quietly went about the business of finding a job.

In what I considered an act of loyalty, I offered my services to FSU first, but like most Florida universities, found them particularly uninterested in their own history, content to hang on to Europe and suck up to Ivy League rejects, a category I might have fit into if not for a reputation I seemed to have garnered for departing on short notice. So I shook the Tallahassee dust from my shoes and hit a few community colleges, but found them, if possible, less obliging than FSU. Most of them were small vocational/academic institutions run by xenophobic locals, and the sight of my Volvo with its New York license plates sent me down for the count before I could even open my mouth.

Then, to add insult to injury, some mailing list hooked onto my new financial status and I was suddenly barraged by FSU and UNC and Harvard, all intensely interested in my assuming my position as a proud alumnus. First, there were little cards asking for my $1000___, $5000___, or $____ donation; then there were personal letters from their representatives, kindly offering to fly down at their own expense to discuss endowment opportunities with me. I found the FSU one particularly irritating in light of the cavalier way they'd treated my resumé, and on the little prepaid RSVP card, scribbled a profane variation on: *In your dreams, bud*.

However, this small revenge in no way resolved the problem at hand, namely my lack of employability, and I was desperate enough to consider putting in an application at the bank when Clayton, of all people, came to my rescue, bursting in on me one afternoon while I was writing upstairs, his best friend Kenneth in his wake. They had run all the way from the bus stop and were too breathless to speak for a moment, Clay pointing at Kenneth, gasping, "Tell 'im. Tell 'im."

"What?" I asked, but Kenneth could only pant.

Clayton finally managed, "Mister Nair. Got in a wreck."

"Who?"

"Mister Nair. Teacher. Hurt bad. Won't be back."

"Oh," I said. "Well, I'm sorry. Kenneth, was he some kin of yours?"

"No," Clayton gasped. "He teaches history," he pointed at me, "like you."

"Oh," I said, sitting back.

Kenneth finally added his contribution. "Kemp had the sub. She's a jerk."

"That's right," Clayton said, pulling my arm. "And Mr. Nair'll be out all year. Come on, Gabe; they'll give it to somebody else. History's the only thing I get A's in. I need you."

Spoken like that, he could have talked me into robbing a convenience store, and within the hour I was back in my suit and Rolex and at long last succeeded in impressing someone, the personnel secretary at the school board office. She sent me to the principal for an interview, a very nice man, a little in awe of me, not because of the suit or the watch or even the Volvo, but because I was a *Catts*, and by Michael's labors it was a name that had come to be locally synonymous with supreme wealth.

He hired me on the spot, and when I got home, I swore a high-fiving Clayton and Kenneth to secrecy and invited everyone, including Mama, to supper at the Steakhouse. When the food was finished, I stood very grandly with my tea glass in hand and announced that after careful

examination of career options in North Florida, I had accepted a position of enormous responsibility shaping young minds at Lincoln Park
Middle School. Everyone seemed to take it at face value, and they were
pathetically eager to congratulate me.

Myra kissed me, and Mama, poor Mama, wept tears of sheer relief,
for her excuses on my behalf were beginning to edge her close to the
lake of fire and brimstone, and now she had something to brag on, her
son Gabe, the professional. And while I might downplay it all, she was
perfectly sincere when she proudly announced my occupation to all and
sundry, for to her, a teacher was as good as a lawyer who was as good
as a doctor who was as good as the President. They wore ties, and they
didn't get grease under their nails, and for the first time in twenty years,
even Harvard was eclipsed by it.

"I'll start at eighteen thousand dollars a year," I proclaimed. "Missy
will have to shop at Wal-Mart."

"*Ma*ma," she cried, and Myra, her arm around me, was annoyed.

"You better watch yourself, Melissa Anne. There ain't nothing
wrong with Wal-Mart. Don't you start playing the snob with me."

A small display of loyalty for my benefit, I am sure, and nothing for
Missy to take seriously, for my salary wouldn't keep this household in
underwear, Wal-Mart or otherwise, but something in their support made
me begin to get a little excited.

"I'll show these yokels how to teach history," I said more than
once, and when I read over the state-approved text in bed that night, I
made so many exclamations of outrage that Myra began to have second
thoughts.

"You're not gone do these children like you done Brother Sloan,
are you?"

"No, no," I murmured, but when I'd come across another
absurdity, I'd let out another yell, and the next morning, Myra warned
me to go easy on them.

"Clayton'll catch it if you get anybody mad."

I assured her that I knew how to comport myself in a classroom, that what did she think I'd been doing up North all these years?

"Those were Yankees," she said. "These people know your phone number."

I promised to be the picture of passivity, and I truly meant it, for I was beginning to see that the marriage of an alcoholic mama's boy and a schizoaffective babygirl would be one that required a certain measure of insincerity to succeed, and dear God in heaven, I wanted it to succeed.

So I behaved with impeccable manners, keeping my utter disgust with the school system to myself and relying on the guerrilla tactics taught me on my dear mother's knee to get my way without causing so much as a ripple of unrest on the calm pond of public education. Only rarely was I ever challenged, and then it was usually at my own table.

"Why do you teach slavery so long?" Simon asked one morning at breakfast. "Mr. Nair didn't."

"Because LP Middle is eighty percent black and one hundred percent ignorant of black history," I said.

He chewed reflectively. "Well, where does that leave Clay? And Kenneth? Black history ain't their history."

I gladly rose to the point. "History is not the memorization of facts and dates, but the science of interpreting events in a reasonable and informative manner that enables us to better understand our motivation as a people and deal with current events and plot future goals. So whether Clayton studies white history or black history or junebug history is immaterial as long as he is being trained to establish facts and interpret them in an intelligent fashion."

Simon looked at me a moment. "Then why not train his mind with white history?"

"Because teaching white history wouldn't make anyone mad." This contribution was from Myra, as she hurried us out the door, and not an entirely accurate assessment, for I was not being merely contrary here, but trying to make these children aware of their heritage. I mean, these children were from poor black-belt families who had a tremendous sense of place among themselves, a whole thriving subculture in their churches and oral history, but you'd never know it to read the state-approved texts. So in a fit of desperation, finding the school board completely apathetic to anything I cared to try at the black middle school, I organized a living history project, with truly fascinating results.

My work in Indiana had been interesting, but this was raw, fallow ground, and I was truly astounded with my students' dedication and their families' cooperation. We worked on it two months, and by May had collected taped recollections of life in the turpentine camps, worn remnants of old slave quilts, first-hand accounts of lynchings and trials and murders, superstitions and tall tales and magic spells, most of which I'd never seen documented anywhere, even in Washington. When the physical evidence (including a mojo hand and a lye-stained washboard) began to pile up in our classroom, I talked the librarian into giving us the little room behind the periodicals and went about the task of showing the students how to meticulously order and preserve everything, assuring them this history was as vital as anything they'd ever heard about Columbus and fourteen hundred and ninety two.

So we were on a roll there at LP Middle, starting our final projects, and I found myself looking forward to Mondays, a sure sign of occupational satisfaction, when Clayton and I would ride to school together and discuss school issues, who was stupid, who was smart, who was pregnant (a fairly common occurrence, especially in the eighth grade), why algebra was so incomprehensible, why girls liked jocks. And between and around all this, I'd tell him about Michael, for he'd once confided to me that he could hardly remember his father anymore, and it had only been a year and a half, how could that be?

"You were young when he died," I told him. Then, on sudden inspiration, "Why don't you make him your final project?"

"Daddy?" he asked doubtfully. "Won't it be silly? Doing your own father?"

"Of course not," I said. "Michael lived and died. He moved in time. He has just as valid a claim to historical preservation as Ronald Reagan, for God's sake."

"Oh," Clayton said, and with no more ado, he quietly went about it as I'd taught him, carrying around a tape player for a week or two, getting Myra to describe how they'd met (she gave the uncut version, which the children found mighty amusing), where they lived, and why. Then he went to Mama, who cried through most of it, but donated memorabilia, baseballs and pictures and his first pay stub from Sanger (sixty-nine stinking dollars for forty-seven hours' work), then hit the secondary rounds, Candace and Sam and Benny and Brother Sloan; then, last of all, he came to me.

We talked out by the pool on a balmy spring evening, the mimosa in bloom again, the air sweet and clear and almost achingly reminiscent of the fence line on Magnolia Hill, but once the tape was rolling, I had a hard time discussing Michael, for there were so many doors I could not open. I think my viewpoint was the weakest in the bunch, nothing more than a patchwork of anecdotes and wistfulness, lacking Myra's detail or Mama's grief or Sam McRae's powerful, moving words that Clayton said made him cry.

"Like a baby," he said. "I was ashamed."

I assured him it was not an unknown phenomenon around the Catts household and, let me tell you, when I came upon his project, a simple three-sided display with two tapes and a written report, I didn't get past the title page before I was going strong. Hand-written in his fat, child's script, it was simply entitled: "My Father, Michael Catts" and in the white space below, he'd been cocky enough to include a dedication:

"To Gabe, with love." I tell you what, if I hadn't been crying so hard, I would have laughed, for it was a classic piece of Catts family irony, but I would have given him an A even if he'd dedicated it to Carlym Folger, for somehow, by some talent (nothing he'd inherited from me, that was for sure) he'd reported on Michael unemotionally, with no trace of sentimentality, letting the facts speak for themselves. He included the baseball, he included Sanger, he even picked up on the social stigma of living on Magnolia Hill in the forties and fifties. From Sam he'd learned of the Klan attacks and chronicled them with details I'd never heard before—how they'd hung him in effigy from the rafters at Sanger, how they'd burned a cross in Sam's front yard three weekends in a row, how very close they'd come to shutting the plant down for good.

It was an accumulation of hard, raw facts that made for compelling history, and if he left out a few essential ingredients that had in some ways shaped it all—Myra's insanity, my infidelity—it wasn't his fault, for they still resided in the realm of the unspoken. And as any good historian will tell you, no history is history until it is recorded; but at that point, the words were just not there.

I *guess you could call it a spring of* promise, and when the school board included a continuing contract in the envelope with my last check, we celebrated lavishly, as if I'd been appointed an eminent scholar at Oxford, throwing a big fish fry, inviting all the old boys from the men's class, even Brother Sloan, whom I hadn't spoken to since his public accusation. He didn't seem the least bit repentant; in fact, there was still a smile of victory playing around his mouth whenever I looked at him, but I let it pass, for the other old men seemed pathetically eager to make amends. Myra told me Brother Folger had taken the class in my absence, and I think sitting under his teaching two hours a week was making them fear dementia had set in.

They all showed up hours early, dressed in their best leisure clothes, ancient khakis and cotton shirts, their hearing aids affixed with new batteries, their wives in tow bearing indescribably good dishes like cheese grits and banana pudding. Before the oil was fairly hot, one or two had cast out a bit of bait ("Now thet Dukakis' wife, hear she's an alcoholic—"), hoping I'd hit, but Myra had made me promise to be agreeable, so I could make nothing but the most disinterested replies, and had a feeling they left full, but intellectually starved. So I took pity on them and called Brother Sloan aside and agreed to take the class back and the next morning, the first of June, gave them their money's worth, standing at the podium with my *Quarterly* open in case the Sunday school superintendent happened by, addressing their eager old faces with narrowed eyes.

"Why," I asked them, "did we fight a Civil War?"

They gave me all the old standards, and I let them fight it out between themselves for most of the class time, saving my opinion for the last sixty seconds.

"Money." I grinned, and after an extended pause for breath, we were back in action, but only for thirty seconds, when the bell rang and we had to go back to the sanctuary for church.

They were furious with me for pulling such a stunt, Brother Sloan most earnestly tortured of all, having to let such blasphemy go unanswered while he sat on the deacon's bench for two solid hours of hymns and Brother Folger's drivel before he could catch me at the salad bar and scream:

"It was slavery, Gabriel Catts. Ain't you ever heard of the Missouri Compromise?"

"Slavery was money," was my patient reply as I stood there and chewed lettuce.

That night in bed, Myra tried to be helpful. "Gabriel, honey, Dr. Williams would see you for free. You'll have plenty a time this summer—"

"I do not need psychiatric treatment because I think the Civil War was nothing more than a business transaction gone awry."

"I don't give a hoot about any war. I just don't think all this fighting is healthy. Are you *sure* you weren't beaten as a child?"

Her years in therapy had made my wife a healthy cynic where matters of neuroses were concerned, but perhaps she was a bit serious, for passionate confrontation was not her strong suit (it wouldn't have been mine if I'd lived one house down on Lafayette), and she was honestly perplexed by my love of needling.

"Not beaten by my parents," I told her, kissing her neck, "but emotionally scarred by my love for an ambitious red-headed woman who rejected me to marry my less sexually satisfying but infinitely richer brother—"

"Gabriel—"

"So I take out my angst on these harmless old men and their blood is on your hands, woman."

So I laughed it away, but later, when I couldn't sleep, I went downstairs for a glass of hot milk and found myself at the French doors, staring into the quiet, hot night. A little brown owl nested in the old yellow pine beyond the fence, and on a hot night it would fly close to the pool looking for prey, snakes and field mice drawn to the cool water. I stood there listening to the low, mournful hooting in the perfect stillness of the night, waiting for that sharp flick against the white of the deck that meant a strike, when my eye caught the pale gleam of a lamp I'd left on upstairs in the servant's quarters, and after a moment, I sighed.

Yes, yes, maybe she was right. Maybe I was projecting a little nervous tension here. Not about the war or Reagan or any other Dilemma Facing Modern Fundamentalism, but about Clayton, dear Clayton, who would sneak into the men's class whenever he got the chance and always side with me, no matter what. I could have championed bestiality, and he would have been there beside me, backing me up a hundred percent, for Clayton was only a storm trooper in that his loyalty was his honor. It wasn't carved on his knife; it was carved on his heart, and you talk about seeing the writing on the wall. Sooner or later, someone—probably a Sims—was going to let him in on a fascinating little rumor they'd once heard, and poor Clay. Poor Gabriel. Poor Myra. What could we do? Deny it? That'd be the easy way out, a laugh and a look of hilarious disbelief ("Don't believe everything you hear, son—"), but damn, I wasn't sure I could do it.

Not sure at all. It'd be a lie, for one thing, and it would somehow demean us all, even Michael. *Especially* Michael, for how could I explain how much my brother loved me unless I explained how much he'd forgiven me? It just wasn't possible, and I wanted to discuss it with Myra, set some plan of action in order, but found it difficult, for the closer we became, the more protective she was of Michael's memory, and I didn't want her to think I was trying to claim Clayton out of some petty middle-aged need for ownership.

I agonized over it a few weeks there at the beginning of the summer, but in the end, simply kept my mouth shut, which was stupid, inexcusably stupid, for if anyone knew how denial could heat normal reaction to explosion point, it was me. But that's what I did, all right, plain old-fashioned denial, the kind I am very gifted in, while I surreptitiously tried to improve my odds by spoiling Clay rotten, laughing at his jokes (which were funny), encouraging him to be as sarcastic as his mother would allow, hoping I could ease him over any shocking revelations with a tight relationship. So it was much later, July Fourth—or, no, it was Labor Day, at the end of the summer, when the blow finally fell, by Mama's hand, of all people, who would have put a gun to her head before she'd have touched a hair on Clayton's head.

It happened around the dinner table on Magnolia Hill, the same table where Ira had once made the shocking little announcement that had changed our lives forever. We had gathered there for the holiday, eating something festive, ribs or steak, all of us a little nervous over the new school year, painfully conscious that this was the last day of an era. After today, Simon would become an official employee of Sanger Manufacturing for one year, then an official freshman at FSU, a plan he'd made long ago with Michael's blessing. Tomorrow would also mark the first year Missy could drive to school alone, in a restored '64 Mustang I'd found her in Montgomery and liked so much that we were negotiating a trade with the Volvo, for, with all the genetically engineered pragmatism of her nature, she valued air-conditioning above style.

As for Clay, Tuesday would be his first day of high school in town, a landmark he was not at all concerned with, though Missy was dedicated to urbaning him up for the experience, lest he do something publicly humiliating and shame her good name. All summer long she'd been on his back, going so far as to supervise his selection of school clothes and now, with time growing short, she went into overtime, using this last meal to try and humiliate him into better table manners, telling him, at one point, he chewed like a pig.

"Don't you even *think* about talking to me in the cafeteria," she said, and Mama, always Clayton's ally, took it upon herself to give him a few tips on good manners.

"You never talk with your mouth full," she said sagely, "and when one hand is on the table, the other one ain't."

"Where is it?" Sim asked mildly.

Clayton cracked, "On your crotch. That's the polite place to rest your hand while you eat."

Simon laughed, and Missy was saying something about him doing her a favor and never speaking to her again, when Mama stood to get the dessert.

"He's a-getting more like his daddy every day," she said, passing me on the way to the kitchen and giving me a little slap to the back of the head. "Now you'll see what I went through a-raising *you*, Gabriel Catts."

She didn't even realize what she'd said, going to the kitchen for the dessert, leaving the rest of us paralyzed, Myra's face suddenly very white, Simon and Missy talking quickly, trying to cover the silence (I hadn't realized till then they knew), Clayton and I staring at each other across the table for about five strained seconds before dropping our eyes and finishing in silence.

Mama came back with the ice cream and ladled it out without a sign of unease, allowing the meal to regain a normal pitch, but when I chanced little glances at Clay, his face was averted and oddly squinted, as if he were trying to remember a date on a test. I knew well enough what he was thinking, remembering Myra's words from his project ("I came back to see Gabriel, he was the brother I remembered"), plus bits and pieces of other things, how everyone commented on our likeness, how I'd told him the maps on the walls of the servant's quarters were exactly as old as he was, that I'd put them up the summer before he was born when I was down here working on my book.

("Why'd you leave them?" he'd asked, and I'd been vague. "Well, I left in kind of a hurry—")

But not a word was spoken, not a word, for repression creates a false little parallel world of its own, and once the conversation picked back up, there was a hint of enormous relief in the room, as if everyone (except Mama, who still hadn't realized her slip) was thinking, "Well," sigh, "at least *that's* over."

But I knew better, and when Curtis came by to pick Clayton up for one last run to the river, I followed him to the truck and took him aside, my voice trying for normalcy. "I need to talk to you tonight."

He wouldn't look at me, but Curtis assured me they wouldn't be late. "We're only going gigging. We'll be back by nine."

I nodded and smiled and told them to be careful, then went inside and suffered through another one of those horrific afternoons of waiting. I tried to keep everything low-key and harmless, going down to Sanger with Sim to see his rabbit-hole of an office, finalizing the car swap with Missy, teasing her on her preference for a Volvo, predicting she'd vote the Democratic ticket on the next presidential election, but beneath the smiles, my head was pounding, and Myra's blank, introspective face was scaring the hell out of me.

Finally, around dark, she said we must go, that the children had to get to bed, and as we said good-bye to Mama on the porch, the jagged windows of the house next door seemed to grin at me in triumph, and I mused aloud, "One of these days I'm gone burn that son of a bitch down."

"Gabriel Catts," Mama cried (at my language, not my intent), but I would not apologize, and when Sim and Missy came home later, just after nine, Myra sent them straight to bed.

"It's nine o'clock," Missy cried, but Myra was firm—pale and firm, her small hands clenched behind her back.

"It's the first day of school. You need your rest."

Simon, who at eighteen had plenty of reason to balk, didn't argue though, and as he started up the stairs, he paused as if to speak, then turned and left us with a good-night, and I knew Michael was the reason for his silence. He must have spoken to him, given him the authorized version, somehow made it right, and God in heaven, I wished he would have put it on tape because Myra and I were scared to death.

We sat at the kitchen table and looked at each other a few minutes, then made our only plan. It was: "You talk first."

This was spoken by Myra to me, and I nodded. Then we sat there a little longer, our hands on the table in front of us, till I broke the silence.

"Myra," then hesitated, "does Clayton know—" then paused again. What I wanted to know was if he knew of the lithium, of Dr. Williams, and all that went before it, but the way I asked it was: "Does he know about your father?"

She didn't answer, but only shook her head, slowly, and after a moment, a tear rolled silently down her cheek untouched. One single tear, and I stood and went to her, holding her against my chest.

"I don't want him to know," she whispered fiercely. "I told Missy and Sim, but not him, and I don't want to, Gabriel, none of it. I can't—"

"It's all right," I kept murmuring, then stood her up. "Here, baby, you go on to bed, get some sleep. This'll be better, one on one—"

"No, I have to tell him—"

"No— listen, baby, Curtis said they'd be late," I lied. "You go on, I'll take care of it. You saw how he took it. He loves me. He'll be fine—"

She was so desperate to believe me that she let me take her upstairs and talk her into a pill—not lithium, she couldn't take that without a blood test, something else, a synthetic, she called it, with a name about twenty letters long. Then I went downstairs and waited on the couch. The clock ticked, the locusts shook in the trees, the little owl watched for its prey, and I tried to remain calm, listening for the door, denying the passing hours till suddenly, I stood, going to the kitchen, telling myself it must be past eleven, that Curtis knew better than to keep him out this late on a school night.

The clock on the stove read two fifteen.

I jerked the phone off the hook and dialed Curtis and Lori's, and on about the fifteenth ring, a sleepy voice finally answered.

"Curtis?" I said. "This is Gabe. Listen, where the hell is Clay? I got up and he's not—"

"I dropped him off at eight." He yawned, and I immediately backed off.

"Oh. Well, listen, he must be downstairs—no, no problem, y'all get anything?"

"Too many snakes," he said, and when we hung up and I dialed the sheriff's office, I agreed: too many snakes.

The deputy on duty was sympathetic, but unable to file a report until twenty-four hours had passed, so I got in the car and drove around town, to the bus station, the church, along the highway, the cemetery, anywhere I thought he might be hiding. But I found nothing; nothing but a still summer night, one so damn reminiscent of the night he was conceived, in a seedy motel room during a festival, the hot lights of the midway making it happy and harmless, nothing more than a child's game as I pitched the condoms and decided it was time to play hardball with my brother Michael.

When early light began to cast a rose glow along the pines to the east, I swung back by the house to see if he'd shown up, and was half way across the deck when I remembered the servant's quarters and wondered if he'd sneaked up there last night, afraid to face me.

"Of course," I murmured, and berated myself for not having thought of it before, taking the stairs to the rooms two at a time, but stopping at the door, my hand on the old brass knob, hit by a premonition of evil so strong it almost sent me over backwards. After all, this was where it all began, right up here in this small room, given to me out of kindness by my brother, a kindness I repaid as I repaid all his gifts, and I had a primeval, heart-pounding certainty that this was where the dues would be paid; that Clayton was here all right, but he wasn't hiding; he was hanging from a light fixture or lying in a pool of blood in the old porcelain tub, a pathetic last message scrawled above his head.

The impact of the image was so strong that I was paralyzed there at the top of the stairs, one hand still gripping the cold metal knob, aware of a movement somewhere below, the click of a French door, then a woman's voice. It broke my paralysis, and I jerked the door open, hoping, praying, I could save him, but when I burst in the room, it was just as I'd left it fourteen years before, hardly changed at all. Even the sheets on that narrow bed probably the same, and I was so relieved I went to the window and leaned on it for support, my forehead on the glass. I rested there a moment, then realized the sound I'd heard was Myra, down on the deck, calling my name. I tapped on the glass to get her attention and saw the tip of her nightgown as she went around the corner to the stairs.

Softly she came, up, up, and when she opened the door, her face was bloodless but even.

"He's at Candace's," she said in a light, dry voice. "She's on the phone. She says he's very upset. She made me promise I wouldn't call." It was as if she'd memorized the words on Candace's urging, and she finished in that same light, paced voice: "She said, Gabriel, that if you call him or try to see him, you will lose him. She said for me to tell you that."

After the horror of my vision of ropes and blood and death, this calm, level-headed advice was the sweetest thing I'd ever heard in my life, and I was speechless with relief, answering wordlessly with a nod, then resting my forehead back against the cold glass while Myra went downstairs to the phone. I watched her pass below and saw she walked with an odd stiffness, possibly a side-effect from the medication, and thought I'd better go see about her, comfort her, tell her Clayton would understand. That he was thirteen, but he was old for his age, he wasn't like me—

And suddenly I realized what I'd done: how in maintaining my own protracted innocence, I'd sacrificed my son's. It was so searing, so bitter, that I closed my eyes at the impact, then lifted my face with deadly deliberation and slammed my forehead against the heavy sash of the old window, making it crack, then shatter. On the deck below, Myra turned, and after a second of wide-eyed horror, started for the stairs, calling my name, but I ignored her, drawing back and hitting my forehead, one blow after another, in senseless, thoughtless punishment, trying to produce a greater pain, but not quite able, consumed by the hopeless, futile cry of the king: *Would God I had died for thee, my son, my son.*

Chapter

19

I *thought he'd be gone for two days,*
tops. Then Candace would call, and
I'd go over there and tell him my side of the matter and maybe he'd call
me a few names, bastard and SOB and the like; then he'd break down
and both of us would cry and that'd be the end of that. He'd come back
home, and we'd begin again, this time on a firm foundation of truth,
older and wiser and conscious of the imperfectability of man.

That's what I thought.

Hoped. Told myself over and over again those first few days as I
went about my first-of-the-year routine, introducing my classes to the
theory of history, eating supper with Missy and Sim, trying to smile and
make the best of it while every second my ear was straining for that
damn phone to ring.

But it didn't.

Not once, and on Wednesday afternoon, I said to hell with it and
left school early to pick up Myra and go over to Candace's and straighten
this thing out once and for all. But when I pulled in the back drive, I

saw Ed's truck was already there and ran inside in a backwash of relief, prepared for battle, truce, surrender, whatever I had to do.

What I found was Candace, sitting primly on the sunroom couch, surrounded by suitcases and boxes and bags full of clothes, and for a moment, it didn't connect. Then I saw the edge of Clayton's skate-board sticking out of one of the bags and began shaking my head.

"No, Candace," I said. "Not at all—"

"Yes, Gabriel," she answered just as evenly, slowly coming to her feet, but before we got into it, Myra came down the stairs, a pair of ragged hightops in her hand, her face blank as she set them on the pile.

"These are his old ones. I can't find his new Nikes. I just bought them last week. He won't wear them; they hurt his feet."

She was speaking in a tired, puzzled voice that Candace answered very pleasantly. "They're on his feet, you idiot. But pack the old ones too, he'll need them for fishing."

There was something hideously wrong with all of it, Candace's forced gaiety, Myra's blank obliging face, and I waited till she had gone back upstairs before I turned on my sister. "Clayton is not leaving this house. No, not at all. Forget that shit—"

And instead of a reply, Candace stormed past, snatching at the sleeve of my shirt.

"Shut up, Gabriel, just shut up," she hissed, pulling me through the kitchen to the laundry room and closing the door behind us.

"—no, not at all," I was still saying. "I don't know what you and Myra think you're up to, but no, never, not Clayton—"

Candace, looking not so much like Mama as she used to, but more like Daddy's people, small and wiry, her hair frosted where the blonde had prematurely grayed, leaned against the door and watched me with a hard, unsmiling face, letting me rage on without a word.

"—I mean what d'you think'll happen? He'll figure it out by osmosis?"

"I told him," she said, and I looked at her.

"You told him? *You* told him? And how the hell was it any of your business to tell him anything?"

"He asked me and I told him. Everything. Everything, Gabriel."

Now I don't know why it made me so mad, hearing she'd spared me this ordeal, but I was mad, I was shouting mad, pacing the room, calling her a wide variety of all the profanities I could conjure, minced with a few deadly observations on her character, but she was unmoved, just standing there against the door, watching me with eyes that were tired and disgusted.

"Are you finished yet?" she finally asked, and it only made me madder.

"Hell, no, I'm not finished. I won't be finished till I see Clay, find out what kind of lies you been feeding him—"

"Lies?" she repeated, annoyed at last. "Lies? Well, here, Gabe, you don't have to run to Clay, I'll be glad to tell you what kind of lies I been feeding him: That his grandfather was a child molester, that his mother is mentally ill, that his uncle he loves more than anyone *on earth* is really his father, and his father, who he is hanging onto by the skin of his teeth is just his uncle. That's the kind of *lies* I been feeding him, *Gabrielle*, and d'you know, for some reason, he's just not taking it very well. I mean, God knows it's simple enough, losing a father to cancer when you're eleven, then finding out he isn't your father at all. I don't know why he isn't over here apologizing this minute for all the trouble he's put you through."

Disgust, anger, even hatred, I could take from my sister, but sarcasm, never. Suddenly, everything was her fault.

"You had no business telling him anything. I was going to tell him. You don't know—you were in goddamned Germany!"

On this, she finally left the door and approached me quietly. "When were you gone tell him, Gabe? When?"

"Last night—no, Sunday. I had it all planned. I would have told him, made it right—"

"Then, listen," she said, stopping just short of my nose, "You tell me all about it. You're right, I wasn't here. All I know is Myra's version, and it don't make a hell of a lot of sense, so come on, let's have it, brother. How is it you come to have a child by Michael's wife, I'd love to know."

For a moment, I just looked at her, then I turned aside. "It's none of your business," I whispered, standing beside the washer and pressing my forehead against the edge of the pantry shelf, feeling the sore place where the stitches still stung, but her voice at my back was quietly sing song, reminding me of something, something a long time ago—

"Of course it's my business," she said. "Your son's asked to move in with me. It's been my business ever since he showed up on my doorstep Sunday night, crying, calling his mother a whore—"

"No," I cried, suddenly remembering Ira, and turned. "Just shut up, Candace! I don't have to listen to your *shit*—"

"Sure you do," she said. "I heard you, boy. Myra's heard you, everybody at Welcome's heard you, so why should we spare your feelings? Whore sound a little hard to you? A little raw? Well listen, bud, it ain't nothing compared to what he's calling you, and he'd say it to your face if I let him. He's just like you, boy: *know the truth and the truth shall set you free*—"

"It's not true," I whispered.

"Well, as far as Clay's concerned, it is. And until he sees it different, I'm sorry, Gabe, he's mine."

She faced me off evenly, and after a moment, I turned away, pressing my forehead against the shelf that smelled of bleach and Downy, finally whispering, "I'll speak to him, Candace. Tell him how it was, convince him—"

"*Convince* him?" she breathed. "You mean *mow him under*,

scream and cry and blame it on everyone else, and I'm sorry, Gabe, I can't let you do that."

"I love him," I said, in final, desperate appeal, and Candace laughed, just as Ira and Michael had, and it was so strange. I really did, how could they doubt me?

"You know," she said, "I've been waiting for that. I mean, waiting, and it kills me, Gabe, it really kills me, the things you do in the name of love. Listen, why don't you ask your wife about Gabriel Catts love? Her father used to tell her he loved her all the time. Called her to his death-bed, crying, asking her why she never called, never came to visit, when God in heaven knew he loved her more than anyone on earth—"

I felt a wave of the nausea that always hit when I heard the more putrid details of my wife's torment, but I knew better than to mention it; Candace would probably tell me to go ahead and puke, that it was all private here, she'd seen men puke before, use to run them till they puked, tell them it was good for them. So I just pressed my twelve new stitches hard against the shelf and let her finish.

"—and you will not do that to Clayton. No, not at all. I promised Michael I'd be there for his children, and I'll be there all right. I'll raise him till he's grown if that's what it takes, and you, Gabriel Catts, will stay clear. Do you hear me? *Stay clear.*"

"You don't know what you're asking," I whispered. "I lost him ten years already."

"And you had him one, which is more'n you deserve, and if he never comes back, you'll have Myra and Sim and Missy and it'll have to do. It's nobody's fault but your own." She stopped to wipe a tear, and for the first time, I realized she was crying. "Nobody put a gun to your head."

My forehead was still pressed to the shelf, pressed so hard I could feel the tiny, stiff ends where the ER doctor had tied off the sutures, and with a sudden flash of anger, I drew back and struck the sharp edge of the shelf, exploding those neat little puckers of skin and spraying the washer with drops of blood, while Candace pulled me back, screaming, "And you will not do this to yourself, Gabriel Catts. You will live through this and you will see it out, d'you hear me? Do you hear me?"

I didn't care. I was shaking the blood off my face, trying to shake off her words, but she had the front of my shirt in her fists, and was screaming in my face. "And you will *not* drink and you will *not* leave because I love you and Mama loves you and Myra and Sim and Missy and Clay love you, and you will be there for them." She shook me the way she must have seen Ed shake raw recruits. "Do you hear me?"

At that point I wasn't hearing much of anything. Stimulation over-load, I guess you'd call it, and to this day, I have no other memory of that afternoon, how I cared for my stitches, whether I helped pack the truck or lay on the couch and cried. Nothing but a blank. And for the first time in my life, I realized how her childhood must seem to Myra: bits and pieces of vivid memory and a few scars like the one on my forehead that I will wear till I die.

I do know that I went back to work the next day, where my Frankenstein-like forehead elicited a great deal more interest from my students than the exploration of the New World. After fielding an hour's worth of questions and speculation first period, I assigned library passes and started them on their first oral reports, and when they'd left, I found a ream of legal pads in my file cabinet and sat down at my desk and began to write, not another historical revision or a character assas-sination, but the explanation I could not give Clayton because the words were so hard to put into motion.

First, I wrote of Michael's funeral, then, for some reason, I found myself writing of my childhood on Magnolia Hill, with Benny and Daddy and Cassie Scales, and my good friend Ira and his little sister, who was not so remarkable at all till I saw her with her hair unbraided in the sun and fell in love.

It was so sweet, bringing them back to life under my hand, the smell of mimosa, the crack of the screen door, the rise and fall of voices on the porch at midnight, and when the final bell rang at three, I went straight home to my desk in the servant's quarters and continued to write the long, spiraling sentences that flew off my pen like magic. On and on, they came, and as the night passed and dawn was upon me, I thought how convenient it would be if this were mere fiction. Then I could delete the closets and the cruelty, I could make Cassie kiss me, I could kill off Old Man Sims the night Myra was conceived and have her come to Magnolia Hill by a kinder route—the niece of a preacher, the cousin of a friend of a friend. And when she came knocking when she was grown and asked for me, Mama would give her my address, and we'd marry the week after I finished FSU and move to Durham and conceive our children—

I stopped in mid-fantasy, for where would that leave Sim and Missy? In the realm of the unborn? Or would they have been born to Michael and another woman, some woman who might not read books and tell him of other worlds outside the pounding walls of Sanger Manufacturing so that he would die at forty-three with nothing to show for it: No Sam, no broken Klan, no Simon or Missy or Clayton to grieve him.

So perhaps the truth suited me better after all, and I couldn't have changed it if I tried, and I found myself smiling when I thought that maybe we had won, despite everything—the closets and the cruelty. Won by virtue of something, I couldn't say what. Then I remembered Myra's words at the grave that day, on innocence and insanity and the paths to salvation.

I was still pondering it, yawning, when she came upstairs in her gown, and I noted with relief that her eyes were no longer blank, but merely worried, squinting in the new sun.

"Where've you been all night?" she asked irritably, kissing me lightly on the mouth, not a good-morning kiss, but a have-you-been-drinking kiss.

"Here," I said. "Working on a new book." I hesitated to go any further, and she didn't look too interested anyway, only relaxing when she tasted my breath and found it sober and going over to the bed and lying down.

"This Pamalor," she yawned. "A hundred milligrams is too strong. I'm gonna have to call Dr. Williams. I can't live like this—"

She was asleep before the words were fairly out of her mouth, and I went over and kissed her forehead, blessing the pharmaceutical industry, for despite her great distrust of their intentions (*bloodsuckers*, she called them) I couldn't see her standing the loss of a child without a little numbing.

My watch said seven, so I went downstairs to make some coffee and found Missy pouring orange juice at the refrigerator, her face relieved when she saw me.

"Well, thank God," she said. "We thought you'd hit the road, too."

Her blunt honesty was so much like Mama, so damn much, that I found myself laughing and laughing, for the first time in days, and she started in, too, then hugged me, and we got a little teary there for a moment, which she sidetracked by filling me in on all the juicy tidbits of gossip she'd picked up by keeping her ear to the ground.

"I'm gonna have to drive him to school every day. He's too stinking lazy to walk three blocks from Candace's, and I'm gone ask him just what the heck he thinks he's pulling here. It's just like him to show himself to get a little attention."

"No," I told her, relieved, painfully relieved, the whole nightmare was finally resurfacing in the light of routine breakfast conversation. "Let him alone. He'll come around."

"Oh, sure he will. After he's been a pain in the tail long enough. I mean Mama told *me*, and I didn't get in such a *snit*."

"Did she?" I murmured politely.

Missy was her usual imperturbable self, buttering a waffle, saying, "Sure. Told me right after Daddy died 'cause I kept bugging her to call you. Told me about good sex and bad sex and about her father and Ira and why he was in Raiford." She made a face. "And she told me Clay was my half-brother because she'd had sex with you and got pregnant the summer you stayed here."

This was a bit strong for my stomach, and I could feel my face suddenly growing very hot, but Missy only chewed her waffle. "I guess she thought she'd better get it out in one shot, but it worked out all right. I just kinda figured everybody's mother sat them down like that." She started laughing. "But I was a little bit curious, you know, wondering if everybody had this kind of stuff in their families, so the next time I was over at Grannie's I asked her if we—you know, the Catts—were pretty normal, and she said yes, but that we were better Christians than most people."

She laughed long and hard, but I was a little sad, knowing it was my fault we'd joined the Sims as moral underachievers.

"But Clayton now," she continued, "he's just such a *twit*. I mean, I saw him in the library yesterday and I said, 'Clay, are you really moving in with Candace? Uncle Ed'll make you mow the yard and you know you hate that.' And you know what he said? He said he'd *work a saw at Sanger* before he'd live in a house with *that* man." She rolled her eyes, "I mean, he has to be so *melodramatic* about it."

She went back to her waffle. "Candace's right. I think we should just ignore him. Listen, Saturday morning rolls around, he'll be talking out the other side of his mouth."

But he didn't. Not through the red flush of a lovely autumn, not in the brittle ice of a raw, Gulf-blown winter, nor any of the December anniversaries—the funeral or the wedding—or his birthday in March. From Missy and Sim we followed his year: the Latin he was failing, the ankle he sprained in gym (faked, Missy surmised, to get out of the six-hundred-yard dash), the new haircut Sim described as spiked, the girl in algebra he loved, who wouldn't so much as look his way. At Christmas, Myra and I huddled back at the kitchen table like a meeting of the general staff and selected his gifts with many disagreements.

"Nothing on Vietnam—no, Gabriel, I'm sick of it. . . . Chess? Why does everything have to do with war? Listen, I bought his presents twelve years with no complaints. You do Missy's. You're good with her."

So I chose Missy's presents and left Clayton to Myra, but whether he opened the carefully discussed, artfully wrapped gifts was open to speculation, for Missy and Sim were very quiet about it, so quiet I had a feeling he'd left them under the tree, untouched. Candace never said during her weekly Sunday afternoon calls, made on the sly while Clayton was at Mama's, and Myra and I couldn't stand to ask, only listening on the upstairs and downstairs extensions while she caught us up on his life. Sometimes Myra would stop her to clarify something or give a little advice, but apparently she and my sister were close enough not to have to bother with details, and as for me, I had nothing to say but that I loved him—a little phrase I was learning to keep to myself for fear of being likened to a child molester, or worse.

The only concession I made was going out a little more, occasionally attending freshman football games or slowly circling the high school at lunchtime (à la child molester, now that I think of it—) in hopes of seeing a glimpse of a blond spiked head somewhere in the crowd. But I had no luck, none at all, and had no choice but to go home and scribble out more of my apology, and it was on a clear spring night, a year almost to the day from the evening I'd sat out by the pool and conjured Michael for Clay's project, that Myra suddenly became curious about my nocturnal activities upstairs in the servant's quarters, and found me painstakingly typing my little work, producing, at best, one page a night.

The first draft was all written, so I was no longer worried about hiding my intent, but when I proudly showed her my stack of legal pads, she was far from enthusiastic.

"Not my life, you're not," she said, "nor Michael's either."

It was hardly the response I'd expected from a woman who'd been open enough to discuss adultery with an eleven-year-old girl, and with no argument strong enough to plead my case, I handed the typed pages over with one request: "Don't decide till you read it. At least read it."

She took the typed first quarter, spotted with Wite-Out and editorial scrawls, and I tried to give her time, plenty of time, to make up her mind, but after only an hour went upstairs and found her sitting up in bed, most of the pages face down beside her, staring into the air with a look of calm bemusement.

When I sat on the edge of the bed, her face reclaimed a little life, but was still a little puzzled as she looked at me. "Gabriel, Gabriel," she said, "you almost make me miss Magnolia Hill. Lord, I never thought anyone could do that."

It was such a sweet reaction, such a Myra-like acceptance of dreams and ideas and hopeless stabs at reconciliation that for the first time in a long time I remembered why I'd loved her in the first place, not for her hair or her lingerie or even her Mercedes, but for her kindness.

"I love you," I told her, thinking to hell with Candace, it was true.

She smiled a small, sad smile. "Poor Ira," she said, tapping the paper in her lap, "he never had a chance, Gabriel, never—"

She began to cry, for her brother was the grief of Myra's life, more so than Clayton, who was a car drive away, being cared for by a loving aunt, while Ira, Ira was lost to us forever.

I pushed the papers aside, and I lay down beside her. "Poor Ira? What about poor Myra?"

She wiped her cheeks. "I haven't got that far yet."

"Oh," I smiled. "Well, save some tears for Myra Sims. She never had a chance either."

"She had Michael," Myra said, very gently.

I agreed. "Yes. She had Michael."

"And she has Gabriel." She smiled.

I held her face in my hand. "She always has Gabriel."

So we were in agreement there, at least until I typed my way through the summer of '74, and I found myself at the mercy of a guilty Baptist conscience.

"I have never worn a transparent bathing suit in *my life*! You made it up, Gabriel, you made it up!"

"It was only transparent when it was wet. I noted that very clearly, see?"

"But it's a lie! I've never owned such a thing!"

"You were loony that summer. You don't know what you owned."

"Well, I know I didn't wear a see-through bathing suit. Michael wouldn't have let me, and if I did, I don't see how it's necessary. I mean this is for Clayton, not *Hustler*."

We were arguing over it in the servant's quarters, and I sat her down on the narrow bed that had once been the battlefield for this war and tried to explain.

"Listen baby, I know it's not *Hustler*. I tried to ride the fine line between being needlessly explicit and—"

"And *what*?" she cried. "Just say you got me pregnant. Good Lord, Gabriel, he'll figure out the rest."

"*No*."

"Well, why not? Are you trying to make yourself out as some kind of king stud here?"

"Don't be an idiot," I snapped, then took a calming breath, and tried to explain. "It's just—I just want him to understand why I did it. I mean it's easy for you, you can get out of anything. You're like Ira, mentally incompetent to stand trial, but me—I want him to know it wasn't something casual, that it was—" I paused, then found the word, "— serious. I want him to know he was conceived in love, that I loved him and you did and Michael did, too. I don't want him to think it was some kind of hideous *accident*."

She softened a little at that and patted my hand, and I thought she was going to give in, but she only said, "Well, then write it like you want to, but listen, I'm gone cut it when it gets—" I tried to interrupt, but she waved me away, "—offensive. And inaccurate, which this part about the see-through bathing suit is."

So we were right back at square one, and when I refused to budge, she withdrew her support entirely, calling me many names and analyzing my motives with something less than Christian charity till we came to a reluctant compromise: I could describe the bathing suit in some detail, wet and all, as long as I noted it was relatively modest when dry, and as long as I documented on a page-to-page basis that Myra's affection toward me never seemed what you might call reciprocal.

It was a small, not altogether untruthful concession that brought about a truce that lasted about three pages, till she came across the phrase "white and painful."

"You're describing an *orgasm*!" she shouted. "I can't believe you, Gabriel. Why don't you call this thing *Deep Throat*?"

I assured her the adjectives had come innocently to mind with no pornographic symbolism intended, but she was hysterically firm on this one, wanting to jerk the whole project.

"I'd rather he didn't know anything than *this*."

"This," I said, "is true, and anyway, who cares what it suggests? I mean, this is adultery we're talking about here, not needlepoint."

She really wept at this. "You're just making a joke out of this. It's just another game to you. God in heaven, why did you ever come back?"

I tactfully ignored what had become a common theme around the Catts household, but it was a solid month before we worked this one out, finally agreeing to relative honesty, white and painful and all, but putting the whole narrative away in a safe deposit box for Clay to open on his fortieth birthday.

"By then," I told her, "nothing will shock him."

She only looked at me. "How can you say that? I hope he cries."

Then I remembered the closets and Ira and apologized many times. From there on out, we rolled along with remarkable speed, only having a short breakdown when I went into a little intimate detail about Adele and really found myself in hot water. But after a few tears and a lot of fast explaining, we made it peacefully to the end, with Myra holding steadfastly to two inflexible dictates.

The first was that Michael never be recorded using offensive profanity (that is: profanity personally offensive to Myra Louise Catts). The second, that the exact nature of the crimes that sent Ira to Raiford never be discussed or alluded to in any form or fashion. I found both exceptions unrealistic and painfully misleading, but Myra stood firm, pointing out that Michael's language was not the issue here, and that Ira's crimes were of such a nature that they should never even be spoken of, much less explained away.

"Michael worked in a factory," I argued. "He played baseball. He picked up profanity. Who cares? Damn, Myra, don't paint him as some kind of plaster saint."

"I'm not painting him any way. I just never heard him use the word and I'm not so sure he did."

"Why would I lie about such a thing?"

"I don't know—but listen, honey, it makes him sound trashy, and Michael was never that way."

When I pointed out that she'd let *me* be recorded using *that word* with no undue concern about how I sounded, she just looked at me.

"Hey, I let you be recorded doing all kinds of wild and trashy things."

I saw we were losing ground here and quickly assented, so

Michael's words of disgust at the Klan and bad football have been down-graded to shit and SOB, and Ira's crimes left out all together. However, I will give one indication of their magnitude to say that to this day there meets in Duval County a victim support group that spends about six evenings a year crying over their losses and promising Ira Leldon Sims will see the electric chair, no matter how many pissant bleeding-heart liberals try to plead otherwise. But that's as far as I can go, and I guess I should be grateful that I got by with only two inadmissions, for if Myra'd had her way, Clay would be left with the mystery of another immaculate conception. In the meanwhile, I have quit telling my students that the recording of history belongs to the winners, the revision of that history to the losers. Now I know it belongs to neither, but to their conjugal partners. A small but possibly revolutionary slant on recorded history.

But enough of that. When it was all typed (the second half by Myra, which went a lot faster) and numbered and ready to lock away till 2015, Myra made an interesting observation that was really quite startling when she asked me why I had never mentioned my hand. Never. Not once, and I was so fascinated by the omission that I lay in bed that night and reread the entire manuscript and found that she was right. Except for one small reference after Daddy's funeral, I made no hint that since Old Man Sims' squeeze to my wrist, I have never been able to use my right hand.

Oh, it's not withered or unusual in any way. When it first came out of the cast, Doctor Winston downplayed it as a little ligament damage and gave me exercises to strengthen it, but after a year or so, he finally admitted there must be something more, a something we were never able to properly investigate due to the incredible burden of Daddy's hospital expenses. By the time I was old enough to do something on my own, the muscles had atrophied until it had became what it is today: a normal-looking, but useless, slightly curled hand that I still hold instinctively to my side, though it hasn't hurt me in twenty-six years.

"How could I have left it out?" I asked Myra when she woke up briefly at six, but she only looked at the clock, then curled back up.

"I don't know. Maybe it doesn't bother you."

"But it was such a wonderful symbol. I'll have to rewrite the whole damn thing."

This woke her up enough to look at me. "Well, I'm not retyping it, I'll tell you that."

"I'll hire a typist—"

"You will not. You'll do it yourself. I don't want some stranger reading my life."

"It'll take me ten years to type it myself."

She burrowed into her pillows. "Make a footnote."

"I hate footnotes."

She offered one last piece of advice. "Then make an addendum. It won't make any difference anyway, just explain why you're so easy to beat up."

An odd way of looking at it, I thought, but she fell asleep before I could argue, and the more I sat there and considered it, the more convinced I was that my hand had shaped me into the man I am today. For one thing, it placed me in a special category, that of a cripple, a stigma that has lessened now that I am grown, but was a pretty narrowing thing when I was young. Being a cripple meant I could stay inside and read books. I could not play baseball with any skill, or work a saw at Sanger. It meant I could use verbal gymnastics to get my way, but not resort to physical violence. And when I was fifteen, it meant I was not expected to go to work and make my way, but stay late at libraries and ponder abstractions, which I did, till I was seventeen and had no choice but to leave Magnolia Hill, for I was unable to compete in any market—I didn't have the skills; I was a cripple.

So I went to college and got an education and eventually a job, but maybe it was my hand that held me to Magnolia Hill. Maybe it was the tie, the small piece of unfinished business that drew me back, time and again, to the woman unintentionally responsible for it all: Myra, who is very protective of my hand, who holds it on her lap in church and kisses it sometimes, one finger at a time, in a way that makes me wonder if she will one day restore it to full use.

Well, like I say, it was a hell of a good symbol to overlook, and metaphor aside, it also explained more clearly why Michael always wanted me to throw baseballs, since Dr. Winston once (and only once, I might add) mentioned it might be therapeutic. It also explained why he never laid a hand on me, for he knew any fight between us would not be fair, and Michael was, if anything, a very fair man.

I lay in bed that morning—a Saturday, I think it was; Myra and Missy and Lori were going shopping at the outlets in Graceville for bathing suits—and tried to figure out a way to insert my handicap in a moving way that didn't require major retyping. When Myra woke up after nine, she was groggy and disoriented, courtesy of the pills, squinting at the clock.

"What time is it?" she asked. Then, "It's nine, Michael. You're late."

"It's Saturday and I'm Gabriel," I said, not offended, for I'd grown used to this particular side-effect of the meds. At first, it really threw me, her calling me Michael, but she was horribly embarrassed, threatening to pitch all the pills, till I assured her it was all right. So now I answer to Michael or Gabriel, or if she's really having a bad day, Missy or Cissie or on one inauspicious occasion, Ira.

"Sorry," she murmured, sitting up and rubbing her face.

"My hand's the reason I yell at the old men," I told her sagely.

She looked at me. "What?"

I held it up. "My hand. It's why I yell at the old men."

She took it and flattened it against her chest the way she does sometimes. "Don't blame your poor hand. You'd probably yell at people anyway."

"No, I wouldn't," I said, and offered my startling new revelation that she didn't seem to grasp the significance of, and after a while, I grew annoyed. "You just don't want to retype it. You're just lazy. And practical. I hate it; it's like I'm married to Mama."

She only yawned at what I thought was a bare-faced insult, and I tried to give it my best shot, sitting up so I could look her in the eye. "See, Myra, I've never been able to *shake hands* with other men. And *your father* did this to me. And listen," I was really excited about this one, "I used to be afraid I couldn't perform sexually because of my hand."

She looked a little perplexed at this, and I explained quickly, "I mean, the missionary position was the only way I thought you did it, and I couldn't bear weight—never mind, that's not the point. The point is, it changed my life. I'll have to revise, I'm sorry."

She just sat there a moment, and I thought I'd won her over. Then she said, "Gabriel," then, after a small sigh, "have you ever thought that all this fuss over your hand could be nothing more than a try for the sympathy vote? Have you thought of that?"

You know, sometimes I really did hate this woman's guts, and I jerked my hand back. "Go on, Cissie," I said and she left me alone, calling for Missy to wake up as she dressed.

"Don'tchu even remember your youngest son anymore?" I asked with more than a touch of sullenness, and she looked at me a moment with narrowed eyes, then went back to brushing her hair in the mirror, her voice light.

"Ah, yes. I think his name's Clayton. I'm watching him play baseball tonight."

Baseball was a sore subject with me, and I could only resort to sarcasm. "Oh, well, that's a tight relationship for you. Sitting in your car while he ignores you on the field. Boy, I wish I was that close to *my* children."

But she paid me no mind, only kissing me good-bye, leaving me in a sour-grapes kind of mood, pretending I didn't care that she and Candace wouldn't let me go with them to the ballpark on Saturday nights when Clayton took the field as probably the sorriest outfielder in the history of organized baseball.

"One of these days," Missy predicted, "somebody's gone hit a line drive to right field, and Clayton's gone be standing there scratching his tail, and it's gone konk him right on the head and kill him dead." She shook her head. "I mean, Uncle Gabe, he *never* hits the *ball*. Never. I mean, everybody knows he only made the team 'cause Sanger's the sponsor, and I tell you what, it embarrasses the crud out of me every time he takes the plate."

"Maybe he'll improve," I offered.

She snorted, "Improve, my foot. He don't give a hoot about baseball. He's just doing it to suck up to Rachel Cole, who wouldn't touch him with a ten-foot pole."

I didn't argue, though I knew Clayton wasn't out there to impress Rachel Cole or anyone else, for that matter. That he didn't care how humiliated he got. He was playing baseball, he was being Michael's son, and I loved him so much for his loyalty I would have paid a thousand dollars a night to watch him stand out there and scratch his tail, but once again, Myra and Candace prevailed.

"No!" they cried in these shocked, horrified voices that would have made you think I'd suggested some unheard of perversity.

"Well, why not? Myra goes, why can't I?"

"Myra is discreet," Candace said. "She sits in the car—"

"I can be discreet. I can sit in the car—"

"*No*, Gabriel, you'll *ruin* everything." This from Myra, on the bedroom extension, her voice trembling like she was about to cry.

"Well, my God, Myra, I'm not gonna—"

I was cut off by Candace, her voice patient and even, like she was informing me I had cancer. "Gabe. Listen. Baseball is the first thing, the *only* thing Clay has shown interest in."

"I'm not disput—"

"*And* he wouldn't even take the plate the first few games; he was so busy looking around, hoping you hadn't come to make some kind of scene—"

"I will sit in the car, Candace—"

"*And* if you do show up, you'll show yourself, you know you will. Everybody laughs at him. He's so sorry—"

"*Who* laughs at him?" I shouted. "Do you mean to tell me you and Ed just sit there on your ass and let people laugh at him?"

"*See? See?*" she shouted in triumph, while Myra actually wept.

"—ruin everything, everything—"

So I gave in, slamming down the phone and sulking a record two weeks, though it made not one bit of difference to my wife, who started dressing for these damn baseball games at two thirty in the afternoon and would sometimes even go out and wash the car.

"So, you think a clean car'll impress him?" I asked, but she was hot and soapy and determined.

"Leave me alone."

When she'd leave at seven, I'd sit around and fantasize about the other love of my life (Johnny Walker) till she returned home at nine with the bright eyes and flushed cheeks of a thoroughly satisifed woman, but no details of the game at all, unless Clayton happened to do something miraculous, like make a hit. And on the night he actually made a run in, she dashed up the stairs screaming, "Gabriel! Gabriel!"

I came out of the shower dripping wet, expecting a reconciliation, to say the least, but she only jumped up and down.

"Clayton made a hit. He ran around the bases. He won the game."

It truly seemed nothing short of a miracle, and indeed, when Missy gave her version at breakfast, it was considerably revised. "Well, he got on base because the shortstop was tying his shoe when he saw Clay was up to bat, and when he actually hit this little pop, I think they went into shock."

"But he made first? How'd he get in?"

"Oh, Ricky Vaughn was up next, hit a homer that went about seven miles, cleared the bases—"

"But it won the game?"

She made a face. "Good Lord, no. We won eight to two. Their pitcher was out. The relief guy walked four runs."

I tell you what, it was enough of a myth-debunking tale to make you forever skeptical of the validity of oral history, but I could not investigate firsthand without causing more of an uproar than I cared to deal with. My only revenge was a true hatred of Saturday nights, a hatred that did not lessen when Myra confided the real source of her excitement that night.

"When he made that run, everyone in the Sanger crowd stood and cheered, for Michael, I guess, but I was parked way to the side, and when he crossed home, he turned and looked to see if I was there, if I'd seen him, just like he used to do when he was a little boy. It was so sweet. I tell you what, me and Candace cried the rest of the game."

Well, it sure didn't sound too sweet to me, that I was left sitting home alone while my wife fell in love with a fourteen-year-old rebel without a cause, and in the end I was forced to play the last, the only, card I had left in my hand, when I woke up the next morning in a puddle of blood.

Chapter

lbeit, a small puddle of blood.

But the relatively small showing didn't calm Myra, not for a second. Suddenly, she was my wife again, holding my hand, calling Dr. Williams.

"He's bleeding," she told the nurse at Sanger. "Yes, from the mouth—"

"It's just the ulcer, honey," I told her. "It's nothing. I'm fine."

Though actually, I wasn't so fine. I hadn't been since Christmas when I ate fruitcake at the Sanger party and realized after about my fifth slice that it wasn't the pecans I was enjoying with such frenzy, but the rum they were soaked in. And since I'd been on Antabuse since September as a sort of insurance policy against self-pity, I spent the remainder of the evening (literally) puking my guts out.

I wasn't proud of the fact I was back on Antabuse, or that I'd made such an amateur's mistake, so I kept it to myself and passed it off as a virus, but my poor stomach wasn't letting me off that easy. For six months I'd been eating Tagamet and drinking Maalox and all the other things that used to work, but the baseball tension put me over the edge, and I crossed the border from active to bleeding ulcer in the space of one night.

"Margaret said Dr. Williams is out," Myra said. "We're going to the ER."

"Myra, no, I'm giving finals today—"

"A sub can give finals," she said, throwing on some clothes with a firm expression. "You're going to the hospital."

So within the hour, I was sitting on an examining table in the ER waiting for the doctor, feeling like a complete fool, asking Myra if she realized how much all of this was going to cost.

"I'll sell some shoes," she said absently, strolling around the room, nervously clicking lamps on and off, stopping every few steps to take a deep breath, and when a very young doctor came in and asked me what my problem was, she blurted out, "He's bleeding. The pillow, it was *covered with blood*. I told him we can't ignore it; it won't just go away."

The doctor looked rightfully surprised at her vehemence, telling me to pull up my shirt and lay back, and I felt like even more a fool and tried to downplay it.

"Listen, she's exaggerating. I have an ulcer. All I need is a little Tagamet—" I stopped to scream when he pressed my stomach, "*Damn*, boy, that hurts."

He ignored me, moving around the table, his voice thoughtful. "Have you had some kind of blunt trauma recently? A punch? A fall?"

"No—" I began.

Myra just about yanked me off the table, saying, "Tell him the truth, Gabriel. He has to know—" with such intensity that I looked at the doctor.

"Well, I did puke Antabuse Christmas. Ate some—uh—fruitcake with rum in it."

"Yow," he said lightly, but was a little disconcerted by Myra, who was still clutching my arm.

"See?" she said quickly. "And they can do things for you. They can fix you up. They've got medicines now." She looked at the doctor. "Don't they?"

The doctor was looking at her with earnest perplexity now, saying he'd have to order blood work, that he couldn't venture a diagnosis until he saw the labwork.

Myra ignored him, her face blank and white as she reassured me, "That's all right though, because they can do things for it now. Nowdays," she said, "it never kills anybody."

The doctor and I both were watching her now, wondering just what the hell she was talking about, when I finally noticed her eyes, and felt a tight claw at my throat and reached up to hold her hand. "That's right, baby. It'll be fine."

For they were squinted, distant, connected by a tiny marker of memory to another voice, another time by a cue so strong her face was panicked, far-off, trying to fight an old forgotten battle, but not sure, not sure—dying of not being sure. Overall, it was a look that I would liken to the eyes of an animal two seconds after the spring of a steel trap, and in a light, dry voice, I asked the doctor to please call my mother and tell her I needed her.

He said he would and left, saying something about ordering blood work, and when he was gone, Myra broke down and cried against my shoulder.

"It's all right, baby, it's fine—" I said, thinking that waking up on bloody sheets was a hell of a lot more serious a matter to Myra Sims than it'd ever be to me, but when she spoke, it was not in that nervous, shifting voice, but in her own: impatient, mad, trying to set me straight.

"It's not *that*, Gabriel, it's never *that*—" she cried, but was too flustered to finish, and it was a while longer before she was finally able to enlighten me. "Michael died here," she said. "He came in just like this. He had the flu, we thought. Then it was just gallstones, but—" I pulled her to my chest, but she finished. "He was never the same again. He kept losing weight. He got so thin, so weak. He *died* Gabriel, he *died*. I'll never talk to him again—"

I finally realized there was a betrayal larger than Old Man Sims looming here and held her tightly, trying to calm her, but was getting close to tears myself when my mother came to the door in one of her old housedresses, looking like she hadn't stopped to brush her hair when the doctor called. And you know, I have problems, deep philosophical problems, with this woman who bore me and gave me such an idiotic name, but I tell you what, she is nobody's fool, and sized up the situation in about two seconds flat.

"Well, Gabe, son, I toldju to quit eating so much of thet hot sauce," she said irritably, when I told her my complaint, neatly deflating all the ends and pieces of old memories of defeat that still lurked in these clinical halls, then turned to Myra. "Myra, baby, while he's getting these tests and whatall, why don't you come home with me?" Without missing a beat, she added, "Clay's coming by after school. He's heping me move my azaleas and cut back thet kudzu. It's sa blame hot I can't stand it more'n an hour, and if I leave it to Clay, well, it'll never get done."

Myra's tears came to a sudden and complete halt at the mention of Clayton's name, but Mama politely ignored it, making a pretense of having to talk her into it. "We get done in time, you can stay to supper. I got a ham and potato salad and we'll send Clay to the store for ice cream or frozen yogurt or whatever it is you women eat these days."

"I need to stay with Gabriel," she answered in a small voice, the voice of a responsible child who cannot attend a birthday party because she's promised to visit a sick aunt.

I proved I could play this game as well as Mama, pushing her off the table, saying, "Go, go. I'll be fine. Listen, when he gives me the Tagamet, I'll pay him his thousand and go grade my finals."

It took a little haggling, but she finally kissed me and left, just as the lab technician came for the blood, and an hour later, the ER doctor was back, a stack of little yellow slips in his hand, looking somehow annoyed.

"How long have you been bleeding?" he asked.

I was vague. "Oh, awhile. I've had it before, though. No problem."

"As a matter of fact," he said, "it is a problem. Your hematocrit is low, your white blood count is high, you're anemic, and your stomach feels like spaghetti."

I just shrugged; I mean what was I supposed to say? That I was sorry?

"You've been ignoring a very serious condition, Mr. Catts. I think the least radiology will find is a sizable perforation, and my only recommendation is surgery."

I rubbed my eyes for a long time, then tried to explain why this was impossible. "My wife is emotionally fragile. She lost a husband to cancer here a couple years ago. I just can't see putting her through another surgery this soon."

"Well, you may be putting her through another funeral here soon if you hemorrhage again with that blood count."

I cursed long and hard at this, then gave him my conditions: "Only if I can get it done today. As soon as possible. I mean, right now."

"I'll have to call surgery. They're probably booked—"

"Tell them I'm bleeding to death, threaten malpractice—I don't care, just do it quick, or I can't get it done at all."

He left with a look of moderate disgust, but returned slightly mollified, telling me I was in luck, the one o'clock colostomy had taken a turn for the worse, and he could slip me in at two.

"If you need to call anyone, the phone's in the drawer. Dial nine to get out."

So I lay back and dialed nine in combination with every number

I knew, feeling like Jackson at Cold Harbor, amassing my troops, telling everyone where Myra was, where I was, what to do and say, and what to avoid.

"But are you all right?" Missy asked, still sniffling, for they'd called her out of geometry finals to speak with me, and she'd convinced herself en route to the office that either Myra or me or Sim or all three of us had died in a car wreck.

"I'm fine, fine," I assured her. "The nurse gave me a blue Valium and a Zantac and I'm sitting pretty here."

"Well," she began, then finished nervously, "take care. I don't know what to say. Try not to bleed to death or anything."

I promised her I'd give it my best shot, and when the Valium kicked in, decided I might as well lay back and enjoy this perfectly legal little buzz and put the phone away.

Sometime later, an orderly came and rolled me down the hall to surgery, and I remember asking him what time it was. One thirty, he said, and I thought how Clayton would be out of school already because of early dismissal, and he and Myra would be in Mama's yard clipping the kudzu, pulling it off the fence that separated us as children. And if the conversation lagged, maybe she'd tell him how I once showed her how to make a hopscotch board there, once a thousand years ago. . . .

The next thing I remember is waking up in a sterile, white-walled room, my mouth dry, my stomach tight. I tried to investigate, but my good hand was taped up with an IV, so I could only lie there and stare at the ceiling till a nurse came by to check the drip.

"Can I use a phone?" I asked, and at first she said no. Then she told me to lie back and returned with Simon in her wake, dressed in his dirty khaki work clothes, looking so much like Michael that I was too bewildered to speak.

"The doctor says it went off without a hitch," he said, leaning on the rails and taking my hand.

I only whispered, "Myra?"

"She's still at Grannie's with Clay. Grannie says they've talked more than they've pulled kudzu, but I guess that was the point, wasn't it?"

I nodded and closed my eyes and remember telling him how much he favored his father, but that was all. When I woke up, much later, I was in a regular private room, not sure if Simon had come, or if I'd had some weird twilight vision of Michael. It was the first thing I asked Myra when she came to see me that night, nervous over the tubes and IV, but the Myra I knew and loved, not the skinny one, as Michael would say.

"Yes, baby," she said, "he stayed the whole time. Him and Candace and Brother Folger."

"Brother Folger?" I asked, still a little light-headed. "Who's that?"

"Carlym Folger? Why Gabriel, he married us."

"Oh. Knute. I'm glad I was unconscious."

She let down the bed rail with sure, experienced hands and climbed into the narrow bed beside me.

"Why do you have to be so nasty?" she asked, and I tried to move over to give her a little room.

"He wasn't visiting me, he was visiting my checkbook—"

"Hush," she said. Then when she had settled in, "The doctor says you can go home Monday. Said everything went fine. He had to remove part of your stomach, but the part that's left will stretch out. You won't even miss it."

"Good riddance," I murmured, feeling safe and happy with Myra there beside me. "Did you see Clayton?"

She hesitated a moment, which really hurt me, for that slight pause before she spoke said volumes more than her careful words. "Yes. He's fine. His hair's not as bad as it sounds. It's kind of a moussed-up flat-top."

She offered no more, and I didn't press her, thinking that if she could see him, explain her side of the matter, then all would be well.

That maybe in a situation like this, where there was a jagged loss of innocence, someone had to bear the blame, and after her horrible, furious words in the ER, I was perfectly content to be the scapegoat. For it was like my sister said, nobody put a gun to my head.

So it was with a calm sense of acceptance that I returned home four days later to the house on Thomasville Road, the beautiful house built in 1903 by a wealthy banker, the house that fell into disrepair in the forties and fifties but was reclaimed by my brother and his wife, one broken window, one painted baseboard at a time, and as we rounded the last curve in the drive, I said the same thing I always said: "This is the most beautiful house in Florida."

And as always, Myra replied, "Lord, you should have seen it when we bought it. We only paid for the land. The house was just a structure on the deed description."

"I think," I said, very wisely (for I was still on Percoset, which affects me something like whiskey, making me full of profound insight), "that we can safely say you and Michael reclaimed it magnificently."

As long as it lasted—a week, I think—I was a source of great inspiration, and so kind, even to Carlym Folger, that I believe Myra considered asking the doctor for a permanent prescription. But she didn't, or he wouldn't, and with no warning at all, I was out, flat out, the little bottle all gone, and I found myself not only wrestling a savage desire for whiskey, but facing my fortieth birthday with no children to comfort me. Simon had moved to Waycross to get in a little practical experience at the Georgia plant before he started FSU in August, and Missy was resolutely preparing for her senior year, full of college plans and dedicating two hours a day to convincing her mother she needed to study at least a year in (get this) France—an indecent obsession I took full responsibility for, since I was the idiot who'd introduced Napoleon to this otherwise Celtic bunch. But she paid little mind to any of my very compelling arguments, and about the most any of us saw of her these days was the back of the Volvo as it drove down the drive.

However, on the eve of my birthday, she came into the kitchen one night after a date and found me sitting alone in the dark, wondering what kind of God would let a man have six million dollars and not one drop of whiskey, and told me she was ordering me an ice-cream cake for my birthday.

"That's all right, baby, save your money," I told her, but she would not be satisfied until she and her mother had hit the mall, presumably on my behalf, though they returned home with more bags than one small birthday could warrant.

They left after lunch with many warnings I not attempt the stairs unaided, and with nothing better to do, I lay in bed and stared at the old ceiling boards, thinking about the day I was born on Magnolia Hill.

The sun was high, the house already hot, smelling of cedar and camphor and after Mama's water broke, the fresh, pungent smell of amnionic fluid. I could hear the excitement in the voices of the neighbors, someone running for the doctor, someone taking the children. Candace, five, excited with the prospect of a live babydoll, and Michael, just over six, worried, not wanting to leave, kicking and crying, showing himself and calling for Mama as they dragged him down Lafayette, having to spend the hot, endless morning on the curb down the street, watching the trail of women come and go in and out the front door, then the doctor, then, finally, Aunt Mag, waving him home.

With no eye for traffic, he crossed the street in a dead run, up the porch and into the hot, strange smell of the house, going room to room till he found Mama in her own bed, her face white, her hair tangled on her shoulders, but smiling, happy, a tiny baby wrapped in a towel in her arms. A boy, she told him. A fat little boy, pretty as he could be. Did he want to know what she was going to name him? Michael only stood there with his finger in his mouth, frightened by the strange smell, the nervous excitement, the exultation in the women's voices, not able to speak, and Mama smiled, "Gabrielle."

Someone, an uncle—or maybe it was the doctor—laughed, but she ignored him, pulling Michael to the bed, kissing his small dark head, showing him the tiny face, saying, "See? You boys looked like angels when you were born, and I named you for angels."

And suddenly, the morning lost its awful nightmare cast and returned to a normal, happy day; for he was a good boy, he'd gone to Sunday school every week of his life, he knew all about Michael and Gabriel, the archangels, one sent to rebuke Satan, one sent to proclaim a King. And he wasn't mad anymore; he wasn't afraid. He climbed on the bed, kicking his dirty feet on the cover, and when he heard Daddy at the door, he ran to meet him, leading him into the bedroom by the hand, presenting him to his wife and new son, saying, "See? See? I'm Michael and he's the other one. He's Gabrielle."

I could see him so clearly, I could almost reach out and touch his little hand. God, I wished I could. I wished I was the father who walked through the door and lifted him above his head and laughed in his face, but I wasn't. I was alone in my bed, with scars on my belly and scars on my head, and I fell asleep to the sad, wistful dream, waking up late in the afternoon to long shadows and the strange, disoriented heaviness that comes from oversleep.

I could hear Myra and Missy moving around downstairs, their voices a confidential whisper, but I waited patiently till Myra finally came up, still dressed in her mall clothes, carrying an armload of boxes and bags.

"D'you want me to wrap 'em or just give 'em?" she asked with an excited, flushed face.

I yawned. "Just give them," I said. "Why waste paper?"

She dug around in one of the bags awhile, then presented me with, of all things, a Pierre Cardin robe and pajama set.

I was not only disappointed, I was perplexed. "We're in Florida.

Nobody sleeps in pajamas. I'll burn up."

But she paid me no mind. "Missy's sixteen now, too old for you to be walking around here in your underwear."

"I have never," I told her sternly, "walked around here in my underwear."

But I could have saved my breath, for she had connected her children's welfare with the pajamas, and was very firm about it, shaking them out of the cellophane, saying, "Here, try 'em on. Then I'll give you your next present; I promise you'll be thrilled."

Something in her bright eyes made me think I was in for something big here, an evening of careful sex, or maybe something truly wonderful, like Clayton, and I went to the bathroom and put on the idiotic pajamas (noting the price, and you wouldn't believe what she paid for them, I mean, *you would not believe*).

But when I came out, I found no Myra in a G-string, no Clayton with a bow on his head calling me Daddy, nothing but my fully clothed wife, sitting there on the edge of the bed with a smile, and I was so bitterly disappointed I lay back down,

"What?"

She smiled brilliantly. "I'll retype your story."

"Wonderful," I said with a stunning lack of enthusiasm, for I'd boxed it up in the closet after I came home from the hospital, deciding it was simply impossible to insert my hand without rewriting the whole damn thing. Besides, after one last particularly objective reading, I'd come to the unavoidable conclusion that if you separated the wheat from the tares in my life, Michael and Daddy and Mama and Brother Sloan and Sam and Brother McQuaig and Myra and Candace and the children would comprise the former group, while I held the company of Old Man Sims and Jack Kin and the stinking Ku Klux Klan in the latter. I mean, I wasn't the Nathan Bedford Forrest of the bunch, the Old Man still held that honor, but I was miserably, undoubtedly, Jeb Stuart:

the lovable, romantic ass who rode circles around battles and got a lot of good press when, in fact, all he really did was compromise the position of the real armies.

It was a painful revelation, one that was causing me many hours of alternating self-pity and resolution, and between times, I asked myself why and oh, why was I knocking myself out to make sure Clayton had a sound, black and white, three-hundred-page documentation of my lack of moral worth? Why not let time heal all and hope I was remembered for Harvard and the Oral History Project and my many droll jokes? But I didn't bother to favor myself with a reply; the answer was as plain as the nose on my face: Michael. Michael was the reason I was willing to bare my sorry little soul to the world, and while I never doubted I'd get back to it eventually, it was certainly no reason for celebration.

"And," she said, her face still beaming, "you can go to baseball with me tomorrow night. Lay down in the backseat. Candace says we can take a quilt to throw over you in case Clay comes by."

"Wonderful," I repeated with such a stunning lack of enthusiasm that her smile dimmed.

"I thought you'd be pleased. It's the city-wide tournament. Maybe he'll hit a homer."

If I had bothered with a reply, it would have been something about when pigs fly, and Myra's face was actually frowning.

"What a disagreeable man you've become," she said, snatching up the bags and wadding them into balls with tight, angry fists. "And poor Missy bought you a ice-cream cake, ordered it special in Tallahassee, and you're gone lay up here and show yourself—"

What I was doing, in fact, was lying there thinking she was getting as good as Mama at slapping on the guilt. She even had that pained sing-song perfected.

I got up slowly. "Hush, I'm coming. I'll behave."

But she was not convinced. "She also got you some old book, and

I'd appreciate it if you wouldn't tear it apart the whole time you read it."

I looked at her. "What book?"

"Some book on that war—the Civil War."

I had the gall to grimace at this, and she turned a little nasty. "Well, you just stay up here and sulk, Gabriel Catts. We did fine without you a lot a years. I'm sure we'll make it a few more—"

"I'm coming, I'm coming," I said, standing. "Has she read it yet?"

"No," she said, helping me up.

"Good. I can fake it."

"Gabriel—" she murmured in a low, annoyed voice, but did let me lean on her as we went down the stairs, still murmuring something about me *behaving* myself as I concentrated on not tripping on the hem of my new robe, when a sudden blast of music hit me, Madonna or the like, and I looked at her.

"You run tell Missy I ain't sitting down here listening to her nigger music, I don't care what kind a cake she bought me—" This being Magnolia Hill slang for rock-and-roll, that after three decades of enlightenment, I used in a pinch. But before she could answer, the room was suddenly full of laughter, and I looked over the stair rail to see all the old fish-fry gang gathered around the French doors with punch glasses in their hands and possumlike grins on their faces, while my dear wife stomped her foot with glee, for the choice of welcoming song at my fortieth surprise party had been hers. It was "Like a Virgin," and she just thought she was so hilarious, laughing till tears ran down her face at having pulled one over on me, while the old men joined in with happy abandon, knowing they'd finally had the last word on the Yankee-liberal-intellectual and our fights over affirmative action would never be the same again. But what can I say? They had me cold, and I hobbled down the stairs and shook their hands and admitted that yes, they got me that time.

As for Myra and her little knife twist in an old wound, I forgave her outright. Listen, she could have arranged for someone to be singing: "Like a Crippled Alcoholic Occasionally Impotent Homophobic Narcissistic Ass," and I would have kissed her and told her I loved her, for as soon as I looked down on that roomful of people, my eyes had fallen on a young man with blond spiked hair standing next to Curtis, and I knew that by some act of grace, I'd not only broken even, I'd actually won.

From that point on, the party never lost its hilarity, for frayed nerves had me at my shameless, most sarcastic best, and though Myra and Candace seemed a little worried, afraid I'd suddenly lose it and run across the room and scream at Clayton that I loved him, I was cool as a cucumber, walking around in my designer robe like Hugh Hefner; for, as I say, when it suits me, I can exhibit patience that would put Job to shame.

It was only when we opened presents that I spoke to him at all, nothing more than a spontaneous thanks for the book he and Missy bought me, that was not on the Civil War, but a very fine biography on Martin Luther King, Jr. I'd been wanting to read. Missy kissed me when I proclaimed my (sincere) thanks, but Clayton looked away. To divert the moment, I saw Jack Kin standing there with a look of unashamed disgust and lifted an eyebrow. "Hey Jack, you want this when I'm done?"

He turned his head and said "Shht," making everyone laugh, even Clayton, and I saw Myra smiling at me, for, as she would put it, *behaving myself*. So the evening went, not hindered by expectation or accusation, and the old men found my new tolerance so engaging that they hung on long after the others had left, sitting around the pool and discussing, of all things, Chappaquiddick, while Myra and Missy helped Clayton move his stuff back in.

"—girl was pregnant, sure as I'm sitting here—" Brother Gaines was saying, shaking his hand at me for emphasis, when I noticed Clayton was standing at the French door, looking at me. I don't believe the irony of the situation escaped him for a minute, and when the old men saw him, they paused long enough to wish him good night.

But his eyes were on me when he answered, very levelly, "Good night, Uncle Gabe."

I accepted the revision without pause, wishing him good night with no shock or hurt at the very significant *uncle*, and he seemed satisfied, going back inside, leaving Brother Gaines to resume, "—plain old-fashion cover-up is what it was."

On and on they went, far into the night, and for once I let someone else take the self-righteous lead, too relieved with my own forgivenness to get real worked up over another man's indiscretion.

It was well past midnight when their wives finally dragged them home, and as I walked them out to their cars, they assured me the second half of a man's life was a hundred percent better than the first. I was in no position to argue the matter, and when they left, I watched the red pinpoints of their brake lights flicker at the highway, then stood there in the yard awhile, savoring the night smells of summer—ligustrum and tea olive and, underneath, a hint of raw earth from a neighboring farmer's newly turned field—before I went inside.

The house was empty, Missy gone home with Mama, Simon on the road to Waycross, Clayton's door shut, and after pausing there long enough to press my hand to the wood and reassure myself that life actually lived and breathed behind those four walls, I went down the hall and found Myra reading in bed, her head wrapped in a towel, her *Sunday School Quarterly* in her hand. I didn't find it too much of an anticlimax, for I knew by now that if a nuclear device hit us ground zero, these Baptists would crawl out of the rubble on Saturday night to study their lesson. So I took off my robe and sat on the edge of the bed, and after a moment, I said very clearly, "I'm gonna have to cry."

"Well go outside," she said, glancing up. "Don't let him hear you," proving that in some ways, she has truly grown the way of all country-born women: hard-headed and practical in the extreme.

But I didn't argue. I only pulled my robe back on and pretended to take out the garbage, but kept on walking till I was at the fence line, then leaned against a post and cried till I was hoarse. When I was finally done, I washed my face at the faucet and came back inside with a calm, perfectly normal expression and found Myra sleepy, but still awake, her face tender when she saw my red eyes.

"Gabrielle, Gabrielle," she murmured. "He looked like an angel when he was born and I named him for an angel."

She laughed lightly when she said it, quoting Mama, who'd had to defend her taste in masculine names to Brother Kin at the party after Missy put the official spelling on the birthday cake, but later, when I was about to turn out the light, she asked in a much smaller voice, "If you found out he wasn't yours, would you still love him so?"

I was surprised at the question, but maybe such relentless uncertainties are the curse of all indiscretions, and I lifted her face so I could look her in the eye and lay this one to rest, once and for all. "Well, honey, I look at it this way: He's either my nephew or my son, so we're blood kin one way or the other." I paused to turn off the lamp and finished in the darkness. "Anyway, that boy in there and whose blood is pumping in his veins is the least of my worries."

And such was the love, the unqualified acceptance in this gentle, no-nonsense answer, that she kissed me and fell asleep, and her face looks very young, very innocent, in the half-light, like that of the smart, sassy, red-headed child she never was, but always meant to be, fought to be, has, in some good and innocent ways, become.

And I am left alone in the darkness, in a position that has befallen me at last: that of the survivor, the revisionist of my own life. For I cannot tell her—it would hurt her so—that these are really not my words at all, but those of my brother Michael. You remember him: The one who played baseball. Who pulled for the Braves. Who left me a million dollars. And a house and a car, and a pool and a deck. And a wife and a son and a soul. The one who walks with God. My brother Michael.

*J*anis Owens was born in Marianna, a small town in the Florida panhandle, about fifteen miles south of the Alabama line, about thirteen from the Georgia line. Her father was a preacher and insurance salesman who moved his family to Mississippi and Louisiana before settling back in north Florida. She earned a degree in English and Southern History at the University of Florida and continues to reside in rural north Florida with her husband and daughters. The story of the Catts family continues in her two novels after this one: *Myra Sims* and *The Schooling of Claybird Catts.*

The Writing of My Brother Michael

MY BROTHER MICHAEL has its roots at my great Aunt Izzy's funeral years ago in the West End of Marianna, a small town in the Florida Panhandle. She was my beloved Grannie's only sister and the last of her generation, and her passing was dearly felt, her small house packed with story-telling relatives and rivers of food, as we do in the South. I had my baby daughter with me, and late in the afternoon, Mama and I went for a walk to quieten her, just around the corner to Magnolia Hill, an adjacent neighborhood of small shotgun houses where Mama had lived as a child, when her father and uncles all worked at the heading mill, making wooden barrelheads.

Mama is a storyteller of some skill and imagination, and as we went up the slant of the Hill, she told me a family story that I'd heard many times before—the tragic story of the death of a nameless young girl who'd briefly lived next door to them on the Hill, in a small row house that was still standing that day; she pointed it out as we passed. With her usual attention to detail and evocation of mood, Mama described the girl as she always did, as pre-teen, maybe thirteen, a plump and pretty child, with red hair and far-off eyes, who moved in next door with a reclusive mother and a stepfather; they never seemed to fit in with the bustle of life on the Hill. She said they kept to themselves, but she remembered one encounter with the red-haired girl. She came up to their porch one afternoon in late autumn while Mama played dolls. Mama says the girl didn't say a word, just stood and watched her for a long, quiet moment, then went back inside her own house, and was never seen alive again.

The next morning, Dr. Whittaker came for Grannie and asked if she could assist him next door, as rural doctors used to do in small towns when women and birthing and female trouble were involved in a case. When Grannie went next door, he stopped her on the porch and swore her to an oath of secrecy to never divulge the secrets of the house—an oath Grannie took seriously for many years to come. Mama says she only knew the young girl was deathly ill and that none of the children on the Hill were allowed to play outside or make any noise that day for fear of disturbing her. The next time Mama saw her, it was late at night after she died, after Grannie had bathed and dressed her and laid her out for burial in a small coffin in their living room, where the neighborhood children—Mama included—were allowed to stroll past her coffin for their last goodbye.

She was buried shortly after in the paupers' section of the local cemetery, and her family soon left the area. It was only years later that Grannie broke her oath of silence and told Mama what had really happened next door: that the child had been found in the outhouse that morning, unconscious from blood loss after a self-inflicted abortion. What was worse was that the father of the baby was rumored to be her own stepfather—a charge never proven, and thanks to the oath of silence, never even voiced, though it haunted Grannie till her death, and in one of our last conversations in '76, she mentioned the incident, her face full of horror, even after sixty years.

That was the story my mother recalled that day—*The Story of the Little Redheaded Girl Who Died Next Door*, which, as I say, I had heard many times, though somehow the combination of postpartum hormones and grief over losing Aunt Izzy brought her tragedy home more sharply than ever before. When I returned home the next day, I had mastitis and woke up with a temperature of 105° and an image from a dream. The image was of a man watching a woman through a French door; the woman was in great emotional distress, though the man didn't know it. I had no idea who the man was, or why the woman was in distress, but before I got out of bed, I knew the story from beginning to end and wrote the last page first, then the rest, straight through in five weeks.

So unconscious and instinctual was the writing that it was only on a much later reading that I realized what I'd done: that I'd rewritten the tragic story of the voiceless child next door on Magnolia Hill. But with the magic of fiction, I'd done what even Grannie couldn't do: I'd rescued her in time, had given the girl a name, a story, a voice. In fiction, she becomes Myra Sims. In short, I did the same thing that Mama had done that day on the Hill: kept her story alive and bore witness to what had happened to her, broke the oath of secrecy over a tragic end.

—Janis Owens

Questions

1. Author Janis Owens is not afraid to label her writing unashamedly Southern. What do you think makes a book Southern? Could *My Brother Michael* have taken place anywhere? What about the story is different and what is similar to, say, a Willa Cather or Eudora Welty story?

2. Some readers are exasperated by Gabriel Catts to the point of irritation; some find him likable and redeemed. Did you find him a sympathetic figure, or a true anti-hero?

3. Most readers bring their own histories to their reading of novels. Did you find Ira Sims a sympathetic or a sinister character? Did you find Cissie overbearing or wonderfully nurturing?

4. The search for the father is one of the underlying themes of this book. How was each character's fate determined by their relationship with their father? Were there exceptions?

5. *My Brother Michael* was written by a woman in a man's voice. How do you think it would be different if a man had written it?

6. The author makes many references to Cracker Florida and Cracker architecture. The term "Cracker" is sometimes considered derogatory. How would you define the Cracker culture? How is it different from mainstream Southern life?

7. Religion plays a large part in the life of the characters of this novel and the theme as well, with an almost Victorian sensibility of right and wrong. Does this stark contrast lower or strengthen the tone of the story for you?

8. Janis Owens' second book is *Myra Sims,* which tells the same story as *My Brother Michael,* but from Myra's point of view. Do you think this is a good idea? If you haven't read *Myra Sims,* how do you think Myra will tell her story? If you have, compare how it differs from Gabe's telling of it.

To request a complete catalog or place an order, write to Pine-apple Press, P.O. Box 3889, Sarasota, Florida 34230, or call 1-800-PINEAPLE (746-3275). Or visit our website at www.pineapplepress.com.

Myra Sims by Janis Owens. This novel tells the story of the Catts family, the same story as in *My Brother Michael,* but from the point of view of Myra Sims as she evolves from voiceless victim to survivor. "Once you meet the Simses and Cattses, you'll want to read both books....Owens is the Pat Conroy of west Florida mill towns and forgotten crossroads all over the rural South." — *Florida Times-Union*

A Land Remembered by Patrick D. Smith. This best-selling novel tells the story of three generations of the MacIveys, a Florida family who battle the hardships of the Florida frontier to rise from a dirt-poor Cracker life to the wealth and standing of real estate tycoons. But in the meantime the land changes too, from a wilderness teeming with wildlife to an overdeveloped wasteland: a land remembered.

Classic Cracker: Florida's Wood-Frame Vernacular Architecture by Ronald W. Haase. The history of Florida wood-frame architecture from the simplest "single-pen" homesteads to the latest homes at Seaside. 46 color photos, 17 b&w photos, 56 line drawings, including floor plans.

Visiting Small-Town Florida, Revised Edition, by Bruce Hunt. Combined and updated version or the previous popular two volumes, covering seventy of Florida's most charming, historic, and often eclectic small towns, places with names like Sopchoppy, Ozellow, and Two Egg. You'll learn the town's history, meet some of its unusual characters, and learn where to shop, eat, and stay in these remnants of old-timey Florida.

Dog Island and Other Florida Poems by Laurence Donovan. The title poem of this book records a sojourn to a small island off the Florida Panhandle. Reachable only by boat, Dog Island provides a quiet respite where Miami poet-artist Laurence Donovan contemplates the sea, sand, and sky and transforms them into words and etchings.